WHATEVER HAPPENED TO CATHY MARTIN

by Mim Eichmann

Paperback ISBN: 978-1-953686-12-1
eBook ISBN: 978-1-953686-13-8

Library of Congress Control Number: 2022933901

WWW.LivingSpringsPublishers.com

Cover photo: taken by the author at Cricket Creek Forest Preserve, Addison, IL -- all rights reserved
Cover design: Frank Wegloski, Maximum Printing, Downers Grove, IL

Dedicated to Alison, Brad and Todd

Author's Note

"Whatever Happened to Cathy Martin"
(Working title: "*The Argonaut ~ 1968*")

In 2018, I attended my 50th high school class reunion back in the Washington, D.C. area after having lived in the Midwest for almost my entire adult life. Many of my classmates had drifted apart and we had eventually lost track of one another over the decades. Having an opportunity to reconnect with those classmates in attendance as well as learn the fates of others unable to do so, brought to focus the joyous, humbling, pitiful, and sometimes shocking lives of those promising kids with whom I'd once roamed the halls of Northwood High School in the late '60s. In many cases, however, no one had any idea where our classmates had ended up. Our generation, ultimately named the Boomers, fell victim to its own diaspora, scattering throughout the U.S., Canada, and Europe without the benefit back then of internet intervention. While at the reunion, a bizarre question came to mind: could any of them have simply disappeared without a trace immediately after graduation? And could another classmate have carefully crafted that disappearance? Who would even know?

When I'd attended the reunion, newly retired from my full-time job, I'd just completed writing my first two historical fiction novels, "*A Sparrow Alone*" and "*Muskrat Ramble*" and was feverishly querying literary agencies searching for representation. Although still in that maddening querying stage, I began writing "*The Argonaut ~ 1968*" as something of a refreshing experiment in penning an upmarket fiction thriller, set in a time frame about which I was obviously quite familiar: 1968-78. The original

Prologue

Berlin, Germany 1947

In a flash, while the guards' eyes were averted, the prisoner scraped five seeds from the apple mash. He'd just extracted the mash from a vat of boiling apples, painstakingly wringing them through the prison's large hand-cranked grinder. Within the light, sticky film, the tiny black seeds adhered easily alongside the others pasted discretely inside his tightly shackled wrist cuffs. Although scalding his fingertips each time, he still needed to dredge at least another dozen seeds tonight. Maybe two dozen if possible. Nonetheless, this was a good haul.

He knew that today was the last time the kitchen would be canning applesauce -- the last time he'd be able to obtain seeds. No more apples were outside in crates. Unless he waited another year, which was not an option. He didn't have another year. The gallows shimmered in the late fall sunshine less than a block away, awaiting the travesty of a swift trial before a mock military tribunal.

When he got back to his cell, he would grind the seeds, crushing them to a fine black powder, using the small stone he had carefully loosened from his dank cell wall. Then, he would pinch the powder into the bottom of the torn envelope he'd hidden within the rusted toilet. Even though chained to his bed every night, he needed access to the toilet, of course.

In total, he had accumulated about eighty-five black seeds. Enough to make someone instantly ill for several hours but hopefully not a lethal dose. Cyanide poisoning was a tricky business. But it was one of the businesses he knew very well.

title was based on a fictitious high school yearbook, but since the bulk of the story transpires in 1978 and the prologue takes place in 1947, there were just too many confusing dates at the beginning of the book. Leaving the year 1968 off the title would have been equally confusing ... no one was searching for the golden fleece! Also, please note, the book is entirely fiction.

I'm not sure I really expected to get caught up within my own net so to speak and actually complete the manuscript for "*Whatever Happened to Cathy Martin*", but rather surprisingly, it has now emerged!

~ Mim Eichmann

Many thanks to my early manuscript readers including: Luisa Buehler, Odette Cortopassi, Nancy Crocker, Todd Eichmann, Kim Kreiling, Cherie Little, Doug Lofstrom, Gina Mitchell, Jim Ross, Joyce Tumea, the SGV book club, and the Room 7 Writers Group at the Downers Grove Public Library in Illinois: Rod Brandon, Pat Camalliere, Michael Cebula, Jon Payne, and Lee Williams.

Lights automatically flicked off at 10 p.m. Cell check occurred at random times throughout the night. Usually two guards on cell check. Occasionally three. Huge men armed with spiked metal batons. They needed to keep these prisoners alive for their trials, but that never stopped the guards from the brutal torture they liberally meted out for the smallest infraction. For reasons of security, the guards' visits were never made on a regular schedule. Ninety minutes could intervene between two cell checks, but the subsequent visit might occur less than twenty minutes later. The prisoner knew he would have to act the moment he heard the metal doors banging open at the end of the hall.

Lying awake in the dark, he listened to rats scuttling close by. At first, he'd kept his envelope of ground seeds under another stone in the wall, but two massive rats had eaten the cyanide, immediately gone into violent spasms and choked to death within seconds. After that he had to be more careful. A dead rat in one's cell rarely caused any suspicion among the guards. The vermin swarmed everywhere. But two rodents? Simultaneously? The prisoner knew he had to find a better hiding place or risk much closer scrutiny. Something he couldn't allow. Not now.

He was startled awake by the sound of a door clanging shut down the hall. Damn. He hadn't meant to doze. He clamored to his feet, quickly retrieved the envelope, and then dumped the black powder into his tin cup. He flushed the toilet to collect water into the cup and swallowed the pungent mixture in several noisy gulps.

The room began spinning immediately as he crashed forward onto his hands and knees on the filthy floor. Bloody vomit spewed like a molten fountain creating a thick pool of bile, visibly widening in front of his hands.

He heard his cell door crash open as the two guards entered for their routine check. When their flashlights hit the prisoner, they ordered him to look up at them. Still on his hands and knees, heaving in agony, the prisoner somehow forced himself to squint into the blinding light. Blood now oozed freely from his nose; the whites of his eyes flamed with crimson. One guard rushed out to call for the medics. The other one released the prisoner's wrist cuffs, forcing him to sit back against the wall. He began pouring water from his canteen into the prisoner's mouth hoping to stop the foul retching. Reeling, far more nauseated than he'd anticipated, the prisoner grabbed the guard around the neck, first beating his head against the wall, then yanking him onto the floor and began squeezing. His grip wasn't as strong as usual, but it was strong enough. Before the other guard returned with the medics, the man lay immobile, eyes rolled back into his head -- dead.

Swaying, the prisoner pushed himself to his feet, ripped the dead guard's concealed pistol from its holster and staggered out of the cell. The dark hallway undulated around him. He could hear the voices of several men echoing from the opposite hallway. Probably the other guard with the medics. Having memorized a zigzagging route staffed by few guards, who proved to be easily subdued by the prisoner's stolen pistol, he forced his limbs to continue moving, finally reaching his destination -- the deep tunnel that led to the city's underground sewer. If he didn't perish within the vermin-infested waters he would emerge with a new name, a new country … and a new life.

"If you must record my exploits, I do wish you'd put less emphasis on the melodramatic and more on the intellectual issues involved."

Basil Rathbone as Sherlock Holmes in

"Dressed to Kill" (1946)

Chapter 1

Indianapolis, Indiana 1978

Looking across the immense, ostentatious living room, framed by a breathtaking mosaic of skylights set into massive cathedral ceiling timbers that soared over plush Persian carpets, I wallowed in an atmosphere that screamed of untold decades of carefully invested old money as I sipped my glass of champagne covertly watching my husband Hank. He was engaged in close conversation with one of his attractive colleagues, Ms. Dorothea Dixon, better known as the Double D or simply the DD, both for her well-displayed measurements as well as initials. Lest I give the erroneous impression that the woman is an incompetent bimbo, however, the Double D was one of the first female graduates of Notre Dame once the University had gone co-ed in the early '70s. She could zero in on the tech problems of any huge deal with a major corporation, offer specific strategies and a precise breakdown of associated costs and minute details mapped out within a matter of a few days, sometimes even within a few hours. Hence my husband's undivided attentiveness on several levels.

Growing up I used to belt out "*Some Enchanted Evening*" from our well-pitted LP of "*South Pacific*" attempting to match Ezio Pinza's passionate rendition much to my parents' amusement. One of my favorite sections was: "*Who can explain it, who can tell you why? Fools give you reasons, wise men never try*!" This may well provide something of an explanation to the circuitous road map of miscues in my often-thwarted attempts to find true love. Forget rushing across a crowded room in *Bali Hai* ... I couldn't even have managed to locate that special someone in a Winn Dixie parking lot on a Saturday night. I still maintained that Hank had been thoroughly intoxicated the night he'd proposed to me in front of a group of his coworkers at a raucous bar and had to follow through with the wedding simply to save face.

Hank and the Double D had been an item -- or more than likely -- were still an item, which had been the root cause of the havoc in our four-year marriage and the impetus behind our increasingly volatile conversations with a psychiatrist. Hank correctly presumed that my reluctant attendance at this gathering tonight was little more than a spy mission on my part. The lavish celebration was an engagement party for his upper-level boss and fiancée being thrown by the groom's aunt and uncle, who were major shareholders with the Eli Lilly pharmaceuticals dynasty and hot on the trail to open the first winery resort to be based in southern Indiana down in Brown County. Thus, for reasons both social and financial, the expansive celebration was being held within said magnificently gated enclave in Indianapolis since the couple-to-be would also be shareholders of this groundbreaking venture. Earlier in the afternoon the young couple had flown in from New York City and had been temporarily waylaid due to construction delays involving huge traffic detours as they attempted to reach their own party, already in full swing.

Although I held a journalism degree from Franklin

College, a rural liberal arts school outside of Indianapolis and currently worked as a copy desk clerk for the Bloomington office of The Indianapolis Star, I had limited expertise making small talk and no great desire to improve upon said lack of skill. By contrast, my husband was a bona fide snake charmer from birth, wielding an Indiana University marketing and finance B.A., successfully grabbing the brass ring immediately upon graduation. He was a quickly rising nova within the expansive marketing ranks of Idyllic Security, Inc. -- known simply as Idyllic -- a state-of-the-art corporation developing customized security equipment for large and small corporations as well as for individual wealthy clients around the globe. His work required frequent trips to Chicago, Philadelphia, and New York City, often accompanied by the lovely, graciously obliging DD. He'd recently been assured by an inside informant that he was soon to be promoted to his current boss' position in Indianapolis, thus making his appearance at this party essential since he would then be reporting directly to the groom, David Fowler.

Rather like the Ewing family on "*Dallas*", the Fowler dynasty tentacles stretched into stockholdings from cheese factories in upstate Wisconsin to off track betting in Las Vegas to secret experimental crop farming techniques in India. The corporations that didn't actually fall under their wing, such as Lilly Pharmaceuticals, for example, were nonetheless heavily invested-in concerns by the extensive Fowler clan. If you checked into the roster of backers for any publicly offered major corporation, you would trip over at least one Fowler or Fowler offspring within the first dozen names.

Excited shouts from the guests echoed in the massive hallway behind me announcing the arrival of the long-awaited couple. Surrounded *en masse*, the duo migrated towards the great room, the noise level escalating by several decibels. Someone had simultaneously cranked up the Bee Gees' "*Night Fever*", now booming from speakers clandestinely positioned throughout the entire house. At first, I only saw the back of a perfectly maintained blonde flip as the couple roared in, mimicking John Travolta's well-known dance moves. After about fifteen minutes or so the crowd finally thinned out and I was totally surprised to see that the fiancée was Janet Lynn Webster. Janet Lynn had graduated in my high school class down in Columbus, Indiana. I'd never known her particularly well, but my best childhood friend, Cathy Martin, had thrown me over for Janet Lynn's adoration and, more precisely, that of Janet Lynn's wealthy parents' adoration, mere weeks after we'd started our freshman year of high school. I remained in what I'd hoped a fairly incognito spot, attempting to blend in with the monumental jungle of Ficus plants towering above me.

Two other company wives strolled my way, soon joined by a third, and we introduced ourselves, hoping to relieve some of the tedium we all shared as outsiders. Discussions centering on casserole recipes and the recent uptick in chicken pox cases surrounded me, but Hank refused to eat casseroles and we had no children with or without chicken pox, so I simply nodded with a smile, contributing little to the conversation. Misery loves company, but it also loves good food, which was plentiful everywhere around us. We helped ourselves to additional flutes of champagne, courtesy of the uncle's extensive private cabinet, along with huge, broiled shrimp, skewered with a wedge of sausage drizzled in a tangy smoked sauce said to be the favorite appetizer at the French Quarter restaurant in New Orleans where the couple's wedding reception would be taking place in a few months. None of us in my little group were expecting to be included since our husbands simply weren't high enough on the roster. If Hank was promoted, however, I shuddered to think that our status would probably change. Attending this party was complete Nirvana by comparison.

I hadn't noticed that Janet Lynn was working her way around the perimeter of the room, flitting from one small group to the next amid a flurry of congratulatory toasts. As she walked towards us, she stared at me.

"Well, now, I know you from somewhere," she smiled, in that soft, slightly husky Southern accent I vaguely remembered from a decade ago, "but I'm afraid the name escapes me at the moment, so you'll have to help me out there."

"Denise Prescott," I replied, extending my hand. "We graduated from Columbus High together back in '68. My husband's Hank Taylor … um, in marketing at Idyllic here in Indy."

"Of course!" she laughed, her hand gracefully touching my arm. "Now how could I forget that!"

Well, quite easily, I surmised, since we'd probably exchanged fewer than a half dozen sentences with one another our entire four years at CHS – if that. Something about her exotic manner seemed unnatural, fake even, but I let it slide by. Wealthy people had always made me nervous. And, after all, she'd probably had a long grueling day already, what with the delayed flight from New York, traffic, detours, and whatever else entitled people found overwhelmingly daunting. She gave a small nod by way of acknowledging the other women hovering in our ragtag clique.

"And congratulations!" I added, echoed by my little group's titters, truly in awe of the glamorous vision in front of us, as we lifted our flutes in a toast. "Someone mentioned these delicious shrimp appetizers are from the restaurant where you're planning your reception down in the French Quarter." Whenever appropriate, turn the conversation to food … this was a rather transparent trick of investigative journalism that I'd attempted to perfect many years back.

Janet Lynn failed to take the bait, however.

"I do feel badly that I've lost track of so many of our classmates," she continued, her long golden eyelashes sweeping momentarily downward. "Have you been able to keep up? Probably so since you still live out here, I imagine."

I shrugged. "A few," I replied. "Not too many."

"Same here," she remarked, punctuated by a theatrical sigh. "Practically none, in fact."

"Are you still in touch with Cathy Martin?" I asked. "For some reason I remember that both of you were planning to attend Wisconsin at Whitewater."

She smiled rather thinly, eyes narrowing almost imperceptibly.

"Cathy Martin. Now there's a name buried in the past. One that can certainly remain buried in the past. I haven't thought about her in a long time. Yes, we started out together, but things got, well … everything became rather messy almost immediately."

I nodded and took another sip of the champagne. The statement struck me as one of those 'don't ask me for any further details' type of remarks, so I was surprised when Janet Lynn continued.

"Cathy got pregnant right at the beginning of our freshman year and had to drop out and get married," she stated evenly, looking straight into my eyes. "The man had been my boyfriend actually, Tom Miller, a senior at Wisconsin. So you can see how that completely severed our tenuous friendship. I haven't heard anything about her for almost ten years now. And even though I'm obviously quite over her incendiary deception, I still have no interest in renewing her acquaintance as you can well imagine."

A wistful shadow stole momentarily over her face. It was very difficult to perceive the Janet Lynn of old as a victim somehow. It was even more difficult to perceive her uttering phrases like severing our tenuous friendship or incendiary deception since it was well known that Cathy Martin had ghostwritten all of Janet Lynn's papers back at CHS.

"Oh my," I replied, aware that my spoken reaction was quite underwhelming.

She brushed her blonde flip back behind her ear, momentarily flashing a large diamond-encrusted, silver drop earring and glanced around the room before speaking again.

"So, do you still live in Nashville? Weren't your parents also artists or something ... like Cathy's dad Chomp Martin?"

"Yes, they were. Still are in fact," I replied, quite surprised that she'd known anything about my family, shuddering to hear my parents' names coupled in any way with Chomp Martin's.

"And I'll bet all of your stuff from high school is still stored at your parents' since none of us have enough room to house it in our own apartments. I know most of my things were still at my folks' place."

Somehow, I completely missed the fact that she'd mentioned this in past tense.

"Hard to say and even harder to ever find," I laughed rather nervously. "My mom has never wanted to part with anything of mine. But it would take a spelunking crew to locate anything. They've hoarded so much stuff for their pending art projects over the years it would be impossible for me to put my hands on anything in particular. That's assuming it hadn't been inadvertently tossed in one of my mother's occasional purging outbursts."

"Well, I suppose that's somewhat comforting ... what I mean is, you won't have any old love letters or anything, well, embarrassing, carelessly drift into the wrong hands in years to come."

"Doubt there's much of that," I laughed again. "Had a rather boring past as a teenager I'm afraid. My folks only have the stuff from my high school days. Everything from my little kid days when I was growing up in Nashville I've hung onto. Don't ask me why … maybe just an offshoot of my parents' hoarding instincts or something. That stuff was a lot more interesting actually."

"Really?" inquired Janet Lynn, slightly raising an eyebrow. "How truly … unusual."

"Cathy Martin and I hung out a lot together back in our grade school days. I guess we had a lot more in common back then. Kind of fell out in high school. You know how it is with kids."

Janet Lynn nodded, far more interested than I would have anticipated, which was oddly unnerving.

"Anyway, we put together these really bizarre scrapbooks and whacky photo albums, even recorded a bunch of dumb Sherlock Holmes' type mysteries we'd concocted on this ancient tape recorder we'd found somewhere. Completely nonsense stuff that no one could possibly ever find even remotely interesting! I think I still have a lot of it with me somewhere. But then, who knows?" I laughed, self-consciously reddening, embarrassed for having brought up this subject at all.

"Indeed. You've hung onto all of that from your childhood?" she remarked dryly, her eyes narrowing slightly yet again. "How … um, interesting. That's quite miraculous I must say."

"Sad to say, a much more interesting part of my life. Are you planning on attending our reunion next month, by the way?"

"Oh, I'll be much too busy with the last-minute details for our wedding, so no, unfortunately, I'm afraid I'll have to miss," she shrugged.

Janet Lynn then gave me an odd look, voiced a limp compliment about my earrings, which was undoubtedly a prompt for me to rave about hers. Then with one of those breathy "thanks-so-much-for-coming" sweeping adieus, waved to another small group of her guests and glided away effortlessly, an undulating vision in her low cut, tan-line revealing golden-silk tunic with matching wide-legged trousers -- a clingy outfit that would have probably been categorized as pajamas only a few years ago, but was now a much sought-after designer pantsuit.

Hank and I got home from the party around 1 a.m. I was thoroughly exhausted, but Hank, as usual, was horny as hell. My husband had always been a huge believer in the benefits of mega vitamins – even injecting them if necessary -- primarily to combat his serious cluster migraine headaches, but also to achieve a heightened sexual prowess. Sadly, I typically was a disappointment to these amorous proclivities. In fact, when we saw Woody Allen's movie "*Annie Hall*" where Diane Keaton's spiritual persona levitates from their bed to do some sketching, while their physical selves were engaged in the preliminary throes of unbridled ecstasy, Hank guffawed so loud most of the people sitting directly in front of us in the theater glanced back at me. We'd now been in couples' therapy with a male shrink, Dr. Racine, for almost two years. Hank's affair with the DD (and I suspected one or two other women who'd preceded her) was fueled by my lack of attentiveness to his needs and tepid expressions of affection. Tonight, at least, Hank had lapsed into an orgy of snoring immediately following our own throes of unbridled whatever, but I was left wide awake. On a whim I decided to look through my high school senior yearbook.

Cracking open the front cover with the faux gold embossed relief of *Columbus High School -- The Argonaut -- 1968*, there we were, captured from the shoulders up along with our classmates in black and white for all time: Cathy Martin, Denise Prescott, and Janet Lynn Webster in our identical, slightly scooped-neck, long-sleeved black sweaters and single row of small fake pearls. Cathy and Janet Lynn were both very fair blondes, complete with porcelain complexions and shiny, shoulder-length straight hair, with that perfectly lacquered slight flip to the ends. My own hair refused all attempts at straightening thanks to my Italian grandmother's genes, and remained a very thick, curly dark brown, typically bordering on sheep wool snarls in high humidity. Cathy's and Janet Lynn's pictures could easily have just been the negative printed in reverse – in fact, I remembered an odd rumor that Janet Lynn had skipped school the day her photo was supposed to have been taken and that it actually *was* Cathy's picture. This was so Janet Lynn wouldn't catch hell from her parents when they found out she'd skipped school with her then boyfriend, Mr. Columbus-Football-Player-of-the-Year, Mr. Paul-Newman-Eyes (as was noted on his page), Edward Hutchinson.

"*Young! Expectant! Ready to Devour the World with Boundless Curiosity*!" boasted the banner across the page displaying twenty young seniors on Cathy's page. My page stated simply: "*Our Graduates, 1968*" and Janet Lynn's boldly proclaimed: "*Heading off to their Next Exciting Chapter in Life.*" Janet Lynn had done surprisingly well for herself, I thought. You would never have known she'd been that student in eighth grade math still counting on her fingers for her eights and nines multiplication tables. Both she and her husband-to-be, David Fowler had briefly addressed the crowd earlier tonight. Despite that same coy breathiness and soft Southern accent, her having uttered phrases like incendiary deception and tenuous friendship were apparently not anomalies. She'd smoothly delivered a gracious, impressively articulate, extemporaneous speech without the slightest pause or occasional 'um.'

But I was far more shocked to learn that math and science expert Cathy Martin had become derailed from her educational aspirations, gotten pregnant and then married! Cathy Martin had rarely even dated throughout high school and never had time for any men in her life, even as a casual friend. In fact, if Janet Lynn hadn't dated one football hunk after another during our junior and senior years, tongues would undoubtedly have wagged about those two girls enjoying just a little too much togetherness at Janet Lynn's parents' various estates. No one ever so much as whispered a word about homosexuality back in those days, but without question, that specter hung over several other students' unusually chummy same sex relationships that were thinly disguised as friendships.

So, whatever happened to Cathy Martin?

"My very dear fellow, musical talent is
not the evidence of innocence.
As a matter of fact, the late Professor Moriarty
was a virtuoso on the bassoon."

Basil Rathbone as Sherlock Holmes in

"Pursuit to Algiers" (1945)

Chapter 2

Big Ben clanged us awake to a steady thudding of grey rain against our bedroom window. Flooded roads and chugging traffic into Bloomington underscored our dismal Monday morning commute as Hank dropped me off at the newspaper building just south of town. The Indianapolis Star had converted to a computer system within the last couple years and up until a few months back, the linotype operators had still been picketing in front of the building, protesting the paper's conversion to computerized typesetting. Those of us scabs, basically a handful of wannabe newspaper junkies desperately flaunting our practically worthless journalism degrees, would rewrite hard copy or convert information called in by our correspondents to the paper's style. This was accomplished on a menacing computer terminal featuring a black screen, flashing green square cursor and a badly designed "kill" button capable of instantaneously relegating untold hours of tedious work to outer space, never to be retrieved.

The paper had recently fired its obituary editor, so we now handled obits called in from funeral parlors throughout the state, as well as countless local police beats, district court cases and basic human interest stories including details of weddings, engagements, and awards. As assistants to the copy desk editorial staff, everything we typed was sent to the main desks for approval;, almost nothing went to press directly from our hands unless the editors were swamped on deadline. Then we were obligated to tackle those stories ourselves, a daunting task absolutely none of us relished since repercussions for incorrect information could easily result in instant termination coupled with serious fines. And, although the modern age was upon us, the actual printing was still done from the same massive heavy metal plates that had been in use since before the turn of the century. We had only usurped the linotype operators, not the end process.

The first call I took was an obituary from a funeral home in Greencastle about an older couple who had died of carbon monoxide poisoning resulting from their blocked furnace. As I listened to the funeral director, I made a mental note to visit my parents in Nashville immediately. They still lived on the edge financially and were far too cavalier about health issues. My dad was slightly diabetic, and my mother had never been a very strong woman. She'd almost died in childbirth delivering me and her recovery took far longer than normal despite her sturdy maternal lineage. They overlooked even the most obvious maintenance for themselves; their horribly cluttered little frame house was the stuff of a Stephen King nightmare. Whenever I visited, a huge part of my time was expended clandestinely disposing of piles of magazines, newspapers, and advertising circulars, along with many varied items my father thought he might ultimately use for his sculptures. These raw materials, as he referred to them, included anything and everything cardboard, plastic, or polystyrene, which he collected by wading through dumpsters and garbage cans throughout Nashville. In many ways, my parents were much like a pair of adorable, innocent puppies that needed constant supervision.

Since I didn't work on Wednesdays, I decided to make the trek then instead of waiting for the weekend. There had been several additional feature articles spurred by the carbon monoxide deaths in Greencastle and I felt compelled to act immediately. My dad had recently taken a part-time custodian's job at the grade school, so only my mother was home when I arrived. She was on her way to a local convalescent home where she volunteered once per week helping serve lunch and assisting with the ladies' various knitting projects. Many of the women were devilishly driven to knit or crochet, resulting in a lot of scarves, pompom hats and vests for various relatives as well as for church bazaars. My mother wasn't even remotely adept at any of these crafts, but that seemed to be of small consequence. When a ball of yarn went rolling off into the corner threatening to unravel a knitter's last several rows, she was still nimble enough to retrieve it before too much damage had ensued, so she was certainly useful.

"Oh, Deensie," she said, giving me a huge hug and kiss, using the nickname that had resulted from my own mispronunciation of my name as a toddler. "I just have a few minutes before I leave for Erskins House. Did you forget that I help out over there on Wednesdays?"

"I guess I did," I replied. "I wanted to look through some of my old stuff actually, and then, um, maybe do a little sorting."

"Honey, you said a long time ago that there wasn't anything left here you wanted, remember? And, as you know, Daddy has a detailed catalog of everything that he's brought in," scolded my mother, gently. "I wouldn't go rifling about and just pitching things willy nilly! As Daddy always says, y'know darn well that very item will be *exactly* what he needs to complete his next big project."

"Oh, of course! I wouldn't dream of pitching anything

that Dad's collected, Mom!"

"That's certainly a chance I wouldn't take, but if you're very careful we could use a bit more space around here if you see anything that could be … tossed," she reluctantly agreed. "Are you looking for something in particular, honey? I thought you'd taken everything you wanted when you left for college."

"No, nothing specific. I met someone I knew from high school at a party the other night and I just wondered if there was anything that I might have left here. Just curious, that's all. Oh, but you know whose name came up out of the blue? Chomp Martin. Is he still doing those huge chainsaw monuments around here?"

"Oh my, mercy no, thank the heavens!" shuddered my mother. "I think he stopped working here back around 1970. Maybe even before that. Nobody would buy that awful stuff that he made. And such a horrible temper on that man! Oh my! He was something to behold as you probably remember, Deensie. I think maybe the town council ran him off because of his outrageous behavior. His reputation had reached the point that it was creating problems in getting the public into town to see all our good artwork that was available," she added, lovingly gesturing to the endless piles of detritus encircling her, as though they were the unfinished mounds of clay fervently awaiting Rodin's formative hand or a slab of Carrara marble glistening expectantly beneath Michelangelo's quivering chisel.

"So then, where'd he go?"

"You'll have to check with Daddy to verify my memory," she replied, tapping her forehead with her index finger, "but best as I recollect, he moved down near Shepherdsville in Kentucky. You know, right off 65. Out near those river bottoms. Awful murky swamps down there. That place just plain gives me the creeps. Probably a much better place for someone like him though, I expect!"

"Do you know if he still lives down there?"

"Well, now that you're asking about him, I'm pretty sure he died a few years back. Frozen to death in his cabin I think it was. Well-deserved if it's true. You know, there were always these rumors that Chomp Martin was a Nazi soldier with the Germans back during World War II. But somehow the government couldn't ever prove it and … get rid of him. Unfortunate for all of us living here, that's for sure. He had some kind of thick foreign accent you know. Might have been German, I guess. I stayed my distance so never heard him speak. You'll have to ask Daddy about it. I'm sure he'll have the full story straight. I just never trust that I have these things exactly right in my head these days."

"However, it's often a mistake to accept something as true merely because it's obvious."

Basil Rathbone as Sherlock Holmes in

"Dressed to Kill" (1946)

Chapter 3

I distinctly remember when Cathy Martin showed up in Nashville, just a few weeks before we'd both started fourth grade. She'd moved into a lichen-shrouded shack far from town, down near the widest section of the creek bed, a low-lying breech almost always wallowing in thick, coarse mud. At one time everyone had dumped their garbage in that area, undoubtedly contributing to the miasmic atmosphere, but a town ordinance had prohibited the practice right after World War II when mandatory regular garbage collection commenced. It was still referred to as 'the dump' for many years afterwards however, until finally enough newcomers had arrived ending the odious designation.

Cathy was riding her bike, a dark green two-wheeler with badly pitted chrome fenders and a poorly spliced, greasy bike chain. We'd both slid to a stop as a motorbike suddenly roared through a sparse outcropping of trees from the opposite direction. The motorbike skidded directly in front of us, showering us with a torrent of stinging pebbles. Cathy fell in avoiding the collision. Then after a tight swerve off the path, my bike fell sideways into a small ditch, dumping me into wet leaves.

"You brainless moron!" Cathy had yelled as the motorbike swerved up the hill. "What kind of half-ass ignoramus plows over that rise, huh? You troglodyte!"

I didn't know if I was more shocked about the motorbike swerving into us or this girl, who appeared to be about my age, referring to someone as a half-assed ignoramus. Up until that time the word ass was unquestionably the worst cuss word I'd ever heard coming out of the mouth of the crudest boy in my school. And I had no idea what a troglodyte might be, but it sounded equally nasty. The girl looked over at me as I struggled to unearth my bike from the leaves.

"Hey, you ok?" she asked.

"Yeah. You?

The girl shrugged.

"You know, your knee is bleeding," I commented.

She glanced down then just shrugged again.

"What's your name?" I asked.

"Cathy Martin."

"I'm Denise … Denise Prescott. You should get some mercurochrome on that cut. It's mighty ragged looking."

Cathy flipped down her kick stand and walked out to me, extending her hand. I don't remember ever shaking another kid's hand before that moment. Cathy's chopped hair, a greenish dirty blonde, looked as though it had been combed with an eggbeater to use one of my mother's favorite expressions. Her blue jeans were badly frayed at the pockets and folded up to just above her socks – socks that may have been white at some point in history. A faded blue t-shirt with a torn, jagged collar, also well-streaked with dirt, topped it all off.

"Naw, it'll just bleed itself out an' scab over. Worse is when it don't bleed, y'know? That's when you get an infection."

I'd heard the rumor about some crazy mountain man

named Chomp Martin with torn off sleeves baring upper arms the size of Smithfield hams according to Mark Stephens, a kid whose mom worked at the same restaurant as my mom. During the summer months when the restaurant was swamped dealing with the tourist trade, Mark and I would pick up a few extra dollars rolling utensils into napkins and helping clear tables. Most of my information about the outside world in the summertime came by way of Mark. He claimed he'd heard stories from his cousins over near Spencer Lake, that Chomp Martin (no one ever dared call him Chomp to his face and certainly never addressed him as Mr. Martin either) had been accused of strangling a man with his bare hands just for the sheer fun of it. He was tried in a lower court, but those following the proceedings were surprised when he was acquitted for lack of evidence. The coroner said it was inconclusive whether it was Chomp's stranglehold or the deceased man's high alcoholic intake that had resulted in the victim's demise. Nonetheless, Chomp's rough reputation had arrived in tandem with the man himself and all skirted a wide path, heads down, just in case that jury's conclusion proved incorrect. However, I didn't connect Cathy with Chomp Martin at first.

Cathy rode over on her bike the next day. She had on the same jeans, rolled up higher, and the same ragged, though now also blood-stained, socks. The cut on her knee sported a thick dark brown scab. A dented aluminum pail jangled over her handlebars.

"Wanna go blackberry pickin' with me?" she asked.

"Sure. You mean that spot over near the state park cabins? I heard those bushes were pretty much picked clean a few days ago."

"There's a better place way further down that hill. Three or four huge bushes. Juicy and burstin' in fact. We can sell 'em in town."

"That's over in the dump," I replied, wrinkling my

nose. "They say those berries are full of poison or something."

Cathy's laugh came out as a loud croak. "My dad and me live down there right by that dump as everybody calls it. Been eatin' those berries all summer long an' neither of us has heaved 'em up yet!"

That's when I realized that this girl named Cathy Martin was Chomp Martin's daughter. I knew what it was like to be the girl that no one ever wanted to be around because of your parents' weird artistic proclivities. I'd certainly encountered that stigma on many occasions. However, I was grateful that my own folks didn't possess Chomp Martin's violent reputation.

"Dirt never killed nobody, but stupidity does every day," she tossed out. "That's what my dad always says."

I nodded. "Hey, I like that. Can I ask you one question?"

"Sure. Shoot."

"What's a troglodyte?"

"You know what a Neanderthal is, right?"

"Sure. Early man."

"Same thing more or less," she shrugged.

"Oh, ok. Yeah, show me those blackberries. Let's go."

And that's how our friendship was born.

*****

Over the next few days, we collected and sold about two dozen pouches bursting with ripe blackberries, then made ourselves sick eating candy bars that we'd bought with our profits. Our subsequent profits were far more wisely channeled towards acquiring mystery books and board games as well as taking in the occasional movie. During those first weeks I learned that Cathy's mom had walked out two weeks after Cathy was born. "Soon's she could stumble outta that dugout we lived in and head back to the closest bar, according to my dad," Cathy mused. "I only met her once and that was years ago."

"And? What was she like?" I still hadn't met Cathy's father but couldn't imagine living without my own mother. Mom had always been quite frail, rather silly, almost like a cartoon character with her chirpy little voice, but she did her best to encourage my father's artistic pursuits and somehow managed to get food on our table every day, despite juggling the various collection agencies that defined our precarious existence. If we'd lived out in Hollywood, you'd have sworn she'd been the role model for Edith Bunker in "*All in the Family*". But fortunately, my dad was no Archie.

"What was she like? Eh, nothing special to talk about. She was never any part of my life, so I never had reason to want her around."

"Makes sense, I guess," I remember answering. It was hard not to agree with Cathy. She seemed remarkably self-assured. Maybe that came from not having a mother. Cathy taught me Morse code and we would broadcast brief messages to one another either with flashlights or squibs of paper in school. We were both already fearless tree climbers, even making a paltry attempt to build a tree house that completely disintegrated that winter. Cathy had laughed when we'd spotted the random bits of bark strewn along the thick bed of pine needles. "Oh well, so much for our expertise in architecture!" she'd guffawed. "Frank Lloyd Wright had Fallingwater and we've got Falling Needles!"

Her vocabulary and reading skills far outshone mine, even though she claimed she'd skipped school most of the time they'd lived out in Spencer and had rarely resided anywhere close enough to go to school prior to that. Although there was a tiny lending library in Nashville, the supply of mystery books, our favorite genre, was incredibly puny. Cathy had brazenly stolen, or to use her phrase, "had borrowed on long-term loan" two dozen Nancy Drew and Beverly Graves mysteries back in Spencer that summer, on loan from the Indianapolis library. We immersed ourselves in those books, later graduating to Sir Arthur Conan Doyle's *Sherlock Holmes* stories and constantly bantered about in our atrocious attempts at a British accent. Undoubtedly, this prepared me for my newsroom coworker Thorwald's antics a decade or so later.

I taught her Parcheesi, Hearts and double solitaire. She taught me Chinese checkers, Monopoly and Poker. She would stop over at my house or, more commonly, taking a cue from one of her favorite pilfered Nancy Drew mysteries, we would leave notes written in our own reversed mirror codes, detailing a time and place to meet, stowed in a hollowed space in a gnarly oak. This cryptic exchange worked for several months until a large barn owl fought to reclaim mailbox rights over his territory and won.

Over the next two years we picked wild blackberries, raspberries, and blueberries throughout their seasons, along with brashly stealing squashes, pole beans and tomatoes from a neighbor's garden and selling them alongside the road, undercutting other vendors' prices. We earned enough to purchase an Instamatic camera. The camera itself was reasonably inexpensive compared to other cameras. But the cost of those film cartridges, not to mention the processing, was exorbitant. During a required marketing strategies class in college, I learned that successful businesses always followed that model of drastic markup. Make it too cheap and too easy and you'd never make a decent buck off it because the public won't put any value in it and the item simply won't sell. The Kodak Instamatic camera was certainly a stellar example of that financial philosophy.

Anyway, insofar as the Instamatic was concerned, we were hooked. And we didn't want pictures of ourselves posing in those fashionable short mesh gloves complementing a billowy, pink taffeta Easter dress topped off by a blue-ribbon sailor hat or seated with all the aunts, uncles, cousins, and grandparents impatiently waiting for someone to say grace so we could dive into the Christmas goose. Oh no. We sought outlandish pictures. Nothing was sacred. Our photos were comprised of chicken pox and vaccination scars, moles, warts, scabs, gymnastic antics, ugly toes, crooked teeth, anything unusual … clearly identified and very snugly positioned between the black photo corners on every page of our scrapbooks. One summer afternoon while pretending we were Tarzan and Jane swinging on a branch across a rushing creek, the branch snapped and Cathy fell into the creek, suffering a badly broken right ankle and deeply lacerated calf. We documented our creative paint job of blue and gold amoebas on the cast in a short series of photos along with the black stitching that threaded up her leg. Leave the cute family pictures to the Norman Rockwells of the world, we'd chanted in unison. (We did like one of Rockwell's latest pictures, though, called *Girl at Mirror* since the girl was clad only in a white slip and seated in front of a cheval mirror. That one was quite daring for old man Norman in our opinion.)

By the end of that school year my parents were working for a local diner. My mom waited tables and my dad washed dishes and handled other custodial chores. I'd finally met Cathy's father Chomp Martin, a gruff man with a thick foreign accent who very rarely spoke to anyone. Watching him wield his roaring chainsaw splitting huge logs in preparation for his crude, often shockingly indecent totem pole creations, was a terrifying experience. Fortunately, any closer contact with Chomp was almost nonexistent. I'd always meet Cathy outside her place, a tiny shack with an outhouse. I'd never been invited inside and had no desire for such an invitation.

Cathy was one of the taller girls in our class. When forced to clean up for school that fall, I was surprised to discover that she had almost white-blonde hair and what had looked to be freckles was just plain old dirt. Chomp Martin by contrast was a huge, powerfully built, weather-beaten man, his massive arms duplicated in scale by a broad chest, and what was visible of a thick neck beneath his jet black, bushy beard. They'd always lived off the land as far from civilization as possible until they'd moved to Spencer. Cathy said her dad knew she was really smart and wanted for her to attend school. She claimed to have taught herself to read and figure out her numbers by the time she was five years old, and that Chomp didn't want her to grow up a "drug-whacked whore" like her mother.

In Spencer there had been numerous threats on Chomp's life stemming from the court's decision regarding the homicide. As a result, he decided to try his hand at chainsaw art in Nashville. Cathy maintained that her dad was a good person, but nobody could see beyond the beard, tire tread muscles, strange accent, and treacherous reputation. Nonetheless, the man terrified me. I was grateful that whenever I stopped by her place she was already waiting outside, sometimes munching on a heel of bread or pegging stiff new playing cards to her bike spokes with clothes pins so they would emit as loud a motorcycle noise as possible. Her father's motorcycle had been stolen when he was in jail awaiting trial back in Spencer. Stolen by one of the cops in fact. If he ever found out which one had nabbed it, that man had just drawn his last breath snickered Cathy, cop badge or no cop badge.

"Meaning exactly what?" I'd asked.

"You don't wanna know," Cathy had replied, running to the nearest pine tree while shrieking, "race you to the top, Curly Locks!"

She wouldn't have required the head start anyway; she was by far the stronger athlete.

"Perhaps there's method in his madness."

Basil Rathbone as Sherlock Holmes in

"The Woman in Green" (1945)

Chapter 4

When I got to the newspaper Thursday, I checked through the back obits during my break. Sure enough, there he was:

ΔPD//: Shepherdsville, KENTUCKY: Harold Chauncey ("Chomp") Martin, age 56, died late December 1972 or early January of this year. He was found frozen to death on January 21 in a rural cabin near the river bottoms. Tentative identification of the deceased and additional information provided by Bullitt County Sheriff Ernie Carstens and the Bullitt County Coroner's Office. Exact date or cause of death unknown. Possible surviving daughter, Cathy Martin, last known address Nashville, Indiana; current whereabouts unknown. ΔET

Another of the copy desk clerks as we were known -- the only guy in our section in fact -- looked over my shoulder as I pulled up the obit from the archives. "What's that?" he asked, pointing at my screen.

"Nothing actually," I replied, as I quickly killed the search. "Just wondering what happened to a girl I was friends with back in high school. This obit was for her dad. Not important, just curious."

The clerk's name was Thor – not Thor as in the massive hammer-wielding god associated with thunder and lightning of Old Norse mythology, but after Lars Thorwald, Raymond Burr's character in Thor's mother's favorite Hitchcock thriller, "*Rear Window*." And to complete the effect, our Thor's last name was Larsson. At any rate, *our* Thorwald, who had retained a slight British accent from his early childhood years in London, simply nodded, crumpled another stick of Juicy Fruit gum into his cheek and walked aimlessly away obviously disinterested. He had this maddening way once he was almost out of earshot of finishing conversations over his shoulder and ended this one with "didn't know you even 'ad any friends from prep. I sure's 'ell don't." Somehow, this revelation came as no surprise.

Hank had left on Tuesday for a two-day trip to Chicago. He was driving with two women, the DD with whom he was having the affair, and Gloria Camponella, whose face reminded me of a basset hound, sadly lacking both the brains and the build of the DD. She always introduced herself with an off-key rendition of "you know, G-L-O-R-I-A," while seductively undulating her scrawny hips and shoulders. Sadly, G-L-O-R-I-A was one of those poor women who by the time she turned forty would probably look closer to sixty.

Of the two women, the brilliant DD was by far the more venomous. She'd had the audacity to ask me to lunch just days after I had walked into my own bedroom to discover my husband greedily biting one of her enormous breasts as she sat astride him on our bed, their clothes tossed freely about the room. While calmly tucking into her *chateaubriand* at lunch -- graciously offering to pick up the check after I'd already ordered a tuna salad plate -- she'd stated that she had taught Hank everything he knew about sex. As far as she was concerned, he was now hers during their regular working hours, as well as any business trips, of course. I could have him the other times. Having expected extensive apologies for her outrageous actions, I was so stunned I could barely stumble blindly from the table. As I looked back at her, the bitch calmly crossed her long, well-tanned legs, wriggling slightly to make visible a little more cleavage beneath the tufted lavender lace camisole that subtly peeked out of her deeply vee'd blouse. She smiled demurely, signaling the waiter for another glass of pinot. "I never intend to get married. Why should I?" she continued loudly as I walked out. "I plan to retire early while I'm still young, travel, see the world. But in the meantime, I may nibble about the edges of any men whom I find attractive … their marital status is quite irrelevant as far as I'm concerned." By then I was out of earshot.

That episode was the beginning of Hank's and my bumpy road of couples' counseling, which thus far had merely served to underscore my insufficient attention towards my affectionate spouse, which any normal woman – case in point, Ms. DD -- would certainly have been able to gratefully provide. This analysis was delivered on a bimonthly basis by our counselor, Dr. Racine, who couldn't understand my indifference. Hank was devoted to his dad and stepmom, a brainless twit of a woman who'd somehow wriggled her way to the front of the casserole line a couple years after his mom's death. Hank had a very good-paying job, complete with staggering annual bonuses, got along excellently with his coworkers and superiors, and was a man with a lucrative future with Idyllic. We were actively saving for a down payment on a nice house outside Bloomington or Indianapolis, hoped to one day have a family, get involved with the church community … this last truly surprised me since neither of us were much into organized religion. All the dots should have cozily lined up to produce an excellent bonding within our marriage. But to me, it all just looked like wayward football strategy scribbled by a three-year-old across the tv screen.

"Oh? It's not uncommon for a woman traveling alone to carry a revolver?"

Basil Rathbone as Sherlock Holmes in

"Pursuit to Algiers" (1945)

Chapter 5

I desperately needed something occupying my thoughts other than Hank and traveling companions DD and G-L-O-R-I-A. If there were any office intrigues operating under my nose in the newspaper office, I sure hadn't heard of them. All appeared to be androgynously fretting to verify information before going to press. God forbid we might make an error by misquoting a source, misrepresenting a story, or fail in our assessment of the information pages. The reporters stuck late Saturday nights in the Sports office might toss back a few celebratory beers, but that was certainly the extent of any partying.

Some weeks the entire copy desk clerk section was smothered in calls and paperwork coming in from outlying correspondents. Other times it was so slow – what Thor referred to as a 'snoggy snoozer' -- we were sent endlessly boring assignments from sister locations such as The South Bend Tribune, to replicate recipes, property tax evaluations and such.

This had been one of those snoggy snoozer weeks thus far. Bored, attempting to keep focused on something other than Hank and his travel companions, I thought back on Cathy Martin and Janet Lynn Webster. Thor had once mentioned that he'd been an editor for his college yearbook in Ohio and I asked him if he thought it possible to obtain a copy of an old edition.

"If it's a larger school, yeah, sure," he'd replied.

"How about the U of Wisconsin?"

"Sounds plausible, but man, that'll cost you, Prescott! Besides you don't want the whole yearbook. Just order copies of the pictures that you want from their office. And, whatever you do, be careful that Old Man Jenson doesn't find out you were diming it long distance courtesy of the newspaper's piggy bank."

During the deadline rush, editors were rarely at their desks in the newsroom. I used those few free moments to call the yearbook office at Wisconsin to ask about acquiring old photos. A student named Mary Jamison answered stating she would also need each student's year at school and their hometown to locate the pictures. Their yearbook was known as *The Badger*, Mary informed me, proudly adding that it had been printed almost every year since the mid-1880s.

"Cathy Martin -- usual spelling?" she'd continued.

"Cathy with a "C", but usual spelling of Martin. She would've been a freshman in '68-69, from Nashville, Indiana. I'm also looking for a senior, Tom Miller, but I don't know where he's from. Oh, also, could you send me any photos of Janet Lynn Webster? She would've been a freshman that year from Columbus, Indiana," I added as an afterthought.

"And you're certain they went to Whitewater? Also, the name Tom Miller's pretty common. We have several other campuses in the state, you know. Sometimes people forget that and assume everybody attends up here. You'll need to send a check for six bucks to cover the copies and mailing costs. I can't send you anything until I receive the money. Sorry if that's inconvenient, but you know … rules!"

She gave me the address and I sent the check with the

afternoon mail. I hesitated to have the photos mailed to my home, but ultimately decided that was probably best.

About a week later a small envelope arrived with a note from Mary. It only contained two pictures -- one of graduating senior Thomas J. Miller, of LaCrosse, Wisconsin, with a secondary education degree, mathematics major, who was just shown as a grey silhouette captioned "Camera Shy" and one supposedly identifying Janet Lynn Webster, Columbus, Indiana with about twenty-five girls also living in the same wing of her dormitory. 'Sorry, no pictures of anyone named Cathy Martin,' wrote Mary on an enclosed note. And Mary had also checked with the registrar's office and found that no one named Cathy (or Catherine or any other spelling) Martin had enrolled at the university that year or the next in case my dates were off. Of course, she might have been at another campus, urged Mary.

I wrote her a quick note of thanks and posted it from the newsroom.

Tom Miller would have been quite intelligent if he'd planned to become a high school math teacher I surmised. It seemed very odd to me that Cathy hadn't even enrolled, however. Maybe she got to the school a few weeks early, fell hopelessly in love at first sight and just decided to give her own education the heave-ho so she could marry this guy. But he was originally Janet Lynn's boyfriend? Some mental synapse was misfiring over this situation, although maybe the two girls had been up in Wisconsin that entire summer and that's when all of this had happened. I recalled having seen a photo of a Frank Lloyd Wright-inspired mansion nestled into cliffs high above the Mississippi River that had been the Webster's summer enclave. Probably one of those House Beautiful-type spreads boasting seven or eight bedrooms with adjoining bathrooms, a dining room that comfortably seated fifty guests, gaming areas, a cinema room, tennis court, small riding stable ... my imagination went into overdrive. There were probably a lot of back roads to get from the university over to the mansion, but not more than a two-hour trip. For some strange reason I remembered that the town's name was Rutledge.

At that point I should have let the entire matter go, but something kept nagging at me, and I took one further, possibly foolish step, encouraged by my friend Marcy Callaghan, a former roommate from my Franklin College days and now a colleague at the newspaper. In Thor's opinion it was a totally boneheaded move, but nonetheless, I persisted. In the personals section of the LaCrosse Sentinel I placed a two-line note, which was a free listing:

"*Looking for Thomas J. Miller or Cathy Martin (Miller) – please contact Denise Prescott at …*" and I brazenly left the newspaper's main number and newsroom extension.

"Come to think of it, old fellow, some fish'n chips might go very well just now. Thank you for your suggestion, sir!"

Basil Rathbone as Sherlock Holmes in

"Pursuit to Algiers" (1945)

Chapter 6

Much the way that waves slam up onto a concrete barrier, sending towers of spray in every possible direction, Hank's and my relationship remained unpredictable. Some Saturdays we lay in bed together for hours, reading the newspapers, laughing hysterically through favorite passages of various books, making love, taking the occasional shower together, drinking lots of red wine, ordering in Chinese or thin-crust cheese & mushroom pizza, and watching re-runs of old television shows from the late '50s or early '60s like *"Maverick"* or *"Bonanza"* or Thor's and my favorite detective tv offering, *"Columbo"*. *"Columbo"* didn't have nearly enough episodes each season, which was too bad since it almost always included some terrific guest actors and intriguing police work, despite Lt. Columbo's bumbling investigative reasoning. *"The Rockford Files"* boasted a lot more episodes, occasionally including a decent guest actor, and the inevitable car chase with screeching tires and totaled vehicles. James Garner did all his own stunt driving work which was pretty damn amazing … I mean, how old was that guy anyway?

I would start to think we were finally back on track

and then, out of the blue, Hank would disappear to play golf with his buddies on a Friday after work and not return until late Sunday evening. He would claim to have fallen asleep at one of the guy's places after a long night of drinking and smoking a few joints and had simply forgotten to call. Or he'd insist that he had called repeatedly, but that I'd failed to pick up. However, he never could pinpoint just exactly what time any of these aborted phone calls had occurred, leading me to question their authenticity.

Each time he played this little game I became angrier, as did my two best girlfriends. We'd meet for pizza and beer at one of our favorite local dives every couple of weeks and inevitably my careening marriage received my friends' renewed scrutiny.

"Why are you staying in this dead-end relationship with this narcissistic, brutally demeaning man, Denise?" pleaded Marcy Callaghan, my newspaper coworker. "He's just twisting your mind, your emotions, your health, just for the hell of it! Why do you insist on torturing yourself week after week?"

"We've been telling you this same thing now for months," agreed Linda, Marcy's sister-in-law and Franklin College graduate, now in her first semester of law school at Indiana University. Her husband had been ecstatic when she'd received one of the highest grades ever on her LSATs and had immediately urged her to try to enroll at the best law school in the country. Hank had merely hooted in disdain when I'd conveyed Linda's exciting news.

Brushing crumbs from her hands Linda signaled our waiter for another pitcher of beer. "Get out now! Divorce is nothing like the old days, you know. Nobody finds fault on the other party. It's so much easier. Two months of legal separation, split everything down the middle and then, voila! All done. You're finally free of this self-centered moron so you can find someone who respects and actually loves you!"

"I'm still not ready to throw in the towel," I sighed, as both women shook their heads in disgust. "I don't want to get divorced."

The waiter exchanged our empty pitcher for a full one. "Other couples go through therapy like we're doing and manage to miraculously pull it all together. But somehow, we always seem to start out okay immediately after a session and then gradually roll farther and farther apart."

"What's the name of this guy again?" inquired Marcy, twisting cheese strings off a pizza slice.

"Racine," I answered. "I think his first name's Richard, but I've only seen his initials, R.L."

"Ooooh, la dee dah," shrugged Linda. "He's been counseling you and Hank for how long now?"

"Almost two years," I sighed. "Although we don't always get there twice a month like we agreed to. He kind of reminds me of … I can't remember the actor's name off the top of my head … you know, the guy who played that weird devil worshiping gynecologist in "*Rosemary's Baby*?"

"Oooh, Ralph Bellamy!" shuddered Linda, whose incredible memory for trivia never ceased to amaze me. "He played Dr. Guy Sapirstein. Oh wow! Now *there's* a creepy dude if I ever saw one. Although I think John Cassavetes is even scarier looking. Those eyebrows! He played Mia Farrow's husband, Guy Woodhouse, remember? And then there's Sidney Blackmer as Roman Castavet. Head honcho of that coven they all belonged to. But this guy Racine actually reminds you of Ralph Bellamy?"

I nodded as we clinked our mugs together, a toast to celebrate our second pitcher.

"Yeah, he does. Hank thinks he looks like Sapirstein too. He's the one who found him. I knew if I looked for a marriage counselor he would never bother going, so I just let him choose. It made that part a lot easier, believe me."

"Figures," stated Linda, disgusted, as she thumped her

mug down with a loud clunk. "It's all about control with so many of these guys nowadays. That's the stuff that our mothers had to put up with after the war for Chrissakes! Our moms were considered fully competent designing and building armored tanks, jeeps and bombs in factories during the war, then the men all came home and uh oh, guess what, now you're replaced. Now you're far too puny and unskilled to even hold down a factory job building a damned two-slice toaster or single-pull gas lawn mower."

Marcy and I nodded in agreement.

"Oh my god! All of those stupid coffee klatches that our moms were forced to endure with their little pink fluffy mules scruffling along … I don't even know if that's an actual word, but you know what I'm talking about … that awful sound those slippers made slapping across the kitchen linoleum. I lost count of how many trays of burnt chocolate chip cookies my mother scraped into the garbage pail. I can still hear that lid banging down after she let go of it. I can't imagine having to deal with that shit every day, and for the life of me, I can't figure out why our mothers just sat back and let it all happen." Frowning, she shook her head and pushed back in her chair, crossing her arms in disgust.

We were all silent for several seconds and then Linda added, "you know, my mom was one of the best fighter plane mechanics during the war. Every Allied pilot out there wanted her working on their control dash panels when there were any problems, can you believe that? She was considered the absolute ace in her field. But the war ends and guess what? Well, goll-lol-ee, just like Gomer Pyle would have said. Now, she can't even get a simple job retrofitting a dead sparkplug. They placed her over in the mess hall punching meal vouchers. *Punching vouchers*! Then, she finally worked her way up the line to the toaster brigade. What a joke."

"Ok, ok, I know," I interjected, laughing nervously.

"All that aside, Hank thinks if I agree to start a family that all of our problems are going to magically roll right out our sliding door effortlessly, completely whisked away like kitchen orts."

"Orts?" questioned Marcy, coughing mid-sip of her beer. "What in the hell are orts? Roaches?"

"No, crumbs," I replied, smiling, taking a small sip of my own beer. "You know Thor in the newsroom?"

"Oh God, who doesn't know Thor in the newsroom?" groaned Marcy, rolling her eyes.

"Ok, well he's really into all of those oddball words. I'm pretty sure that's where I learned that one."

"So do you really think you're going to stick this out and actually try to get pregnant, Denise?" asked Linda, frowning, shaking her head in distain. "Seriously, that just seems so, well … foolish. You know, like a final nail in your coffin or something. Having kids right now scares the absolute Bajezzus out of me."

"You certainly don't make it sound very appealing," I mused. "And, I'd still have a philandering husband, a stream of kids redolent with rashes, temper tantrums and colic and no job to lose myself into every few days in an attempt to maintain a crumb of dignity."

"You mean ort," winked Marcy, grabbing another slice of pizza. "Great word. I'm gonna remember that one, Thor or no Thor."

We clicked mugs again in a mock toast while I attempted to change the subject to the summer's drought and the economic impact of Indiana's projected corn harvest nightmares, about which I'd been editing a couple of lengthy articles over the past several days.

Although I'd previously managed to keep my feelings bottled up regarding Hank's bi-monthly disappearing episodes, at our next counseling visit, still fueled by Linda and Marcy's outrage, I started screaming at my husband. Dr. Racine had pinned my arms against my sides trying to calm me down, while Hank shook his head with that "see I told you she could get crazy like this" smug expression plastered across his face. It was decided by the two men that Hank should move into a hotel room for a week or so while I was getting back in touch with reality, aided by a low dose prescription of valium. Hank came back to pack after four days – not to move back in or out -- but just for another three-day business trip. At least this trip to NYC was without the DD thankfully.

I was becoming less willing to share any of my feelings at these therapy sessions. I felt myself constricting into an ever-tightening ball, shutting out all outside interference. I'd picked up an additional eight hours at work when another part-time clerk needed to get home earlier every day because her babysitter had quit. This meant I was now working almost full time, with no breaks, no lunch and was completely exhausted all day. At the time I wasn't certain the valium was the culprit, but nonetheless gradually eased off Racine's recommended dosage.

"Precisely. I smell the faint,
sweet odor of blackmail."

Basil Rathbone as Sherlock Holmes in

"The Woman in Green" (1945)

Chapter 7

Almost two months had elapsed since I placed the personal ad in the LaCrosse Sentinel. I had completely forgotten about that notice, Cathy Martin, Tom Miller or why on earth I'd even felt the necessity to place it at all. My life had been caterwauling so much out of control that I certainly lacked the energy reserves to look for some long-lost childhood friend.

"Hey, Prescott," yelled Mr. Thompson, the city desk editor, "call on line five."

"This Denise Prescott?" asked a deep, obviously annoyed voice. I fully expected it to be one of our correspondents, Frank Jacobs, whose six pages of tedious handwritten copy about an upcoming fundraising event for a local Catholic parish I'd unceremoniously slashed into three tidy paragraphs in our earliest edition today.

"Yes," I answered.

"This is Tom Miller," the man growled. "Remember me?"

I couldn't place the name. He also had a slightly unusual accent.

"Who? Oh … oh, right. Uh, hi," I stammered, as the reference became clear. "Um … it's good to hear from you."

"What's goin' on this time?" he barked.

"Going on? Sorry, I don't follow…"

"Yeah, what's up with this Cathy Martin shit again? You some other crazy ass relative thinkin' I know this woman?"

"No … no sir." I was now truly embarrassed for having ever contacted this man.

"I told her old man when he called up here, what, five or six years ago, that I'd never heard of the dame. And that same explanation goes for you, whoever you are. Whoever answered the phone said this was the newsroom … this some kind of story and you're trying to frame me or something? What newspaper you work for anyway?"

"No, not at all, sir. No … sir. Nothing like that. I was just trying to find a friend that I'd lost track of a long time ago. Another friend gave me your name. Thought maybe you had ma ... married my friend. I should never have placed that personal ad. Please accept my apol --"

"What. Paper. Ms. Prescott."

"The … the Indianapolis Star, Mr. Miller. The Bloom … Bloomington newsroom," I replied, my voice quavering as he slammed down the phone.

Thor and I were the only ones in the copy desk clerk section at that moment. Marcy had departed about an hour earlier. Despite the usual underlying din within the newsroom, he heard both ends of my conversation.

"I definitely shouldn't have sent that ad," I confessed, rubbing my forehead.

"Yeah, well, I told you back then it was a really dumb ass idea," Thor replied with a shrug. "In fact, I think those were my very words. Hope the guy's not a serial killer and you've now moved up to the *numero uno* slot on his hit list, you twit."

"He lives way up in Wisconsin, practically in Minnesota, if I remember correctly. I seriously doubt he's going to make the trip all the way down here to Bloomington," I shot back.

"You don't know that he lives in Wisconsin. That's just where you ran the ad."

I sighed in exasperation.

"Prescott," barked the city desk editor, "line five again. Can't anybody else around here answer the goddamn phone? What am I today, the newsroom switchboard operator?"

This time it *was* the correspondent chastising me for my hacksaw treatment of his article. Just who did I think I was anyway? He'd been sending his well-edited copy to The Star for well over two decades now and he'd never received such shallow treatment from a low-level clerk like me! I hung up mid-tirade claiming another call.

I had almost forgotten about the threatening phone call by Friday afternoon. Just as Thor and I were leaving the newsroom, however, a man seated at the entry stood up, blocking our way as we rounded the corner.

"Denise Prescott? Tom Miller. Need to talk with you. Over coffee's fine." His arms remained folded. I mumbled a startled hello and wondered how he had picked me out unless he'd questioned every woman who'd left the building. He started griping about the snarled trail of traffic coming down his entire trip from Chicago.

"I didn't ask you to come down here, Mr. Miller," I countered quietly, attempting a small smile. "And unfortunately, we really don't have time to meet with you for coffee right now. I'm so sorry."

"Make time. Ten minutes'll do it ... no need to detain your … uh, friend here," Miller smirked with a disdainful chin thrust.

"My coworker, Thorwald Larsson," I said by way of introduction. Neither man acknowledged the other.

"There's a place just down the block from here. Open for another hour," Miller stated brusquely.

Thor's thick, expressive eyebrows were working overtime. "I don't relish taking down your obit when I come to work on Monday," he hissed loudly in my ear, grabbing my elbow. "I'm coming with you!"

Mr. Miller didn't apologize for his boorish phone behavior earlier in the week, but once we were seated and had ordered coffee, my investigative journalism roots cautiously surfaced. I asked him if he ever *might* have met a freshman named Janet Lynn Webster at Whitewater, but maybe didn't remember her name. I quickly described her as a very attractive blonde, quite stylishly dressed and undoubtedly well known for her fingertip-grazing skirt hemlines.

"Well, maybe. Yeah, there was some kind of mixer to meet students in the department before classes started," he grumbled. "Ordinarily I skipped out on all that social crap, but my department insisted the seniors meet the incoming freshman, help steer them from making bad curriculum choices, warn 'em against letting homework lapse. Usual crap they should've learned back in high school."

"I see," I nodded. Janet Lynn Webster at a math department function. Um, yeah. Right.

"I left to do my student teaching up in LaCrosse the next day and only showed my face back on campus for a couple of mandatory department meetings and to collect my diploma in June. That was it."

"But you don't think you ever saw her again?"

"Positive. If that was even her in the first place."

"Ok," I replied, smiling, trying to be friendly. "So … um … you were a mathematics major, correct?"

"Well, gosh, I sure am glad to learn you're able to read since you work for a newspaper, Ms. Prescott."

Both Janet Lynn and Cathy were supposedly liberal arts majors I thought to myself. Why would either of them have been at a math department function in the first place? And Janet Lynn had claimed that this man had been her boyfriend prior to Cathy Martin's snagging him in the sack? Something sure wasn't adding up. Even more puzzling, despite his abrasive demeanor, I had to admit that Tom Miller was actually a very attractive man. Certainly not the type one thought of as a high school math teacher. But maybe math and science teachers were a lot different up in Wisconsin … grew up shooting cougars *en route* to kindergarten or something. I plunged on.

"And do you remember what Janet Lynn was like? Or at least this person who might be Janet Lynn," I countered quickly.

"I dunno. Blonde. Pretty in that blonde kind of way if you like that type, I guess. If she's the one I think she had on this sparkly skirt – real short. There weren't a lot of girls majoring in math or science anyway, but the other girls there were wearing those real, ugly, you know, long dumpy skirts, kind of looked like a garbage hauler's bag, y'know?"

"But you didn't even talk with her?" I asked, thoroughly doubting an affirmative answer. "I mean, not even a 'hi how are you' or anything?" This entire conversation was getting weirder by the minute.

"I remember she wanted to sign up for advanced calc for her first semester and asked me if I thought that would be foolhardy for a freshman."

"And your answer?"

"You'd practically be begging for a failing grade, but naw, I figured she'd come to that conclusion all on her own," he snorted.

"So, nothing else?" You know like, do you want to go out next Friday? I said to myself.

"Nope."

"So, if I could just ask one more question … did you eventually meet Cathy Martin's father, Chomp Martin?" I asked carefully. It occurred to me that I still had no idea as to exactly why Tom Miller had driven down here. Thor's unwavering, practically bug-eyed stare just past my right elbow, magnified by his John Lennon-style glasses, was beginning to unnerve me. On the other hand, I was glad he was listening to this bizarre conversation so I could compare notes with him later.

"Never met the guy, but he's totally nuts!" Tom scoffed. "He ranted at me on the phone about his daughter, this Cathy Martin -- wanted to know where she was. I kept telling him he had the wrong Tom Miller to which he kept yelling, 'oh no I ain't! It's you, dammit, you sombitch an' you damned well know it. You better keep lookin' over your shoulder young man 'cause soon's I find you, them shoulders uh yours gonna be missin' themselves a head!"

I had to admit, that certainly sounded like Chomp Martin.

"When did all of this happen anyway?"

"Hell, I dunno. Just before Christmas in '73 probably. I'd just gotten married then … but not to anyone named Cathy Martin!"

"And are you still married?" I blurted out.

Thor grunted out a barely disguised expletive.

Eyes narrowing, he stated quietly, "now that's really none of your business exactly is it, Ms. Prescott?"

I felt a swift kick in my ankle from Thor and shot him an angry glance.

"Right. No. Of course not. Sorry. Chomp Martin died right after he spoke with you, Mr. Miller. He was found frozen to death out in his cabin down near Shepherdsville, Kentucky in the swamp area of Bullitt County."

"Huh? That right?" Miller mused, leaning back further in his chair, taking a long sip of his coffee. "Well, well, now, that's interesting news. Very interesting news. You're absolutely sure 'bout that?"

Or you found him first I thought warily. The assumption was the man had frozen to death. Rural autopsies were rare when the probable cause of death was deemed obvious. A middle-aged drunken Neanderthal, sporting a gut thoroughly pickled after years of imbibing his own moonshine, out in the middle of nowhere in an unheated cabin in the dead of winter was only asking for trouble. Nobody would even care unless some close relative raised a fuss. And if no such relative persisted? Case closed. A stereotypical situation, yes, but Chomp Martin fit that on all fronts.

"It's late, I need to get home," I said, standing abruptly. "My husband will be getting concerned."

"Ok, well here's what I wanted to deliver to you in person, Ms. Prescott. If I ever find the faintest whisper anywhere in your newspaper down here or anywhere else about me and this Cathy Martin person, I'll know you've lied to me. I advise you to keep any further hearsay completely to yourself. You got that?"

Extracting a five from a wad of cash he stood and threw the bill on the table as he stomped out.

Thor and I walked out together after I'd paid. I was grateful that the block was well lit all the way to the parking lot next to the news building.

"Nervous yet?" teased Thor.

"Ok. Yes, Thor. I'm terrified. Happy?"

"You gonna relay all this nonsense to the happy little hubby when you get home?"

"No way."

"Hey, ya want my advice?"

"Not especially, but you're probably going to give it to me anyway, so shoot."

"Drop thinking about any of this crap. That guy means trouble. I can smell it and it totally reeks, let me tell you. Maybe he dumped Cathy's body somewhere … oh, and yeah, so here's another thing to think about: what about this woman he says he married back in '73? He was mighty edgy when you asked him if he was still married, don't you agree? And, hell, just for the fun of it, maybe he actually assisted with old Chomp's demise as well. Stranger things have happened! He reminds me of those grainy pictures you see of terrorists throwing bricks at our returning 'Nam vets during a fourth of July parade!"

*****

Hank was in one of his rare 'let's pretend we're the perfect husband and wife' moods. Although a rainy weekend, we headed over to Bloomington Square for a late Saturday brunch and even agreed on the purchase of a Tiffany style floor lamp that was way out of our price range but perfect for our sparsely furnished living room. I agreed to an early pizza which was so-so and the newly released remake of the movie "*Invasion of the Body Snatchers*" that had recently opened at a neighborhood theater and was truly awful. I decided to keep the information about Tom Miller to myself and just enjoyed being together for the weekend.

Back at work on Monday I received a letter from Mary at the University of Wisconsin. Out of curiosity she had checked back further regarding Cathy Martin and found that the young woman had accepted a full academic scholarship to the university that summer but had never enrolled or even inquired about on-campus housing. This was quite unusual, especially since Cathy had excellent grades and her application essay was one of the best any of the scholarship admissions committee had ever received stated Mary in her letter. The school assumed she had taken another college's scholarship at the last minute and neglected to contact them.

"There is a possible explanation. Yet I venture to say, that the average petty thief has more extensive knowledge of the value of objets d'art than the average collector."

Basil Rathbone as Sherlock Holmes in

"Dressed to Kill" (1946)

Chapter 8

Although I'd kept more or less in touch with my few remaining contacts from high school, I eagerly attended our tenth reunion in mid-September over in Columbus. Hank groused about going, particularly since there was a Bengals/Oilers game he wanted to see in Cincinnati with his usual golfing buddies. During the entire reunion he sat at the bar tossing shots with a bevy of equally bored, grumbling husbands of other alumnae.

Cautiously, as nonchalantly as possible with several friends while discussing old classmates, I asked if anyone remembered Cathy Martin or knew anything about where she was living, if she was married, or if anyone had heard from her since our graduation. Not a soul had even given her a thought for years, but everyone certainly remembered Cathy … and without question, everyone remembered Janet Lynn Webster.

"Do you remember that Cathy Martin's favorite movie was "*Rosemary's Baby*"? She bragged about seeing it dozens of times!" stated Christine Lewis.

"Yeah, I can so see that!" agreed a guy named Alex, whose last name was so scrunched up on his name tag it was completely illegible, although I vaguely remembered him from one of my English classes. "I always thought that both Cathy Martin and Janet Lynn Webster looked exactly like Mia Farrow. You know, with that goofy flippity blonde hairdo all you girls had back then."

"Yeah, perfect check bones and blonde hair, before that hideous rabbit-skinned look. Oh, and those amazing transparent blue eyes, like cat's eye marbles," sighed Christine. "You have no idea how much I wanted to look like either one of those girls, starched-to-the-limit blonde flips or not!"

"They looked exactly alike by senior year that's for sure. But not quite as thin as Mia Farrow, thank goodness," I agreed. "Funny that Cathy would have liked that movie so much. Before we started to high school over here, we were totally in love with the Sherlock Holmes films. But only the ones with Basil Rathbone and Nigel Bruce. The only theater in Nashville showed all fourteen of their films one week every summer. We would just camp out there from the first to the last show every day. I've never eaten so much rancid buttered popcorn in my life!"

"Huh, interesting," chimed in Mark Stephens, my old napkin-folding companion from our Nashville restaurant days. He had also been Cathy's lab partner in a college-level physiology and anatomy course. A relentless organizer, Mark worked with the reunion search team sending postcards to everyone's last known address, attempting to locate some of our former classmates who seemed to have evaporated over the last decade.

"Do you guys remember that Cathy graduated only one person shy of being valedictorian of our class? Beat me by half a decimal point but lost out to Joe Swenson," added Mark.

Christine nodded, but none of the rest of us

remembered that fact. We all agreed that it seemed very odd that she would have just given up on her education to opt for dirty diapers and a marriage license.

"But you have to admit, she really started getting very weird our senior year," added Christine.

"Weird meaning what exactly?" I asked. "I just don't remember anything about her by '68."

"For one thing, she was experimenting extracting stuff from plants that had unusual qualities. Uh, not for anything as dumb as believing in witches like "*Rosemary's Baby,*" Mark chimed in. "She was way too pragmatic for anything like that."

"Like what then?" I frowned.

"She mentioned once that she was trying to create spontaneous combustion without any obvious source of ignition – you know, like sunlight or any direct beam of light. One weekend I remember that a mixture she'd left in a Petri dish the day before had started smoldering just as the janitor was cleaning the hallway."

"Did she get caught?"

"I think she wriggled out of it by claiming she didn't know the chemicals would interact that way. Claimed she was trying to concoct a natural kind of fertilizer for her dad to use on his crops."

"His crops?" I almost spit out my wine. "Wow! I sure wouldn've thought ole Chomp Martin would have been into anything as domestic as raising feed corn and soybeans!"

"The entire Petri dish eerily disintegrated over the next few days once the smoldering stuff was completely extinguished," Mark added. "I was the only one who noticed, but she refused to explain it."

"Did that strike you as odd?" I asked.

"Actually, I figured it was a pretty good trick and not one she was willing to share. A lot of us got totally bored in advanced chem – it moved way too slow – and just kind of worked on our own stuff in there without the teacher's knowledge. Mr. Harris knew a lot, but man, presentation? Ugh. Bad news."

"Did you invent stuff as well?"

"Well yeah, sure. But my stuff was just routine nonsense, you know, like enhancing sparklers. Kid stuff. Given Cathy's science ability, I was surprised to hear she'd accepted a full ride in liberal arts. But maybe she was just bored with the pragmatic stuff in the chem lab and found English and philosophy a lot more challenging."

"Did you talk with her much? Consider her, well, something of a friend at any rate?" I pressed. The intriguing, extroverted girl with whom I'd spent so many carefree days of childhood seemed to have completely withdrawn once we'd hit our teens.

Mark laughed and took a large gulp of his beer. "I tried! Hey, I even asked her out a couple of times," he chuckled. "Once to the Winter Wonderland dance and then again to senior prom, but she always said she already had a date."

None of us remembered having seen her at either function, although to be fair, we probably wouldn't have been looking for her anyway. We did remember Janet Lynn comically pouting when she wasn't crowned Queen, however. In reply to Mark and Christine's queries regarding my sudden interest in Cathy Martin, I said I had discovered several notebooks in Cathy's handwriting at my folks' place and wondered if she'd want them returned. I also mentioned having attended Janet Lynn's engagement party.

Christine had graduated as a music major from Wisconsin but claimed she'd never run into either Janet Lynn or Cathy on campus. She was currently working at a small bank in Columbus as a receptionist – great use of her music degree, she'd shrugged. She was impressed that I'd learned to work with the computer system at the newspaper, complaining that she was still struggling with the newest version of the IBM Selectric with the self-correction tape.

"Just using whiteout is *so* much easier," she'd grumbled. "Watching that aluminum ball clattering about doing backflips all day gives me a real headache."

I refrained from admitting just how many times I'd been forced to completely rewrite a story having erroneously hit the evil kill button, devilishly positioned just above the numeral one on the top row.

Christine agreed to bring her freshman Wisconsin yearbook to work with her the following Wednesday, my day off, so that I could look through it during her lunch hour. The rest of the evening was spent in frivolous conversation with various people reminiscing over our crazy teen years at Columbus High.

There had been a bad accident on State Road 46 just past the State Park entrance. Once you're on that stretch there are no side roads or shortcuts, so we were stuck until the wreckage had been moved to the side. Rain pelted down mercilessly as we sat for a good half hour waiting for a Chevy pickup and a paint-over-rust-hippie mobile to be extricated from one another. Angered from having to sit through a boring evening fueled by far too much liquor and the loss of a sizable football wager, Hank had been driving too fast for the slickened black pavement as well. I was grateful for this long wait so he could sober up. I was equally grateful that we weren't in that mangled heap further down the road.

He slapped the steering wheel, punched through a series of radio stations and finding nothing to his taste, exhaled loudly and pushed back, looking up at the roof of the car.

"So, was it worth it?" he finally asked, glancing over at me. "Think you can make it another ten years until you see all your little giggly piggly high school friends again? Any of 'em have as exciting lives as you do, writing obits for the local rag?"

I knew he was pushing for a fight but refused to let him goad me. Anything he could use as bait these days was fair game; the smallest complaint I might utter met with considerable embellishment for Dr. Racine's notes at a subsequent counseling session.

"I did, yes," I replied, smiling at him in the dark, even though his head was still tilted back facing the roof and he'd closed his eyes. "A few of the girls I used to hang around with have gotten married and moved out West. I was kind of surprised about that. It was great to hear what they've been doing. Some of them already have a couple of kids. I just can't imagine being that far along with my life I guess."

As soon as the words escaped my mouth, I regretted uttering them.

"Gee why's that?" snorted Hank, finally looking over in my direction. "You think you're too good for motherhood or something? You know, my brother was born when my mom was only twenty-four and that was even considered late. Hell, you're five years older than that already and I sure as hell don't see that you're any closer yet to starting a family."

I swallowed, not wanting to be led once again into this constant argument.

"Hank," I replied, trying to keep the usual exasperation from creeping into my voice, "even Dr. Racine has agreed that we have some really major issues to work through before adding kids to our problems. Babies are a lot of work; even your stepmother agrees with me about that."

"Women have been having babies and raising 'em without all this worryin' an' carpin' about it for thousands of years. Now you dames are all on the pill. So, for whatever reason, now you have to stop and analyze it.

What the hell else you gonna do with your life for Chrissakes?"

"A lot of women have careers, or at least rewarding jobs, making their own money, Hank. You work with a lot of them and so do I -- " I began, but was interrupted.

"The point of going to college is to meet your husband. Simple as that. Bring some class and integrity into the relationship. Be the anchor for your kids. You know, make sure there's homemade cookies warm from the oven and a mug of hot chocolate when they get home from school. My mom, God rest her soul, always did that for me. Every goddamn day."

"Your mom was apparently a saint, Hank," I sighed. "My mom sure never did that for me. Not from neglect though. It was rare that she was even home since she was usually washing dishes or waiting tables for some dive or other in town. We couldn't have pulled through without her income, that's for sure."

"So, is that what you have as a goal? Same as your old lady? Or are you planning on making a living working for a lousy hourly wage for a flea-bitten rag like The Star? No pension? No medical benefits? No possible chance of any worthwhile promotions? Hah! Don't make me laugh!"

Thankfully, the cars ahead of us began starting their engines and we slowly began worming along in a long queue off onto the shoulder with the aid of blazing police flares, through a huge drainage ditch that splattered thick mud onto our windshield, and then finally back onto pavement to continue our journey home.

What exactly did I expect from my marriage? How could Cathy Martin, obviously a brilliant, promising young woman, practically our valedictorian and scarcely out of high school, who had never even dated, have met some guy, slept with him a couple of times, gotten pregnant and decided to ditch anything resembling higher education without blinking an eye? Or had she? That doubt began creeping over me again. That doubt called Tom Miller. Tom Miller who had done an extraordinary job completely terrorizing me. My thoughts eerily drifted back into Thor's and my conversation with the man. I suddenly jumped just as Hank reached over for my hand.

"Jesus, Denise! I can't even touch you anymore without you jack-rabbiting all over creation!"

"Proof my dear fellow! We must have proof!"

Basil Rathbone as Sherlock Holmes in

"Dressed to Kill" (1946)

Chapter 9

The Badger was easily three times larger than *The Argonaut* with smaller photos, tightened white spacing in the layout (a pet peeve of mine from my short stint in advertising), and an 11-point Times New Roman print size versus the standard 12-point. I found the 'camera shy' page for Tom Miller and then finally located Janet Lynn's dorm photo that Mary had mailed to me. She hadn't pledged a Greek social sorority which, knowing the social gambits of Janet Lynn from high school, struck me as rather odd. Her parents could certainly have afforded it. Maybe she thought a sorority might somehow cramp her style, I mused. Or maybe she had tried to pledge but was refused. Girls rumored to have loose reputations were rarely accepted into the better sororities.

I paged through the math department section. A banner titled "*Freshmen Shown the Ropes*" captioned one page of asymmetrically arranged photos, cleverly lassoed together (hence the witty "ropes" cutline presumably), with a creative chaining of "greater-than-or-equal" and "less-than-or-equal" algebraic notations.

"Look!" exclaimed Christine, pointing out one of the photos towards the bottom of the page. "That's Janet

Lynn! I doubt I've ever looked in the math department section. What's she doing over there?"

In the photo Janet Lynn wore that fingertip defying sparkly skirt that Tom Miller had described, in a picture that identified several other students, both male and female. Lassoed to that photo, which showed many of the freshmen students in the background, obviously taken at the same occasion, was the label "*Senior Math Dudes*," identifying Rory Dunlap, Chet Parker and Tom Miller.

Either the yearbook had misidentified Mr. Miller or the man who'd stormed into The Star's newsroom was an obvious impostor. I was in line with version number two. This young man was very small in stature, with thick, black-rimmed glasses, somewhat stooped, thin shoulders visible within his white short-sleeved shirt, sporting a skinny dark tie, prominent pocket protector and an even more prominent Adam's apple. The guy definitely *looked* like a high school math teacher. Rory Dunlap and Chet Parker certainly weren't the Tom Miller I'd met either. The man who'd claimed to be Tom Miller looked more like, what … a liar? A thief? A murderer? Maybe I should be more worried about my own safety as Thorwald had urged or even contact the police about this man. I remembered his powerful shoulders, strong arms and those blunt, square-tipped fingers gripping his coffee cup that somehow reminded me of breaded fish sticks. Deep within my subconscious lurked thoughts that he'd killed Cathy Martin, Cathy's father and who knows, maybe even his own wife as well, just for the sheer hell of it. Without question the man had a vicious temper.

I carefully examined the rest of the photos on that page. There was a partial profile of another blonde woman very much in the background of a different photo. It might possibly be Cathy I thought. I asked Christine if she had a magnifying glass to which she laughed, "of course! We're a bank, Denise! We have to identify every tiny mark on every document that finds its way across our desks!"

Magnifying glass trained over the photo, I reasoned there was a slim possibility that the image was Cathy. But this created a host of additional questions in my mind. Had both girls originally been at the campus I wondered? Yet Cathy had never enrolled according to Mary Jamison, the girl on the current *Badger* staff. Was it possible she had simply forgotten to send in the paperwork, arrived at the school only to find she wasn't enrolled, still attended a couple of functions anyway and then just left with this impostor claiming to be Tom Miller? What had happened to the real Tom Miller shown in the photo and where did the impostor Tom Miller fit in? I wondered if it was wiser to talk with the police or simply let the entire matter rest. If there was any kind of missing person case it was probably already a decade old, I surmised. More than likely someone would have raised questions about this before now. Then it hit me. Of course, someone had -- Cathy's own father. But even that was over six years ago. And the man was dead now anyway. Involuntarily, I shivered.

Thursday was a train wreck at the newspaper from the moment I walked in the door. It wasn't until early in the afternoon that I had a chance to send a cryptic message over to Thor's station about *The Badger* photos. Thor's reaction was pretty much what I expected.

"Yep, yep, man's an impostor. Told you. Stolen identity. Body pile's stacking up," he typed back furiously. "TMi popped the Martins & TM."

"TMi?" I queried.

"Tom Miller - impostor."

"What's the motive?"

"Crap. Incoming police sheet. Gotta trot."

Thor wasn't working the next day, so I never had a chance to talk with him.

****

My husband alluded to some vague destination with

his golf buddies and left early Saturday morning. I doubted he'd be showing back up until late Sunday evening. Rather than pacing our apartment in intensifying frustration all Saturday afternoon, I paid an impromptu call on my parents. I'd just visited a few weekends earlier and they were quite surprised for me to arrive yet again upon their doorstep. Since they had several art pieces submitted to the Fall Folk Art Fest being held in Nashville, they apologized that they wouldn't be around too much. I just barely caught my mother at home as she was picking up some lunch to take back to the Fest. I lied and said I'd come in to see the Art Fest anyway – in truth, I had completely forgotten about it -- and was excited to see their display and would see them later. Since they were out of the house this gave me *carte blanche* to delve into their crawl space, crammed to the gills and almost completely black, defeating my dim flashlight beam.

I was specifically looking for the photo albums I'd filled with the pictures that Cathy and I had taken with my little Kodak instamatic camera, as well as a couple of overstuffed scrap books, several notebooks and possibly a few small, reel-to-reel tapes. I was quite certain that none of these items were still at my parents' home, just as I'd rather embarrassingly detailed with Janet Lynn at her engagement party. An earlier superficial search in my apartment, however, had turned up zilch, and at this point, both boredom and curiosity propelled me forward.

Due to the camera's expense, my parents had understandably refused to buy one. I remembered saving every penny I could towards that $16 expenditure because I was so determined to have one, however. Cathy and I split the cost of the film and the development of the pictures each time. I remembered rushing down to the Rexall with the film cartridge requesting our two copies of each shot, then carefully fitting the photos into the black corner edges of our identical photo albums, even adding the same information next to the pictures so all would be identical. I wasn't certain just how many albums we'd accumulated over those few years. Our usual clandestine Monday morning scavenging in the cabins within Brown County State Park's campground had fortuitously netted us a forgotten tape recorder and used tapes on which we recorded a glut of badly plotted mysteries. A pair of new scrap books, boasting fifty pages each, materialized as well, displaying our many bizarre treasures.

I only located one photo album during the search containing several boring shots. Among them, we were taking turns flying a large kite that actually lifted us up momentarily into the air, doing cannonballs into the public pool (neither of us were very adept swimmers) to see who could produce the biggest splash, trying to do the splits in the air while doing a handstand. Then there was some really goofy stuff pasted onto the last pages pretending we were Tarzan and Jane jumping from tree limbs across the river which had resulted in Cathy's not-so-funny broken ankle. I remember laughing, thinking she was only acting like she was in pain and then discovering that she was seriously injured. Other than that, however, they were just laughable photos documenting a fun childhood. Cathy had completely changed when she'd met Janet Lynn in high school. I'd wondered at the time if there had been some kind of idiotic misunderstanding but surmised that the alluring prospect of new friends and activities had eroded what was probably by then simply a waning friendship.

I scribbled a quick note wishing my parents luck with their art entries, pleaded a last-minute engagement, and drove home.

****

Dr. Racine had been out of town on vacation for several weeks. Once the doctor had returned, Hank was caught up in a huge project, so we'd missed yet another week's evaluation. Then, scheduled quite out of the blue,

Hank announced that he now had a series of mid-week meetings up near Rockford – just a straight shot up Illinois route 39.

"It shouldn't be too bad unless traffic's a mess getting over there from here," he'd snorted.

I asked if I could go with him.

"If you're worried about protecting me from Ms. Dixon she's not in on this project."

"Actually, I wanted to drive up to Wisconsin to see the Webster's summer home. Everyone at my reunion was raving about what a gorgeous place it's supposed to be. It's just an hour or so northwest of Rockford apparently. I could drive over early in the day and be back to have dinner with you after your meetings."

"No harm in your tagging along, far's I know. It's a really long, boring drive complete with lousy radio stations unless you're hot for guaranteed salvation into the hereafter."

"I imagine we've reached our destination."

Basil Rathbone as Sherlock Holmes in

"Pursuit to Algiers" (1945)

Chapter 10

Traffic was an impossible snarl, due in part to the unrelenting downpour that accompanied our drive up to Rockford, putting Hank in the foulest of moods. Fortunately for me, however, the following day dawned bright and clear for my excursion over to Rutledge, located right on the Mississippi River, eight miles north of the state line. Why the Websters would have established their summer retreat in this remote outpost was certainly an enigma. The Dreamland Café sign, advertising that it was the Home of Rutledge's only Bottomless Cup of Coffee, appeared to be the only mention of the town's name on any signage throughout the entire place. The closest towns were each at least twenty-five minutes away: Dubuque over in Iowa and Galena down in Illinois shared that dubious proximity prize. But maybe that was the whole idea. Get back to nature, away from everything, and enjoy time spent with one's guests in an exclusive, intimate setting. My parents' idea of kicking back, spending money and enjoying nature was to splurge on sno-cones at the local Topps on a sweaty summer night while swatting dirigible-sized mosquitoes feeding off our exposed pink flesh.

I stopped at the Dreamland Café to ask for directions,

reasonably assured that there couldn't be too many summer homes in a town that didn't really appear to be a town. The young gum-snapping waitress had no idea and had to call back to the cook. He came out from the kitchen wiping his hands along a brown-spattered apron, easily a decade past its last successful bleaching. If my mom was the model for Edith Bunker in "*All in the Family*", this guy was definitely in the running for greasy spoon owner Mel Sharples in tv's "*Alice*", albeit without the acerbic personality.

"Won't shake yer hand, miss. Pretty greasy from all them burgers an' meatballs," he chuckled. "I'm Ned. Angie here says you was lookin' for directions. Whatcha need?"

"I was just in the area and thought it would be nice to see the Webster's estate. I knew the family a long time ago. I mean, they weren't expecting me or anything," I added nervously. "I … I was just curious to see it since I was up here an' all."

"Webster place?" he echoed. He shook his head slowly, staring at me, frowning. "Property got sold what, maybe five, six years ago. Maybe even longer. It's all real overgrown now far's I know. 'Course, you can't see a helluva lot from the road anyways, y'know? Just the fence. Real wrought iron surrounds the entire property – not a lick of rust from what I've seen, which is pretty amazin'. We get some mighty fierce ice storms up here every year, especially up there along the top of them bluffs. Nasty winds and snow too, well, 'cause of the river."

"Oh, I had no idea they'd sold it," I replied, disappointed. I could already hear Hank (and Thor as well even though I hadn't apprised him of my trek) snickering about my having driven all the way up here for absolutely nothing.

"Well, *they* didn't exactly sell it," replied Ned with a strange grimace. "The daughter sold it. What there was left to sell of the place, that is."

"I'm sorry?" I replied, jolted back to attention.

"Heck, it burned down. You didn' know 'bout that? Oh yeah. Geeze. Terrible fire back in, well, '72 I think. Yeah, that sounds 'bout right. Made all the papers. Don' see how you could've missed it. Mr. an' Mrs. Webster, they both died in their beds in the fire. Jes' awful!"

"I'm from down near Indianapolis," I replied, my hand shakily moving towards my mouth. Surely the information would have been printed in the Indiana papers since the Websters had been residents of Columbus for so many years and Mr. Webster had even served on the Columbus town council for ages! How could we all have missed something as gruesome as a fellow classmate's parents' deaths in a fire? Wouldn't someone have mentioned it at the reunion? One heard constantly that our generation was totally self-absorbed. For the first time I truly believed the accuracy of that statement.

"Guess the daughter had just gotten back to school the day before, right after stayin' out here durin' Christmas break," continued Ned solemnly. "I think she was a student over at Whitewater. Crazy of the Websters to build a place so high up on the bluffs in the first place everyone thought. Nothing down here to see 'cept the river fer cryin' out loud. I mean, all those raggedy steep switchbacks on them shiftin' sandy roads to get up there … treacherous for anybody let alone a fire brigade trying to mount any kind of defense, y'know? When they did their investigation, the fire chief said he was amazed the place hadn't gone up in a blaze before then. Them folks didn' have any chance of escape according to investigators. Place was an absolute tinderbox, ready to flare up without even the smallest provocation they said in the papers."

I shook my head in disbelief, just staring at him.

"Anyway, the daughter come back and sold the place practically before the embers'd cooled which seemed pretty odd to all of us up here. I'd only spoke to the girl a coupla times. Very pretty blonde and smart. But she always struck me as real cold somehow. Them eyes or somethin', y'know? Icy blue. Brrrr. Not my type."

Somehow I doubted Janet Lynn would have found Ned particularly appealing either but kept that opinion to myself. If Hank had ever mentioned anything about his boss' future wife having lost her parents in a devasting fire, I certainly hadn't picked up on that information. Maybe men just never talked about things like that. Something about the whole tragedy struck me as oddly familiar, but I had no idea why. Probably what comes from working as a news jockey. At any rate, I knew it would be the first question out of my mouth when I saw Hank tonight.

"Thanks for all of the … um, information," I finally stammered.

"You mentioned you knew the family at one time? Real sorry ma'am that you had to hear 'bout all this from me. More coffee? How's about a donut? I gotta fresh-toasted coconut with your name scribbled right on top of it, eh? On the house, ok?"

"Sure, thanks," I nodded, attempting an appreciative smile. I sat staring at the orange and turquoise vinyl daisies in the plastic vase on my table as Angie brought over the donut and refilled my coffee. Absentmindedly, I broke the donut into three sections, folded it into my napkin and put it in my coat pocket to eat later. What came fiercely to mind for the thousandth time was that I needed to get all of that hoarded flammable mess out of my parents' home before this kind of tragedy might sweep them away. I vowed to refuse any and all excuses they might offer as soon as I arrived back home. I was just ready to ask for my check when the door opened behind me.

"Hey there Holmes!" called out Ned, who was now dismantling a juice fountain. "What, you slummin' over in this part of the world this afternoon?"

I looked over my shoulder and there stood Tom Miller. Or more exactly, the man who actually *wasn't* Tom Miller. What on earth was he doing up here? He probably still lives just a few miles away in LaCrosse, I said to myself in answer to my own dumb question. As nonchalantly as possible, I slowly looked away, loosening a few curls to partially mask my face. With any luck he would stand there shooting the breeze for a few minutes with Ned, order a cup of coffee to go and leave without noticing me. I had the coffee to go part correct, but he walked over to my table, turned the opposite chair around and straddled it. Snapping off the lid he blew across the hot liquid and then looked up at me.

"Well now, this is quite a coincidence."

"Not exactly," I muttered, still averting my eyes. "Are you following me or something?"

Instead of answering my question, he continued with, "let's see now, as I recall, last time I saw you we were drinking coffee down at that cozy little diner way down in Bloomington, Indiana. So just what are you doin' up in this neck of the woods, Ms. Prescott? On assignment researching a human-interest story on Ulysses S. Grant?"

I frowned at him, obviously confused.

"Ulysses S. Grant … uh, 18th President of the United States?"

"Yes, Mr. Miller, I know who Ulysses S. Grant was, thank you," I retorted coldly.

"Maybe you didn't remember that he lived over in Galena, Illinois after the Civil War, that is, before he became president," smirked Tom.

"Oh, of course. Right. Well, yes ... partly … at any rate," I fumbled inarticulately. "Actually, I drove up to Rockford with my husband yesterday. He has several business meetings. Just on a whim I drove over to Galena to do a little shopping and then thought I'd head up this way, following along the river. You know … um, just to enjoy the view."

"Not much to see along through here," he smirked. "Guess nobody mentioned that to you, huh?"

"Well, there's still some beautiful color up here. You know … the trees. But you're right about any view of the river. Guess I was poorly informed on that account. I stopped here for some coffee and was just ready to head back to Rockford actually. Another few minutes and I wouldn't even have been here at all."

He nodded slowly and took a long sip of his coffee, staring at me over the rim.

"She was asking about the old Webster place," remarked Ned from his eavesdropping vantage point.

I cringed. Damn. This man was the last person on earth with whom I wanted that information shared.

He folded his arms over the back of the chair. Somehow, he seemed even more powerfully menacing than our first meeting.

"Did you know them?"

"I don't think I need to answer that question," I replied, adding cautiously, "particularly to someone who claims to be someone he isn't!"

"Oh, but I *am* that very person!"

"Right. You're Tom Miller," I stated as matter-of-factly as I could muster, my heart beating erratically in fear. "That same Tom Miller who graduated from University of Wisconsin as a math major in June 1969."

"Yes ma'am, that very same one," he nodded.

Pushing back my chair I stood up abruptly.

"I don't know who you are, sir, but you're definitely not that Tom Miller," I hissed between clenched teeth. "There's a picture of him in the Wisconsin yearbook and you certainly don't look anything like that man!"

"Misidentified," he shrugged. "You're talking about that same picture I described to you, correct? That insufferable department soirée with that blonde chick in the short skirt? Yeah, that guy wasn't me obviously. I look a lot more like my camera-shy silhouette -- the grey ghost image -- doncha think? Now just sit back down. I don't bite."

"Ok," I replied, still standing, crossing my arms. "Obviously not you. So, then who was it?"

"Guy named Russ Miller. He was also a senior that year. Actually, I was at the party, just like I mentioned. I'm just not in the picture."

"So, if I go back and look up this Russ Miller, he'll look like the one captioned in that group photo? You're certain about that?"

"Yep, quite certain," he replied. "And now, with that deep mystery cleared away, just why are you really up here to see the Webster place? Sit down, dammit, Ms. Prescott. You're makin' me nervous."

Maintaining a belligerent stare, I slowly sat back down.

"Curiosity, Mr. Miller … or whoever you are. Just plain old curiosity. Janet Lynn Webster is marrying my husband's New York boss in a few weeks. I had no idea that her parents …"

"Ahha, I see," he grinned, nodding his head. "That 'just plain ole curiosity' factor. You can call me Tom or a lot of folks just call me Holmes … if you'd prefer."

I made no reply. My preference was just to call him gone.

"I have a key to the gate. That's the only way you'll get past that twelve-foot-high wrought iron fencing topped with razor wire. There are just some charred remains yet of the buildings still standing. The pool has some mighty impressive trees sprouting out of it now too. Come to think of it, I believe those are mainly sugar maples, so maybe they'll have some of that nice foliage you were hoping to enjoy."

I bristled at the obvious taunt.

"Why are you entrusted with a key? Are you the

caretaker or something?"

"Yeah, or something," he shrugged. "So, you wanna see it or not?"

No woman in her right mind waltzes off with a guy like this just to see the remains of a burned-out house. Every neuron in my brain fired with major warnings. Naturally, Tom picked up on my hesitation.

"Hey Ned," he called out over his shoulder, "tell this very fine lady that I'm just an ok, ordinary guy, huh?"

"Holmes?" laughed Ned. "He's a total pussy cat. Definitely a-okay lady!"

So now I'm taking the word of a local greasy spoon's cook who has referred to the man twice using some arbitrary nickname. A cook I'd just met less than fifteen minutes ago who, admittedly, at least served up a decent cup of coffee with real cream … at a café in a town with a population topping out at less than fifty more than likely. Cue music from "*The Twilight Zone*" right here, whispered Thor's voice in my head.

"Ok," I finally replied, "I'll follow you."

"Be easier in my truck – there's some steep climbs along with some nasty switchbacks."

"No way, José."

"Ok, your car's mechanic bill. Be sure to keep it in low gear."

Even though the sun still nestled low in the clouds, the warmth of the day had now disappeared. A cool breeze smacked me squarely in the face. I shivered slightly, buttoning my coat as I walked to my car. This won't take longer than a half hour I repeated under my breath. Then I'm back on the road to Rockford. Should make it back to our hotel in ample time to meet up with Hank for a drink or two before dinner. I'm sure as hell going to need that drink by then, too. I had gone on many assignments for my college newspaper as well as for *The Star* and made a paltry attempt to convince myself that this was no different than any of those treks. However, of course, I couldn't fool myself: this was different. Way different. Interviewing some woman who refused to adhere to zoning laws and rebelliously hung out her wet laundry in full view of a pricey upscale Bloomington neighborhood or a ragtag group protesting a small corner grocery store with an inventory consisting solely of cigarettes, cheap booze, and illicit magazines, highlighted my most recent interviews. Probably my most terrifying assignment had been a one-on-one interview with Vincent Price during a power outage while a vicious thunderstorm raged last year. Thor was furious he hadn't landed that interview.

Within a few moments, it seemed as though we were driving straight up into the air as the narrow dirt road spiraled upwards, with harrowing switchbacks along rock-lined cliffs. No view could be worth this kind of danger I reasoned, wondering again why on earth the Websters would have chosen this aerie. Finally, we arrived at an ornate front gate. After unlocking it, Tom pushed the huge gate back several feet motioning for me to drive through. The gate banged shut behind him as he pulled into the lead, and we continued to climb along a heavily tree-lined and overgrown, serpentine gravel drive for maybe another quarter of a mile. Suddenly the charred remains of what had obviously been a huge wood and stone estate came into view on a bluff visible through the tree line. He rolled down his window and motioned for me to pull alongside him.

"Kind of reminds you of Manderley after the fire, doesn't it?" he said. "You know, in '*Rebecca*'?"

I nodded, completely speechless, looking out at the extraordinary panoramic vista of the Mississippi far below. A faint scent of burned wood still drifted in the cool air even after six years. "This must have been an absolutely breathtaking place."

"It was," answered Tom, following my gaze as it

traced the beautiful view.

"If I remember correctly, you said you'd never met Janet Lynn except possibly at that math department party. How could you have been here unless she was here?" What in the hell was I doing out here with this guy in the first place? Were all victims this stupid and trusting?

"Turn off your car and I'll walk you through what were some of the rooms. Five minutes, ok? I'm not the big bad wolf. Don't worry."

Reluctantly I killed the motor and slowly got out of my car keeping my keys firmly tucked between my knuckles, my hand poised deep within my pocket. Tom was already picking his way through what had been a wide brick walkway, now a sea of waist-high weeds, as he walked up to the ragged timbers that straddled the former entrance.

"This main entry hall rose up over thirty feet," he stated when I'd caught up to him. "The chandelier that was hanging here was well over a hundred years old. Thing was absolutely breathtaking. The history traced it as having been brought over from France in small pieces during the first World War, and then reassembled here on site. The workmen had to construct a fragile circular staircase to rebuild it because the space above was so narrow and the chandelier absolutely massive. Only one man could be on the staircase at a time because it swayed so badly, and it took months to get the chandelier fully in place. Total loss in the fire, obviously."

We continued into what had been the great room according to Tom. A cavernous, smoke-blackened fireplace stood at the end, with a jagged segment of its burned chimney's stonework stretching up at least fifteen feet above our heads. Next to that had been the dining room, where part of a filthy, faded velvet drape lay under shattered, blackened glass remnants from what had probably been a series of enormous bow windows looking out over the panoramic display of the river far below. We carefully stepped through a large pile of charred timber into what had been part of the library. The fire had consumed all the books as well as eaten chunks out of the bookshelves. The fractured remains of the main stairway twisted up into the afternoon sky.

"Reminds me of Twelve Oaks," I murmured.

"Reminds you of what?"

"Twelve Oaks. In *'Gone with the Wind'*. The plantation where Ashley Wilkes' family lived, next to Tara. You know when Scarlett comes back from Atlanta after the war."

"If you say so," he shrugged. "Sorry, don't remember a lot about that movie except I always thought that Vivian Leigh got a really bum deal considering all her efforts to save her stupid family from starving to death."

"So, you never answered my question," I blurted out. "How do you know what the house looked like if you didn't know Janet Lynn?"

He gave me kind of a lopsided smile. "Well, that's actually fairly easy for me to answer, but kind of a longer story, so I have a suggestion."

I waited.

"What if we drive down to Galena, grab a couple of drinks and I'll tell you. Then you'll be on your way back to Rockford."

"My husband's expecting me to meet him for an early dinner," I replied firmly.

"No, he's not," laughed Tom. "He's planning to have a few drinks and probably dinner with one of your least favorite people."

My mouth dropped open. How did this man know about anything pertaining to my personal life? "She's not up here for this trip," I replied curtly. As soon as the words tumbled out of my mouth, I realized that rather cleverly Tom hadn't actually mentioned that it was even a woman, much less the DD, so I could easily have just fallen for some clever fishing line.

"Oh yes she is," he laughed again. "Kind of a last-minute arrangement apparently – had to check into a different hotel since yours was already at max. But you can verify all that later. So, here's the deal: I'll meet you at the Algiers Pub in about twenty minutes. Just follow me out from here. With those clouds scrolling in off the river the light's going to be fading real soon anyway. And even though it's easier driving down from these bluffs, you add an element of darkness or foul weather and it's downright treacherous as you can probably imagine."

I'm going to follow you out of here, but I'm just going to swing right past you once we reach route 20 and head back to Rockford I seethed inwardly. Was Dorothea Dixon up here entertaining my husband after all? They had pulled that little innocently framed stunt on me one other time when we'd all been in Indianapolis for the premiere convention of cutting-edge security equipment in the U.S., supposedly after their relationship was over. Hank had finally shown up for bed at around 3 a.m. having freshly showered elsewhere. But for whatever reason when Tom pulled into the Algiers' parking lot, I followed him. Without question this was a subconscious minor retaliation on my part if the DD was really partying up here with my husband.

The place was already teaming with senior citizens ordering early bird dinners.

"I can't imagine being so old that I'd want to take the old lady out for dinner at 4 p.m. just to save a buck fifty," Tom joked. "I mean, then what would you do the rest of the night, y'know? Watch Jackie Gleason reruns? Play Parcheesi?"

I glowered at him.

"Bar ok?" asked the hostess. "If you're not ordering dinner that's our usual policy. And miss, I'll need to see identification."

"Bar's fine," answered Tom as I fished my driver's

license from my purse. "What're you drinking?"

"Chardonnay," I replied.

"Two chardonnay and a dish of those pretzel and Chex mix combos," he said to the bartender. This surprised me. I would've pegged Tom as the draft beer type.

"So, guess you need to start talking," I said once we were seated. "Tell me what's going on. My limit is one drink and I'm certainly not hanging out here to talk with you after that, although I do appreciate your tour this afternoon."

"Well, not real sure where I should start," he replied.

"Ok, let's start with how you knew everything about the Webster home, but supposedly you never met Janet Lynn. That's the information you said you'd give me once we'd gotten to the Algiers. And by golly, here we are."

"Ok, that works," he answered, nodding. *"Touché.* You're getting spunkier, Prescott. Looks good on ya."

I waited. Sorry Mr. Miller, your transparent attempt at a compliment was not swaying me.

"George and Sylvia Webster hired me."

"Hired you to do what?"

"Well now, that's a little more complicated."

"Try me," I responded sarcastically.

Our drinks arrived and Tom paid the bartender.

"*Slainté*," Tom said, raising his glass as a toast. "That's Irish for 'to your health'."

"You're Irish?"

"Nope," he replied taking a couple of slow sips. "Not bad, not bad for your basic bar brew … hey, is that considered alliteration?"

"Hired to do what?" I asked, ignoring his attempt at levity.

"How well did you know Janet Lynn back in high school?"

"You know you're very adept at trying to change the

subject," I countered, taking a sip of my wine. He was right; the stuff was pretty decent.

"True, true, but bear with me on this. There's a reason I'm asking."

"I never knew her well. I grew up in Nashville – Indiana, that is – but when my class started high school the schools in Bloomington were so overcrowded, we were bused over to Columbus. That's where I first met Janet Lynn. I think we might have been in gym class together our freshman year, but I don't remember that for certain. Anyway, she ended up becoming best friends with a girl who'd been *my* best friend when we were little kids …" I continued, still uneasy about bringing Cathy Martin's name into general conversation.

"Cathy Martin, correct?"

"Well … yeah. I didn't want to risk setting you off again by mentioning her name."

He sat back and stared at me for a few moments rubbing his chin, then took another sip of his wine.

"So, the quick and dirty answer as to why the Websters hired me is that they didn't think the woman claiming to be Janet Lynn Webster was actually their daughter."

"How does he scare them into believing they may have committed those atrocious murders themselves?"

Basil Rathbone as Sherlock Holmes in

"The Woman in Green" (1945)

Chapter 11

"So, you're some kind of cop then," I stated bluntly. "Undercover division or something? Is that the Holmes reference? A rather unusual use of a math degree, wouldn't you say?"

He smiled. "I do tutor incoming college students in calculus occasionally just to keep my hand in it. One year of actually teaching high school kids was my limit, so I, uh, redirected my interests early on."

"And without the slightest leap of faith, since the two girls now looked so much alike, I'm assuming that the Websters thought that maybe Cathy and Janet Lynn had somehow exchanged places and that's what they intended for you to, what … investigate? When exactly was this?"

"Mr. Webster contacted me through one of his Wisconsin business associates in late summer '71," Tom acknowledged. "I came out to talk with them just after Janet Lynn had headed back to Whitewater that fall for her senior year."

"What made them suspicious?"

"Actually, they'd had odd misgivings for a few years at

that point but had both assumed it was their own memories of certain events."

"Several *years*? And they were just getting around to looking into it?" I stammered. "That seems unlikely!"

"They'd put their house in Columbus up for sale in '68, the same summer that Janet Lynn and Cathy Martin had started college -- probably you as well I bet -- and temporarily moved up here for about six months while their New York apartment was undergoing some major renovations. That's the last time they had any actual contact with someone named Cathy Martin, so they told me. Then in '71 the commercial real estate investment business was getting a little dicey and George Webster felt he needed to be closer to the nuts and bolts of keeping an eye on the company coffers in New York City rather than his Indianapolis office. He chartered a private plane that flew him from Dubuque out east every week and back for weekends. If I remember our conversations correctly, the missus occasionally accompanied him, but most of the time she elected to just stay up in Wisconsin during the week. She was never a big fan of the Big Apple; even Indianapolis was too outsize for her tastes. Nice lady. Very old-fashioned manners. At any rate, that was a large part of the reason they built down in Columbus originally – away from the big bad city. You ever at their place out there?"

I shook my head.

He took a handful of the pretzels and a couple sips of wine. "Warning: Chex mix is pretty stale."

"So where was Janet Lynn that summer? You said 1971, correct? Out here?

"Supposedly she was interning for some small Hearst publication in upstate New York for the month of June. I never could get a tracer on that one, so I'm assuming it was totally bogus. At any rate, she was back out luxuriating at the Wisconsin manse after that."

"Well, that makes sense."

"So, since Mrs. Webster was the one interacting with her most of the time, she's the one who first became suspicious on a more heightened level. Things like not recognizing her two cousins from California when they stopped by for a visit."

"Maybe it'd been a long time since she'd seen them," I offered. "People can change a lot. Especially kids. The fact that she didn't recognize them seems pretty harmless actually."

"They visited the Websters in Columbus back when all three kids were still in high school, and the kids had gone out to see a movie together.

"Ok. But, that said, it's still kind of unusual that Cathy wasn't there with them anyway. She practically lived with the Websters during the entire school year and took a lot of summer trips with them."

"You're absolutely right. Interestingly, however, at the time of the cousins' visit, I discovered that Cathy Martin was in Nashville listening to testimony about her dad's most recent altercation with another artist. Ultimately her dad was released to her custody for a two-month probation. Cathy had no choice but to keep him close to home. She was already eighteen, a year older than Janet Lynn, which is why the judge released the ol' man to her."

"Huh. A year older? Really? I didn't know that. Anyway, what about the movie?"

"So, the story goes that the three kids bought slushies to take into the theater and the nephew really spiked his up with vodka. He got so sick that they all had to leave about a half hour into the flick and he, uh, just managed to make it into the bushes outside before heaving. Then the niece and Janet Lynn walked him back to the Webster's house – a good three miles from the movie theater – because Janet Lynn was terrified that he'd barf again and ruin the interior of the car. None of the kids had told their parents about this at the time, but now the story was unveiled by the niece since almost five years had passed."

"Well, it certainly makes sense that they'd kept that embarrassing an escapade a secret from any of their parents!"

"Before the niece had mentioned the fact that they'd walked home, however, Janet Lynn suddenly intervened that she now remembered the whole ordeal and how worried she was about the prospect of having to scrub out the interior of her brand-new car."

"Sounds like a good reason to me."

"Except it was her dad's car, not hers. She didn't even have a car, new or otherwise, until her birthday several months later since she wasn't sixteen yet. But at the time, no one mentioned the story's inconsistency."

I waggled my hand back and forth. Maybe just an innocent mistake in her recollection. "How'd the car get back to the Webster house if nobody drove it?"

"You'd make a good detective, Prescott," Tom smiled. "Very early the next morning the nephew high-tailed it back to the theater and drove the car to the Webster place before anyone was the wiser. The niece was furious for years that her brother had gotten away without any reprimand."

"Ok, I'll agree it should have been a memorable situation, but it seems pretty, well, I don't know, small potatoes or something to me," I shrugged. "Hardly a matter for the courts as Thor would say."

"Getting back to the summer when I was hired, there were three distinct issues that made Mrs. Webster suspicious. Janet Lynn had never been particularly interested in plants, but all of a sudden when they moved up there, she'd insisted on having a small climate-controlled greenhouse and apparently spent hours researching and cross-cultivating various exotic plants. She kept it padlocked as well claiming she had lost valuable cuttings to the estate's staff members' nocturnal poaching."

"And maybe she did," I shrugged.

"Ah yes, because 'poison is a woman's weapon' you know," smiled Tom.

"Who said anything about poison? Anyway, that's Basil Rathbone in "*Pursuit to Algiers*".

"Ah, very good. Excellent in fact. Give the lady a gold star."

"Let me guess. You're probably plum full of Sherlock-isms," I replied, then adding smugly, "patience is its own reward."

"Ah, ah, ah! Not quite! The quote from "*Pursuit to Algiers*" is actually: 'Patience is an admirable quality.' You're confusing it with: 'Virtue is its own reward.' That's from *Kismet* -- the song '*Rahadlakum*' specifically."

I thought you were a math major I mumbled to myself. Since I'd listened to my parents' LP of *Kismet* almost as much as *South Pacific* while growing up, I was mortified that I'd blown that one.

He then added, pantomiming lighting a Meersham: "elementary my dear Watson, elementary."

I rolled my eyes. This guy's feeble attempts at charm were falling far short of any intended target.

"At any rate, the greenhouse was located a fair distance from the mansion but was completely consumed by the fire, even though a small wooden shed remained intact between the two. The police investigators assumed that air borne cinders had somehow embedded in the structures further down the embankment causing the fire's ignition at the greenhouse and a handful of other select small surrounding outbuildings. A rather far-fetched conclusion in my own opinion. Fire doesn't simply pick and choose like that; if it's that voracious, it consumes everything within its path."

I assumed that Tom had not been part of that original investigation but remained silent.

"Mrs. Webster said Janet Lynn had never shown any

interest in science prior to that summer back in 1969," Tom continued. "She detested the subject in fact. That's why she'd originally opted to be a liberal arts major. She only needed to take earth science her freshman year and then be done with it according to Mrs. Webster. She distinctly remembered having that conversation with her daughter when first looking at Whitewater's curriculum while Janet Lynn was still in high school."

"Well, earth science. Okay. So, there you go. Obviously, there were some plants involved. There it is. New hobby?" Admittedly foraging about in the dirt didn't strike me as something that would have appealed to Janet Lynn as I perceived her, but I really had never known the girl.

"Well, the last one is somewhat more damning, and it was immediately after that incident occurred that the Websters had contacted me. Janet Lynn had tripped over some loose stones and badly twisted her right ankle and was also stung by several wasps at the same time. Mrs. Webster frantically drove her to the hospital in Dubuque fully expecting her daughter to go into a mild anaphylactic shock from the stings since she'd experienced a brief, life-threatening coma when she'd been stung as a youngster. But quite surprisingly, her daughter remained completely unaffected by the venom this time. No fever, no swelling, no coma, no nothing."

"Well, maybe she'd outgrown the allergy. Doesn't that happen sometimes?"

"Very rarely, since subsequent stings are very often lethal. But, ok, you're right. It can happen," Tom concurred, waggling a hand back and forth. "But when looking at her ankle, the doctors mentioned to Mrs. Webster that Janet Lynn would have to be on crutches and completely off that foot for several weeks due to the severity of the sprain. Fortunately, though, the x-rays showed that her ankle wasn't broken … again."

I took a sip of my wine, frowning at this statement.

"Except that Janet Lynn had never broken her ankle," continued Tom. "And that's where everything was suddenly thrown right out into the open for everyone."

"No … but Cathy Martin did," I replied slowly, a strange cold worm slithering high within my chest. "Somewhere I even have pictures of her in her cast in one of my photo albums. Or at least I did. I don't know where those albums are anymore. We'd been pretending we were Tarzan jumping over a river embankment and she slipped on some moss and fractured one ankle and really sprained the other one. Also ripped a long tear in her calf that needed stitches. Ok, ok, so that may well be damning."

"What else do you think you might still have, Denise," Tom inquired quietly, his dark green eyes peering deeply into mine.

I took a sip of wine and settled back on the stool, momentarily lost in thought.

"Go on with your story," I replied, suddenly feeling uncomfortable with having mentioned anything about those old mementoes again. What was I thinking, for heaven's sake? The chardonnay was loosening my tongue. I needed to be far more cautious.

"Ok, so Janet Lynn discovers that Mrs. Webster had hired an investigator to pry into her activities at school. She'd already spread the story about Cathy Martin getting pregnant and running off with me, although I didn't know about it at the time. I suspect that's actually why she attended that math department party – to locate a senior who wouldn't be around at all during the year and had no interest in sticking around after graduation either. Cathy Martin could therefore just disappear into thin air."

"I'm sorry, but to me that still seems, well … a rather contrived explanation," I replied, scarcely veiling the sarcasm in my voice.

"I literally fell into her story as the perfect scapegoat.

A man that she'd supposedly been dating at Whitewater who got her best friend pregnant and then that girl had obviously dropped out of school to get married. The perfect scenario to immediately sever all contact, yes?"

"So where is Cathy Martin then? And why were you so hostile towards me about my having placed that ad mentioning the two of you and simply asking you to contact me?"

"A better question would be where is Janet Lynn Webster. Cathy Martin and Janet Lynn Webster left the Webster's Wisconsin estate together driving over to the Whitewater campus in Janet Lynn's light blue Corvair convertible on August 16th in 1968. Janet Lynn arrived on campus alone, however, on August 19th and attended that math department party on August 20th."

I nodded my head, frowning.

"And only one of them was ever actually enrolled -- Janet Lynn -- even though Cathy had originally accepted a full scholarship," he stated.

"Well, if Cathy Martin didn't end up with you, she ended up with some other guy I guess," I replied rather flippantly. "Why can't you assume that's the reason she didn't end up there?"

"No, not quite," said Tom quietly, taking another sip of his wine. "It's my belief that Cathy Martin became Janet Lynn Webster at that point. The real Janet Lynn Webster is, I suspect, buried along a rural route somewhere in Wisconsin. That's a lot of ground to cover to say the least."

"That just seems so far-fetched. I'm sorry, but --"

"And worse," Tom interrupted me, "once the Websters became wise to her and hired me a few years later, it's my belief that she used a remote, untraceable fire-starting device to set the place on fire and killed them as well. The local police found no trace of any accelerant or hot point of ignition and concluded that the fire was a tragic accident, probably caused by an ember that had bounced out from the great room fireplace igniting the rug."

"But you obviously believe otherwise."

"It was winter. A roaring fire to warm that cavernous room was certainly normal. According to several of their longtime employees, the Websters expected it to be kept going from the early morning hours typically until about 10 p.m."

"So then, were any of the house staff injured or killed in the fire?" Not having grown up in a mansion run by an armada of trained house personnel I hadn't even considered their necessity to the site.

"Quite by chance, no. On Sunday evenings except for the very rare, occasional visitor remaining past the weekend, the half dozen full time staff members were responsible only for serving a very simple dinner in the late afternoon to Mr. and Mrs. Webster and then had the remainder of the evening free. Their cook, a Mrs. Abbott, had an apartment in the back of the house, but Sunday nights she almost always went home to see her husband over in Dubuque. Fortunately for her, that's exactly what she'd done that night."

"Admittedly, there are some huge holes in this," I conceded.

"Most interesting to me, but apparently not to the local investigators, there was a fire alarm system installed within the house. Mrs. Abbott sheepishly admitted to having set off those alarms on more than one occasion and stated that when those things started clanging it was enough to wake the dead."

"So, you're going to tell me that the alarms had been tampered with and weren't working."

"No, no, that would have been pretty easy to figure out. They hadn't been tampered with. The Websters were burned almost beyond recognition, while sound asleep in their beds. They had separate bedrooms. The police thought it was smoke inhalation that got them first. My guess is that they were poisoned first and were dead before the fire even began lapping about the bed skirts."

"Poisoned? What makes you think … this all seems so … incredibly brutal. I can't …" I stammered.

"I've been stumped by how this woman pulled off all of this and other atrocities within this case for six years. Since I was no longer on the Webster's payroll to investigate any of it obviously, I've continued to clandestinely pursue the whole mess on my own as time has permitted until some other evidence brings the case back into the forefront and it's reopened. And in doing so recently, I've placed myself in Janet Lynn's, or Cathy's, if you will, dangerous gun site. Somehow, she learned through an unfortunate leak that I'm the one who bought what was left of the Webster estate. I'd used a bogus corporate name but knew that anyone with more than an ounce of grey matter could unravel that fantasy."

"What other atrocities?"

"Most obvious, the distraught Janet Lynn left for London immediately after her graduation, now comfortably girded with what she presumed was her sizable inheritance."

"It wasn't?"

"Unknown to anyone except his trusted, tight-lipped accountant, ol' George's funds were stretched to the max trying to keep his real estate investments solvent. In addition to far more expensive land redevelopment costs, especially to bring in electric, gas and city water systems on two mammoth projects facing serious environmental backlashes and hostile demonstrations on the East Coast, he'd been hit with a series of expensive lawsuits, all of which he'd lost. Those hefty litigation expenses and extensive fines had almost ruined him financially. Unfortunately for our Janet Lynn – well, Cathy, that is – George Webster's legal team had done an excellent job of hiding these massive indiscretions from his family as well as the papers. There was some early speculation by the police that the fire might possibly have been a suicide on ol' George's part, but that was quickly discounted. At any rate, Janet Lynn, certainly a beautiful, seemingly wealthy, and exquisitely professional young woman in every sense of the word, presented herself as an excellent catch over in Europe. And lo and behold, within a mere eight or nine months she was engaged to a deep-pocketed London toff, not too terribly long in the tooth, who oozed many generations of the bluest ancestry eloquently squirting from every vein."

In spite of myself, I laughed slightly at the imagery. "I take it you don't have much time for British aristocracy. And I assume that engagement was broken off since she's marrying my husband's boss shortly?"

"Nope. She married Sir Henley Clarke. Huge ceremony in fact. Even included a few of those rather distantly removed plastic relics from London royalty according to accounts," replied Tom.

Both of our glasses now sat empty. Reluctantly, I agreed to a second chardonnay.

"About six months or so after their honeymoon – which in typical well-to-do European fashion lasted almost two months ..."

"Eat your heart out Edith Wharton," I murmured, to which Tom nodded in agreement as the bartender switched out our empty glasses.

"Sir Henley began experiencing serious, often debilitating leg pains, very similar to gout. Mind you he was still a reasonably active man of normal weight and no excesses in habit as they say over there. He was hospitalized several times during increasingly severe outbreaks of this mysterious illness. His doctors were baffled by the problem and tried various therapies, both physical as well as medicinal. But the man died in agony about a year after the mysterious attacks began."

"And you obviously suspect something that Janet Lynn orchestrated, maybe this time from her bilious plants," I said quietly, "coming right back to your Sherlock Holmes quote I suppose."

"As noted earlier: poison is indeed a woman's weapon. We've homed in on what is most likely her method -- specifically adding very minute amounts of abrin that can trigger a lethal dose within a surprisingly accurate time frame. Quite easy to hide it within vitamin capsules, for example. Doesn't alter the taste or bring on immediate symptoms like most poisons. The real trick is having the victim ingest the vitamins within an exact time frame."

"Abrin?"

"Look it up," nodded Tom. "Nasty stuff."

"Well, at least this time she was rolling in dough afterwards, assuming you're correct and that she actually murdered her husband intentionally," I countered.

"Unfortunately for Janet Lynn, Sir Henry's will stipulated that he would have to be married for at least two years in order for his spouse to collect. A bit of an oddity, but one that Janet Lynn unsuccessfully fought against in producing a codicil to that original document. But that revised will was ruled invalid by the courts based on an inconsistency of some wording and an unverifiable witness' signature. All of her late husband's wealth went to his nephew which will be distributed in full upon the lad's 25th birthday in a year or so.

"Holy cow," I muttered. "Possibly strike two. Or is that three? So, getting back to the Websters, why the massive fire at the Webster's summer estate? Why not just the house?"

"She needed to get rid of George and Sylvia Webster as well as torch any of the plant evidence, I think. We'll assume she had several abrin seeds. The seeds look like little lady bugs – red with one or two black dots. Tiny but deadly. At any rate, that to me would have been the most expeditious plan."

"Good lord," I muttered.

How did someone plan out this kind of thing? If all this was true, the woman made Sherlock Holmes' nemesis Irene Adler look like a saint by comparison.

"Although not officially hired, I looked into the investigation of Sir Henley's death, which unfortunately, brought me back under Janet Lynn's microscope once again. Her current fiancé originally had no idea that her deceased husband had become terminally ill so soon after they were married. But once he did find out, he quietly hired an investigator in New York. I've worked with that detective on other cases as well and we exchanged quite a bit of information. Interestingly, the wedding date's been pushed back a couple of times already at the groom's request. I think she's now hell bent for leather to bury any information that exists about Cathy Martin's earlier years. Anything that might zero in on her having killed off her rival and the remaining family a few years back. She certainly can't keep doing away with people hoping to inherit their money."

"Why would he want to marry her anyway with those suspicions? I mean … that seems absurd!"

Tom shrugged. "Eh, you know … that's *amoré* … David Fowler's really questioning several sources of this darker history, believe me. He thinks that because she's a beautiful woman with several unexplained tragedies in her wake, a reputation of mistrust has unjustly evolved, like an unwelcome shroud. But, nonetheless, being a cautious man, he wants things quietly investigated all the same."

"Talk about love being blind. And all of this still puts you at risk I assume."

"And you as well, Prescott. If I'm correct, your possession of anything from that deranged woman's past puts you at risk simply because you have real proof of her actual heritage. She can't mess up on this attempt to grab that glistening brass ring. But there's additional information now unfolding in this saga which is basically why I've been forced to re-emerge at least unofficially on this case. And I'm not able to go into that right now."

"And you're sure about all of this. These accusations and her, well, role or whatever you call it?"

"Sure's my name's Thomas Miller," he replied with a half-smile, raising his glass in another toast.

Silently skeptical, I wasn't convinced of that name at all, despite the man's well-played, poker-faced sincerity. Too many years of Thor's automatic disbelief in people, coupled with years of Columbo and Rockford episodes, not to mention a husband who could innocently look me in the eye, while still reeking of his girlfriend's shampoo, and vow complete chastity regarding his whereabouts during an entire weekend.

Stale or not, Tom requested another bowl of the pretzels and we sat silently for a few moments, deep in thought, sipping our wine.

"*Verstehe?*"

I nodded, even though I wasn't familiar with that word. Was it German? I stared at my reflection in my glass rather than looking into those mesmerizing hazel eyes.

"Allow me to congratulate you
on a brilliant piece of deduction."

Basil Rathbone as Sherlock Holmes in

"Dressed to Kill" (1946)

Chapter 12

Hank tiptoed into our hotel room around 2 a.m. but even though wide awake, I feigned sleep. I'd eaten dinner by myself, portions of my conversation with Tom Miller replaying in my head. Hank's childish indiscretions were light years from my thoughts at present. His foolhardy escapades with the DD were nothing compared to the deadly history of Cathy Martin, even if Tom's account was only partly true.

Tom and I had exchanged phone numbers, although by his own admission, he was very rarely reachable by phone. He could usually be contacted via a pager number that he also provided, but his ability to return a call within a short period of time was sometimes compromised. I wasn't certain that giving the man my home phone number was wise, but some insistent inner voice urged me to do so, nonetheless.

Even though Hank had originally insisted we weren't going to be invited to Janet Lynn's wedding down in New Orleans, he now informed me that we'd suddenly been included on the guest list and that he had accepted for us. He was ecstatic. I was terrified. Why on earth would I purposely place myself in this woman's path if she was as dangerous as Tom Miller contended? My preference would be to stay as far away from her as possible. If Tom was correct, at least five people – including Chomp Martin, in what Tom referred to as a piece of the collateral damage body count since the man scarcely had a nickel to his name – had suspiciously perished over the last four or five years.

It wasn't until our lunch break the following Tuesday that I was able to corner Thor in the hallway outside the newsroom and talk at any length about my tour of the burned-out estate and my surprise meeting with Tom Miller. Thor was horrified that I'd followed the guy onto the estate grounds and then recklessly agreed to meet him at a bar in Galena.

"Prescott," he hissed, looking around to be certain no one could hear him, "are you absolutely off your frickin' nut? This guy is totally feeding you a complete line of first-class bull puppy crap. Investigator my ass! He acted like some B-grade movie street punk the way he talked to you when he showed up here. You need to cut off all contact. Like right now. I mean it! Did you ask him what happened to his own wife? Eh? No! I can tell by that dumb look on your face the answer to that question."

"Thor --" I interjected, but he brusquely waved me off.

"And you say his nickname is Holmes? Yeah, no way. I don't follow on that one either. Let me guess – he's discovered that this supposed poison Cathy Martin used on her parents and husband were from the *lycosa carnivora* – that deadly spider whose venom was untraceable in its victims after a few hours in "*Sherlock Holmes and the Spider Woman.*"

"No one but you could quote every Sherlock Holmes' movie ever made, Thorwald," I replied, shaking my head. "Although to be fair, Tom's pretty decent at quoting that stuff too. He thinks that Janet Lynn ... or Cathy ... or whoever she is ... take your pick on names ... was growing abrin in a greenhouse on the Webster's estate in Wisconsin. Then she crushed up the stuff and poisoned both Websters before the fire even started."

"And nobody discovered the plants where this abrin was supposedly being grown? I've never even heard of abrin, Prescott!"

"It's called rosary pea. I looked it up. She probably managed to get some cuttings on the black market, so it was less suspicious."

"And then nestled them right in with the tomato plants in the ol' back garden at the Webster place, eh?" Thor scoffed.

"No, she had a greenhouse on the estate if you remember. Tom Miller said it was always padlocked. Tom also said that the greenhouse mysteriously burned to the ground even though other small outbuildings in between were spared. For better or worse, I believe Mr. Miller at this point," I stated emphatically.

Thor shook his head in disbelief.

"Your middle name 'gullible', Prescott?"

I remained silent.

"And did you mention this adventure to Hank-the-worthless-husband yet?"

"No and I don't plan on it. Speaking of Hank, though, I need to finish up a series of articles the main desk just sent over so I can leave fifteen minutes early today. Appointment with Dr. Racine."

Thorwald rolled his eyes muttering, "boy, some people sure know how to waste their hard-earned money. I could tell you how to fix your marital problems for free: just admit you're not compatible and leave that tuna of a husband as soon as possible. All he really needs you for is to administer those vitamin injections in his ass since that's the one site he can't reach on his own."

"I shouldn't have ever told you about the Myers cocktails," I sighed. "He claims that taking the vitamins by mouth doesn't help when his migraines are really severe."

"That's all pure industrial-size paddock paddies and

you know it. JFK made it a fad, that's all. Didn't exactly help him in the long run, did it?"

"Thor," I sighed, "that's just plain rude."

"True though, eh?"

****

Dr. Racine was running later than usual with his clients prior to Hank's and my appointment. We sat silently outside his office, Hank killing time by flipping through the Spring 1977 issue of *Golfing Today,* evidently absorbed in the sport's comparison tables that were now well over a year old. He'd arrived first, only slightly acknowledging me when I walked in. Definitely one of his chilliest greetings to date. Nervously, I'd started rearranging the contents of my purse since the magazines on hand were either about golf or fishing. One ancient Better Homes & Gardens slopped over a corner shelf, raggedly honeycombed by many female hands eager for any useful coupons, recipes, or ads.

The office door finally opened and a stooped, homely couple about our age shuffled out, the woman visibly pregnant and sporting a badly swollen black eye. At least Hank had never hit me. Well, not yet anyway.

"Sorry for the wait. Please come in and have a seat."

My chair was still quite steamy from its earlier occupant.

"Since I haven't seen you for the last several weeks, let's start with some of those couple's games suggested by Eagen to warm things up. I'm assuming by now you've had a chance to read through the pamphlets I gave you during our last meeting?"

Hank shook his head. "Really not so much into games," he snorted, thrusting his feet out further.

"And I guess I forgot all about those handouts," I admittedly sheepishly. "I'm really sorry, Dr. Racine."

"Well, that's rather unfortunate to hear," he frowned, sitting back in his chair. "I'd hoped to be able to build somewhat on the premises that Dr. Eagen puts forth in his writings. Well, let's start then with examining some positive interactions that you've had with one another since we last met – interactions that you've found particularly enjoyable. That is, some small thing that Hank did or said that you especially appreciated. Denise, my dear, why don't you answer first."

My mind raced. Sadly, not a single thought sprang into my head other than Thor's parting words that I should just admit that Hank and I weren't compatible. I finally mumbled something about appreciating Hank's replacing the inflexible, grinding hinges on our bedroom closet door last weekend.

"Yeah, after being nagged about it day in and day out for six months straight, guess I really didn't have much choice," retorted Hank, fully absorbed in gouging a thin line of dirt from under his fingernails.

"I should think there was some measure of wanting to please Denise by fixing the door, correct?" asked Dr. Racine.

"Not particularly. Just to get her to shut the hell up about it."

Dr. Racine cleared his throat. "Ok and can you think of anything that Denise has done for you in the last few weeks that you've appreciated, Hank?"

Hank stopped picking at his nails and surprisingly, gave a slight affirmative nod.

"Well, I have to admit that I wanted to get invited to my upper level boss' wedding that's coming up in New Orleans in a few weeks. You know, to better position myself -- move up in the firm. Turns out Denise was an old high school friend of David's fiancée which nobody knew until their engagement party up in Indianapolis a couple months back. So, as it turns out, we got an invite after all. You know, based on that. Great, I have to admit."

Rather puzzled, I stared at Hank. Janet Lynn and I certainly hadn't been 'old high school friends!' I couldn't remember any occasions where we'd even said hello when we'd passed one another in the hallway throughout four years of high school. We'd moved in entirely separate orbits. Our invitation to that wedding couldn't possibly be due to that. Something really wasn't adding up.

"Well, that's wonderful!" exclaimed Dr. Racine, rubbing his hands together and beaming as he looked over at me. "Did you mention your appreciation to Denise?"

"Uh, yeah, I uh, guess so," he shrugged, bouncing his leg up and down, "but that still doesn't alter the fact that I just really don't like being married. Maybe it's just Denise. Dunno. I'm just not into this death-til-you-part shit, y'know? The whole marriage thing is too damn confining. Unless there were kids, y'know? I mean, that's a whole different story. I've told her that. Don't want my kids growing up in a broken home, y'know what I'm saying? But she's never been willing to discuss kids, which is crazy I think."

"But you were appreciative about the invitation to your boss' wedding, correct?"

I was surprised that Dr. Racine attempted to bring Hank back on topic. Usually, he just let the conversation meander along, wherever it took itself.

"My boss' boss actually. Yeah, sure. I'm happy that I'm going … I meant that *we're* going. It's gonna be some killer affair with a Second Line and everything, you know?"

Dr. Racine shook his head slightly, smiling. "I don't think I've ever heard of a Second Line, Hank."

"Eh, you know, it's a parade that the guests participate in after weddings – funerals too, apparently. Everyone at the wedding heads outside after the reception and follows this small combo of musicians playing that early jazz stuff, you know like Louis Armstrong. It continues as a parade through a mile or so of streets in the French Quarter, with all the wedding guests waving handkerchiefs and twirling parasols. The onlookers stand on the sidewalks and cheer.

Then the parade drops off the newlyweds at their hotel. Best part of the wedding they say."

"My, this all sounds quite magical! Do you plan to stay for a day or two afterwards? Soak up a little sun? Maybe being together for a few days in a fun city like New Orleans is exactly what's on order!"

"Actually, my flight leaves early afternoon on Sunday so our only full day together will be Saturday," I replied. "Hank has several meetings on Sunday, so he'll be catching a Monday flight."

"Well, then I guess you'd better really live it up on Saturday!" laughed Dr. Racine.

"If one isn't willing to pay the penalty,
one shouldn't play the game."

Basil Rathbone as Sherlock Holmes in

"Pursuit to Algiers" (1945)

Chapter 13

Our flight was over two hours late arriving at New Orleans International Airport. The torrential rains causing the delay had flooded the entire city with several inches of standing water making the trip to our hotel wildly challenging for our cab driver as he circumvented vehicles as well as hordes of oblivious, umbrella-toting tourists persevering along the incredibly narrow streets and slivers of buckling sidewalks.

Even with the steeply discounted wedding guest rate at the Place d'Armes Hotel, this expense would set our budget back for the next several months. But, dripping in the rain, which had finally eased up to a steady drizzle, the restored old brick hotel with its ornate, black-scrolled ironwork posts and balconies, complete with large flickering gas lit coach lamps, helped justify the financial outlay just to experience something this gorgeous. The hotel was located at Bourbon Street near Jackson Square; everything we might wish to visit was within easy walking distance another couple assured us in the lobby while we waited to register. After quickly unpacking we joined a few of Hank's colleagues for dinner at Palm Court, a very expensive restaurant noted for catering to the well-to-do palate for over a century. I knew anything I might order would be far beyond our usual meal allowance since no prices were included. Hank was right. I always worried far too much about what everything would cost.

"Just order your meal and enjoy it," he hissed in my ear when he saw my eyes widening in horror at the blank price column. We rounded out our evening by heading over to Frenchmen Street to hear a couple of blues bands at various bars where the locals typically hung out. At least the suggested cover charges and drink prices were more in line with my chintzy Hoosier standards Hank had chided.

After burning through the dense morning fog, spurred by yesterday's heavy rains, the sun's intensity quickly rendered the air a pervasive sauna. We spent the early part of the day sightseeing, sampling the ubiquitous little sugared square donuts known as *beignets* and freshly broiled shrimp dunked in spicy sauces, while shopping in both the open air and enclosed French Quarter marketplaces. Tired but exhilarated, we headed back to our hotel room for a quick nap before getting dressed for the wedding. Somehow, however, our warm bodies nestled together after mid-afternoon margaritas defeated any attempts at slumber … maybe Dr. Racine was right to suggest that a fun city like New Orleans was exactly what was on order to rekindle the heat within our marriage. Hank was on the borderline for a migraine, so I gave him a vitamin shot to help deflect its potential onset. He shrieked that I must have hit a nerve straight on. Thankfully, the burning subsided within a few moments.

Not surprisingly, Janet Lynn's creamy white satin bridal gown rivaled that on any cover of *Vogue* or *Today's Bride*. Studded with seed pearls throughout the lace overlay, her veil shimmering with diamond chips, Janet Lynn walked unescorted down the center aisle smiling brightly while photographers' bulbs flashed from all corners of the room as she joined her handsome groom, David Fowler.

None of her attendants, also exquisitely attired, were familiar faces from our high school years. The ceremony was quite short, a Unitarian pastor's message leaning far more towards the pragmatic rather than the spiritual, bookended with performances by a string trio providing perfectly rendered Mozart. Afterwards, two of the ushers threw open a pair of heavily carved oak doors and we all followed the newlyweds into an immense dining room just as a fifteen-piece jazz orchestra tore into Louis Armstrong's "*Mahogany Hall Stomp*."

Unlike most weddings, other than the head table there was no pre-arranged seating, so guests could sit wherever they wished. Squeezing through the crowd, we moved to a table towards the back. Hank immediately took off for the bar to find us drinks as I sat down. Other than the two couples we'd dined with last night and a handful of people I vaguely remembered from Janet Lynn's engagement party in Indianapolis, I wasn't familiar with anyone when I scanned the room.

After several moments Hank handed me my drink and sat down. Another couple, obviously more our parents' age than ours, sat down and we exchanged the usual small talk while competing with the increasing din of the band's performance. Janet Lynn and David floated by our table flanked by the inevitable swoon of photographers and posed for several pictures, thanking all of us for "joining them on this truly glorious celebration of their boundless love for one another" as I overhead Janet Lynn reiterate many times in her slightly throaty Southern accent. The couple flitted from table to table, encouraging everyone to visit one of the many *hors d'oeuvres* tables positioned strategically around the room.

"Save room for the buffet, though! We have both authentic Creole and Cajun entrees and sides – shrimp the size of your fist, I swear! I thought I'd gain ten pounds just sampling everything when we came down last month to make our menu selections," she added with a hearty laugh before they moved on to the next table to deliver the same anecdote. If she even glanced towards us, I certainly didn't catch it, although I'd noticed Hank and David shaking hands earlier and talking for a minute or so.

Hank and I danced a few slow dances together, but neither of us were particularly adept dancers. A lot of the New York City guests were excellent swing dance enthusiasts, however, and the band continued to pump out one fast tune after another adding to the fever-pitched excitement. His arms wrapped around me as we stood with many onlookers ringing the floor, Hank commented with amusement on the antics of some of the dancers. This was my old Hank. The Hank I'd fallen so deeply in love with our senior year of college. The Hank who would gently tuck an unruly strand of my curly hair behind my ear or lightly kiss my neck, slowly running his hand over my skin left bare by my low-backed dress.

"My God you're sexy, sweetheart," he whispered in my ear. "Why can't you be like this all the time?"

Although my first reaction was to say, 'why can't you?' I smiled and pulled his arms even tighter around my waist, then turning to kiss him deeply, murmured, "I don't know but I'm ready to start now, honey. Just give me that chance!"

Another series of slower tunes brought us back out on the crowded dance floor for the last few dances, culminating with a stunning blues singer belting out in perfect Billie Holiday style "*Do You Know What It Means to Miss New Orleans*?" Then we were guided out into the cool night air following the Second Line musicians, waving lace-trimmed handkerchiefs that the restaurant had handed everyone. The sidewalks were packed with well-wishers, hooting their approval of the black and white parasol-toting bride and groom as we all wended our way back to their hotel.

I was attempting to unlock the door to our room as Hank unzipped the back of my dress and whipped it off over my head in the hallway, both of us giggling. Once inside we dropped our clothes on the floor and I made a move towards the bed. Hank shook his head whispering, "no, no, shower first, baby, shower, shower!"

I was always so conscientious about being too noisy in hotel rooms, but here I was at 2 a.m. laughing raucously as we lathered one another up, then rinsing every part of our bodies with our hands and mouths before finally stumbling into bed. Why can't we always be like this I kept asking myself? This was so easy. This was so much more damn fun than worrying about having enough money left at the end of the month for rent or car payments.

If we could only have left our lives in this blissful cocoon. But that was not how things played out.

"No, my dear fellow, this is not the work
of a homicidal maniac.
It's something infinitely more sinister."

Basil Rathbone as Sherlock Holmes in

"The Woman in Green" (1945)

Chapter 14

Now that Hank had been promoted, he needed to remain in New Orleans for another day -- fortunately on the Idyllic payroll at a far less ostentatious hotel -- for a series of meetings before the newly wedded couple departed for their honeymoon. I headed back to Weir Cook Airport in Indianapolis on Sunday afternoon, touching down during the first flurries of a minor snowstorm. I still found it odd that our invitation to this New Orleans extravaganza supposedly hinged on my non-existent friendship with Janet Lynn Webster, now Fowler, especially given the fact that the woman had never even acknowledged my presence at her wedding. Involuntarily I shivered, lost in thought, as I mulled over a lonely dinner of scrambled eggs and burnt toast.

Monday morning while I was in the process of editing a long-winded handwritten copy from a rural correspondent, I looked up to see Mr. Thompson, our city desk editor, standing in front of my desk. He'd never walked over to the copy desk clerks' section, preferring to bellow out our last names from the tight circle of editors' desks -- comically referred to as *the raft* because of its resemblance to a flotilla.

"Hey, um Denise," he said nervously, "I need to talk with you, uh, privately. Could you meet me over in my office in just a few minutes?"

"Uh, yes sir," I replied, immediately breaking out into a cold sweat. Since Thompson's primary work desk was prominently affixed in *the raft*, the only time I'd ever seen anyone called into his dark glass office positioned along the perimeter was when they were being brutally reprimanded and subsequently fired. Also, I couldn't think of any time he'd ever called me – or anyone else in the newsroom for that matter – by first name. I mentally scanned through my last week of copy edits. My second day on the job I'd inadvertently misspelled Shipshewana, Indiana as Shitshewana, which fortunately was caught by another editor before the edition went to print. I'd learned to read, re-read, and re-re-read everything before it was sent over to *the raft*. However, I couldn't think of anything that had plopped on my desk that was earthshaking before I'd left last week for the Fowler wedding in New Orleans. What the hell had I done wrong? With the massive expenses we'd incurred while in the French Quarter, I sure as hell couldn't afford to be fired right now! I shot off a fast interoffice note to Thorwald who looked up with legitimate concern as I crossed the newsroom to Thompson's office.

When I walked into his office, Mr. Thompson was standing next to his desk and a woman in a tweed jacket and dark brown skirt was sitting just inside the door. She stood and shut the door as I entered.

"Have a seat, Denise," said Mr. Thompson, pointing to a chair opposite the door. He sat on the edge of his desk. "Please … please sit down. This is Sergeant McDermott from the Indianapolis police."

With a strong grip, the sergeant shook my hand, murmuring something of a hello. My parents, I thought immediately. Damn. I still hadn't made a dent clearing all that hoarded junk at their place. But that didn't explain why a policewoman from Indianapolis was here.

"Is this about my parents?" I asked, swallowing weakly.

Mr. Thompson and Sgt. McDermott exchanged glances.

"No, Ms. Prescott, it's not about your parents," answered the sergeant.

I breathed a sigh of relief. They were ok. This must have something to do with an article I'd incorrectly edited. Maybe I'd inadvertently omitted the all-hallowed term "alleged" when referring to a suspect prior to sentencing. Keep it all in perspective, Denise, I said to myself. If you're fired, you're fired. Praise God it's not about your parents.

"It's about your husband," said Mr. Thompson evenly.

"Hank? He's still down in New Orleans today for corporate meetings with Idyllic Security – that's who he works with. I think his flight's due to land at Indy around seven tonight," I frowned.

It was just barely early afternoon. I considered some kind of drug bust – I knew he used grass frequently – but I was positive he'd never used anything stronger than that and I was also certain that he'd never done any kind of drug dealing … well, reasonably certain anyway. Unless he was incredibly reckless. I couldn't imagine him getting involved with drug sales and jeopardizing his new lucrative standing with Idyllic!

"Your husband was found dead in the bathroom of his hotel early this morning, Ms. Prescott," stated Sgt. McDermott. "A Ms. Dorothea Dixon identified him for us."

"Hank? What?" I stammered, horrified as I shrank back in the chair. I started shaking uncontrollably, strange sounds coming from deep within me. There had to be a mistake. This couldn't possibly be true. Hank was extremely fit. Other than the occasional joint, he didn't even smoke. He did drink, but nothing like some of those minimum two six-packs per night drinkers in his crowd. Tightly grasping the chair arms, still shaking, I looked back and forth from Mr. Thompson to the policewoman.

"What … happened?" My voice came out a strangled whisper.

The policewoman cleared her throat.

"I understand this is a terrible shock, Ms. Prescott. And I'm sure you'll want to have your husband brought here as soon as possible. There are some unusual, well … suspicious … circumstances surrounding his passing, which is why I'm here to ask a few questions," said the sergeant quietly, digging out a small notebook and pen from her purse. "Could you tell me when you last saw your husband?"

"Yesterday morning," I stammered. "At our hotel in New Orleans. We both checked out at the same time. We had the cab driver drop him at another hotel downtown and then take me out to the airport." Yesterday … yesterday when I'd lived in a completely different world.

"Thank you," she murmured, jotting down a few notes. "Time?"

"Early. I'm sorry … I don't know exactly what time."

"Was there anything different about your husband's meeting compared to other times? Concerns?"

"He'd just been promoted to a new position a few weeks ago. Earlier than he thought the promotion was going to happen, but other than that I … I can't think of anything else he's mentioned," I replied, feeling very numb. Truth to tell very little that Hank said to me in the morning made anything of an impact. I was typically pretty cotton-headed for at least an hour most mornings until two cups of java had burned their way through my veins.

"Did you speak with him last night?"

"Last night? No, he was in New Orleans," I frowned, confused by the question.

"I meant on the phone, Ms. Prescott," she said

flashing a fake smile. "Did he call you last night or you him?"

"No," I answered, still shaking, tears now coursing down my face. "He's usually quite … bu ... busy with these meetings. Or sometimes there's … you know, drinks … or dinner. New client discussions. I don't usually expect a phone call from him."

"And you didn't call to check on his welfare? Well, that's convenient I suppose. Not all couples have that kind of understanding."

I shook my head again. What was this woman driving at exactly, I wondered? Was she chastising me for not interrupting Hank's business dealings during his day? None of my married girlfriends would dare interrupt their husbands while they were in strategic conferences either. I vaguely wondered if the officer was married; I didn't see a wedding ring.

"So … can't you at least tell me what happened?"

She flipped to the front of her notebook and began reading.

"Our preliminary investigation shows an approximate time of death to be somewhere between 10 p.m. last night and 4 a.m. this morning. Probably closer to a 10-11 p.m. time frame according to the coroner."

I shuddered. Coroner inquest. Victim no ID. Found in dark alley. Tentative identification. Preliminary investigation. Slugs for stories I'd typed hundreds of times over the last several years suddenly swam in front of me.

"Was this a heart attack? A mugging?"

"Possibly heart attack or stroke, but there were indications that it was not a naturally incurring incident," she replied.

"Not a naturally incurring incident," I repeated dully. "What the hell does that mean?"

"Your husband regularly takes enhanced vitamin supplements, correct? Do you know exactly which supplements exactly?"

What on earth could all this have to do with Hank's vitamins?

"He has several bottles of different pills that he takes. I don't know what they all are. Vitamins C and D, I think, maybe iron and … uh, potassium."

"Capsules?"

"Yes, well, at least some of them are. He also has shots at times to help control his migraines. It's called a Myers Cocktail. Occasionally he has treacherous migraines that he has a prescription to self-administer a shot. They said that President Kennedy had been prescribed that same shot, or something very similar to it anyway. Hank … um … prefers to have those in his backside … less painful than in his arm or thigh, so I give him the shot when he needs it."

Sgt. McDermott remained silent as she wrote down my last couple of sentences. I swallowed hard.

"And when was the last time that you gave him one of those shots, Ms. Prescott?"

I thought for a minute.

"Well, he felt a migraine coming on and I gave him an injection on Saturday night a few hours before his boss' wedding."

She nodded, her pen rapidly scrawling at the bottom of the page and then she flipped to a new page.

"And that was in New Orleans, correct? And how often can you use that same … syringe, I guess is the correct term?"

"A syringe, yes," I nodded. "You can only use it once and then discard it, so it's an expensive treatment. It's really a kind of, well, last resort when the regular capsules aren't effective."

"And there's no way that he could inject himself you think?"

"In his arm or thigh, yes," I answered. "But that really

leaves his muscles sore – he said that's almost as bad as the migraine itself. To inject himself in his … um, buttock … he would really have to twist around … I … honestly don't think it's possible."

"And Ms. Dixon? From what I was told she was seen, well, partying Sunday night with your husband. I'm told you fully approved of their … rather close friendship, yes?"

"No, I don't approve but I'm certainly aware," I replied, the bitterness evident in my voice. "I didn't realize she was at these meetings since she didn't attend the wedding. Are you asking if he'd ever have asked Dorothea Dixon to give him an injection? I doubt it … scarcely the prelude for an exciting sex romp if that's what you're insinuating!"

No answer from the sergeant other than the annoying scratching of her pen. I glanced up at an expressionless Mr. Thompson who still straddled the corner of his desk, arms folded, eyes focused on his shoelaces.

"Any drug use other than the vitamin shots?" inquired the sergeant.

"Drug use? Not … no…" I replied, rattled by this question.

"You're certain?"

"Yes, ma'am …" I stammered. "Well, occasionally he smokes … marijuana. Very occasionally."

Sgt. McDermott abruptly flipped her notebook closed and stood up. Wobbling, I stood up as well.

"I'm sure you're anxious to get home and make phone calls, Ms. Prescott," said the policewoman, putting her hand on my shoulder in what I deemed a less-than-sincere gesture. "Please understand that you're not to leave the state of Indiana at the present time. Also, I'm sure you understand that we won't be able to release your husband to you and your family until we've fully completed our investigation."

I swallowed and then asked incredulously, "are you

implying that I'm a suspect or something?"

"Everyone who was a part of his life is currently considered a person of interest as we try to reconstruct the events leading up to Mr. Taylor's unusual death. As I mentioned, you're not to leave the state until we've completed our investigation," she reiterated firmly. "Are Mr. Taylor's parents still living?"

"His father's remarried and lives up in Mishawaka. His mother died a few years back. And Hank has an older brother who lives up that way also. I'll need to get in touch with all of them immediately," I replied. "His dad hasn't been in the best of health recently either. This will be a terrible shock for them."

"I'll take you off rotation immediately, Denise," added Mr. Thompson. "You'll need several weeks to get yourself … well, settled. Your own parents live over in Nashville in that artists' colony, right?"

I was surprised he'd taken the time to research anything about my folks. Inwardly I shivered. Thor had undoubtedly been assigned a quick background report on me for our boss.

"Don't worry about anything," he smiled, falling short of anything resembling television's Lou Grant's compassion.

My mind reeled. What had really happened to Hank? Was he into something deadly like shooting up heroin? Why had the sergeant asked about drugs? How could I possibly have missed those signs? I thought back on people I'd known in college who were habitual druggies. Not one of them even snorted coke. Everyone was way too poor for that kind of dalliance. Those few acquaintances were cheap potheads who'd smoked grass or passed around a bong at parties.

I walked back over to my workstation, picked up my purse, killed the story about the Presbyterian Church's annual pancake breakfast fundraiser on my screen, placing the original copy back in the communal work basket, and signed out of my computer. Thor was on the phone taking down information. He put the person on the other end on hold for a moment and motioned for me to come over to him.

"Hey Denise," he whispered, "I just heard about Hank. Man, what a total shock! You doin' ok, girl?"

"No," I swallowed, feeling tears starting anew. "Hell, I don't know what's going on. I'll drive up to Mishawaka to talk to Hank's dad and stepmom early tomorrow. Will call them when I get home. Should go over to my folks now … after I stop at our apartment."

Our apartment I swallowed. I wouldn't be calling it that anymore.

"I'll be gone from work for a while. I don't know how long though," I whispered.

"You're coming back here eventually, right? Don't you dare leave me in this mechanical zoo, Prescott!"

"Thompson indicated he'll take me back when I'm ready. I think, anyway. He's never been eager to keep jobs available for us part timers. There's a lot to sort out. And I think I'm even a suspect even though I was up here and Hank died down in New Orleans. I don't really understand how any of this adds up."

"Possible suspicious death, the spouse is always a suspect. You know that. Even if you're several hundred miles away. Elementary my dear Watson," he attempted to joke lightly, giving me a brief hug.

I gave a weak smile in return.

"I'll call you in a few days, Thor," I replied. "I'm not sure where I'll be. My parents maybe … who knows."

"You're gonna be ok. Don't let all this rattle you, Prescott. Promise?"

"Yeah, ok. Sure. No rattling. Yeah, I'll try," I replied, smiling through my tears.

"Atta girl."

*****

Hank's stepmom answered the phone in her excessively treacly voice as Thor would have expressed it. Bill was asleep she told me sweetly. And unless it was "really, really, really important" she certainly didn't want to wake him. His doctor had just prescribed a new medication to ease his breathing; the poor man hadn't gotten so much as a wink of sleep for the last several nights and was truly exhausted -- beyond exhausted, in fact. So, I told her about Hank. She'd inhaled sharply, uttering abstract sentiments. I told her I would drive up to South Bend to see them tomorrow morning. That information was met with a rather weird, exaggerated pause.

"Will you be … expecting breakfast?" she finally inquired. "I don't have any eggs or anything … I'd have to leave Bill to go out to the market …"

"No, no, of course not. I'll just grab something before hitting the road."

"And do you want for me to, well, relay this information to Bill or do you want to take care of it yourself when you get here?" she continued, clearing her throat.

"You decide, Nancy. Whatever you decide is just fine," I stated, trying to keep the exasperation from my voice. "I'll see you tomorrow."

Where was any concern for the widow's welfare, I wondered as I hung up the phone. Granted Hank and I had been experiencing problems, but we'd still been a married couple, trying hard to get our marriage back on track. Or so I'd thought anyway. I pushed out of my mind the fact that the DD had been the one to identify him. In New Orleans. They worked together … just leave it at that, Denise. Get a grip on it. This is 1978. No one swoons these days. I sighed remembering Scarlett O'Hara's scatterbrained Aunt Pittipat constantly declaring she needed her smelling salts whenever encountering the smallest of confrontations. I decided to wait and contact my own parents after my trek up to Hank's. At least my mom would take the time to make hot chocolate and sit down for a lengthy heart to heart.

I also placed a call down to the police in New Orleans and was informed that there were several autopsies scheduled before Hank's. His wouldn't be started for at least three days, possibly four. The toxicology tests could be run simultaneously, and all results would be sent immediately to the police. The coroner and the police would be contacting me separately as they gathered information. I left my phone numbers and other information with both departments. Then, I fell across our bed and cried myself to sleep.

The next morning, Bill Taylor was completely stunned by the news, especially any possible allusion to street drugs when I mentioned the police hinting about drug use. "Leave it to that scum down there to try to point fingers! My boy was always clean! Clean, dammit! You hear me, girl? Clean! Clean! Squeaky clean!" he shouted again and again, so angry that he was often slurring his words, fists slamming on the sides of his armchair as Nancy worked feverishly to calm him down. "I don't wanna hear nothin' about him using any kinda drugs! Not now, not ever! You hear me? I'll stand up to any cop, any judge in any court of law that tries to shovel out that kind of defamation on my son! Tries to ruin his good name now that he's gone! Dammit!" he bellowed, phlegm percolating deep in his throat.

"Bill, sweetheart, your language," chirped Nancy, scolding sweetly. "And you're getting yourself all worked up. I don't think that Denise was actually implying --"

"I just asked the question because they asked me," I interrupted. "I've never seen him do any drugs either." Well, except smoking pot or hitting the bong with his office buddies most weekends, but I figured ol' Daddy Bill certainly didn't need to hear about that.

While Nancy worked to get him sedated, doubling his new medication, I volunteered to take their shopping list and headed out to Kroger's. A pair of specialty-cut, petite filet mignons, imported asparagus tips, large Idaho potatoes, sour cream, fresh garlic chives, fresh Italian bread, fresh strawberries (was she kidding? It was almost Thanksgiving for Pete's sake!), heavy whipping cream, ladyfingers (the crusty kind not that awful spongy kind she'd double underlined), Makers Mark whiskey (obviously I was not living right) … and then finally a few regular items with which I had at least a passing acquaintance. It was obvious from the quantities that I was not being asked to stay for dinner. Nancy seemed put out that she couldn't just repay me later and begrudgingly wrote out a check that I cashed at their bank. When I returned with their groceries, Bill was snoring loudly in his armchair.

"I had an absolute devil of a time getting him to calm back down," Nancy stated icily. "You have no idea how much all of this has upset him."

I stared at her for several moments, trying to compose myself as I set the bags on her kitchen table.

"Well Nancy, I'm not exactly thrilled either!" I retorted, unable to further repress my growing anger at her callous remarks.

Her large blue eyes blinked myopically behind her tortoise shell glasses. "Well, it seems a certain young lady I know was pretty busy trotting around with every man in sight while our poor Hank was valiantly slaving away to try to make ends meet --"

"Wait! What?" I exploded. "Is that what Hank told you was going on in our marriage? I absolutely can't believe it!"

"You know, Denise," she retorted, her hand reaching up melodramatically as she touched her cheek, "Bill and I have never really approved of you, I must tell you. Or your parents either. I mean, they call that … that garbage they make out of what … gluing cardboard and glass shards together like a kindergartener some kind of 'modern art'? My goodness! And they consider themselves artists? Artists of what for heaven's sake … providing fodder for the local landfill? Bill and I both tried to talk some sense into Hank. I mean, we really couldn't hold it against you personally that you had such, well … such poor models for your upbringing. But Hank certainly didn't need to saddle himself with … as Bill often refers to you … such a tragic *denouement*."

I grabbed my coat and purse and walked to the door, so furious I didn't trust myself to utter one more word.

"Oh, and my change?" Nancy added, her saccharine voice having sufficiently returned after her lengthy cataloging of my deficiencies.

I threw a handful of nickels and dimes on the tile floor, smugly watching the bouncing coins noisily scatter in all directions and slammed the door behind me.

*****

I played out endless conversations on my drive home as I raged at Hank, his father, his stepmother, my own parents, Thor, the DD, Dr. Racine, Sgt. McDermott, even Tom Miller, whom I erroneously referred to as Mark at first, having forgotten his actual name. My parents *were* like children. I would certainly be the first to admit that. But somehow, having a ridiculously immature woman like Nancy Taylor ruthlessly attacking my parents in that pathetic Tweetie Bird voice of hers was a foul punch in the gut.

Just as I pulled into our complex it started snowing.

I stormed into our apartment and threw my shoulder bag across the room where it slammed up against the closet door spilling out most of its contents across the floor. My coat and shoes were hurled next, ricocheting off the adjacent wall. Tossing several ice cubes into a goldfish bowl-size brandy snifter, I poured myself a huge glass of whiskey. Not Makers Mark to be sure, but the best stuff that we'd ever been able to afford. I didn't particularly care for whiskey, but there was no wine in the place and I was determined to drink myself into as catatonic a stupor as possible. Shouldn't be too hard to accomplish I figured, since my only meal today had consisted of a stale biscuit, an overripe banana, and a roll of fragmented peppermint lifesavers.

I sank down on the kitchen floor staring up at the yellow wall phone, toasting it as I took my first long swallow. The phone casing was cracked straight through the center, top to bottom, from my having attacked it with the receiver when I'd discovered that Hank was back humping the DD despite all those lovey-dovey, gooey promises he'd made during our first counseling sessions. He'd then taken a picture of the damage to prove to Dr. Racine that I had difficulty dealing with anger. What wife wouldn't be furious with her husband, I'd shrieked in reply.

Racine had then spewed out some reassuring, low key bullshit as I now remembered. My mind somersaulted from one angry confrontation to another while I gulped down the whiskey, topping it off several times after rattling the cubes into an angry vortex.

Suddenly the phone started ringing loudly, the bell thunderously shrill within its cracked casing. Still slouched on the floor I stared at it assuming it was my whacked-out imagination. After what had to be at least a dozen rings I reluctantly pushed myself up against the wall, removed the receiver saying nothing and then slithered back down to the floor. Award for the best invention of the '70s … those extra-long cords that one could relentlessly twist into permanent spiral chunks.

"Prescott?" said a male voice, vaguely familiar, but not Thor.

I didn't reply.

"Is that you? Denise?"

"Who's this?" I replied, surprised how slurred and husky my voice sounded already. How long had I been sitting here and how much whisky had I put away?

"It's Tom Miller."

"Who?" Mentally I searched for a face to attach to the name, but nothing registered.

"From Wisconsin, the Webster estate, your friend Cathy Martin, Algiers Bar in Galena … you know, 'Holmes'," he added. "Hey, don't hang up. I really need to talk to you."

I stared at the receiver in my hand.

"Okee dokee, sooo talk," I replied haltingly. "Free country … free speech … or so they say."

"Denise, just listen," he continued. "This is important. I know you're upset but --"

"Hah!" I laughed, interrupting him mid-sentence, my words still slurring badly, but I'd now ceased to be concerned. "*Moi?* Upset? *Au contraire, Pierre*! Give the man a thousand dollars! Ding, ding, ding, ding, ding! And, my friends, we're gonna throw in that mint green Mustang V8 convertible as well to sweeten up the deal. Whoever you are I'm upset because there's nothing about my life that's ever amounted to so much as an anthill, y'know that? Real artists always laughed at my parents. And me. And so has the rest of the world. Laughed at me that is. Somehow, I just can't ex … ex … *escape* … being the uh … personification, the *grande dame* of ridicule, y'know? Whoever you are just go away! I sure as hell don't need your goddamn pity." I sat glowering at the phone in my hand.

"No, Prescott, please! Don't hang up! I can tell you're drunk."

"Think so? Well, damn, this shit mus' be workin'. Ain' that grand?"

"You're not thinking clearly. If I was any closer right

now, I'd be there in person, but I'm working a case up in Michigan and I can't leave right now."

"Ooooh, Michigan. How nice! Where on the mitten are ya dimin' me from? Mus' be cold up there. Brrrr. It's already snowing down here, y'know? Oh wait, hey, now I remember you. You're that detective guy, right? Holmes, the chardonnay guy. Hey, I'm just about finished with this humongous glass of some kinda whiskey … shit, can' read the bottle from here or I'd let you know. And there's still more in that bottle. Too bad you're in Michigan or I'd pour you a glass too. An' I just defrosted the freezer last week so there's lots of nice fresh ice cubes to … swizzle aroun'. D'ya know my father-in-law drinks Makers Mark. This ain' Makers Mark, I can assure you. Pfft. Like you'd care."

"Denise, the police are going to be at your apartment early tomorrow to question you about Hank's murder," Tom stated emphatically. "Do you understand what I'm saying?"

I sat looking dumbly at the phone, whirling the ice cubes around in the empty glass. Once they'd jump over the rim and skip out to the faded linoleum, I'd throw them back, spinning like dice.

"Hank? He wasn't murdered. The cops haven't even started their … investi …gation thing yet. They said four days or something."

"Yes, he was murdered, Denise. The preliminary investigation indicated that he was poisoned. That's why that cop visited you yesterday at the newsroom. It wasn't some nice social call to let you know about your husband's passing. Trust me, they'd have just crudely handled that by phone."

"And you know this exactly, um … how Mr. Smartypants?"

"Never mind how I know, it's just true," he answered tersely. "Don't go at this alone, mad at the world. Promise me that you won't talk to the police until you have an attorney lined up. You have the right not to let them interview you when they show up tomorrow morning. Even if they assure you everything is off the record, you know full well as a journalist that there's no such thing as any comments related to a crime being completely off the record. And for God's sake don't let them tape anything you say either."

"Oh, heck yeah, you bet yer Buster Browns! Hey, did you 'ave Buster Brown shoes when you were a l'il kid? I did. Only once. Saddle shoes. Thought those shoes were the pen … penultimate cat's meow, y'know? Whoa. I pronounced that right! Amazin', eh?"

"I'm going to try to get down there by tomorrow. I'll help you. Ok? Are you listening?"

I nodded my head slowly, his words scrambled within my thoughts. Hank. No police. Got it.

"Ok, Holmes – see? I remembered you after all -- whatever you say. Yep. Thanks for the call."

Wobbling, I stood up and crookedly jostled the receiver back on the phone. A few moments later a recorded voice repeated several times "if you'd like to make a call, please hang up and try again" and then started a loud electronic bleeping that went on for a good minute. Finally, it shut up. I tossed the old ice cubes clattering down into the sink, cracked open another aluminum tray of cubes, and then liberally refreshed my glass of whisky.

"Hullo! We've had company!"

Basil Rathbone as Sherlock Holmes in

"Dressed to Kill" (1946)

Chapter 15

Fortunately, I passed out before I'd made much of a dent on my second glass. Thunderous knocking on my apartment door jolted me wide awake several hours later. I futilely glanced at my watch in the dark and then struggled to stand, a massive hangover immediately turning the world sideways as I stumbled to the floor lamp and flicked it on. Now there was a key fitting into the deadbolt. I'd failed to attach the chain on the door last night. I was surprised that I'd remembered to lock the deadbolt.

The door crashed open, slamming into the wall, and the apartment manager and two police officers walked in. I remained near the lamp, holding onto it, swaying slightly.

"That's all, Mr. Sims," said the one officer to the manager. "Thanks for your assistance. Denise Prescott Taylor?"

I nodded, frowning. As I glanced outside over the stairwell's railing, I could see that it was quite dark and now snowing steadily. Mr. Sims walked out, closing the door behind him. The officers flipped open their badges introducing themselves as officers Ross and Nickerson and gestured towards my couch.

"If you'll have a seat, we'll keep this interview as short

as possible."

I asked to use the bathroom as they pulled over our two kitchen chairs. The one officer walked in the bathroom ahead of me, taking note of my shoes, coat and the entire contents of my purse still strewn all over the floor in front of the hallway closet. He walked through the bathroom and then nodded that I could go in. I had no idea what he was looking for. After using the toilet, I raided the medicine cabinet and swallowed two aspirin with the limited hope the tablets might ease my spinning head. Bad as my head churned, however, I was grateful I was only harboring this hangover and not worshiping the porcelain goddess with these two policemen here. Someone had warned me last night they'd be showing up today I suddenly remembered. A phone call. I couldn't remember who though.

"So, Ms. Prescott, we just have a few background questions first. Do you have a problem if I turn on this tape recorder? That way I won't have any confusing notes to make sense of later. You're a reporter. You know how that can be when you're writing a story, correct? Since you're not under any caution agreement nothing can ever be used as evidence, of course."

A dim memory flickered about not letting myself be recorded as I sat down on the couch. Officer Ross placed the recorder on the small steamer trunk that we used as a coffee table and stated who he was, who I was, spelling out my full name, Denise Lynne Prescott Taylor, the time (6:13 a.m. – wow, no wonder it was still dark …) and the date, Thursday, Nov. 16, 1978. Officer Nickerson didn't ask any questions, but I noticed he was briskly taking notes, recorder or no recorder.

"Now, I'm told you prefer to go by Ms. Prescott as opposed to Mrs. Taylor, correct?" Officer Ross inquired. "Is that because of your journalism connections?"

"I use both names. My byline is still Prescott."

"Byline?"

"The person who rewrites a story off the wire service or an editorial or opinion piece. Or the original source as well. You know, their name is typed underneath … because they're responsible for the article itself or for the rewrite … that is, the interpretation."

"Ah, I see. Ok then, so Prescott."

"Yes." I had no idea what he was driving at. Maybe nothing. Come on aspirin, I silently urged, do your thing. Even though I was freezing, my armpits were sticky. I also realized my apartment must smell like a distillery. Probably I did as well.

"Your date of birth?"

"March 23rd, 1950," I replied.

"And you were born in Nashville?"

"Yes."

"Nashville Indiana that is, correct?"

"Yes." As an afterthought I added, "sir."

At that point Officer Ross threw out the first curve ball.

"Would say that you and your husband had a happy marriage?"

I hesitated a minute before answering. I certainly didn't appreciate where this query might lead.

"We've been … seeing a counselor for maybe a year or so. So, I'd have to say we were working out some … well, a few very … minor … difficulties. I mean, what family doesn't have its ups and downs, right?"

Neither officer reacted with so much as a grimace.

"And how long had you been married?"

"A little over four years."

"Big wedding, all the trappings? Grandma and all the cousins flown in from Omaha and all that?" he snorted.

Why on earth should that have mattered I wondered. What a bizarre question!

"Quite small actually. No Grandma or any other

relatives from Omaha or much any place else for that matter," I replied, wary of this line of questioning. "Small family. Small wedding."

"So that's not much time, is it? I mean before things in your marriage started going, well, a little sour as they say in the movies, yes?"

"I suppose not. Some marriages never have any problems; some start out with them I guess."

"When was the last time you saw this marriage counselor? A doctor? Psychiatrist?"

"Regular shrink."

"And you and your husband believed that he or she was helping, correct?"

"He. Yes, sure, I guess so." Why on earth would we have continued to fork out a chunk of our salary every month to the man if we didn't think he was helping? Those sessions were one of the priciest parts of our budget.

"You guess so?"

"There's not like a yardstick or something that you can measure progress exactly. It just takes time," I answered, slightly aggravated. At least that was the excuse that Dr. Racine shelled out every month.

"I noticed when we walked in that your handbag had, er, spilled out and some other items had obviously been recently thrown in the corner. Is that typical for you to display your anger in that manner? Is that one of the things that you were working on with the counselor, Ms. Prescott?"

The officer taking notes showed him something he'd written. I wondered if they'd already contacted Dr. Racine's office and knew the answer to that particular question.

"And while you were in the bathroom Officer Nickerson noted that your wall phone in the kitchen was cracked apart, definitely having been beaten in with the receiver. Was that bit of destruction your handiwork or your husband's?"

I momentarily considered pinning that carnage on Hank but thought better of the idea. If they'd already gained access to Dr. Racine's notes from our counseling sessions, illegally obtained or not, they knew damn well that issue had been obsessively discussed during a recent session. I glared at him and then lowered my gaze.

"Mine."

"So, you might say that you have problems with anger, correct? Has your psychiatrist ever prescribed any medications to aid you with your tendency towards such angry outbursts?"

I surmised they already had the answer to that question as well and if they hadn't, the one officer's quick romp through my bathroom vanity would have produced the bottle containing my few remaining valium tablets.

"He prescribed valium at one time, but I haven't been using it for a while," I replied.

"So, it didn't help?"

"I just didn't like being on it."

"Any particular reason you didn't like being on it?"

"It made me feel tired all the time. Confused."

"Ok, I see. I assume you also take the vitamin supplements that your husband did, correct?"

Another quick subject shift. The aspirin was not working. I didn't feel like I was going to throw up, but I was shaking very slightly.

"Sometimes."

"But not regularly."

"Not regularly."

"From Sgt. McDermott we were informed that Mr. Taylor typically took vitamins every day, correct?"

"Yes."

"What kind?"

"I don't know what they all were. That woman …"

The officer interrupted me. "I assume you're referring

to Sgt. McDermott?"

"Yes. Anyway, she asked me the same question. Some of the bottles are Vitamin A, D, C, maybe B, I think. There are other ones, but I don't remember them all."

"Were these capsules, tablets, some of both?"

"Both."

"And on whatever occasion that you would have taken one of his vitamins, would that have been a tablet you think or a capsule?"

"Just a tablet that he would insist I take occasionally. Thing was huge – a horse pill I always called it -- so I had to grind it up and stir it into applesauce to swallow it."

"And when was the last time you took one of those, um, horse pills?"

I thought for a moment. "I don't know."

"You're certain that you don't remember?"

"No, I don't."

"Recently? Say anywhere during the last six months or so?"

"Maybe … but I really don't think so."

"You don't think so or just plain no, Ms. Prescott?"

"No."

He scratched his ear and nodded to Officer Nickerson who flipped to a new page in his notebook.

"But either way you wouldn't ever have taken any of his actual vitamin capsules, correct?"

I shook my head.

"Did he keep all of his vitamins separate? I'm assuming they're all here in your apartment. In the medicine cabinet?"

"There's too many bottles. He always buys everything in bulk, so the bottles are in a kitchen cabinet."

"So, for his trip, though, since it was only for a couple of days, he probably didn't take all those bottles, correct?"

"Well, no. When he traveled, he'd put all he needed in a couple of old prescription containers. Those plastic ones."

"Did he always take samples of all the pills? More than he'd need?"

"I don't know. He probably took along more than he might need. Just in case. That would be my guess. Vitamins were the only thing that combated his paralyzing migraines. I think I might have said that before. If I didn't … then, well, that's why."

Officer Ross nodded, glancing over at the other policeman.

"Were the capsules and tablets mixed together or in separate bottles? The ones he took along, that is."

"I really don't know!" Exasperation was creeping into my voice despite my attempt to remain civil.

"Ok, but he had those smaller bottles with him when the two of you went to New Orleans I presume?"

"I guess so. I wasn't typically watching over his shoulder while he was packing up, officer!"

Calm down, Denise, I warned myself. I was being cornered by these questions and didn't appreciate it one bit. I then remembered last night's phone call. That guy who may or may not be Tom Miller, warning me about these officers showing up this morning, saying something about Hank having been poisoned.

"With your permission, Ms. Prescott, we'd like to take all of the original bottles that are still here in the apartment with us to determine if any of those pills were possibly, well, tainted in any way."

"Tainted?"

"Some of the wholesale distributors we've contacted have mentioned that recently they've been acquiring bad batches of various vitamins and drugs. It would be easy for us to check the batch numbers against any known recent sales to determine if there were any underlying irregularities."

"I … um … see," I replied, frowning slowly. I knew he was handing me a complete load of buffalo chips.

Determine underlying irregularities my ass.

He nodded to Officer Nickerson who flipped his notebook closed and then both men stood up simultaneously.

"You said that all of the original bottles were in the kitchen, correct?"

"Yes, highest shelf in the corner cabinet," I replied, as they snapped on plastic gloves as though preparing for surgery, shook out a large plastic bag, and strode into the kitchen. They returned a few moments later, the bag folded over and held together by a large metal clasp.

Officer Ross stopped the cassette player, carefully tucked it back into its case. Both men mumbled something of an incoherent goodbye, indicating they would be in touch within the next few days and to stay in town. The first weak rays of sunlight were randomly speckling the small fresh snow drifts as they walked out.

Coffee first, I said aloud and began rustling through the cabinet for all the necessary accoutrements. Hank had always liked his coffee so strong a spoon could stand straight up in the stuff. Although I preferred a milder brew, I opted for something closer to his just to jolt me awake. Once the coffee was brewing, I scavenged for breakfast makings, unearthing a rather desiccated, yet serviceable, orange. I took a quick shower then hit the road to my parents over in Nashville to tell them about Hank. I would do a somewhat truncated revision detailing my conversation with Hank's dad and stepmom. Being the innocents they were, my parents had always spoken highly about Hank's family and were clueless that their adoration was totally one-sided.

A churning grey sky lurked above, more than hinting at additional snow, but I made it to my folks' place without incident. Although I had a key, I always knocked first and waited a few moments before using it, primarily so that I wouldn't startle my mother. Clad in her favorite green pin dot apron covered in flour, my mom answered the door.

"Well, bless my stars! What a lovely surprise!" she exclaimed, planting a huge floury kiss on my cheek. "Why you're just in time for blueberry coffee cake. I still had some blueberries frozen from last summer and Daddy insisted that I make a coffee cake this morning – so, voila! That's exactly what I did."

My mother's cakes tended to be based on several obscure Polish recipes that called for lard, making them rather heavy in texture, but typically edible.

"Sounds terrific!" I replied, kissing the top of her head. She just barely stood at five feet and now that she was getting older, she was definitely shrinking a bit, so maybe not even touching that five foot mark these days. "Here, let's brush a little of this flour out of your hair, Mom."

"Oh, goshers! Who would know? Blends right in with all of the grey and white ones already in there, sweetie," she laughed. "Can you believe I just happened to make a huge pot of coffee this morning, so there's still plenty left. Help yourself and then scoot on in to see Daddy. He'll be so glad to see you. You should see his newest art project. Well, actually it's hard to miss since it takes up our entire living room."

And sure enough, it did. The badly sagging brown sofa, my dad's ancient recliner, both floor lamps and a rickety coffee table were scrunched over in the corner. The tv console, which had originally straddled the opposite corner, was now flattened against one wall where no one could comfortably watch it. On the floor was a huge three-dimensional mosaic of various-sized, Clorox-white plastic lumps.

"Well, lookit who's here!" laughed my dad, holding a small can of paint and paintbrush, standing barefoot on the mosaic in the far corner. He was carefully dribbling a small swirl of cobalt blue onto a corner section devoid of the plastic pieces.

"Wow," I said, looking over his handiwork and forcing an enthusiasm I certainly didn't feel. "This is really … something, Dad."

"Yep! Now, who am I? C'mon, sweetheart, you should know this one!" he winked slyly, adding another small dribble of paint over another section.

"Um, well, let's see … Kandinsky?"

"Aww, come on, Denise!" he scoffed.

"Hmmm, ok, how about Picasso … you know his Blue Period or something…"

"Denise!" he frowned at me, his bushy eyebrows beetling over his broad nose.

"Hmmm, definitely not Andy Warhol. How about Gauguin? Van Gogh? Dali? Um, let's see, maybe Jackson Pollack …"

"Yep! You guessed it baby girl!"

This was part of a game we'd played since I'd been in third grade. The answer was almost always Pollack, although there'd been one time when he'd actually stumped me with a piece made of bright glass shards that he claimed was in the style of Paul Klee.

"Now can you guess what the flowers … those white pieces … are made of?" he continued, obviously eager for my attention.

They were all cut from what appeared to be the same type of curved white plastic. Some were glued on by the edges, lined up like dominos, others were face down almost like a triangular cup of sorts and still others were glued down on their center backs with all the edges facing upwards. In the center of each flower was my dad's signature item: a brass postage stamp holder shaped like a large mailbox that appeared somewhere on all his works. He'd found the stamp holders from a fortuitous -- his definition -- dumpster dig outside a bank that had discontinued the item as an incentive for opening savings accounts many years back. Acquisition of said stamp holder didn't quite create the bank's expected motivation, so they disposed of them. Brass stamp holders graced the ends of the pull chains to light bulbs in our closets and storage areas, as well as serving as drawer pulls, candle holders and pot handle replacements on my mom's casserole bakeware. They were part of the decorating scheme … if there was one … everywhere in the house.

"I really can't tell, Dad," I apologized. "Kinda tough to get any sense of perspective standing at the edge here, you know?"

"I'll let you in on a great trade secret," he stated in a loud stage whisper. "Those L'eggs plastic eggs, you know, those egg-shaped containers that the ladies' pantyhose come in these days? I just carefully sawed 'em into all kinds of sections. Your mom got a little weary of vacuuming up all of the plastic dust, but it was worth it, doncha think?"

My mom's canister-style Electrolux, a pre-World War II vintage relic that she'd acquired very cheaply at a resale shop shortly after their marriage, hadn't worked efficiently since before I'd left for college. There was so little actual floor showing anywhere in their house, the vacuum's questionable cleaning acumen certainly wasn't missed.

"How are you going to get it out of here?"

"It's actually in several sections and comes apart. It's what they call a triptych – d'you know what that is? I just happened across that term and realized that's exactly what I was creating."

I nodded.

"But I need to have it all together in one piece so when I'm dribbling the paint it flows from one flower to the next, you know. It's called *Fleurama* -- can't wait for you to see it when I've got it all finished, honey!"

My father's art works were always conceived on a larger scale. His ideas spanned from a twelve-foot-high Hershey's chocolate kiss made of hard plastic egg cartons strapped to chicken wire, to a free-standing calendar fashioned like an abacus that was built with huge children's building blocks rather than colored beads strung along the wires. One of his more promising, useful ideas was a series of scarecrows made of old 45 rpm yellow and black records. These were threaded onto bendable metal rods and were supposed to spin in the wind. However, the records failed to move even in the briskest of breezes, so the crows made a complete mockery of the entire affair.

I was absolved from any further artistic analysis when my mother announced that her coffee cake was now out of the oven and on the table as well as our newly poured coffees. Everything was "gonna be gettin' stone cold if we didn't hurry our little hidies out to the kitchen," she chided playfully. My parents were indeed like puppies, I mused again, but they sure as heck were adorable ones.

The kitchen looked much the same as it had in my childhood. Yellow and white gingham valances hung over the kitchen window with the hand-embroidered little ducks along the hem that my mom had carefully affixed while she was pregnant with me, according to the oft-repeated tale. The biggest difference was the pantry and adjacent kitchen wall were now stacked floor to ceiling with paint-spattered wood crates bursting with my dad's art supplies. I ate a couple small bites of the coffee cake, took several long gulps of coffee, and then sat back.

"Scrumptious as always, Alice. Don't you agree, Deensie?"

"Yes, indeed. Delicious," I smiled.

"Are you okay?" he asked. "You seem, well, a little peaked, sweetie."

"Actually, I … I need to talk with you both. I stopped by because I have some … really upsetting news," I began, a lump already forming in my throat. Maybe my parents were rather simple minded, but they were deeply in love, always respectful and dedicated to one another.

My mom touched my wrist affectionately. "Does this

have to do with Hank, sweetie? We've kind of seen this coming for a while. We haven't wanted to interfere, of course … we've always admired him and thought his parents were such nice people," she murmured.

My eyes blurred over with tears.

"Mom, Dad … Hank died two days ago," I whispered, tears overflowing. "He'd stayed down in New Orleans for a meeting an extra day after his boss' wedding and --"

A chorus of "Oh my God," "What happened?" "Oh baby, no!" followed as they jumped to their feet, my mother's fork clattering to the floor as she rushed over, smothering me in a monumental hug.

"When he didn't show up for a scheduled event, they … they found him on the bathroom floor. The police said he probably died right after he'd gotten back after dinner that night."

"So, was this a heart attack do they think? He always looked the perfect picture of health. Probably due to some unknown medical condition, I'll bet. And good grief! All of those vitamins he took!" exclaimed my dad.

"They don't know what caused it. There's an investigation. I should know more in the next few days. I drove up to his folks yesterday. I didn't want to just call you … wanted to talk with you in person. Like I said, I should know more in a few days. Then I can … make plans for a service, I hope … and everything."

"I was so hoping that maybe you two would finally get things sorted out and get back on the right road," my dad said, kissing the top of my head. "And what's more, you should tell yourself that it was definitely on that track, Denise. You shouldn't harbor any kind of guilt or anything. Promise me?"

I smiled through my tears, looking at him.

"Oh sweetie!" my mother said again, "What a nightmare for you! I just, well, I just can't imagine! Losing your husband when you're so young. Oh, my sweet baby girl! What do you need from us right now? If you want to move back here that's fine. In fact, I think you should go ahead and just do that, don't you, Daddy? The paper's giving you time off I assume?"

I nodded. Time off or a pink slip, I thought.

"Right now, your old room is kind of a worse sight than you might be accustomed to seeing," my father admitted sheepishly. "It was already piled up … as you know … but I've had to store all of my, well, a lot of new art supplies, you know, all of the items I had in the living room so's I could make room for *Fleurama.* And then last week there was this resale shop over in Gnaw Bone that went out of business and left behind some unbelievable, terrific stuff! I couldn't pass up all those goodies, of course. Those crates are kind of crammed out in front of your room, out into the hall. Well, and all down the hall on both sides as well."

"Oh dear, yes, Daddy's right. I forgot about that. It's piled pretty much to the ceiling," my mom agreed, sighing. "Of course, we can get it sorted through in no time – just give us a couple of days -- and then it will be all ready for you just like the old days! We can certainly reorganize the old shed again, can't we Daddy? Get some of those new things stored out there. Oh, and then there's that warehouse that Hank's been letting us store some of Daddy's big items in, too. Maybe we can take more of it over there, don't you think, Daddy? But anyway, it will be just lovely to have you living here with us again, Deensie. We've really missed you so much baby girl!" she cried, hugging me tightly. Whenever Hank had gotten really annoyed with me, particularly if he was accusing me of some childish action, he'd call me Deensie. My parents always meant it affectionately -- my husband, almost never.

"As you know, sweetheart, we don't have much money to help with … well, costs for the service and such … but you know we'll give you everything we have," added my mother, a worrisome expression spreading over her face.

Renewed tears slid down my cheeks, more for my parents' loving generosity than for the hideously confusing loss of my husband. Small talk ensued as she put on another large pot of coffee and we devoured most of the coffee cake.

"Don't know if you can handle some other, well, mighty disturbing news, Denise. Did you hear about the discovery down by that old creek bed near Ogle Lake a few days back?" my father asked, leaning back with a newly refilled cup of coffee.

I shook my head, glad for the change of topic. Nashville's local news was certainly covered by one of our editions of the paper, but contrary to my parents' assumption, I wasn't assigned to that edition and was shamefaced to admit that I didn't typically read it. Since my assignment, Bloomington, was in Monroe County, most of the local news was exclusive to Monroe and not Nashville, which was in Brown County.

"Oh, my, Deensie, it's caused quite the ruckus around here. I'm so surprised you didn't run across the story somehow," shuddered my mother. "Daddy, do you think this is a good time to be talking about --"

"So, what was discovered?" I interrupted, glancing from one to the other.

"You tell it Daddy, please! I may get some of it wrong. You know how bad I am with getting all the facts straight and in the right order these days."

"Well, you remember that old Arlinger dairy farm? Wasn't too far from the state park. Little bitty place but did a fair local trade back in the 1950s, maybe even as late as '60 or '61 is my guess."

I shook my head.

"Ok, well, best as I've heard, that place was still owned by some family member up in, I think they said Ohio ...

does that sound right, Alice? Anyway, this family member sharecropped it out for at least a decade or more. Tenants didn't keep cows -- said to be raisin' soybeans or alfalfa or something along those lines. Can't imagine trying to actually farm any kinda regular crop on that rough land up through there. But guess others have made a successful go of it. Anyway, must've been a good arrangement for everyone because the owner never came here to inspect or nothin'."

"So, let me guess, that original family member passed away and the next of kin inherited. And when they came here to inspect, they found that their place was sky high with marijuana plants with a litany of small pickup trucks lining up after midnight twice a week readying the stash for both coasts," I smiled.

"Oh, that certainly would've been far better, Deensie!"

"Well, you guessed the first part right," my dad continued, nodding. "When those relatives got down here finally to inspect, they opted to just sell the property outright to a developer. The house, the barn and all the outbuildings were in such poor shape they just wanted to get their money out of the land. There are some real wealthy folks up in Indianapolis who've been building summer palaces over near Ogle Lake. You'd be amazed the mansion's that've gone up. Price of land is gettin' so high that those old family farms are just gettin' sliced 'n diced up and sold to real estate developers because the inheritance taxes 'er so damned high nowadays nobody left in the family can afford to keep their own family farm anymore. Gotta sell or watch everything they own just go into huge debt! Ridiculous! Entire farms -- gobbled up in inheritance taxes soon as the owner keels over. Anyway, that property was perfect for them big money Indianapolis folks itchin' to build."

"I can imagine," I agreed, having another tentative sip of my coffee.

"Well, turns out that a company run by some family known as Fowler up in Indianapolis bought it lock, stock and barrel with plans to open the place as a winery, complete with vineyards, huge restaurant, private and public tours, wedding packages, the whole nine yards. The last segment of the property was finally getting cleared just a few days ago … bulldozers came back in, backhoes and what have you. There'd been a lull for some reason. Back tax filing errors or something. Don't remember exactly why. Anyway, they were clearing the part that's near that old, dried stream bed … well, probably wasn't dried up until a few years back, come to think of it. You used to catch smelt in through there, do you remember?"

I nodded. Both about catching smelt but also reacting to the Fowler dynasty's tentacles. This was one of the new investments I'd heard about at Janet Lynn's engagement party. Cathy Martin and I used to ride our bikes throughout that area -- obviously trespassing, I now realized -- and wade along in the small stream to catch smelt and crayfish with our butterfly nets. My mother would fry up the smelt typically, but had no use for crayfish, whereas Chomp Martin had a fixation with Creole and Cajun styles of cooking. According to Cathy, that man threw everything we'd caught in the pot even if no one could identify it.

"So, there was this kind of long, deep hollow, a crevice, I guess, under a ridge of old trees – exposed roots or something they said – that just caved in once they'd started in on the dig. It hadn't been visible at all until then. Probably only accessible from a rabbit hole or something they thought at first. The crew found some old bones down there. Assumed at first that they were just stray dogs or raccoons that died during a winter. You know how that goes. But then one of the workers found a skull that they thought sure as heck looked like a human skull, so then they called the police."

"Oh, this is where it gets so scary," my mom said, her fingers whitening around her coffee cup.

"Naturally, the police called in the coroner's office to investigate. Sure enough, the medical examiner said they were human remains. What's more, since they'd found two right thigh bones, they knew they had two different bodies, even though they'd only discovered that one skull."

"Do they know anything else yet?" I frowned, shocked that I hadn't heard about any of this at the paper.

"They had some kind of specialist, uh, what do you call these old bone specialists …"

"A forensic anthropologist?"

"Yeah, that sounds right. Anyway, this forensic person checks everything out for a coupla days. Runs some tests. In last night's paper they said there were definitely two sets of remains …"

"Oh, Daddy," my mother shuddered, wrapping her sweater tightly around her tiny frame.

"One was definitely a boy. It was his skull they found. Young teen maybe. They think the other might be an older girl. At any rate they were able to date the boy's bones back to somewhere between 1960 and '62 or '63. I don't know if you remember that kid that disappeared back around then, Jimmy Larkins? They're thinkin' it's him."

"Oh Daddy," murmured my mother, folding her hands as though in prayer in her lap.

I nodded. I did remember Jimmy Larkins. He'd been in the class ahead of me. He was a big kid with a big mouth and very well-to-do parents who owned much of the commercial property in Nashville. He rarely missed a chance to mock all of us poor kids and had suspiciously disappeared without the slightest trace from his bedroom one summer night. The Larkins assumed they would receive a ransom note, but nothing ever materialized. The family hired a sea of private detectives, evidence dogs and even psychics to no avail. Police thought maybe he was just a runaway and would come back dragging his tail behind him like so many rich, spoiled, bullheaded kids do. But that never happened either.

"I remember the family was so distraught they sold all their interests in Nashville and moved away a year or so later," I remarked.

"Well, that's certainly understandable!" agreed my mother. "I just can't imagine …"

"But the family said they'd never stopped looking, always hoped maybe he'd been kidnapped and would end up just walking in the door ready to sit down with them and enjoy the Christmas goose," my dad added.

"So, do they know that it was definitely Jimmy Larkins?"

"Well, that was in last night's paper as well. They had some other specialist checking on his teeth, looking at his x-rays from his dentist -- you know they did that during the war to identify soldiers …"

I nodded. "Yes, I know about that. And?"

"So, yes, it's definitely Jimmy. No question there. A couple of molars from his x-rays were very distinctive according to the dentist. They may not ever be able to identify the girl other than she probably died a few years later. The skull and both hands were severed at the wrist according to the report. Police have sent notices out across Indiana, Illinois, Ohio and Kentucky looking for reports of missing young women during those years but far as I know, there's nothin' new."

"Not one report of a young women missing during that time frame?" I frowned.

"Well, just one that wasn't solved. It was from some woman whose teenage daughter had vanished around that time somewhere in Ohio … might have been down near Hamilton. But when the authorities investigated, they'd found that the woman was apparently, well, basically, the town drunk, and had walked out in front of a speeding car a few months after she'd filed the complaint and was instantly killed."

"That's awful."

"Woman's last name was Johnson, maybe? Can't remember the name of the missing daughter though. But here's the really gruesome part," he continued in a quiet voice, glancing with concern at my mother, who was now humming briskly to herself while staring at the embroidered chain of ducks on the kitchen curtains.

"It's snowing again," she stated, still looking at the window. "Look, Daddy, Deensie. It's snowing. It's comin' down might fierce again."

My dad then continued, whispering close to my ear. "They were slaughtered, like hogs, completely hacked up. Examiner assumes that happened after they were already dead, but brutal, nonetheless. Determined they'd been butchered by a chain saw. Same person was responsible for both more'n likely since the same type chainsaw had been used given the size of the chain teeth gouges in the remains. And they were disposed of identically, except at different times and the girl's head and hands were missing like I said."

"Do you still have last night's newspaper?" I asked quietly. Ordinarily I could purchase today's paper on the way back to my apartment. But a sensational local story such as this would have resulted in the entire run selling out in less than an hour after the papers hit the stands.

"Oh, honey, I'm sorry. I think I used it under my brushes – you know they keep dribbling for quite a while. Here, let's go look," he offered. But as he'd feared, the story was stuck fast between thick globs of cobalt blue.

"I have a lot of things to take care of back at my apartment and I should get a move on before the snow really does a number on 46. I'll call you later tonight, ok?"

"Sure have loaded you up with a heap of bad news," replied my father, shaking his head, "especially on top of this horror about Hank, honey. But we'll get started on sorting out all my supplies we've stacked up in your room first thing tomorrow, so we're all set when you're ready to move back in, ok, sweetie?"

"Sounds like a good plan, Dad," I smiled. Right now, I wasn't sure about anything in my life. Moving back in with my folks (along with their clearing even the tiniest pathway leading into my old bedroom without my assistance) seemed about as plausible as my being proclaimed the next Olga Korbut and scoring a wall of perfect tens in the next Olympics. I was still concerned about their place being a fire trap but vowed to start hauling out stuff as soon as I moved back in.

After a lengthy round of kisses and drawn-out hugs, I finally trudged out to my car, scraped off the windshield and started the half hour drive home. The roads were already getting slick. As I was driving, I thought back on what little I'd really known about Jimmy Larkins. There'd been a rumor that he'd forced himself on a girl to have sex with him out in the woods while they were walking home from school one afternoon. It was the first time I'd heard that such a thing as oral sex even existed. In fact, back in those days, I wasn't really all that clear just what constituted regular sex between a man and woman. There had been a day when a female health official had come in to talk with the girls in my class about sex. Well, sort of. We learned that our bodies would start miraculously shedding off eggs every month, along with the teeniest bit of blood (boy was that ever an understatement) for a couple of days in preparation for when our bodies would be ready to make a baby. Exactly how the baby got in there in the first place was skipped over, other than we were assured that your husband helped with that process. The boys had a lecture from a male health official; no idea if their information was any more in depth, pun intended.

At any rate, with respect to Jimmy Larkins, because his parents were filthy rich, everything was completely hush-

hush, but all of us kids gossiped of course. We knew that Jimmy had done something nasty. I also remembered that same girl – Brenda something -- running up to Cathy and me, begging to walk home with us because she knew Jimmy was hiding just down the road, ready to grab her again. Turns out it hadn't been the first time he'd forced her to perform the act and even after he'd been told to keep his distance, he persisted in stalking the girl. Brenda admitted to having originally had an innocent schoolgirl crush on him, but claimed she'd been blindly led into the enterprise. However, Mr. and Mrs. Larkins challenged her entire story. Her mother was a three-time divorcée and notorious alcoholic with multiple arrests for prostitution at a cheap trucker's dive located just north of town near Bill Monroe's Bean Blossom enclave. One certainly couldn't expect the apple to fall too far from that sordid a tree, Mrs. Larkins had sniffed in disdain. The woman was probably encouraging her daughter to get an early start so she could help contribute to their income. That's exactly the kind of behavior one would expect from such a depraved woman. Oddly none of that backstory had come to light when Jimmy had disappeared. I vaguely wondered why.

Also, unrelated, stored somewhere in the far recesses of my memory, was one of Cathy's gorier thrillers that she'd dictated into our tape player. I was thinking she'd called that episode a tongue-in-cheek "Hack in Sack, but not New Jersey." The victim in the story, a young boy, had been hacked apart by a chain saw after having been poisoned and scrunched into a large black canvas bag. The dismembered corpse was then buried under a deep ravine near pine trees along a creek. I remember Cathy excitedly relaying this tale, an oddly absorbed expression on her face that thoroughly frightened me at the time. I'd wanted to erase that story since I thought it far too gruesome, but Cathy just scolded me, stating this was the only decent murder mystery she'd written so far and kept that tape herself. I tried to recall some of the other tales she'd recorded on that same tape but drew a blank.

"The nose of the police dog is long and efficient although it points only in one direction at a time."

Basil Rathbone as Sherlock Holmes in

"The Adventures of Sherlock Holmes" (1939)

Chapter 16

Completely exhausted, once home, I headed straight to bed. My sojourn last night on my living room's gold mini shag carpeting had left much to be desired in the way of restful slumber. I awoke to loud knocking on my door. The bedside clock said 6:09. A.m.? P.m.? It was dark, but that didn't tell me much. Then I heard my upstairs neighbor warbling along to her tepid guitar accompaniment singing "*You Light Up My Life*" which she regularly butchered nightly. Ok, well, that answered that question at least: 6:09 p.m. The knocking persisted. I pulled on a sweatshirt yelling, 'okay, hold your horses,' unaware if the person could even hear me. A glance through the peephole revealed nothing and I carefully opened the door, security chain firmly latched in place.

Standing in the doorway was Tom Miller holding a Jake's pizza box and a bottle of wine.

"Hey, glad you're home. I happened to be in the neighborhood so thought I'd bring us over a little dinner. Tried calling a few times, but your phone seems to be, um, off the hook. Eh, just dead air, y'know?"

Reluctantly I withdrew the chain and stepped to the side as he walked in, stamping snow off his boots.

"I thought you said you were in … Iowa or Michigan or something. Didn't you tell me that?"

"Yep, sure did. I'm surprised you remembered."

He walked past me to the kitchen -- all of about ten steps -- then pointed to my phone. The receiver was precariously straddling the hook rather than cradled correctly.

"See? There's the problem. Not hung up properly. What happened to the casing anyway?"

"Rowdy neighborhood," I replied curtly. The pizza was making my stomach rumble. Damn. My mom's blueberry coffee cake had completely worn off. Hard to claim I wasn't hungry.

"Brought your favorite kind," he smiled, gesturing towards the box. "Where's your corkscrew? I brought cabernet. Hope that's ok. The sommelier at Jake's Pizza said that I should go with a dry red rather than the chardonnay with a bacon and mushroom pizza to go. I tend to agree. Don't you?"

Sommelier. At a pizza joint. Clever.

"Just how did you know that's my favorite pizza?" I shot back instead. Seriously, what was this guy doing here anyway? Why hadn't I listened to Thor two months ago and refrained from sending that stupid personal ad? I still didn't know if the guy was a legitimate detective. Were they even allowed to work in different states?

"Eh, you know. Word gets around," he shrugged, flashing a grin. "So, where's that corkscrew again?"

I gestured to a drawer to his left.

"And glasses? Plates? I've been out there hammering on your door for a good five minutes at least. Hope the pizza's still warm."

"Plates are in the cabinet next to the fridge."

"Have a seat. Your savory repast will be in front of you in just a moment, madam," he winked.

Wine poured, well into devouring our second slice of

pizza, he started talking.

"So, you do remember my calling you last night and saying I'd be headed down here?"

"Vaguely," I answered, licking cheese that had spun a web over my fingers.

"And I'm sure you heeded my warning regarding the police and didn't let them record anything when they showed up."

"Was that yesterday?" I frowned.

"No, actually it was very early this morning. Probably around six or so."

"Ah. Right."

"Maybe her voice will give out soon," Tom laughed, gesturing at the ceiling. Evidently his life wasn't being lit up either by my neighbor's vocal ramblings. "This … uh, concert happen frequently? That's gotta be my least favorite song of all time."

"Always on weekends," I replied, "and most weeknights as well. Always that same lousy tune."

"Jesus, no wonder your husband had migraines!"

"Yeah, maybe," I concurred, smiling slightly.

"So, you did talk with them this morning, correct?"

"Who?"

"The police."

"Oh. Yes. Right."

"And?"

"And what? They asked me a bunch of questions about vitamins … well, Hank's vitamins anyway. That's all I remember. And they took all the bottles of his vitamins. I'm assuming they'd already removed everything from his hotel room down in New Orleans."

"Did you ever handle any of those bottles," asked Tom, his tone deceptively casual.

"The ones here? Sure. There are lots of other things on those shelves. It's an old kitchen. The shelves aren't very wide, but that corner cabinet is deep. I always have to move things around when I want to reach stuff in the back and Hank keeps … kept … his vitamin bottles up front."

Tom nodded his head and took another slice of pizza, took a few bites, and then resumed talking.

"How about the individual pills? Cops ask you anything about that?"

"Not that I remember."

"And did you ever handle any of his pills?"

"Only if he needed to open some of the capsules for one of his shots. Just why are you asking all of these questions?" I interjected tersely. "What business is this of yours?"

"Just curious. I didn't know you could open capsules like that. Thought they were glued shut or something."

"Vitamins aren't sealed. Although I remember that one of the capsules that I tried to open when I gave Hank a shot down in New Orleans was really stubborn and I finally gave up and used a different one."

"What happened to that, uh, really difficult one?"

I thought for a moment then shrugged. "I guess I probably just put it back in his travel bottle. They're expensive little devils."

"And that was …?"

"When we were in New Orleans like I said. What is all this anyway? And for that matter, how do you know about any of it in the first place?"

"The police haven't come up with a cause for Hank's death. They're certain it's linked to the vitamins somehow, but so far, determining the actual poison hasn't come through in any tests."

How the heck does he know any of this, I seethed within.

"So, maybe that in turn makes me … what … less of a suspect?" I smirked.

"Well, hard to say, but I don't think they've exactly crossed you off their list quite yet."

Before I could reply my phone sprang loudly into life.

"Don't you ever answer your damn phone Prescott? I've been a basket case wondering what in the hell happened to you for the last forty-eight!"

Thor.

"I was at Hank's folks and then my own. Obviously, I had a lot to talk over with them, Thor."

"I'd planned to stop by to talk to you earlier but now don't have time, Prescott. You know that smarmy detective weasel wannabe you unfortunately managed to conjure up out of your swamp of acquaintances?"

"Yes," I replied uneasily, purposely avoiding looking over at Tom, whom I would never have described exactly as a weasel or smarmy. I suspected Thor's voice was perfectly audible, unfortunately. Thor, always one for dramatic effect whenever feasible, had perfected the art of the stentorian stage whisper very early in life I suspected.

"Guy's a huge fraud! We're talking mammoth, Prescott! Size of Nebraska!"

Nebraska?

"Had my friend Drake Carson up in Rockford check out his story over the last couple of days. Took a while to fish through all the possibilities. You know, security guards, bouncers, secret police, FBI, CIA, Army, Navy, National Guard. The whole enchilada to quote John Ehrlichman. And guess what? Nooo such detective to be found on anybody's payroll. Private, county, state, fed or military, past or present. Rien. Nada. Nichts. Niente. And worse, I'm absolutely positive I just spotted that Neanderthal picking up a pizza less than a half hour ago at Jake's, so he's skulking around in this area, probably stalking you. You need to be careful!" he hissed into the phone. "Call the police, dammit! Now!"

"Ok," I replied, thoroughly shaken. "I'm … I'm kind of in the middle of something. Can I give you a call back in maybe, like five minutes?"

"Yeah, yeah, sure," Thor answered briskly. "I'm around for the next half hour. Then I leave for my other job. I'm camped out next to the phone 'til then. *Tschüss.*" Why he typically used the German word for good-bye was a mystery, but I'd always found it quite charming.

I hung up and turned to face Tom, swallowing. Hank had always ridiculed me that my moods were so transparently telegraphed across my face it was a good thing I'd never taken up high stakes poker.

"I have a personal call to return," I stated as evenly as possible, walking towards the door. "I appreciate your thoughtfulness in bringing the pizza and everything, but I need to take care of some other business concerning Hank."

Without comment he stood up, dangling a half-eaten slice of pizza in his fingers. I handed him his coat and opened the door.

"I'm legit," he smiled, kissing me lightly on the lips, slightly greasy fingers tracing softly under my chin as I pulled away. "Honest. I'll check in with you tomorrow, ok?"

Despite Thor's dire warning I watched him walking towards his car. Damn. Could I even remember a time when Hank had kissed me with such a simple gesture? It's the wine you dimwit I berated myself. This guy's a huge fraud. Do not lose perspective whatever you do. He is proficient, sneaky, and quite possibly, extremely dangerous. I shivered at the memory of his original trip to meet me -- an enraged bear awakened mid-hibernation as he'd barged into the newsroom.

My phone rang again. Thor was certainly impatient I inwardly grumbled. I doubted that it had been five minutes yet. But the voice on the other end wasn't Thor's. It was Mark Stephens.

"Denise! I'm so glad I finally reached you! It's Mark," he began. "Your line's been out most of the day."

"Yeah, sorry. So I've been told."

"We read about your husband's death in The Star. My

God, what a terrible shock for you! I know that I'd just met him at the reunion a couple months back, but he was over at the bar most of the time, and … well, I'm so sorry that I really don't remember him very well. Is there anything that any of us can do for you here? Jill and I have been trying to call you, but as I mentioned your line wouldn't ring through. Lines down from the ice, I expect."

"Thanks, Mark," I replied quietly. "I didn't hang up correctly from another call, I guess."

"What can we do to help? Anything, you just name it!"

"Nothing I can think of at the moment. I don't know about the arrangements … and such … as yet. Because it was all so sudden … there's a police investigation, of course. So, that just takes, well … time. You know."

"Of course, of course! I'm not at all surprised," Mark replied. "Do you still have our phone number from the reunion invite rsvp?"

"I think so. I'm certain I copied it into my regular address book." The book was sitting on the kitchen counter, and I quickly flipped through to the 'S' section. "Yep, Mark and Jill Stephens. It's right here."

"Ok, good, good. Now you call me when you know, um … any definite plans, please. You know we want to help out, Denise."

"Thanks, Mark," I replied, nodding as though he could see me over the phone line, "that's very much appreciated. I'll be in touch. I promise."

"Oh, wait, before we hang up. I almost forgot. Remember you were asking about Cathy Martin at the reunion?"

"Yes," I frowned.

"Can you believe that I just received our reunion invitation returned to me tucked inside a nice note from Cathy? Her handwriting still looks exactly the same after all of these years. I recognized it instantly from those relentless lab reports we had to prepare together in advanced chem. Always let her write them because her handwriting was so much neater than mine. Anyway, she said that the invite had been delivered to the wrong house – an older couple who'd been out of town for the last several months apparently. It's kind of strange because she wasn't on any of our committee's lists, but Cathy mentioned that she'd received a copy of the invitation secondhand from someone named Patricia. I'm embarrassed to say that I don't know which Patricia since there were at least a dozen Patricias, Patsys, Pattys and Trishas in our class as I'm sure you remember! She said they were going to be moving again soon so she didn't bother enclosing her current address, although the phone would remain the same, so must be a local move. Anyway, she's included her phone number if you're still interested in trying to get in touch with her."

"Sure, why not," I replied. "Let me grab a pencil."

"It's long distance. Looks to be somewhere out in Virginia, but I don't know what part."

"Ok, I've got a pencil."

"The area code is 703, then the number's 527.8162."

"Ok, got it. Thanks Mark. It's great to hear from you."

"Don't forget to call me," he restated urgently. "Anything you might need. I'm serious! I've already been calling a lot of our old friends on the grapevine, Denise. Everyone wants to help however they can."

"Thanks again. I won't forget. I promise," I replied. "Bye."

I had scarcely pushed the bar down to end the call when the phone immediately sprang back to life.

"Hello?"

"You sure have a weird concept of five minutes, Prescott! To me when the sweep hand on my watch – you know, that's the skinny one that ticky tickies around really fast -- has circled completely five times, that equals five minutes, *comprendez amigo*?"

"Hello to you too, Thor," I replied, picturing him impatiently tapping on his watch as he chastised me. "Sorry. Another call."

"So, back to the blue-eyed cowboy," he began, "as I said before, he didn't check out with any of my in-depth research. And you know from my diggings at the newspaper, Denise, that I'm a ruthless bloodhound on this kind of manure!"

Blue-eyed cowboy? Huh, I thought. I wouldn't exactly classify Tom a cowboy and I thought his eyes more of a hazel. I needed to be more observant.

"Are you listening?" Thor exclaimed, "I feel like I'm talking to a Mongolian moose on your end!"

"*Are* there moose in Mongolia?" I queried, falling into our typical conversational banter.

"Good, ok, at least I have your attention! Now, here's what I need for you to …"

"Well, *are* there?"

"Huh? Oh, yeah, but they're endangered. Jesus, woman. Stay with me here, ok? This is serious, you tuna. Now look, here's what I need for you to do as soon as we hang up."

"Thor," I interrupted, "hang on, hang on. Just listen for a second. A few minutes ago, I had a call from one of the guys I graduated with from Columbus High. Mark Stephens. He was on our reunion planning committee. He called initially because he'd heard about Hank, but then he also told me he'd just received a belated reunion reply from you'll never guess who …"

"I give up. Jack the Ripper. Santa Claus. Pippi Longstocking. Nellybelle. Irene Adler. Inspector Lestraude. The Gentleman from Dallas. Lassie. Rin Tin Tin. Toto. King Kong … stop me before I get too far prior to World War II ..."

"Nellybelle?"

"Pat Brady's jeep. Although, I think it belonged to

Roy Rogers. He just let Brady drive it."

"Ah."

"Ok, so a belated reply from whom?"

"Cathy Martin."

Thor whistled. "Whoa there, Kemosabe. Wouldn't've guessed that one! Seriously?"

"Yep. She'd included her phone number with a note to my friend Mark. He gave me the number if I wanted to call her."

"And do you?"

"Well sure, why wouldn't I? After this crazy story about dropping out of college before she'd even started because she was pregnant, marrying Janet Lynn's then boyfriend, and basically disappearing for practically ten years after that … I mean, why wouldn't I want to call her? Hear her side, right? Since she replied with a note to Mark apologizing for not attending, she must want to reestablish contact with some of us out here again. Wouldn't you think?"

"Out *here*? Then she's out *where*?" he questioned. I sensed his brows knitting into one of their deep frowns. "Where the hell does she live now?"

"Mark says it's somewhere in Virginia."

"Ok, so let's say you call her. How do you know that's actually her?"

"Why wouldn't it be her, for heaven's sake? Why would she take the trouble to send Mark a note with her phone number? Oh, and Mark was her lab partner in a couple of science classes. He said he recognized her handwriting from all the lab reports they'd had to turn in."

"Huh. Interesting. Should you call her? You tell me. It's been what, over a decade or something since you've seen her, correct? And you weren't particularly friends with her for most of high school anyway, right? Do you really care that much, especially if there's some voodoo curse over her or something?"

"Voodoo curse? Oh, come on Thor! That's stupid. It might be good to have something else to dwell on than constantly rehashing the circumstances surrounding Hank's death," I sighed.

"Hash. Yeah, that's a great comparison, Prescott."

"Thor, please," I groaned, "give it up. I'm sure I'd still recognize her voice even though she was working so hard to mimic Janet Lynn's back when we were in high school. Obviously, that's long behind her since their friendship fell off the cliff. Anyway, maybe I can just, well, invite her out here sometime."

"School's in session now, Prescott. She's got at least that one kid … age ten by now, correct? She's probably not able to drop everything, pull the kid out of class and just pop on out for a visit."

"You're right. I'd forgotten about school. Well, I can still call her. There's no harm in that. I mean, I don't think there'll be another reunion until '83 and who knows where all of us will be by that time!"

"Probably still scurrying around like blind roaches out here in southern Hoosierville. Well, it's your funeral, Prescott. Gotta trot. I'm gonna be late for old man Casey. He goes ballistic if I'm not on time to get his weekly earnings tabulated and on the books. You know, like the Internal Revenue Service is gonna be on his boney ass within seconds if he's late with his monthly tax filing."

"You work for them as an accountant?" That seemed a stretch coming from a guy who was always looking to borrow five bucks to tide him over for a day or so until pay day.

"Yeah, I'm cheaper, and quite frankly, far better with juggling all his bizarre sales receipt rituals than anybody else he's ever worked with. Can you believe I had to figure out a two hundred and some dollar sale that he just chicken-scratched with the wrong tax breakdown on a greasy McDonald's cheeseburger wrapper a couple weeks back? Good thing I'm as persistent as hell with this kind of stuff."

"That you are. No question there. Thanks. Bye!"

"*Tschüss.*"

I hung up, grabbed a glass of water and plopped down on the battered hassock in front of our television. Glancing through the TV guide, I then started clicking the knob through the stations, which was kind of futile without knowing the time. I was too lazy to take the fifteen steps into the kitchen to look at the wall clock. After countless commercials the station returned to a rerun of "*Columbo*" which I'd already seen at least twice. It was only November, I muttered to myself. What was with the reruns already? My mind churned about when and if I should try to call Cathy as I flipped the dial several more channels. I'd almost flipped through the entire wheel unearthing a rash of dopey-pie-in-the-face comedies as Thor always dismissed them, and none of the Indianapolis channels were coming in clearly tonight, even though the snow had ended. I'll try her on Monday I decided as I landed on some grade B movie, the title of which I never did catch, but that at least lulled me to sleep within several minutes as I settled back into Hank's easy chair.

"Poison is a woman's weapon."

Basil Rathbone as Sherlock Holmes in

"Pursuit to Algiers" (1946)

Chapter 17

I woke up overnight mummy-wrapped in the granny square crocheted quilt that one of my mom's friends had made for my wedding. Even though wrapped tightly, I was freezing. Not exactly that see-your-icy-breath-like-a-dense-fog freezing, but freezing nonetheless, considering that I was inside my apartment. Maintaining my swaddling, I wobbled out of the chair over to the thermostat and inched the pin forward slightly, satisfied as the whoosh of the furnace, closeted just next to the kitchen, heralded future warmth. The television was undulating with shimmering bars of silent test patterns, so I flipped it off and settled back into the easy chair, tightening the quilt around myself. I wasn't certain what time programming began early in the morning, but whenever that was, it wasn't late enough apparently.

I was glad I wasn't in my bed right now, I realized dully. These were the kinds of gothic, early Sunday mornings I'd always craved, where Hank and I would cuddle for a while in a half sleep, slowly make love and then fall back asleep wrapped in each other's arms until late morning. Then we'd usually head out to find a late breakfast or brunch as the European toffs called it these days. Or sometimes I would just make coffee or hot chocolate, heat up a few cinnamon rolls or apple tarts, and we'd grab the Sunday paper, lolling about in bed until well after noon. Each time I'd tell myself that this was the beginning of a new slate, a new life together. That I could completely forgive Hank's infidelities and that he'd be able to see me as something other than just his wife … which was ok … I had certainly wanted to be his wife after all, but desperately needed for him to value me beyond that weary description.

My conversation a month ago fueled by pizza and beer with my friends Linda and Marcy came to the surface yet again. Somehow Hank had found that value in women like the DD but never in me. But then, the DD wasn't his wife and, as she herself had readily admitted, had no intention of ever becoming anyone's wife. I sighed, listening to the heat whistling through the registers on opposite sides of the room. Maybe that was the secret. Just be in it for the fun of it or resign yourself fully to the acquisition of a middle-class motherhood's armor. Maybe for most of us ordinary women, there was no wiggle room in between. But I would never know now I realized as I stared at our large poster of Picasso's *Petits Fleurs* in the darkened room. I hadn't wanted to spend the extra money to buy this mammoth framed picture but was so glad that Hank had insisted. It was the perfect size for our living room, making the wall look bigger, an effect called *trompe l'oeil* I remembered, smiling at a tugging memory from my college days.

College. High school. The reunion. Cathy Martin. More thoughts about contacting her crowded into my head. Now for entirely different reasons, I needed to concentrate on something other than Hank, and she was an excellent candidate. What harm could possibly come from a phone call? On Monday morning I definitely would attempt to get in touch. I wouldn't mention it to Thor and certainly not to

Tom Miller. I should remember to give a call to Mark Stephens after talking with her, however, assuming I was able to reach her.

I thought about my current financial state. I assumed that Hank's paycheck would still show up in our mailbox like always. But what if it didn't? I had no idea how all this stuff worked if your husband had been murdered and you were on the short list of suspects. Stay away from those thoughts, Denise, I scolded myself. Concentrate on the positive, some of Dr. Racine's better advice. I made a mental note to call Racine on Monday morning.

My mind continued wandering. I heard a crow's lone caw echoing off in the distance. What about the bones my parents mentioned that had been unearthed during the new development's excavation? So much had happened since my conversation with them yesterday I hadn't thought about it again until now. Jimmy Larkins. Identified without question it seemed. But the girl. Or young woman. Older, probably buried there a few years later. I shuddered. Like a ghost waltzing across my grave the thought had occurred to me that maybe it had been Cathy Martin down there. But now that Cathy Martin had just written Mark Stephens several days ago, with a friendly enclosure of her telephone number, undoubtedly assuming Mark would be giving her a call, that fear was firmly dismissed. There was certainly nothing suspicious or sinister I reasoned as I drifted off again in the chair.

A pair of women's voices and loud knocking awoke me as sunlight now streamed into my apartment. Still groggy, I stumbled to the door and was grateful to discover Linda and Marcy's red mittens waving through the peephole.

"I'm so sorry to hear about all of this," apologized Marcy, readjusting a cardboard frame boasting three large Styrofoam cups of coffee, as she gave me a huge hug. "Of all weeks for me to be out of town and away from the newsroom. I just got the lowdown an hour ago from Thor at the Donut Hole. I called Linda immediately. Oh my God, what a nightmare, Denise!"

Linda also hugged me, the scent of hot cider donuts floating in her wake, adding sheepishly, "I'm so embarrassed to say that I depend on you and Marcy to keep me on top of all the news. I didn't know anything either until just an hour ago when Marcy called me. I'm buried studying for mid-terms, triple ugh!"

They removed the rest of last night's pizza and wine detritus from the table, unearthed three lovingly mismatched Corelle plates from my cabinets, and we sat down. Within the last twenty-four hours I'd certainly bulked up on my full ration of fat and grease what with my mom's coffee cake, last night's pizza and now donuts. Food, family and friends … if I was willing to count Tom Miller as a friend, that is.

I told them everything that had transpired, including the pre-dawn visit of the police officers and my storming out of Hank's parents' place, marking my exit by throwing down seventy-three cents worth of small change in their foyer. I purposely left out anything about Tom Miller's visit because I still didn't know exactly how he fit into this convoluted puzzle.

"I just can't believe it was that double-crossing skank Dorothea Dixon who discovered Hank on the bathroom floor, Denise," stated Marcy tersely, snapping off a large piece of another donut and thrusting it viciously in her coffee. "Why aren't there any fingers pointing at that bitch regarding this poisoning stuff for Pete's sake? Seems to me she'd be the first one the police would question, not you! You weren't even there with him!"

"I completely agree," argued Linda. "Talk about your prime suspect. I mean, c'mon, good grief!"

"They did apparently, but maybe there's not much of a motive. Who knows?" I shrugged. "She's always made it clear to everyone that her interest in Hank was simply fun and games for as long as it lasted."

"Well, gosh I guess those fun and games with him are certainly over now!" snorted Linda. "Maybe she's like a female praying mantis. They eat the male's head off after they mate."

"Ugh! That's disgusting," recoiled Marcy. "You're making that up!"

"Nope," Linda countered, wrinkling her nose as she reached for another donut. "Sorry, sweetie, but it's for real."

"For all I know that's how everyone on his work team behaves," I shrugged, pushing my coffee slightly away. It was barely lukewarm and tasted more like Styrofoam than coffee. "Maybe they're just a bunch of brilliant, randy misfits. All of them that I've met on that team are young, smart, and extremely voracious for instantaneous financial success the way I see it. And a great affinity for cutting edge electronic bugs that work with complete reliability, so forget your praying mantis example. It's all about the money. That may well have been the prime factor behind hiring them in the first place. Dunno."

"You need to find something else to keep your mind off this mess," stated Marcy. "It's horrible enough that your perpetually philandering husband was murdered just a few days ago and that despite your attempts with a well-known shrink to hammer out marital bliss for your marriage, your husband was still a complete toadstool. I'm sorry, but that's my opinion and I'm not budging from it!"

"Your support has always meant everything, you guys," I smiled weakly.

"And you look really tired, too," added Marcy.

"Well now, that's a dumb remark, Marcy. It's not like she's planning some ooh-la-la romantic getaway right now to the Bahamas or Paris or anything. Of course, she looks really tired! Sheesh, girl!"

"You two are amazing … best friends a girl could

have," I said, squeezing both their hands. "You've been so good listening to all of my problems with Hank over these last couple years. None of this actually seems real yet."

"I've read that in some of my caseload examples actually. A lot of times people just can't bring themselves to face the reality of their circumstances for a long time," remarked Linda. "But you should at least make an attempt to piece together something in the way of future plans … if possible, that is."

"Well, I'm not exactly planning a vacation to the Bahamas, so you're right about that one," I replied quietly, "but I'm thinking of calling a friend that I haven't seen in ages. We haven't been close for a really long time but we were inseparable as kids. Kind of fell out completely during our high school years. Who knows, maybe I'll even try to catch a train out to visit her at some point in the future after everything has settled down here. She doesn't know anything about Hank at all actually … even that I was married to anyone by that name. Her invitation to our high school reunion was delivered to the wrong address so she missed it. But just a few days ago she sent a nice note to the reunion committee and included her phone number, so I'm thinking about calling on Monday."

Until the words tumbled out of my mouth, I really hadn't seriously considered heading out to see Cathy, but now realized the plan had been subtly forming in my subconscious since Mark had mentioned receiving her letter. Train trips had always held a certain allure for me since reading Ian Fleming's "*From Russia with Love*" where a sentence referring to making long slow love in a low berth had prompted several interesting discussions between Cathy and me as curious pre-teens, stating that we definitely wanted that scenario to be our first romantic encounter. We were still tomboys at the time, but those female hormones were inevitably starting to creep through. I'd certainly never experienced anything of that sort; I wondered if Cathy ever had.

"You should just call this afternoon," replied Marcy, shaking her head, dumping some of the cinnamon and sugar from the donut bag into her coffee. "Rates are a lot cheaper on Sundays you know."

"I think that sounds like a good idea too. I suppose the police didn't give you any indication how long it might be until you could make any of your, um … final plans?" asked Linda.

"No idea. And then whatever I do I'll have to work with my in-laws, regardless. He's their son after all."

"I still can't believe his stepmom had the audacity to talk to you that way," said Marcy. "You didn't go far enough just throwing her change on the floor, Denise. I'd have shoved it down her little Tweety Bird gullet."

"Oh yeah, Marcy, that would have helped a lot," replied Linda. "Then she'd have an assault charge hanging over her head as well."

"Ok, so figuratively shoved 'em down her gullet, Ms. Legal Pain-in-the-ass, is that better?"

We were all silent for a few moments, finishing our coffee. I attempted to change the subject to find out about their current problems, but like a boomerang, our conversation continued returning to Hank. I finally promised to call Cathy later that afternoon. We made tentative plans for pizza and beer for the following Friday night.

After the girls left, I tried the phone number for Cathy Martin. No one picked up.

"Only I don't understand why you wish to consult me
about a garden party!
You couldn't possibly find a worse guide
for social etiquette!"

Basil Rathbone as Sherlock Holmes in

"The Adventures of Sherlock Holmes"
(1939)

Chapter 18

I called Thor the following morning, but he was busy taking a complicated story and indicated he'd have to get back to me. Place is a zoo this morning, cautioned one of the other news clerks who had answered my call, so don't expect him to get back to you any time soon. When my phone rang an hour or so later it wasn't Thor, however, but Tom Miller. He'd called to let me know that the poison found in Hank's capsule – that stubborn one that had been tampered with and re-sealed – was not found in the analysis of his stomach contents or other tissues to the surprise of the forensic team. The identity of the actual poison had yet to be identified.

"That wasn't at all where the police expected the evidence to lead," he continued. "Just where things go from here is anybody's guess."

"So, what happens now?" I asked, wondering yet again how he had access to any of this information if he wasn't a cop or detective … unless he was directly involved, of course, I said under my breath.

"What was that?"

"Um, where does that leave things?"

"Damned if I know. Hope you're holding up ok. I'm back up in Michigan, but am staying on top of it, don't worry."

"That was fast. Funny, though, you don't sound that far away."

"Good connection I guess," Tom replied. "I'll call you tomorrow. And, uh, just as a suggestion, Prescott, take it easy on the booze."

Furious at the accusation, my face went crimson. Who the hell was this total fraud of a detective telling me what to do! As I slammed the phone down onto the hook, the crack in the plastic casing quickly snaked all the way to the bottom. On an impulse I angrily punched in the phone number for Cathy Martin again. There were several clicks on the line, and I was almost ready to hang up since I never heard the phone begin to ring. I assumed the call hadn't gone through.

"Hello?" answered a child's voice.

"Oh, uh, hello!" I responded after a moment, caught completely off guard. "Is … is your mommy home? I'm an old friend --"

"Daddy," the child continued, oddly cutting me off, "it's some lady. No, not Auntie Casey." Then it sounded as though someone's hand was muffling the mouthpiece. Very indistinctly in the background I could just make out a man saying, "tell them I'll be there in just a second, sweetheart."

For some oddball reason, my heart was hammering in my chest. Calm down, Prescott, I scolded myself. Cathy had sent her phone number to Mark Stephens looking to reconnect with some of her former classmates. I was a former classmate. Simple explanation behind my taking the initiative to phone her. No big issue. A few more seconds of muffled conversation went by.

"Hello?" said a man's pleasant voice, and then "sure, you can go outside, Jessye. Take Farley with you."

I heard a dog bark and what sounded like a screen door slam.

"Sorry about that," he continued, laughing. He had a resonant, very pleasant voice. Almost like a movie actor's, I thought.

"Um, hi," I laughed nervously. "I'm hoping that I have the right number, actually. I was looking for an old friend, Cathy Martin, and I got your number from our high school reunion committee. I apologize that I may have miscopied the number or something …"

There was a pause of several seconds and some additional clicking sounds, then the man said, "and you would be?" He didn't identify himself which seemed a little odd, but then, so was my phone call.

"Denise Prescott. Actually, um, Cathy and I were good friends growing up … we kind of drifted apart in high school to be honest," I stammered, feeling more and more foolish.

"Oh, uh ok. Glad to meet you, Denise! Roger Dunn. Cathy isn't here right now," he replied, his voice now sounding slightly different. Maybe he'd picked up a different extension in the house. "I'm sure she'll be upset that she's missed you though. You still live out there in the lost hills of Indiana?"

Hills? Well, hardly. But he had the Indiana part correct at least. So, I did have the right number. But Roger Dunn? That wasn't even close to Tom Miller, I thought. But maybe she'd gotten divorced and remarried. Her first marriage had most likely been rather ill-planned, so a new spouse wasn't inconceivable.

"Yes," I replied after a beat. "I do."

"We're out in Virginia, now. Pretty much right where the Blue Ridge starts – closest town is Winchester -- bit of a hike though. Mighty rural out here, but that works out great for Cathy's business. It's really grown, let me tell you. As you can probably imagine, my girl does it all! Everything from raw and cooked honey to her various companies that make cakes, syrups, jellies and such to sell at fairs and fests all up and down the East Coast. She just started another company making honeyed soaps and candles that's going like hotcakes. Hard for her to manage all the orders. She does primarily retail these days, of course. Got the crew going practically day and night. We market under Jessye's Honey Farms, Inc. – that's Jessye spelled with a y-e – same's our little girl. But she's still trying to accommodate some custom orders if that's why you're calling. With Christmas just a bit over a month away, it's tight though, I do have to warn you," he apologized.

"Yes, I can well imagine!" I answered, nodding as though he could seem me. Shows what a college degree will do for you -- hah! I pictured Cathy, a brilliant young female entrepreneur, living on an immense sprawling estate in the shadow of the mountains, with her young, healthy family, toasting marshmallows to make s'mores in their massive stone fireplace while Cathy enthralled her young brood with her imaginative ghost stories.

"I don't know when she'll be home tonight, or I'd have her give you a call. She's keepin' pretty late hours this time of year, of course. You know, with Thanksgiving in only a couple weeks and then Christmas like I said before. Crazy keeping supplies up!"

"Oh, just tell her that I called," I replied quickly. "Please. I'll plan to call again after the holidays. Maybe everything will have slowed down a bit for her by then. Thanks for --"

"Hey, hey, wait a minute! You know, this just dawned on me. How far are you from Swayzee?"

"Swayzee? You mean in Indiana?" I replied, completely confused. Few people who actually *lived* in Indiana had any idea that there was even a town by that name, much less knew where Swayzee was located.

"Yeah, yeah!"

"Oh, I dunno. A couple hours maybe. It's northeast of Indianapolis and I'm southwest. Indianapolis is pretty much in the center of the state. Swayzee's not too direct a place to get to from most anywhere though," I answered.

And there's absolutely nothing in Swayzee, I thought, shaking my head regarding his question. The place was so tiny I don't think it even boasted a stop sign! In fact, I'd always been surprised it even had a post office address. Rutledge, Wisconsin was paradise compared to Swayzee, Indiana.

"Well, Cathy's overseeing this huge warehouse delivery headed out by Amtrak Express – you know they have passenger and small freight service combined right now -- to Swayzee this coming Wednesday. Place has several huge warehouses that store goods for a lot of Indianapolis stores, uh … what did she mention, I'm not real familiar with some of these names since I'm not from out that way … let's see, oh, she mentioned Blocks, LS Ayres, Goldblatts, um, maybe even a Penney's? Not sure I have the Penney's quite right, but well, I think so. Oh, also she has a new baked goods deal going in over to Stuckey's. We've done business with them out here for quite a while – time the Midwest gets some bona fide sweet clover honey with them pecan logs, right?"

"Wow!" I exclaimed, although cringing slightly at his pronunciation of bona fide as bonyee fydee. "That's really amazing, Mr. Dunn!"

"Hey, hey, just Roger, ok Denise?"

"Roger," I replied.

"Anyway, this is a first-time order for these particular stores, and she's had problems in the past with some Midwest locations not completing all the necessary paperwork correctly – you know what I mean. Uncle Sam's got that eagle beak pecking into everybody's business these days, so she's accompanying that first order. Just this one time, you know. Just to make sure everything goes according to Hoyle," he offered. "Maybe you two girls could meet for a quick lunch in between all that boring paper-signing formality. I'm sure that would be a terrific breath of fresh air for her!"

I started to protest that she would certainly be too busy. And since we hadn't spoken in well over a decade, I certainly didn't qualify as that revered long lost chum from her past with whom she would relish spending her few relaxing moments during an exhausting business trip.

"Gosh, I actually have the information right here next to the phone, in fact. Can you believe it?" he laughed. "Yep, here we go. Train #181 and its scheduled stop in Swayzee is one p.m. "Of course, it'll probably be late, then has to unload. Should I tell her that you'll be there around two or so? Is that too late? I'll tell her to be on the lookout for you. I mean if that sounds ok and all."

"No, that sounds great. I should be able to do that," I replied, shaking my head slightly at the same time. If I didn't show up, she would certainly have more than enough to do.

"I'm sure she'll be looking forward to it. I'll tell her as soon as she walks in that front door tonight. She works way too hard, y'know? So glad you called, Denise!"

There was that odd series of short clicks again. They probably still had a party line I realized; someone was just trying to find out when the line was free so they could make a call. My parents still had a four-way party line that included one household with three popular teenage daughters.

"I was never more sure of anything in my life."

Basil Rathbone as Sherlock Holmes in

"The Pearl of Death" (1944)

Chapter 19

When Wednesday arrived, I still hadn't decided whether I wanted to drive up to Swayzee, but my calls to Marcy, Linda and Thor met with a sorry-too-swamped-with-work-to-chat status that morning and no one picked up at my parents. I considered calling Hank's parents in a lame attempt to offer the proverbial olive branch, but just couldn't bring myself to do so. Total silence thus far this week from the police or coroner's office. I held to the old adage that no news is good news.

Dr. Racine's office had called that morning, expressing their sympathy regarding my husband's death and wanting to know if I intended on keeping the appointments that we'd made for the next couple months. I couldn't help but laugh. For *couples* therapy. As a widow. Right. Well, the receptionist had smugly replied, it would probably help me in the future if I were to remarry. Something I should keep in mind, since I was still so young. I managed to keep my temper somehow, thanking her but canceling the remaining appointments and declined their offer to 'review my situation' in the next couple of months for a discounted fee.

So, with absolutely nothing to deflect my course, I was on the road armed with a tattered though detailed road map – not that I particularly needed the map actually -- by noon. From Kokomo off Route 31 the little town of Swayzee was due east on Highway 35. If you blinked, you would miss the left turn onto Highway 13, partially obscured by a sea of dried corn stalks, that headed directly up to Swayzee. I stopped in Kokomo to grab some coffee at a Stuckey's and scanned their assorted shelves of baked goods in their pantry store wondering if I might see anything mentioning Jessye's Honey Farms. Nothing. Since the business relationship was in its infancy, I was probably too early searching for merchandise.

I got into Swayzee a little before 1 p.m. There had been almost no traffic even with my having zigzagged through downtown Indianapolis, so I'd arrived much earlier than planned. Well, maybe I would see the train arrive, I thought. Just as I remembered, the main business district was all of two blocks in length and consisted of small shops carved out of circa 1930's small, faded white or red brick structures, fronted by indistinct diagonal parking lines. I continued through town attempting to locate the train tracks and station. The depot, which was little more than a grey, weathered shed, was farther up a deeply rutted dirt road. I glanced around looking for warehouses. Nothing but snow-dusted farmland stretched in every direction. There would probably be trucks brought in to load I surmised, although it seemed strange that the warehouses would be located too far from this flimsy depot. The land lay flat in every direction with nothing except one silo catching the breeze far in the distance. Maybe there was a newer depot further down the tracks. Unlikely, but possible.

I circled back into town and stopped at one of the two small cafés for better directions. Signs on both storefronts informed me that the establishments opened for breakfast at six a.m. and served lunch until one p.m. daily, except Mondays, when they were closed. Well, if this was Cathy's first trip out here then she wouldn't have known that I reasoned. But something was giving me eerie misgivings about this entire trip -- what Thor referred to as his Hitchcock Hackles. The entire beekeeping enterprise was feeling very fishy. Leaving my bulky coat in the car, I stood at the front register at the Blue Daisy Café after a jangling bell announced my entrance.

"Hi," I nodded, as an exhausted-looking waitress walked towards me, filling several coffee cups on the way, her apron a roadmap of this morning's breakfasts. "You really close at one p.m.?"

"Yes'm," she replied, adding to the small stack of menus next to the register. "I can offer you one cup of coffee, no refill, and a piece of … I think we got peach left … pie, cold, or a donut. Kitchen's closed."

"Thanks, but I'll pass. I was hoping to meet someone for lunch when she got off the train, but we wouldn't be able to get back here until closer to two."

"Nearest place to eat's out in Gas City," she replied. "That's 'bout twenty minutes east more or less. But the nearest train depot's out there, miss. Pretty sure that's just a freight drop, too. Not sure why you'd be wantin' to meet your friend fer lunch in either place."

The Hitchcock Hackles began a frenzied dance to "*Night on Disco Mountain*". I thanked her and had started walking towards the door when I spotted two men looking in the front windows of my car, which was parked a few spaces left of the entry. Both men had on faded, red and black plaid lumberjack jackets, dark mufflers and knit caps pulled low over their foreheads. Ordinarily, I wouldn't have found their attire at all unusual. But right now, suddenly, I was on high alert. I pulled back quickly from the door and went over to the waitress again, who had just stopped mid-aisle to top off another customer's coffee cup.

"Excuse me again," I said quietly, gesturing out the front window, "could you tell me if you know those two men out there?"

She moved slightly left for an unobstructed view.

"No, can' say's I do ma'am, sorry," she shrugged, then frowning slightly, looked at me again. "Don' recognize that car they're lookin' at or the one parked across the street neither. License plate on that other one starts with a 94 so that's Marion County, 'course. You know, Indianapolis. I recognize the others. They belong to folks in here or over at Donna's place eatin' right now."

The first numbers on an Indiana license plate referred to the county, sorted alphabetically, that had issued the tags. There were only 92 counties in the state, but Marion County was so large it had now captured numbers 49, 93 and 94. Bloomington was in Monroe County, number 53.

"Actually, that's my car they're looking at."

"Monroe?"

I nodded.

"Say, you in some kinda trouble or somethin', honey?"

"Well," I laughed hollowly, "I don't quite know exactly. But I think I might want to call the sheriff … or somebody, just in case."

One of the men was now leaning against my driver's door, arms folded, seemingly in jovial conversation with the other one. Just "shootin' the breeze like they got all day" as my dad would have commented.

"Swayzee don't got no sheriff er nothin'," the waitress replied, now concerned, nudging me away from the front window. "Nearest one's --"

"Let me guess, Gas City, right?"

She bit her lip slightly and nodded. "Phone's on the wall just outside the ladies if you wanna make a call. Emergency's free like anywhere. Just dial the operator, honey."

Emergency may have been free, but no one picked up after the operator had rung the police department twice. "They must all be out on calls, miss, or maybe whoever was on desk just ran out to grab a quick sandwich," the operator apologized. "Happens occasionally, you know. Just try again in five minutes or so. Someone's sure to answer by then."

I thanked her, hung up and began rattling through my wallet for coins. I could at least call Thor at the newsroom or leave a message with anyone there who happened to pick up. Let someone know what was going on even if it was some part timer back in the print room. As I continued digging for fifteen cents to make the call, the card with Tom Miller's contact information fluttered out of my purse to the floor. On a rash impulse I nervously pushed the coins into the slot, wavering only momentarily and then dialed Tom's number, stated his pager number when prompted and hung up. My heart now pounding in my ears, I was breathing as hard as a cross country runner badly out of training. Minutes ticked by and no return call. I was freezing in the small drafty hallway yet sweat trickled freely between my shoulder blades.

Come on, dammit, ring! Ring! I cursed silently. I was on the verge of dialing the operator again to ring emergency when I heard the front bell jangling. Either a customer had just left or those two men had now entered. I was more than convinced of the latter. I quickly crossed over into the women's restroom, flipping the lock to secure the door, but refrained from turning on the light since that would most likely activate an overhead fan. A small filthy window just above the toilet, probably last cleaned circa 1955, filtered in greasy sunlight so I wasn't in complete darkness. I now heard heavy boots entering the hallway. No conversation. One man? Both men? Someone else entirely? Maybe I'd let this entire scenario spook me. There might be a completely rational explanation. The men's room door hinges squealed shut as an overhead fan began to drone. All right. At least one man. I tried to calm my breathing. No such luck.

The phone rang. It continued for several cycles and

finally stopped, then almost immediately started in ringing again. After several rings there was a slight pause. Then I heard a man's voice bark "hey, I'm waitin' fer a call here, buddy. Don't keep callin' an' tie up the line," followed by the sound of the receiver slamming back on the hook so hard it echoed loudly in the hallway. I hadn't heard the men's bathroom fan quit or the door squeal back open. Ok. Two men.

Looping my purse handle around my neck, careful not to slip off the toilet seat, I climbed up on the tank and worked to crank open the window. A pen rolled out of the side pocket of my purse and splashed into the toilet. I heard the men's room door hinges squeaking and the fan turn off. No footsteps to indicate the men had left. No banging on my door. Not yet. I was now certain the men had to have concluded that I was in here, however. Had the waitress or a customer told them I was in the café? I doubted the waitress would have done so, but even bumbling Detective Lestrade would've figured that one out by now.

A loud party was in the throes of leaving the café, their voices filling the hallway momentarily. I seized that opportunity to resume wrestling with the flailing window crank; I had to keep refitting the crank onto the base because the contacts were so badly stripped. Still no sound outside but I didn't dare assume the men had given up and walked away. I finally got the window pushed far enough open, cold air forcing in immediately. Somehow securing a toehold despite my thick boot, high up on the cement block wall, I boosted myself up, slithered through the small opening and raced towards the fenced alley behind the restaurant. Wet snow fiercely pelted my face as I emerged. Although I could have run either direction in the alley, I opted to push through what appeared to be a small broken section of the fencing, roughly scraping my cheek on a dysfunctional jagged slide lock, snagging my sweater on the splintered wood. The abrasion, very close to my right eye, burned intensely despite the frigid air.

Just beyond the fence stood a low building partially obscured by the blinding snowflakes. A faded winged red horse on a white oval Esso emblem painted on the side of the building gradually came into focus as I ran closer. Esso Gas was long gone these days, but their flying Pegasus lived on with new station ownerships in most towns. As I neared the station however, I could tell it was abandoned; no old-fashioned pumps with their jolly spaceman-like, round yellow faces stood at attention ready to service one's car when you drove over the snaking black cables signaling one's arrival. Kids had apparently been using the smaller metal sign next to the service bay door for target practice recently; dozens of rocks sprawled beneath the badly pockmarked sign. I picked up what appeared to be a fist-sized rock and was surprised to discover that it was a partially frozen potato. One of Thor's and my favorite early *"Columbo"* episodes came to mind and, allowing myself a brief smile given my half-baked pun of an idea, dropped the potato with a clunk into my purse.

Shaking from both the fiercely driving snow as well as fear, I walked quickly back towards the alley. But rather than cutting back through the fence, I opted to continue following along until it ended, then crossed over to the main street. Now covered with a wet layer of snow, the men's car remained parked less than a block away. There were still several cars parked alongside my own on the opposite side of the street in front of the Blue Daisy. I had no idea if the men were still waiting outside the restrooms, but I could only assume they were either inside the Blue Daisy or had begun searching for me behind the restaurant.

Quickly scanning the empty street, I sprinted towards their car and dumped the frozen potato down into the exhaust pipe. Don't you dare desert me now, Peter Falk, I swore to myself. Unlocking my own car, I cranked the engine allowing no warm-up whatsoever and quickly sped off. No car appeared in my rear-view mirror. Was I overreacting? Had I just sabotaged some stranger's car's exhaust system on some irrational wild whim? I thought of the man's surly voice wanting to keep the line clear and slamming down the phone. An obvious lie. No, I was not overreacting.

I headed straight west, back towards Kokomo. Presumably a bigger town would yield more than the handful of cops available in Gas City. The snow was already slick, though not too deep, and the tread on my steel-belted radials had been reluctantly stretched to face one more season of winter driving to help with Hank's and my expenses. I drove carefully, one eye glued to the nuances of the uneven pavement and the other riveted to my rearview mirror.

As I drove, I tried to figure out what all of this could possibly be about. Obviously, the man I'd spoken with when attempting to reach Cathy Martin was lying; that entire phone call had to have been staged. Had a little girl actually picked up? No way. I remembered hearing those strange clicking sounds. Maybe they'd used some kind of switchover recording device. I didn't know how those switches worked but I knew they were available. In fact, a few months ago my colleague Marcy had researched a story about crooks using line changes to hide from authorities. Great article too. Landed just below the fold on page one of the main section as I recalled. Al Capone had initiated a similar system back in the 1930's so the concept had been around for decades. Hadn't Hank once mentioned Idyllic developing an undetectable device like this? I wished I'd paid more attention. Nonetheless, there was a very strong possibility. I was feeling ice in my veins. What the hell was going on?

This guy who'd claimed his name was Roger Dunn also knew that both Cathy and I were from Indiana. I was ashamed to admit how easily he'd coerced me to drive up here to meet Cathy on what I was now mortified to admit was an incredibly fabricated, flimsy pretense.

But why? Someone had taken the time to send that rsvp and accompanying note back to Mark Stephens after our class reunion. Mark said he'd recognized Cathy's handwriting from their high school lab reports. He had called me specifically with Cathy's phone number since we'd been discussing her at the reunion. Who else knew that I was planning to attend the reunion and might be aware that Cathy's name had surfaced other than those who had attended?

Janet Lynn at her engagement party was the one and only candidate left standing on the dais.

Completely unbidden, parts of my conversation with my father just a few days ago filtered back into my mind. The two chainsaw-mutilated corpses had been found when the excavation for the winery had unearthed the bones. One had been identified as Jimmy Larkins, who'd disappeared shortly after his continuing harassment of Brenda, the daughter of a woman labeled as a cheap, alcoholic prostitute. Although I didn't know that Brenda and Cathy Martin had ever been friends, I distinctly remembered Brenda running up to Cathy for help that one day and Cathy holding her as she sobbed in her arms. This was probably why the scene had stuck with me all these years -- I had never known Cathy to hug anyone. Hard as I tried, however, I could not remember Brenda's last name. Since I knew I would have remembered her from taking the bus, I was certain that she hadn't continued with us over at Columbus High. She and her mom must have moved away shortly after Jimmy's disappearance. Chainsaw. Chomp Martin. Images of Chomp's bizarre, starkly obscene artwork came flooding back to me.

A dump truck suddenly pulled out of a side road immediately in front of my car, swerving on the slick pavement. I skidded slightly to the right of the truck but managed to stay on the road as we both zigzagged yet miraculously continued forward.

Chomp would do anything for Cathy, she'd once told me. Had he killed Jimmy? An accident? An angry gesture originally intended to teach the kid a lesson that had gone too far? On the other hand, Chomp may well have had his own issues with the Larkins. They would have certainly been among the snootier well-to-do folks wrinkling their noses at Chomp himself as well as his ghastly artistic endeavors, which often featured shockingly well-endowed male or female subjects. A chance to cut Jimmy down to size sounded very plausible for a man who'd been on trial for manslaughter in the not so distance past. But a fifteen-year-old kid? I couldn't believe that even someone as ruthless as Chomp would resort to anything that horrific, at least not on purpose.

Traffic was now moving at a snail's pace, certainly in direct contrast to my whirling imagination. The dump truck fishtailed in front of me several times to avoid cars that had spun out on the road and now were down in a ditch alongside the pavement, probably unable to regain any traction.

The dump truck slowed considerably, right blinker now activated, and just barely managed to swerve onto a small county road. A few feet later a sign came into view that Kokomo was a mile ahead and that the speed limit was now dropping to thirty. I was only moving at about fifteen mph at this point, so that did not present a problem. I decided that I was going to stay in Kokomo overnight. There was a trucker's joint just this side of Route 31 that unlike motels, allowed folks to check in any hour of the day. I hadn't stopped looking out my review mirror, now largely obscured by a veil of snow, but I felt confident that my pursuers were not on my tail. The mighty spud had evidently performed its deadly deed.

The phones were on a stub wall located towards the back of the lobby. Room phones would have to patch through from the front desk which would be useless for Tom Miller to answer a page. Why I still wanted to contact him was muddled in my head, but for whatever reason, he seemed my best resource. After I'd checked in, I waited until a man finished his call on a lobby phone then called Tom's service and left the pager number again. I stared outside the adjacent window at what had now escalated into a blizzard according to the radio, hoping Tom would call back. Five minutes ticked by. No call. Another ten. Still nothing. Just as I started to walk away the phone finally rang and I jumped to answer it.

"Hello?" I stammered. The connection was alive with static, doubtless thanks to scores of kids on a recent afternoon's lark, knocking the glass insulators off the telephone poles, thus exposing the connectors to these obscene ravages of the weather. Given my recent conversation with some man claiming to be my childhood friend's husband, however, I trusted no one.

"Uh yeah, hi," said a male voice. "Somebody just paged me at this number?"

"What's your favorite song?" I shot out, taking no chances.

"Um well, let's see, that's gotta be 'You light up my life' – yep, darn best song ever written," the man chuckled. "Denise? That you? Where the hell are you? This number lines up with a pay phone at a pretty sleazy Trucker's Paradise out near Kokomo. Place known for its, uh, reputation of 'lewd and nude just ask me' ads on several men's restroom walls up in that area as I recall. You goin' in for a new line of work?"

"Very funny," I snarled. "Look, Tom, I might be in a lot of trouble. No, let me rephrase that. I *know* I'm in a lot of trouble! I'm scared to death!"

"Okey dokey," he drawled, far too calmly given my

currently crazed state of mind. "Whassup l'il darlin'?"

"Knock it off!" I demanded, somehow keeping my voice low but impatiently stamping my foot. "I'm serious! Where are you?"

"Not too far from you as it turns out. I'd just started moving south when I got what I kinda assume was your first page from Swayzee and I says to myself, well, Holmes, must be somethin' goin' down, after some less than gentlemanly type hangs up on me, so's I starts to meander ovuh in that direction. I jes hit this here snow squall 'bout fifteen miles back, give 'er take."

I exhaled loudly, rubbing my forehead.

"Can you just get here? Please? There are two men after me -- and I'm terrified!"

"On mah way, l'il lady," he replied still affecting the irksome faux cowboy routine. "What's your room number? 'Course y'know, I gotta tell ya, if I see anything else that uh, happens to appeal to my uh, baser, adventuring spirit, it may jes be awhile afores I kin get over to ya."

"Just get here!" I growled between clinched teeth, careful to keep my voice lowered. "Number 231. And stop this lame Texas cornball shit!" Exasperated, I hung up, far harder than I'd intended, glad I didn't break the phone case.

****

When truckers start pulling off the highway in droves late in the afternoon, you know the storm is bringing a city to a complete standstill. My room was located over the entrance facing out to the road. Peering carefully through a small opening between the closed drapes, I saw rigs of all sizes heading in. About an hour after I'd arrived the neon No Vacancy sign -- or at least that's what I assumed the sign had originally spelled since it actually read: "o V can y" with the "y" spluttering on and off -- was lit. I kept glancing at my watch, occasionally shaking my wrist and listening to the ticking. Time was truly standing still. I wondered if Tom Miller would show up soon, simultaneously hoping that my calling him wasn't a colossal error in judgment. A riddle came to mind from the movie "*Charade*" starring Audrey Hepburn and Cary Grant, about asking an Indian whether he was a truthful White Foot or a lying Black Foot. Cary Grant claims to be a truthful White Foot but then counters his answer with, "but how d'you know?" And we honestly didn't really know which side he was on until the last few minutes of the film. You'd better be a truthful White Foot, Tom Miller, I muttered under my breath. I peered through the drapes again. Blackfoot, White Foot or Big Foot, there was still no sign of the man.

After close to another hour, I heard a knock on my door. I peered through the peephole just as a male voice joked in a fake British accent: "Room service, madam."

As I yanked open the door, Tom stomped snow off his boots as best as possible given the fact that the concrete was piled over with a foot of drift at this point. He walked through, looking like the abominable snowman toting a Burger King bag.

"Here, take this," he said, handing me the sack, which was barely tepid. Nonetheless, my stomach growled fiercely in appreciation, as he brushed off as much snow as possible from his coat and hat before shutting the door against the storm. He tossed both clothing items into the corner chair. "Sorry, best I could do about the *haute cuisine* on such short notice. Eh, cheese boogie, no cheese, no cheeps and no fries. Oh, and no Pepsi either."

"John Belushi. Saturday Night Live sketch a few months back. Cute. Wouldn't have thought you were a fan."

He winked. I grimaced.

"And the only wine I could locate was some kind of red swill at the gas station – hope this place provides the regulation church key's pigtail."

"Thanks for coming," I smiled, finally relaxing slightly despite his aggravating banter. "This looks amazing. Honest."

"Just wanted to mention: you do realize that there's a blizzard raging out there, correct?" he began, clearing his throat. "And that this place now has no vacancies, yes? And this means I'm staying in this room tonight, got that? I'm not looking for any privileges, but I just want to make sure we've got that straight up front."

I nodded. I hated to admit that it was really good to see him, sarcasm and all. I mean, a man tromping through a blizzard bearing almost stone-cold Burger King hamburgers can certainly be trusted … right?

"So that means I'm staying here in this room with you, whether you like it or not -- got that? I had to abandon my car in a ditch out on 31 and walk over here. It's not far, but …"

"Yes, yes, I understand," I replied quickly. "I'm … glad that you're here. Thanks."

"Ok, let's eat this crap before it gets any colder and you can fill me in with what's going on."

He sat on the battered chair next to the crudely built-in nightstand and I sat on the bed as we rustled through the bag to divide up the burgers and Tom wrestled with the wine cork.

"Slainté," he toasted. "Ah, pure rot gut circa 1931, eh?"

"Actually, I was just going to say that I didn't think it tasted too bad," I countered. The rubbery cheeseburger on the other hand had probably been parked on the side of the greasy grill sheet since well before noon and took an incredible amount of chewing before swallowing. But it was food. Maybe not particularly tasty, but certainly edible.

"Ok, so what in hell were you doing way over in Swayzee in the first place?" he finally asked.

"Well, after you left my apartment the other day I actually got in touch with Cathy Martin."

He whistled, sitting up straight. "Seriously? You, uh, actually talked with her?" He stared at me, frowning.

"No, no, not exactly. I guess I should say I *thought* I'd

gotten in touch with her. This friend of mine on my high school reunion's committee had received a note from her and when I called the number on the note, the guy who answered said he was her husband -- said his name was Roger Dunn."

I glanced at Tom wondering if he recognized the name, but he shook his head slightly, gesturing that I should continue my story.

"So, this Roger Dunn told me that Cathy has some kind of huge bee keeping enterprise – Jessye's Honey Farms – and that she was accompanying a shipment of products out from Virginia -- which is where they live now supposedly -- to Swayzee to be warehoused before being delivered to major department stores and places like Stuckey's around Indianapolis."

"I'm fairly certain there's no train depot in Swayzee," Tom replied, raising a skeptical eyebrow, obviously dumbfounded regarding my gullibility.

"Yes, well, thank you very much. I found that out too, but not until I asked at a café on the main drag and then spotted these two big goons leaning against my car. One of the waitresses pointed out their car – other than mine it was the only one with out of county plates. Car had Marion tags."

"So, Indianapolis or thereabouts. And they just let you freely waltz past them and drive away?"

"Well, no, not exactly. After I tried to page you, I hid in the women's bathroom. That was one of them that picked up the phone when you called, I'm assuming. Then I crawled out the window and came back around to the front and, well … got away. I assume they were both still in the hallway."

"They didn't catch up with you driving out this way? Only thing that's been open for hours other than north-south along Route 31 is whatever in the heck that road is straight west out to Kokomo."

"Um, I'm assuming that I kind of … well… maybe slowed them down some … I shoved a potato down their exhaust pipe."

"Whoa, impressive, Prescott! Hardly original but … what kind of street gang were you a member of as a kid?" he laughed.

"Nothing like that," I retorted, shaking my head. "I saw it on an episode of "*Columbo*" a few months ago. I really didn't know if it worked."

"*Columbo*, eh? Nothing like advertising how to screw up a car on a syndicated top cop drama I always say. Ok, so that gave you a slight lead and you're probably going to luck out further since everything out there is under at least a foot of snow and ice right now. No idea why these guys are on your tail though? Come on, you must have *some* idea, Prescott!"

"No," I answered, taking another sip of the wine, "but while I was driving here from Swayzee, I tried to analyze some of this stuff. Sort of analyze, anyway."

"I'm all ears," replied Tom. "Hey, look at this! There's about a half dozen or so shriveled fries at the bottom of the bag. Wanna split 'em?"

Wrinkling my nose, I shook my head.

"So, getting back to those men, going with your hypothesis about Cathy taking on Janet Lynn's identity and then getting rid of her, I think I may have a tie in why this is all of a sudden important."

"I'm all ears," replied Tom.

"Her husband's family is going full out with this new wine business down in Nashville ... Indiana, that is. The grapevines, the tasting room, the hotel and cozy little cottages, the wedding chapel nonsense, the whole nine yards. All this is a brand-new operation in a place that basically used to be the town dump until just after World War II. Not everyone is excited about this huge complex moving into the area according to newspaper grumblings either. The townspeople really prefer to maintain a small-town, provincial atmosphere. Tourists are ok, but with a limited timecard as it were."

"Huh," shrugged Tom, scrounging for one last fry at the bottom of the bag.

"But then, about a week ago, the excavating crew at the site discovered two bodies that, according to police, had been placed in this deep trench at different times, but both had been hacked apart with the same chainsaw."

"Ugh. Yeah, I heard something about this. Guess I didn't realize that was over in your patch of the woods."

"Ok, so one of the bodies was identified by his dental records as this really bratty, spoiled rich kid who was a few years older than me, named Jimmy Larkins. He disappeared when I was maybe twelve or so, in 1962, I think. He'd been forcing this girl who was a friend of Cathy's to have, um, I think to have … well, oral … you know … with him. Both Cathy's and Brenda's mothers were rumored to be prostitutes and so no one believed that Brenda had been tricked into it."

"Tricked?" Tom mused.

"Ok, ok, bad verb," I replied in exasperation. "You know what I mean – deceived, coerced, whatever!"

"They never do."

"Well, I was thinking about this a few hours ago while I was stuck behind this dump truck doing about five miles an hour driving here. What if Cathy and Brenda had been trying to teach Jimmy Larkins some kind of lesson, but accidentally killed him? You know, maybe threw a brick at his head or something like that? Or Chomp, for that matter. Just trying to put the fear of God into the stupid kid."

"I've heard that Chomp Martin was well known for those hideous tree trunk carvings with a chainsaw. Cutting up a body wouldn't be much of a challenge I shouldn't think," nodded Tom, offering me the last bite of the French fry, which I declined. "Ok, so let's assume old

Chomp revs up the chainsaw and helps the two girls hide the remains. So, what happened to this girl Brenda?"

"I have no idea. I think she and her mom must've moved out of town very shortly after that because I don't remember ever seeing her again. She never attended my high school over in Columbus, I'm certain."

"What about the other body? You said that there were two. Any leads there?"

"The medical examiner verified that the bones were from a female, probably older than Jimmy, and that she'd been killed a few years later most likely. However, I've read that determining date of death once you're getting into years after the fact is anything but exact. Also, the skull and hands were nowhere to be found."

"Whoa. Now that's nasty! In terms of a year though, maybe around '65? Or maybe later – what, '68 possibly? Ok, so let's think this one through," said Tom, sitting further back in the chair, drawing slow circles on his knee with the wine bottle. "The second corpse might possibly be this Brenda in my opinion, even though we don't know anything about her, or if you want to really go out on a limb here, Janet Lynn Webster. Without question, however, either way Chomp Martin's a suspicious tie in. So completely on conjecture without the smallest shred of proof, let's fast forward about five years. Seem reasonable thus far?"

I nodded slightly.

"Ok, so Cathy Martin heads off to the University of Wisconsin from the Webster's Wisconsin estate with her lookalike Janet Lynn Webster in late summer 1968. They had sent their trunks ahead and Janet Lynn, being quite the party girl, undoubtedly wouldn't have wanted her parents to accompany them on the trip and cramp her style. We're fairly certain that only one girl claiming to be Janet Lynn actually arrived on the campus, right? And we know she arrived a few days after having left the Webster place. Of course, she could have spent a couple of nights with some hot guy along the way, but let's rule that out. You with me so far?"

"Go on." I was curious how Tom would have known that only one girl had actually arrived on campus … had I mentioned this to him when we'd met up in Galena? Or maybe during that bizarre drunken phone conversation? I filed that concern temporarily.

"Let's suppose that part way into their rural drive east they pulled off the road – picnic, scenic overlook, pit stop, whatever – and Cathy kills Janet Lynn."

"How? And more importantly, why?"

"Let's go with poison. Doesn't matter what kind and no idea why. You'd mentioned that Cathy Martin had excelled in chemistry and, as we've agreed before, poison is a woman's weapon. She poisons her beverage before they leave the estate. Something that's going to take effect within the first half hour or so of their trip, so they're still out in the wilds. Janet Lynn's getting car sick – after all it's her car and she's probably driving so she needs to stop … guess that makes it technically a pitstop, so that chalks it up as answer number three. Either the poison completely incapacitates her, or Cathy bludgeons her with a large rock and finishes off the job. Either way she then folds her up in the back seat, so it looks as though she's asleep, and breezes on down to Nashville, Indiana later that night."

Deep in thought as he sketched out the premise, I reluctantly took over the story.

"Then Chomp breaks out the chainsaw and the real Janet Lynn meets with almost the same burial rite as had Jimmy Larkins. Who knows, maybe Cathy had been sending Chomp money all along, siphoning it off from the Websters little by little, or maybe she had a hold on him with some other kind of blackmail, so he's obligated. Whatever the story," I shuddered.

"Let's now move on to 1971," continued Tom,

pouring out another couple glasses of wine. "The Websters are now highly concerned that someone has assumed their daughter's identity and have hired me to investigate."

"But it took them four years to discover this? I still have trouble with that idea. And also, what detective firm was this exactly?" I inquired, my eyes narrowing slightly. I still hadn't figured out how he could be in this line of work assuming Thor's friend was correct. And Thor himself -- truly a bloodhound in that respect -- had about a 99% accuracy rating. Yes, in desperation I'd called the man, but that certainly didn't mean that I'd completely ruled out complicity on his part.

"Legit firm, I assure you, Prescott. Let's not lose our direction here right now, ok? So, the woman claiming to be Janet Lynn had told her parents that Cathy had gotten pregnant with Janet Lynn's boyfriend – attributed to yours truly even though I didn't know the woman, much less in the Biblical sense -- right when school had started. She had then dropped out of school. Janet Lynn – in other words, Cathy Martin -- then tells her parents she never wants to speak about her again. Somehow then, four years later, the impostor Janet Lynn discovers that the Websters have ironically hired me. I make the blunder sometime later of calling Chomp, who cusses me out a blue streak after which he contacts Cathy, putting her on high alert."

"Yes," I agreed, "and according to my folks, somewhere in that time frame, the town council forced Chomp to leave Nashville and he moved down to rural Kentucky. A place known locally down there as the river bottoms; in fact, it has a haunted legacy all its own. Anyway, Cathy pays old dad a visit, slips him with, who knows, maybe the same kind of poison she'd used on Janet Lynn, and then leaves him dead or almost dead, roughly just before Christmas in an unheated shack. Nobody would even think to be looking for him for weeks, even months, if at all."

"Let's say then she drives back up to the Websters' place in Wisconsin, probably poisons both of Janet Lynn's parents as well, and then rigs up some kind of timing device to start the fire at their estate just a few hours after she's headed back for her last semester at the college," added Tom. "It all fits in the correct time frame. But who would ever think to link together three murders committed in the wilds of Wisconsin and out in the swamp land of rural Kentucky?"

"I feel like we're tailoring all these deaths to fit into some totally arbitrary, far-fetched timeline. You know as well as I do that none of this really plays out in the real world."

Tom bunched up the Burger King bag and tossed it across the room to the trash can.

"Rim shot," I said, making note of the obvious. "Meadowlark can breathe a sigh of relief; his stats remain safe."

"Out of practice. Admittedly this is all total speculation and may not exactly jive smoothly," remarked Tom, clearing his throat as he walked over to redeposit the bag correctly into the garbage. "Also, no offense, but none of it explains in the least what this has to do with those two men you claimed followed you or finagled some wacky setup to get you out to Swayzee in the first place. You don't really know if they had anything to do with your waiting for Cathy. The phone call was obviously a setup, of course, but you don't know about those guys admiring your car. There's nothing around that actually ties you into this Cathy Martin anymore, is there?"

"You know," I answered slowly, "I sure wouldn't have thought so. But something flickered way back in my mind after Janet Lynn and David Fowler's engagement party. Janet Lynn, or Cathy or whoever the hell she is, made some comment about our parents keeping our love letters, diaries and stuff."

"That doesn't sound particularly incriminating," chuckled Tom. "Mushy and disgusting maybe, but --"

"No, it doesn't. But Cathy Martin and I had this Instamatic camera that we'd bought together, and we used to take all kinds of bizarre pictures of ourselves. You know, pictures of our scars, moles, webbed toes, broken bones. Even the last of our baby teeth since we'd both outgrown the tooth fairy. Oh, and Cathy had to have several teeth extracted because her mouth was too crowded. We even had those stupid teeth pasted in there! You name it. Totally weird stuff like that. Also, with those Instamatic cameras you could order two prints for the price of one. We each had photo albums and other books full of duplicated pictures, drawings, and all kinds of bizarre ideas we planned to develop into Sherlock Holmes' type mystery stories or movies one day. Or in some cases, we'd record the stories on reel-to-reel tape. As I remember though, Cathy recorded most of those stories. And some of them were really, well, kind of out there, you know? Raunchy for a girl at any rate.

"Anyway, getting back to Janet Lynn at her engagement party, she seemed more than slightly interested that I'd hung onto that junk. I certainly didn't think anything of it at the time, but now … I honestly think maybe that's what might be behind this," I shrugged. "I'm clueless as to where those books might be stored these days! And more importantly, what could possibly be in there that Cathy or Janet Lynn or whoever the hell she is finds threatening anyhow? Maybe on some whim I actually threw them out ages ago. Or Hank did. Any time I tried to hang onto stuff from my childhood he accused me of retaining my folks' rabid hoarding instincts."

"But you don't think so, right?"

"As I said, I'm clueless where the books might be."

"Did you tell her you didn't know where they might be or leave that open?"

"Huh?" I replied, confused. His question struck me as rather odd.

He shrugged.

"I adore my folks, but they're the original Kentucky hillbilly packrats, bless their souls. You can't find anything in that place! For that reason alone, I'm sure I didn't leave those books and tapes back there and originally brought everything to our apartment. But as I've said, I haven't stumbled across them in ages. On an impulse, tired of all the clutter in our place, Hank hauled all kinds of crap to a storage unit somewhere right after we got married. I'm assuming he probably included that stuff. My old high school yearbook, *The Argonaut* was still there at our place, though. It kind of surprised me he'd left that behind."

We were both silent for several moments, lost in thought.

"Tom, assuming the police are correct that Hank was poisoned, do you think there's some chance that poison was meant for me?"

"Um, doubt it. I think your husband was the intended target."

"But why? That really doesn't make sense. Hank was supposedly one of the golden boys of Idyllic. At least that's what Hank had always told me."

"One of their 'golden boys'? Hmm … maybe according to his own interpretation. But there are a lot of guys like him … women too, these days … clawing to get to the top of the corporate landfill. I bet his spot's already been filled."

"That's really cold, Tom."

"Cold, yes. But feel free to prove me wrong. Anyway, assuming you're arrested for Hank's murder, you're discredited in every way possible, held without bail more than likely pending the trial. Janet Lynn then has *carte blanche* to leisurely ransack your apartment, prowl through both your basement storage and this other storage shelter wherever it's located, and then, even your parents' home as a last resort, if necessary, to be certain that any evidence linking her to Cathy Martin has been destroyed. If that other female found in the ravine is the real Janet Lynn Webster, who was never reported missing, there's really nothing to link back to her. End of story."

"This is a mess," I shuddered.

"Astoundingly cutthroat for a woman if you want my opinion," said Tom, rubbing his jaw thoughtfully before continuing. "Ok, so let's get back to Swayzee and assume you were coerced there by a couple of goons who were hired by Janet Lynn as it were."

"Assume I was coerced? Even though there's no train depot in Swayzee?" I retorted sarcastically. "Ok, let me ask you a question then mister detective. How is it that with checking out private, local, county, state, and all federal investigative services your name doesn't show up anywhere? Something doesn't exactly add up on your end either, Mr. Tom Miller, despite the fact that yes, you're quite correct that in utter desperation, I did indeed call you. Not once, but twice today as we're both aware." I held up my hand to ward off any anticipated rebuttal. "Who are you really? And do not lie to me!"

"Well, that's easy to explain. Did you ever hear of *Rumschpringe*?"

"Sounds like some kind of weird purple vegetable I'd leave on the side of my plate," I replied, wrinkling my nose.

"It refers to an Amish youth's brief period of experiencing the outside, or as it's typically known, the English world, prior to pledging to the Faith. A rite of passage if you will."

"Um, no offense meant, but you seem just a tad too old to be classified as an Amish youth."

"To be sure," he chuckled. "For most communities it's age fifteen, so you're right, that certainly was a long time ago."

"Ok, I'm listening."

"How many brothers and sisters do you have?"

"Don't know why you're asking exactly, but I'm an only child," I replied. "So was Cathy Martin. And Janet Lynn Webster for that matter. Why?"

"My parents had fifteen kids. Three sets of twins and eleven of us were boys. I was right in the middle of the pack."

I whistled, frowning, but made no other reply. Imagine having fourteen siblings!

"I was raised just outside of LaFarge over in southwest Wisconsin. Huge Amish settlement up there, almost all farming, other than a few sawmills, the occasional roadside market, bakeries, and legitimate furniture building businesses. Most Amish cabinetry you see in department stores is fake, by the way. I think the smallest family around when I was growing up had six or seven kids."

"You're not putting me on about this? How on earth were your parents able to afford college? There's only one of me and it was a real struggle."

"No," he smiled, "I'm not putting you on. Actually, Amish schooling only goes through eighth grade, taught all together in a one room schoolhouse. I walked out of my parents' home on my fifteenth birthday having just finished eighth grade, more than ready for my *Rumschpringe*. I didn't think I could stomach one more day mucking out horseshit from the barn. But that was just me. Something like ninety-eight percent of Amish youth return after six months or so, marry their Amish sweethearts and follow the strict ways of the Faith. However, I was one of those two per cent who never returned. This results in something known as shunning where you're forever ostracized from communicating in any way with your family or anyone else in the community for the rest of your life … no, uh, Papal dispensations so to speak."

"Do you ever get to see your family?" I couldn't imagine simply walking out on my folks and never seeing either of them again!

"Nope," he replied, shaking his head. "And yes, I do miss them. I'm not as hard hearted a bastard as you may think, Prescott. Anyway, I was very fortunate to be taken in by a Mennonite family in LaCrosse, doing farm work and odd chores to earn my keep, so that I could go to high school and then, after managing to snag a full ride grant, graduated from U of Wisconsin with a math teaching degree. All of that's legit. I started teaching in LaCrosse which is an hour and a half northwest of LaFarge."

"But after all of that you decided you didn't like teaching," I remarked flatly.

"Well, not entirely. By 1969 and 1970 the English world was suddenly spiraling downward faster than ever. Amish youth spilling out into that world were being eaten alive, far worse than their full-blooded American counterparts who'd gradually evolved into that ensuing chaos by watching television, playing pinball machines, and lazing about watching skimpily clad buxom girls in bikinis bouncing out of their tiny bras along the beaches. These poor kids were being turned into alcoholics, drug addicts, prostitutes – both the boys as well as the girls -- thieves, even cold-blooded gang murderers, within the space of a few weeks. That ninety-eight percent return had suddenly dwindled to roughly sixty percent, and most members of the Faith were certain that this was not of the kids' own choosing. The deacon – that's like a minister or a priest -- from my community in LaFarge asked one of his Mennonite neighbors to track me down and then the two of them came out to visit me. Amish aren't allowed to drive cars, but Mennonites are -- not sure if you knew that."

I shook my head but remained silent.

"Even though Herr Bontrager was understandably still furious about my having left the Faith, he begged me to help rescue these kids whose lives were being destroyed by what he called *die Heuschrecke schwarz* which means the black locust. He only had two sons – the rest of his kids were girls – kind of the opposite of my family -- and both boys had simply vanished in thin air. Last contact he'd had from one of his sons was a letter posted from a very seedy area on Chicago's south side. So, now fresh on a full time, decent-paying job for which I had no training whatsoever, I left my teaching position, crammed in some rudimentary police force and detective education over a few months and began tracking down these kids. When no one had heard anything from their son or daughter for over a month I would usually be contacted. Their hope was that I would be able to locate the child and get him – or her – back home."

"So did you locate Mr. Bontrager's sons and bring them safely back to the nest?"

"Well, yes," he replied, looking away from me. "One of them anyway. The other one had died a few months before that of a heroin overdose. Police had found the kid dumped in an alley. The brother didn't know that's what had happened. I was the one who told him. That was hard. Sadly, a lot of those missing kids turned up in the morgue."

"God, that's … awful," I swallowed.

"These kids start out with a lot of money in their pockets, too. A huge mistake, of course, that I couldn't dissuade the community to amend, making them ripe for the plucking," Tom continued, a sharp edge now in his voice. "Add that to the fact that almost all of them also experience something of a language barrier since speaking pure English in our communities *ist streng verboten* and rarely until then did they experience any outside contact. If they were in trouble, they had a difficult time locating the authorities that might have actually helped them. They were guppies fed into the jaws of vicious sharks circling maniacally for the kill."

"Wouldn't it just be easier to deny them the ability to go out into the world?" I frowned. I was the first to admit that even with attending a very conservative college like Franklin out in nowheresville Indiana, the number of kids smoking pot, getting high on pills, and enjoying weekend-long sex orgies had thoroughly shocked me. Without having witnessed newsreels of JFK's or Martin Luther King, Jr.'s assassinations or agent orange being sprayed on helpless women and children in Vietnam or the shooting at Kent State or even watching a man walking on the moon's surface, how could Amish kids possibly understand that world? They were still planting crops using a steel plow drawn by a pair of work horses and using a windmill to pump water from deep wells since electricity was forbidden in their homes.

"Easier, yes, but it's very difficult to alter Amish ideology you have to understand. This was how it had always been done, therefore this was how it must continue. Our ancestors had been the essential, predominant voices for well over two hundred years. I'm sure to you this appears quaint, but to those of the Faith, it's the only logical path."

"So how on earth did you end up on the case involving Janet Lynn and the Webster family in the first place? None of them are Amish."

"Mrs. Webster had gotten my name from the family I'd lived with during high school up in LaCrosse. They knew I was now tracking down these wayward kids. I really didn't want to get involved with the Webster matter at first, especially since the number of kids on my list was a staggering caseload at the time, but she begged me, so I finally agreed. And I confess, the money was very good. Fortunately, I now have a couple of other investigators working with me to locate the kids. Since none of them are actually Amish they don't speak Pensy Deutsch, though, and I typically have to get personally involved fairly early on.

"Most of the time we're searching for kids from southwest Wisconsin, specifically LaFarge, Cashton and Viroqua, since they have the largest settlements, and then over here in Indiana in communities like Nappanee, Middlebury, Goshen and Shipshewana. Occasionally one of us will end up tracking down kids from Arcola and Arthur, which is downstate in Illinois, but for some reason those kids don't seem to go astray quite as easily. The vast majority of the wayward kids have gotten swallowed up by the rampant vice in Chicago, so I tend to concentrate my efforts there. Too many trains and buses with cheap fares emptying out in Chicago. Makes 'em an easy target."

"And I guess the rest is history, as they say," I commented quietly.

"And indeed, the rest is history," he smiled.

We sat quietly for several moments.

"So then, did you leave an Amish sweetheart?"

"Yep. But she went on to marry someone else. It's most unusual for the Amish not to marry."

"Ah," I replied quietly, unable to lower my eyes from his gaze. Definitely hazel, I thought, mentally contradicting Thor's disparaging assessment as a blue-eyed cowboy.

"She married my twin brother in fact and they're very happy – already have three kids and are expecting another any day now. My youngest sister occasionally sneaks a letter out to me, so I do have some very limited contact, for which I'm truly thankful."

"But you never married then?"

"I was married for a few years actually. But she was a little too, uh, worldly, for lack of a better description. Let's just say her reaction to my lengthy treks away from home weren't acceptable from my point of view and leave it at that."

He then sat next to me on the bed, lightly curling a lock of my hair behind my ear for a moment.

"And you live where then – Indiana, Wisconsin, Illinois?" I asked, moving slightly away from him so that I could still face him. I was feeling drawn to him, I had to admit. Keep your distance roared my conscience … but I was no longer certain I was giving any heed to my conscience.

"It kind of depends," he answered, shrugging slightly, which seemed rather an evasive reply, but I let it go. His fingers were still lightly playing with the strand of my hair and then his lips naturally moved to mine. The warmth of his kiss calmly melted over me as he gently pulled me down on the bed.

"My hair is like seaweed," I apologized self-consciously. Static electricity curled the stuff around us both.

"No, no, don't ever say that, Denise. *Du hast schone Haare.*"

I frowned.

"You have beautiful hair," he whispered, kissing me again. "Amish girls never cut their hair, you know, and they always wind it up tightly under their white caps, so no one ever gets to see it. Growing up my favorite day was when my older sisters all washed one another's hair and then brushed it out over the porch railings to let it dry in the sunshine. Always reminded me of glistening corn tassels."

"What an exquisite image," I murmured, surprising myself by encouraging another kiss, closing my eyes. "I can almost envision it."

"Is it ok if we climb beneath the covers and get some sleep?" he asked gently, kissing me on the forehead. "I'll promise to keep to my side of the imaginary bundling board if you'd prefer."

"Imaginary bundling board?"

"Eh, you know. Meaning no … hidden expectations. Refers to a board that runs vertically down the center of a bed … to keep the occupants uh, separated."

"Another Amish image?"

"The idea certainly didn't originate with the Amish," he shrugged. "We probably still have as many seven- or eight-month-long pregnancies as did the American colonists a couple of hundred years back when the board was in constant use."

We both lay on our sides, looking at one another in silence for a few moments.

"Did you and Hank want children?" Tom asked softly, brushing my hair from my forehead again.

I flipped slowly onto my back, facing the ceiling.

"I don't really know how to answer that question. Yes. Well, maybe … not that it matters now, of course … but we weren't on the same, well, timetable or something. I don't know. I still need a couple more years before I'm ready for that kind of commitment. That completely changes a woman's life. Men don't see it that way though. Hank was certain that having a baby would solve all our marital problems. But I never felt that way. It was a constant battle, in fact. There's not some kind of switch that you toggle that moves you right over to desiring motherhood," I stated, slightly louder than I'd intended, still staring at the ceiling. "My girlfriends understand. In fact, I think a lot of women these days understand. But men? Pfft. Why'd you ask in the first place? If I wanted children then it's ok … to have sex with me, and if I don't, I'm some trashy harlot?"

"Who said anything about having sex with you?" he murmured. "Look at me, Denise."

I continued staring at the ceiling.

"Please, my little one," he whispered, stroking the side of my cheek.

I turned my head slowly towards him and our eyes met once again. His lips moved softly down my neck to my collarbone and then to my mouth yet again as he slowly loosened the top button on my sweater.

"I don't know you. And I … I don't exactly trust you …"

"No, you don't know me, Denise. That's true. But whether you believe it or not, you've been trusting me."

I started to quietly protest, but he placed his index finger lightly across my lips. "You've trusted me since you were willing to follow me to see the remains of the Webster estate up in Rutledge and then follow me down to Galena to talk with me in that bar. You've just indulged in my gourmet dinner offering of a semi-petrified hamburger as well as that of your favorite pizza at your apartment. And you trusted me not once but twice just a few hours ago when you called my paging service. Don't question that trust. At least for these few hours we have together right now."

I felt myself melting into those hazel eyes as we slowly removed more of one another's clothing and gently explored those mysteries hidden beneath. Just enjoy this for what it is, I said to myself. That's all you need to remember. If you have absolutely no expectations with this man, you won't be disappointed when he disappears tomorrow. Right? I lay back on the pillow and wrapped my body around his.

"But I think the kind of woman I take you to be,
would rather risk everything on one venture
than live the rest of her life in the shadow of doubt
... and death. Am I right?"

Basil Rathbone as Sherlock Holmes in

"The Adventures of Sherlock Holmes"
(1939)

Chapter 20

I was awakened by an odd pulsing buzz. After several disoriented moments I remembered that I was in a hotel room with Tom Miller, who was sprinting to his coat which was draped over a chair by the door. He pulled a small object out of his coat pocket that I realized must be his pager.

"I need to use the phone," he whispered to me. "I'll pay for the extra charges."

"Sure."

After obtaining an outside line from the front office he began dialing. Without his warm body next to me in the bed I was shivering.

"*Ja*, Jakob?" Tom began tersely, "*Herr* Miller, *hier. Was gibt's? Nein. Wo sind Sie?*"

I could hear what seemed to be a terrified teenage boy's voice on the other end of the phone, sobbing while trying to speak. Although I could only comprehend the occasional word from Tom, there was no question that the caller was frantic. In answer, Tom kept calmly repeating, "*es wird dir gut gehen,* Jakob. *Ja?* Ok? It's going to be ok.

Verstehe? Verstehst du? Es wird dir gut gehen."

Finally, after several long minutes, Tom had gotten the young man to calm down. He finished the conversation with "*tschüss*". I smiled slightly since that was Thor's way of ending our phone calls. I dismissed an inevitable torrent of expletives regarding my behavior if I ever mentioned last night to Thor. Tom looked over at me, raking his fingers through his sandy hair as he began quickly pulling on clothes.

"Sorry, but I need to leave right now."

"But I thought you told me you'd left your car out on the highway somewhere," I uttered in disbelief. "You can't just leave me here like this!"

"Here," he replied, extracting a sea of twenties from his shirt pocket, tossing them onto the bed. "That should cover your expenses, Denise."

Although it shouldn't have, something about the gesture struck me as shockingly demeaning, but I fought off the reaction.

"Also, I have something of a theory about the identities of those two guys who you thought were tailing you," he stated as he finished buttoning his shirt and quickly tucked it into his jeans.

"I didn't 'think' they were … I 'know' they were," I retorted, trying to keep anger from creeping into my voice. From what I'd overheard of the conversation he needed to get to this young man immediately, so I made no additional argument. Tom's voice broke into my thoughts.

"It's imperative that you stay awake. As soon as it's barely daylight head straight home to your place. Or better still, you should go to your parents' place first, then head home. Yeah, that's a much better idea. I'll call you as soon as I can. I'll have to take Jakob back up to his family in Wisconsin and then I'll try to get back down to you when it's possible. Might take a couple days, though. Superman I'm not."

"Where is he?"

"Jakob? Chicago. Bronzeville, specifically … that's on the south side. Not a good place at all for an innocent white kid with too much money in his pockets, that's for sure," he added darkly.

"Tom …"

"Yeah?"

"Kiss me … please," I whispered, feeling foolish as the words tumbled out of my mouth. I was still sitting on the bed twisted in blankets. "I need to know that you're … well … I guess concerned enough to even … I don't know ..."

He pulled me into his arms, kissing me lightly then tucking an errant curl behind my ear. "As they say on tv, 'to be continued'. Just don't let anyone other than your girlfriends Marcy and Linda, your parents, or your weird friend Thor into your place. If the cops show up -- no choice with that -- make sure they show valid identification. And whatever you do, don't drive up to Hank's parents! Plows should get through later today, but you shouldn't risk trying to make it up to Mishawaka until, well, who knows? Use that as an excuse if you should need one. If she's indeed behind this little caper, I suspect Janet Lynn is going to try other schemes since you seem to have foiled her on this one."

"All that doesn't exactly fill me with confidence," I laughed hollowly.

"It wasn't meant to do so, Prescott. *Du hast schone Haare, fraulein,*" he whispered as he walked out the door.

"What does that mean again?" I asked in a loud stage whisper.

"You have beautiful hair, young miss," he replied, firmly shutting the door afterwards.

A few moments after he'd left a disturbing thought came over me. How did he know my girlfriends' names or that Hank's parents lived in Mishawaka? Had I mentioned either of those things? He'd met Thor obviously on his unannounced visit to the newsroom, but I didn't remember having ever imparted any of the other information. Within five minutes I was outside, vigorously scraping ice off my car windows, constantly checking all directions to verify that I wasn't being watched. Although I was famished and in need of a serious coffee buzz, my adrenalin kept those minor issues at bay as I headed south on Route 31. Was there any chance that I'd warded off those two men back in Swazee only to dangerously align myself with a far larger enemy -- sleeping with him in fact? Just drive, I scolded myself. What's done is done. According to the radio the worst of the blizzard had hit just south of Indianapolis and extended well north of Kokomo. Although the snow had stopped falling, it was still a treacherous drive, often a complete whiteout blowing across many miles of tamped down ice.

Exhausted from the tense drive, I was more than ready to stop at my parents' house. Side roads were scarcely passable but since their place was less than a half mile from the main route to the hospital, typically they were one of the first to be plowed. As usual, my dad had already dug out a tiny, jagged path from their front door out to the street. I pulled up behind their car, which was almost unrecognizable under its mantle of white. More than likely my dad was resting up for a bit before returning to that excavation project. He answered the door when I knocked.

"Well, I'll be jiggered! Look who's here!" he exclaimed, wrapping his arms around me. "What on earth prompted you to make the drive over here, Denise? Snow's gotta be almost a foot deep over by you as well!"

"Probably, Dad," I nodded. "I was actually caught in it trying to get back from Kokomo last night, so I just decided I would stop here for a few minutes' breather before heading out to my own place."

My mom surfaced, drying her hands on a tea towel. "Deensie! What a wonderful surprise! My hands are all wet. Give me a sec before I can hug proper! Are you hungry? I just pulled corn muffins out of the oven, what luck! They're just Jiffy, but you know, sometimes that's the best in a pinch. Double batch, with lots of added sugar like I always fix 'em. Oh, and you remember Clara next door? She just sent over a couple jars of her lovely blackberry jam that she put up last Fall. Said her husband was so sick of the stuff he refused to eat one more teaspoon!"

I smiled. It was so good to see them. My sweet, crazy loveable parents. I almost felt tears in my eyes although I honestly didn't know what was prompting that reaction. My dad's project *Fleurama* looked to be in about the same stage of completion as during my last visit. But, as he'd avowed more than once to me, after all, it took Vermeer over two *years* to complete any of his paintings and they were so small! Scarcely see them on the wall from ten feet back! And back then almost nobody lived past the age of forty-five for heaven's sake. No big landscape or triptych artistry like his own. I could almost comprehend his feeble attempts at comparing himself to Kandinsky or Picasso or Modigliani or even Salvador Dali. But Vermeer? I'd always reserved comment on that one.

As my dad started unwrapping the slightly scorched pink wrapper from his second corn muffin, already well-slathered on top with blackberry jam, he commented, "So Denise, it's too bad that you didn't stop by yesterday afternoon."

"Oh, yes, for sure! Glad you brought that up, Daddy. I almost forgot!"

"A very nice young woman stopped by hoping to see you yesterday afternoon. Just a bit before the snow started. She was hoping to have a chance to talk with you since her husband and Hank had worked together up in Indianapolis for several years. She said that she was helping her husband look for information about Hank's life to be included in a memorial service they're planning for Hank sometime next month. Said she'd contacted Hank's parents, but they were much too distraught to talk right now, which was understandable. Not sure why she wouldn't have thought you were equally distraught, though. Fact, I mentioned that very thing, didn't I Alice?"

My mother nodded emphatically.

"That's very interesting," I replied slowly, immediately concerned. "It seems odd that the wife of one of Hank's coworkers would have turned up here looking for information."

"Well, you know, that's exactly what I thought at first," continued my dad, brushing muffin crumbs off his mouth. "Didn't I say that after that young lady left, Alice? But then, she said she was just trying to get some general information without bothering you. How long you'd dated, where you'd gone on your honeymoon. A few pictures if we had them to spare. You know, things like that. I'm sure it was all on the up and up, Deensie. I could kinda see why they might have wanted to keep it on the QT. It's a mighty nice gesture for you I think."

"Uhhh," I murmured. The Hitchcock Hackles were suddenly shrieking … Janet Leigh in that terrifying shower scene. "Um sure. Right."

"Yes, you were a little surprised at first as I recall, Daddy," agreed my mom, nodding. "We both were. I almost said something, but thought it just not too polite, you know. Nice looking young woman, although perhaps dressed just a tad shabby for going out calling, didn't you think, Daddy?"

My dad just shrugged, but then added, "didn't notice that. But she was real interested in my *Fleurama*. I was concerned that maybe, well, you know, maybe she was gonna try to steal my ideas or something. That maybe that was her, uh, undisclosed intention so to speak. Didn't I say that, Alice?"

"You sure did, Daddy, you sure did," my mom answered, nodding her head even more vigorously. Why my mom called my father Daddy and he called her Alice had always been a bit of a mystery to me, I confess.

"And what was this woman's name?"

"I think she said it was Helen something, right Daddy? Or maybe Ellen?"

"I think it was Helen, Alice. But I don't remember her last name. Something kind of long and foreign sounding. She had an accent of some kind. Maybe your age, Denise, or a little older. She did that flip thing with her fingers in her hair that you used to try so hard to do with yours, sweetie, remember?"

I nodded, frowning.

"Such pale skin for such black hair, though, didn't you think, Alice?"

"No, I don't remember pale skin, Daddy. Her glasses had thick black frames, so that might be why you thought she had pale skin. You don't usually see thick frames like that on a young woman. But then she had on this bright red lipstick too and it's kind of unusual to see lipstick that red these days also. Well, sometimes on models or mannequins I suppose. You even see black or purple lipstick on some of those store mannequins at Block's these days which I do not understand whatsoever. So ugly! I mean, why would any woman want to make herself look ugly like that?"

"So, did this Helen person express interest in other things in the house?" I interrupted, beginning to seethe just beneath the surface. Being the kind, loving, horribly gullible people that they were, of course, they had invited this woman in, let her look around at everything asking questions. She didn't look like the kind of person who would be stealing any of his art ideas my dad had finally determined, but no greater concerns had come to mind. Of course, why would they?

"Mainly Daddy's art works like I mentioned before," replied my mother, wiping her hands on a tea towel. "That kind of surprised both of us. It's so rare that you young people take much notice of his unique contributions, but she really did know a lot about Daddy's type of art."

I'll bet she did, I bristled, starting to put two and two together. Of course, she did. She'd heard him prattle non-stop about his stuff every time that she'd been at our house for dinner all those years back.

As they conferred with one another regarding other things they'd shown this woman throughout their home on this impromptu house tour, cold fingers began stretching down my back. There was no question in my mind that it had been Janet Lynn – make that, Cathy Martin. She'd lured me up to Swayzee, then had those two goons verify my arrival so she could pay a leisurely visit to my folks' place. What else had she done while she was in here? Where else had she visited – my apartment? That snowstorm was an incredibly unpredictable piece of luck to grant her even more time. Neither of my parents had seen the smallest vestige of the girl that I'd hung out with practically every single waking moment some sixteen years ago. I could still hear Cathy politely asking my mom to show her how to use a fork to press together her lard, butter, and flour pie crusts. But that Cathy Martin was long gone. I was convinced that a bloodthirsty zombie now thrived in her place – a zombie with a detailed agenda to get what she wanted and anyone in her way might well be pulverized to pulp. Any other carcasses she had to take down by way of collateral damage was of no concern.

Suddenly I was drawn back into my parents' conversation.

"Well, no Alice, I didn't refill your glass sugar bowl," my dad was saying. "You never put new sugar in there until you've washed out all that older crusty stuff and you know

I always forget to do that."

"Maybe I did it yesterday and just forgot," exhaled my mom. "My memory sometimes … it just comes and goes. Mostly goes. Especially these little things that you do all the time, you know, Deensie?"

I stared at her for a moment.

"Mom, give me that bowl!" I ordered, standing abruptly.

"Well, I must have washed it and then filled it obviously …" she began, a startled look on her face.

"No, give it to me! Seriously!" I shouted, lunging at her.

"Honey, you don't need to take that tone to your voice," she added sharply, further shocked when I grabbed the bowl out of her hands.

The sugar had an odd, slightly yellowish-orange cast.

"There might be something wrong with this sugar."

"Something wrong? How silly! I don't see how anything could be wrong. Why, I used it just today, didn't I Daddy? Making those muffins. Or did I just measure it out of the bag? Anyway, that nice young woman, Helen, joined us for coffee. I think she used some as well. Yes, I'm sure she did because that's when I realized it was low and needed washing and refilling. I hope there wasn't anything wrong with it yesterday. I would feel terrible if she got sick or anything!" she exclaimed.

I was more than certain that "Helen" hadn't inadvertently ingested any of what might be her own poisonous sugar yesterday.

"It's ok, Mom," I apologized, gently touching her hand. "I'm just really nervous about everything right now. I'm … I'm so sorry I grabbed it from you and scared you. I'm going to take it with me though. Just to have it tested."

"Tested for what?" exclaimed my mother, her eyes huge. "I've never known a bowl of sugar to go bad in all my days, Denise!" When my mother called me by my given name, you knew she was really upset.

"I don't know exactly, Mom," I replied, as I started looking through her cabinets for small plastic bags and rubber bands. "But just in case, I'm going to take it with me, that's all. There's some really crazy stuff going on in my life right now. Things surrounding Hank's death. I can't explain everything yet. I doubt if anyone can. Are you sure nothing about this woman seemed, well, sort of familiar?"

"Familiar? No, not especially," my dad shrugged.

"She had on this cotton print shirtwaist. Like you'd see at Lerner's or the Fashion Mart. Long-sleeved, of course, in this wretched weather. Not soiled but quite faded. Could have used a good pressing, too, I noticed. Her sweater had a few teensy moth holes and quite a lot of pilling," she added. "You know how wool does."

"Blond hair?" I asked.

"No, Denise, almost black like we said earlier," she corrected me firmly. That constituted two Denises in a row; she was obviously quite peeved. "She wore her bangs way too long so they kind of, well, kind of curled over the glasses' rims. I've seen that kind of hairstyle in *Vogue* and *Cosmopolitan*, but I don't know how girls can stand it."

Probably a wig I thought to myself. Smart move, Janet Lynn. And the glasses, not to mention the pilling wool sweater with moth holes. Nice touches all the way around you deplorable skank, I said under my breath. I had carefully wrapped the entire sugar bowl and its contents in multiple plastic bags held together by three thick rubber bands.

"So, what's this crazy stuff that's going on in your life right now? Is there something your mom and I should know about?" interjected my dad. "I think that the strange circumstances around Hank's death and everything are making you, well, more than just a little suspicious of everybody these days, sweetie."

"Where else was she yesterday? You said she was

interested in *Fleurina,*" I asked, sidestepping his concerns.

"Um, that's *Fleurama*," interjected my dad curtly, as though I'd just misidentified the *Mona Lisa.*

"Oh, right, sorry," I apologized, probably sounding anything but sincere. "*Fleurama.* So, she was obviously in the living room and the kitchen. How about the hallway or the bedrooms? Specifically, my bedroom. What about the bathroom? Did she ask to use the bathroom?"

"Oh, well, we haven't really begun to clear a path yet back there," confessed my mother, refusing to meet my eyes, "so it did take her awhile to climb over supplies to use the … well, you know."

"Great," I snorted loudly. "Ok, I'm heading back to my apartment. If she comes back, or anybody else you don't recognize shows up, please don't let them in, ok? Could you promise me that? Please?"

My mother sat back abruptly, a startled expression on her face. My dad looked at her and then at me.

"Just what's all this about, Deensie?" he demanded, now quite annoyed. "Are you in some kind of trouble? Here you are scarin' your poor mother half to death. And I must admit, somethin' smells mighty fishy here -- an' it ain't last week's catfish heads strung out over my old grandma's clothesline down in Kentucky!"

My mother was now visibly shaking, staring out the window. I made some kind of lame allusion to Rhett Butler's excusing himself rather than ruining the brandy and cigars gathering that surrounded the gentlemen's war talk and left. I was, however, so angry with myself I was ready to chew nails and spit rust, or however that dumb Southern expression went, although I don't think that one was in "*Gone with the Wind*". My journey to Swayzee was only a blind to get me out of the way for several predictable hours – the snowstorm obviously provided an added bonus. Originally, I would have returned as soon as Cathy Martin had failed to show (not to mention the failure of the train depot to show). That interval gave Cathy Martin, now coiffed in a badly styled brunette wig and black-rimmed glasses, more than adequate time to scope out my parents' home. Where else had the bitch been snooping, I wondered? Those two men were simply reporting my arrival and whereabouts up in Swayzee – it was only my off-the-radar paranoia that had even alerted me to their existence in the first place.

I arrived at my own place a little under an hour later. I placed the questionable sugar bowl, still tight within its plastic wrapping, under a loose floorboard in the hall closet. I'd figure out how to have it tested later. Maybe Thor would have some suggestions.

Cathy had been in our home in Nashville constantly many years back when we were friends. She knew all my secret cubby holes, both in my room and in the crawl spaces where I'd originally kept our scrapbooks, tapes, and albums. I was certain she would find a way to paw through my belongings surreptitiously – whether invited or not. I shuddered. Pick the front door lock to canvas the place at a later date when my folks were out? Piece of cake.

My thoughts continued to race. We'd opted to rent a large storage unit when we obtained two rooms of Hank's parents' furniture, including several beautiful carpets that had belonged to Hank's late mother, when his stepmom had redecorated a couple of years back. I wasn't particularly into that heavy mahogany stuff that had been so popular back in the 1950s, but rather surprisingly, Hank claimed nostalgia for the furnishings, hence our decision to save all of it for that elusive date when we would be buying our own home. A lot of other stuff had migrated over to that storage locker since that time because it was a perfect repository for one's basic junk overflow – always a chronic problem in a tiny one-bedroom apartment.

I rummaged in my refrigerator and tore off several hunks of Swiss cheese, then grabbed a handful of Ritz crackers that immediately crumbled all over the counter. The phone rang, or more specifically, clanged, as I was trying to clean off the crumbs. I vowed to call the phone company tomorrow to obtain a new phone. The phone guts spilling out was a disgusting sight.

"Hey, Denise? It's Marcy."

"Hiya! I was hoping to give you a call in a bit. I assume we're still on for pizza tomorrow night?"

"Uh, well, that's … what I was calling about actually," she continued. Her voice seemed strained. "We're gonna have to reschedule next week or maybe the following week since that's Thanksgiving weekend. Or something. Some … other stuff has kind of … well … kind of come up," she added hastily.

"Ok," I replied. She really didn't sound like herself at all. "Is everything ok, Marcy?"

"Absolutely!" she stated, far too quickly. "Yep, no problem! Hey, one of us will give you a call sometime, ok?" Before I could respond she added, "shoot, hey, I gotta go, kiddo! Incoming on line five and Thor's finishing up one story and has another on hold. Phone's been lit up like a Christmas tree all afternoon. Talk with you soon!"

There'd been no indication that anyone had been in my place although the hem in our bedroom drapes was tucked under slightly, leaving a small gap in the middle. Also, the tub curtain was pushed back further than usual. Had I left it like that? Or had Janet Lynn been surreptitiously clawing her away about during my Swayzee sojourn? Bedroom closets and drawers were tightly closed. Books and magazines appeared undisturbed, stacked on shelves, kitchen drawers and both lower and upper cabinets were exactly as I remembered them. But had I really been paying close attention to my surroundings in this apartment over these last few days? Of course not.

Trembling, I dialed Tom's phone number, putting in my own number at his pager prompt. Glass of water in hand, I sat down at my table and waited. No returned call. Fifteen minutes went by. I called again, refilling my water. Another fifteen minutes. Then thirty. I ate more of the crumbly Ritz crackers and glanced through a magazine.

Thor would probably be home from the newsroom by now. After at least ten rings he picked up.

"This better be really important whoever this is," he barked, not sounding at all like himself.

"Thor, it's me … Denise."

"Hiya! What's new pussycat? Bout time you checked in!"

I smiled at hearing one of his favorite goofy greetings and filled him in briefly regarding my disastrous trip to Swayzee, the two men surrounding my car, Cathy Martin's visit to my parents, the orange-tinted sugar and my attempt to discern if anyone had been in my place. He listened quietly, occasionally inserting a comment such as "seriously" or "no way" punctuated periodically by his favorite expletive: "*scheisse.*" I left out my calls and night spent with Tom Miller. Going into what I'd learned about Tom's background really wasn't important at present. Thor had cast Tom as a villain in this saga and I maintained a persistent niggling fear that he may well be correct. I thought back on my husband's and my breathless lovemaking down in New Orleans. That was our last time together I now realized. But by the next evening he was fully enjoying himself yet again in Dorothea Dixon's bed, having completely forgotten about me. Was I really that affection starved that I couldn't objectively analyze my own behavior? Apparently.

Thor exhaled. "There's a lot of stuff just came over the police scanner a couple of hours ago about Hank ... and you. They're back on the injected poisoned vitamin theory with you occupying a potentially leading role in the drama. You can't be charged yet because they don't have enough evidence of course. As you know, the police can only hold you for twenty-four hours unless they actually book you."

"Yeah," I sighed, rubbing my forehead. "I know."

"The actual poison used is still an issue though. The routine labs have come up with squat so they're still in the dark."

"You're talking something like arsenic poisoning, right? Long term doses or something?"

"We can certainly assume they've already tested for anything as obvious as arsenic."

Off-key strains of "*You Light Up My Life*" began filtering dissonantly through my ceiling.

"If we knew that, my dear Watson, we'd be a great deal nearer to the solution of the crime."

Basil Rathbone as Sherlock Holmes in

"The Adventures of Sherlock Holmes"
(1939)

Chapter 21

Finally, just before 10 p.m., the phone rang. I raced to pick it up, surprised at my eagerness to hear Tom's voice. But it was my mother.

"Deensie! Deensie! Daddy's not home yet!" she shrieked. Her voice was so loud I had to pull the phone away from my ear. "Where could he be? Oh Deensie, I don't know what to do! Where is he? I don't know what to do! Daddy never stays out late! Never! Oh Deensie! Daddy's not home yet! What am I going to do?"

"Mom! Mom! Calm down! I can't understand anything you're saying!"

"This man called to talk to Daddy," she finally choked out.

"What man?" I replied, trying to keep my voice even. "When was this, Mom? What time?"

"He called after you left this afternoon. After supper, I think. Yes, after supper. It was just getting dark. Oh, God, I don't remember the time though!" she sobbed.

"Mom, try to calm down. Please! You're screaming! Did this man say what he wanted?"

"He said … oh God, what did Daddy say? I should've been listening better, Deensie! Let me think … oh my poor head. Ok, ok. I think Daddy said … that the man had heard all about *Fleurama* from the … I can't remember her name … you know, that … that, sugar lady."

I fought to keep my breath steady as my fingers tightened around the phone. "Go on."

"He said they wanted him to build something like that in the lobby of this … this building over in Columbus, maybe. Yes. Columbus! He said that Daddy would have to see the space and take measurements because their boss needed to know if it would fit okay. That they wanted to have it installed right away."

"Did Dad mention a company name or anything?"

"No. Well, maybe. I … I don't know," she sobbed. "If they didn't find out today, they were going to sign a contract with someone else. Daddy sure didn't want to lose a big sale like that!" she gulped. "But … but … Daddy's not home yet, Deensie! He *never* stays out any later than nine o'clock, even on his bowling nights! You know that! Never! He knows how upset I get! He's been gone for hours! Where is he?"

"Mom, listen," I replied, my voice shaky despite my attempts to control it. "Did he drive by himself to Columbus? Is there any chance he picked that man up and they drove over there together? Did he say anything like that?"

"Oh, Deensie, I don't know! Maybe, but I just don't remember."

"Is his car gone?"

"Yes … yes, I think so," she stammered. "He was working to get all the snow off."

I closed my eyes. Damn.

"I know if I call the police, they'll just laugh at me, Deensie! They always just laugh at me. They never believe me when I call about things. But Deensie, the police don't know Daddy! They don't know that's just not how Daddy does things! Daddy never stays out this late!"

If my dad was even fifteen minutes late returning from a simple run to the grocery store to pick up a loaf of bread my mother had been known to call the police. How could I have been so stupid to have assumed that Cathy Martin or her henchmen wouldn't have made another impromptu call on my parents after I'd left earlier today? Ok Cathy, I said to myself. Score one point for you.

"Ok, Mom, listen," I replied, trembling, trying to keep my voice as steady as possible. "I'm on my way over. Maybe Dad'll be home in a few minutes. Maybe … maybe he had a flat tire or got stuck in a ditch and the road crew is helping him dig out. Maybe he's already headed back and will walk in the door in just a few minutes. But either way, I'll be there in about twenty-five minutes or so, ok?"

"Yes," she whimpered. "Please hurry, Deensie. Something's wrong! I just know something's wrong. Daddy never stays out this late. Never … nev …Wait, it's that sugar bowl woman, isn't it?"

"Wh…what?" I replied. "What about her?"

"This has something to do with that sugar bowl woman, doesn't it? You shouldn't have taken my sugar bowl with that woman's special orange sugar! Maybe she's keeping Daddy tied up somewhere because she wants that orange sugar back! She must know that you took it! You know, just like in that movie."

"What movie, Mom?" I frowned, thoroughly confused with the subject shift.

"You know the one I mean!"

"No, I don't," I apologized. "I honestly don't know. Which movie, Mom?

"With Audrey Hepburn. She's that blind lady and she has this doll with all these drugs stuffed in its tummy. Heroin bags I think. Oh, and that ugly, scary Alan Arkin. So terrifying. Don't you remember, Deensie?"

"*Wait Until Dark*," I replied under my breath. I'd been totally shocked that my dad had taken her to see something so violent. He'd probably assumed since Audrey Hepburn was in the film that the movie would be sweet and more-or-less romantically sedate like "*Charade*" or "*Breakfast at Tiffany's*". The movie had come out over ten years ago when she was far less frightened by the outside world, but obviously it had stuck with her.

"I don't think the man was looking for that sugar bowl," I replied evenly.

"Well, just how do you know? What else could it be?" she demanded, her voice raising in pitch. "You said that woman put something in the sugar bowl and you acted like it was … well … it was poisonous or something bad like that. Both Daddy and I thought so. But it was drugs of some kind, right? And that man wanted Daddy to bring him that orange sugar so he could get those drugs back. Where did you take it? You didn't just dump it out, did you? It's not yours; it belongs to them! And they certainly can have it!" she exclaimed. "I mean, what would I want with anybody's drugs, for heaven's sake?"

I paused for a moment, not certain if she would be able to comprehend any of my explanation.

"Do you remember Cathy Martin? Chomp Martin's daughter?"

"What would that dreadful man's daughter have to do with the sugar bowl woman? Daddy never had anything to do with Chomp Martin. Besides, Chomp Martin's dead! We just told you that."

"Well, do you remember Cathy and my putting together those photo albums and scrapbooks -- right there on your kitchen table?"

"No. Well … maybe. I don't really know! What difference does that make? Daddy never stays out this late!" she howled, her voice now in ragged breaths.

I persevered as calmly as possible.

"I think those old photo albums and scrapbooks may have some information that the, uh … that sugar bowl woman … doesn't want to have made public."

"What absolute rubbish!" she spat out with surprising vehemence. "I can't imagine why anyone would want your dumb, old stuff, Deensie! I certainly didn't want any of it, I can guarantee that! I mean, young girls taking photos of ugly scabs and scars or broken bones! And those dreadful stories you girls used to write! Awful. Just awful! I shudder just thinking back on it! You took all that nasty stuff away years and years ago! Why on earth would anyone else be interested in it?"

This from someone who raided department store dumpsters for rainbow-colored plastic packing pellets, I thought with a slight smile. Before I could reply, however, I became aware of large tires crunching through the snow outside, just as low beamed lights, probably from a mid-sized truck, flashed through my curtains. My mother began whimpering again about my dad's whereabouts.

"Mom," I stated firmly, "I'm leaving now, ok? Don't let anyone else in … except Daddy, of course. I should be there in less than a half hour … unless the roads are really slick again. But I promise I'll get there, ok? Love you!"

A siege of pounding thundered on my door just as I hung up. I looked through the eyehole but whoever was outside had covered it. Police? Doubtful. Janet Lynn's goons from Swayzee? That was my first guess.

"What do you want?" I growled, my fingers tracing rapidly along the security chain to verify that it was taut.

"What's this? No hello, how ya doin'? Wanna beer?" a man's voice retorted. "Seems we been spendin' a lotta do-si-do-in' time 'round each other these last coupla days. Din' yer ol' lady teach you no kinda manners?"

"What do you want?" I repeated coldly.

"Hey, weren't you jes talkin' to your mom 'bout them albums? Might short memory on your part, doncha think, Deensie?"

I closed my eyes. Damn. My phone was bugged. Why

hadn't I thought of that? I cringed hearing my mom's pet name for me used so maliciously by this monster. Idyllic Security, where my late husband had been employed, was owned by Janet Lynn's husband and his family for Pete's sake! Far from living up to its impassioned idyllic description, it was certainly flexing its exasperating espionage muscle. Naturally, Janet Lynn would have complete access to every state-of-the-art security device developed within that company and would have made it her business to know how to install it. Bug a phone? Child's play for the Janet Lynn Webster impostor Cathy Martin – a woman with a sharp, brutally deranged, scientific mind.

"Be easier if you'd lemme in, Deensie. I mean, ya want all your neighbors to hear us bellowin' back 'n forth?"

Leaving the security chain firmly in place I opened the door two inches. Illuminated in the yellow light spilling over from the parking lot was a man wearing a faded red and black buffalo plaid coat. The same coat I'd seen on the men up in Swayzee. Suddenly he savagely slashed at the chain with a huge wrench, simultaneously kicking the door at the bottom. The door flew open hitting me on the side of my head as I jumped back. He walked in slamming shut the badly dented door.

"Now, that's right more neighborly," he grinned, settling himself against the wall. He was older than I'd thought at first -- weathered, muscular, with a broken eye tooth and long scar slicing a deep crevice from his ear down his cheek.

"So, here's the uh … inventory, of what's missin'. Two photo albums, two scrapbooks, three uh them reel-to-reel tapes an' two uh them old style school composition books that rightfully belongs to … well, that sugar bowl woman as your mother calls her."

"Leave my mother out of this," I bristled. "And where's my father?"

"Now, now, Deensie, let's not jump ahead of ourselves."

"Three little tapes, two photo albums … and a partridge in a pear tree," sputtered an off-key singsong voice. The man had a small hidden microphone clipped somewhere on his coat apparently.

"Heh, heh," he chuckled. "Oh, I should introduce myself: T-Bone at your service. Guy on the microphone's Carl."

If only I'd kept my big mouth shut when talking with Janet Lynn at her stupid engagement party!

"And what if I can't find this stuff?" I stammered.

"She's nuts, y'know? Yer ol' lady's absolutely bonkers," Carl's tinny voice snorted over the microphone.

"Is he in my mother's house?" I panicked.

T-Bone shrugged.

"Dammit! Answer me!"

"Ah, ah, ah, now where's that little magic word, Deensie?" he scolded, waggling his index finger. "And tut-tut using such a naughty word like dammit! What would yer mama say?"

"So, what happens now?" I pleaded, my lips thickly forming around each word. "You already know none of that stuff you want is at my parents' house. You've got their place bugged! You just heard my mother say that a few minutes ago. You're scaring her to death! And what've you done with my dad?"

"Like I said," shrugged T-Bone, "we need them albums an' tapes an' so forth. Pretty straight ahead in my book, y'know?"

"That stuff might be in this storage unit that my husband rented a few years ago. That's really … all I can assume," I replied frantically. "But I don't even know the name of the storage building much less what town it's in! It could be anywhere between South Bend and Evansville for all I know! That's assuming it isn't parked over in Chicago or Cincinnati or God knows where! I've never been there. Can't you understand?"

Was this guy Carl with my mom right now or were they bluffing? I was terrified.

"And what's more, there's a good chance that none of it even exists anymore! How can I hand over something that may not even exist?"

"Well, sadly for you, Deensie, that really just ain't gonna cut it as a good excuse, y'know what I mean? Especially since that uh, sugar lady, she knows from another *very* reliable source that it's definitely somewhere in your possession. An' that very reliable source knows because that someone put it there," snorted T-Bone. "Course, way things came down, that very reliable source maybe ain't willin' or ain't able to help with the locatin', y'know what I mean? So, you an' me? We gonna find that storage place. And soon. An' look through it real good. We got twenty-four hours to, well, get to know one another … cozy up nice 'n tight together, y'know?" he grinned.

I closed my eyes and shuddered.

"And then? Well, I can't really answer for what happens then … probably won't be as cozy as yer evenin' with the ol' Amish cowboy," he laughed. "By the way, you must have one mighty sweet ass, Deensie!"

Was Idyllic spying on us last night? I felt sick thinking of this Neanderthal goon T-Bone and his boorish friend Carl watching Tom's and my lovemaking which had seemed so beautiful only a few hours ago. Would Tom have known we were being watched? No! There was no way any man would allow that – would he? Although maybe Janet Lynn had some kind of dirt on him. Maybe he'd been forced into lying to me. Stupid. Stupid. Stupid move, Denise! This whole situation was appalling. But nonetheless, almost everything Tom had said now struck me as complete fabrication. The bastard probably wasn't even Amish! Had he left me this morning and hightailed it down here to probe about my apartment since he knew I was stopping at my parents' house first? He'd urged me to go there, in fact! His clever appearance with the pizza that night a few weeks ago could easily have just been a scouting expedition. I forced myself to stay calm on the surface, seething beneath as I attempted to purge Tom Miller from my thoughts, concentrating instead on my parents' safe return. Their faces swam in front of my eyes.

"Canceled checks ... or better yet, invoices," I suddenly stammered. "There must be invoices that Hank paid. Those should have an address."

"Well yeah, now you're thinkin' with the ol' bean! Betcha you could find out real quick lookin' over them canceled checks an' invoices right here and now. My escort services are provided free of charge, eh? An' don't think you'll be able to alert the cops or your stupid newspaper junkies. That might just be, well, real dangerous, y'know … for your folks' safety an' all that," he winked. "You remember that nice little Idyllic slogan, right?"

We're with you every minute of every day. The Idyllic corporate logo portrayed a young couple, the woman's ample cleavage scarcely constrained within her string bikini top, flutes of champagne bubbling over as she toasted her ruggedly chiseled date while the duo romped playfully along a deserted beach at sunset. Every time I saw one of those full-page four-color ads in our newspaper I wanted to vomit. I'd always assumed the ad had been a marketing suggestion by the Double D … after all, sex sells everything, right?

"Electricity. The high priest of false security."

Basil Rathbone as Sherlock Holmes in

"The Pearl of Death" (1944)

Chapter 22

A slightly plausible timeline of events came to me as I began searching through a folder of paid bills that Hank had thrown into the bottom desk drawer. Supposing that Hank had mentioned to David Fowler about moving my crappy childhood junk when he'd acquired his late mother's belongings and packed everything away in that storage unit. I remembered that Hank had really hurt his back on the Saturday he'd transferred all that stuff and had then headed out on a late Sunday afternoon flight, high on pain medication, to New York City for a couple days of meetings at Idyllic headquarters. Let's say Hank was socializing either Sunday or Monday evening with David and the-lovely-soon-to-be-Mrs. Fowler, the impostor known as Janet Lynn Webster. Hank, ever the charmer, complains in an innocent, but nonetheless, cozy, little *tête à tête* with Janet Lynn over cocktails -- this is hypothetical after all -- about having to move all my juvenile crap and some other outsized artifacts he'd grudgingly agreed to store of my dad's burgeoning, questionably reusable creations. Hank happens to mention my name and Janet Lynn is suddenly on the alert … bam. Up until then, she's had no idea that he was married to someone named Denise Prescott who had grown up in Nashville, Indiana. Denise Prescott who would have untold relics of incriminating proof to completely undermine her entire identity and unquestionably implicate her in several murders.

As my mind theorized further, here was a simple way to eliminate the man himself, blame his murder on me and then, the *pièce de résistance,* destroy any and all evidence implicating Janet Lynn's true grizzly history. Truly a *fait accompli.* There were probably massive holes in this ill-conceived theory, but I liked it. Oh yes, I *really* liked it.

A soft knock sounded on my apartment door. T-Bone pushed me towards the door, indicating with a chin cock to open it. From his inside pocket he quickly pulled out a small pistol. Outside my door stood the postman.

"Mrs. …uh, Taylor, right?" the postman said to me as I nodded appreciatively. "Here, let me just hand this to you rather than trying to stuff it all into your box, ma'am. Oh, and I'm sorry to mention, there's one envelope here that's postage due. No return address so can't be returned to sender, I'm afraid. Strange thing, too since it's plastered with all kinds of old canceled stamps. I guess the sender didn't think the post office would notice they were canceled. Anyway, I need to trouble you for the fifteen cents. Or if you'd prefer, I can just pitch it."

"Wait just a second," I replied, sounding far calmer than I felt. I walked back over to the desk. T-Bone was still poised behind the door, gun drawn. "It's probably a card from my mom's aunt. She's pretty … well, old and unpredictable."

One of my dad's bronze stamp holders sat on our desk, typically filled with odd change rather than stamps. But there were no coins, just an empty Wrigley's Spearmint gum wrapper waded up inside. Cute. I grabbed my purse, shook out fifteen cents nestled somewhere on the bottom along with other debris, and paid the postman. He gave me a small stack of what appeared to be sympathy and holiday cards, bills, and several Christmas gift brochures. Christmas, I thought to myself. Yeah. That should be delightful this year I sighed. I thanked the postman and then, just as I closed the door, strains of "*You Light Up My Life*" echoed throughout the hallway.

"What in hell's that?" T-Bone grimaced, as he scoured the ceiling for the source of the dissonance.

"Our local entertainment," I sighed, flipping mindlessly through the mail. No paycheck for Hank from Idyllic. Great.

"Man, if that's entertainment, I'm in the wrong business," he snorted as he paced around my living room making faces at the ceiling.

Yes, I suppose the thug business requires a lot more talent, I thought to myself. I pulled out the envelope sporting the pasted-on canceled stamps. Definitely not my great aunt's handwriting.

"I have to use the bathroom," I said quickly, stuffing the little envelope into my waistband.

"Guess you know where it is," he guffawed. "At least this time you can't crawl out the damn window since there ain't no window."

Had he cased my place from the outside? Or had he and Carl been inside?

I locked the door – one of those ridiculously flimsy push button affairs that wouldn't have thwarted a three-year-old from breaking in – and wildly guessed where Idyllic's security cameras might possibly be placed. Trusting to some completely arbitrary instinct from either a *Columbo* or *Rockford Files* episode, I turned on the water in the sink, then slid open the cabinet door underneath to extract a couple of towels. Pretending to be straightening up the remaining towels, my head inside the dark cabinet, I tore open the envelope revealing a scarcely legible, unsigned, cryptic note written by an unfamiliar hand:

Denise -

Don't forget the stamps!

Remember our first Kiss?

~ *V for Victory!*

No signature. No postmark. Bogus stamp treatment. Trick or treat. Great, that helped a lot. I hid the rumpled note inside the folds of one of the towels in the cabinet, flushed the toilet and turned off the running water.

Was there a chance that Hank had hidden those albums and tapes and then threatened to expose Janet Lynn's past that he'd somehow stumbled upon? Were there schemes in which he'd originally played some part, but now, possibly duped, he'd caught on to the fact – probably while he was down in New Orleans -- that he knew he was soon to be eliminated? But what in heck was the scheme? And who would have told him? I couldn't come up with anything other than some outrageous Ian Fleming-type plot starring Sean Connery.

I walked out of the bathroom to the living room. Hank had always been incredibly organized about paying bills on time. I was certain I'd find those on which he'd clearly stamped "paid" for this storage company. T-Bone was now stretched out along my sofa and had settled in with the whiskey bottle, more than half filled, for himself.

"How much longer, ya think?" he asked, taking a long pull on the bottle.

I made no comment.

"Be my guest," he shrugged, taking a gulp after a mock toast and then adding with a wink, "just remember that old Big Ben's a'tickin', an' a'tockin' right? Oh, an' don' forget, we're with you every minute of the day, Deensie." Meaning of course the Idyllic cameras were whirring away, watching my every move, their visual destination being monitored by Janet Lynn and company stationed wherever.

I found the invoice within a few minutes. The place was called Blue Mountain Storage and had four different locations: main office in Gary, one at Speedway Industrial Park in Indianapolis, another outside the Brown County State Park in Nashville, and the fourth a discount warehouse out in Angola. All bets were on the Nashville facility obviously. Then my heart sank as I saw the Protected by Idyllic Security Inc. trademark emblem and the purple and orange banner (sans the scantily clad champagne revelers) running proudly at the bottom of the invoice. Damn, I thought. Would Hank have stashed that stuff in there in the first place? He would certainly have known that it was protected by his own company. At the time though, I reasoned, he wouldn't have had any concerns. He'd probably sold Blue Mountain that protection package in the first place.

On the other hand, he would have known exactly how to time the camera sweeps and hide a small package containing the incriminating items. What was the Sherlock Holmes expression from "*The Pearl of Death*" that Thor always alluded to whenever the lights eerily flickered, or we completely lost power during thunderstorms at the newsroom? Ah yes: "Electricity. The high priest of false security." In Thor's case, it meant save your work every two to three sentences or it might easily evaporate into the eternal ether.

Something made me glance at the invoice again, however. The account was for a Hank Prescott. It was unlikely that this was any kind of error. If for any reason someone inadvertently called my husband by my last name, Hank immediately corrected them. No, this was deliberate. Maybe someone had warned him about Janet Lynn. Did Dorothea Dixon factor into this scheme? If so, why? Was there any chance that the DD knew anything about Janet Lynn's past and was blackmailing her along with Hank? Too farfetched? Not really, I thought. Stay on task, Prescott, I scolded myself.

"I've found an invoice," I finally stated, clearing my throat slightly, turning to face the reclining T-Bone as he swallowed the last few mouthfuls of my cheap whiskey.

"Well, now, ain't that real nice," he grinned. "Good

work, Deensie! And where might this place be exactly?"

"There are four locations listed on the invoice, but I'm assuming near the state park over in Nashville."

"You gotta key?"

I shook my head. It had probably been on Hank's keyring.

"Since we ain't got no key or nothin', take that invoice along so's we can get in."

"Yeah, I kind of figured that," I replied sarcastically. "Where's your uh, buddy Carl?" I then asked, still hopeful that he'd been bluffing about his having been in my mom's house. Anyone with half the brain of a turnip listening in on our phone conversation could easily deduce my mother had more than a few loose screws.

"Eh, seems he found some hot little bimbo rubbin' up against him at the Esso station," chuckled T-Bone. "Went to refuel the truck, after he dropped me here. Ain't nothin' in our contracts says that we can't, well, you know, take a little time off to indulge in those situations that kind of uh, pop up if yer gettin' my drift, right?"

I rolled my eyes as he wiggled suggestively on my couch. I should introduce him to G-L-O-R-I-A I thought in disgust. Definitely a match made in heaven.

We drove in my car to the location, just east of the state park, a circa late-1940s pitted brick and concrete jungle of a warehouse. It was getting dark. Icy chunks of snow were back lit by a few last rays of weak sunlight. T-Bone had dozed off a couple times but immediately jerked awake as I killed the engine at the main entrance of the building. My slender hope of gaining access to Hank's storage unit while the man slumbered instantly evaporated. After showing the front desk clerk my driver's license and Indianapolis Star press identification card, I told him that I'd forgotten my key and would need to have the unit opened. I said that T-Bone was there to help me carry out a couple of large chairs. The clerk frowned and asked for an additional piece of ID, like a credit card. Something that would have Hank's name on it, he stated. My only credit card *did* of course have Hank's name on it, since married women almost never possessed credit cards in their own names. However, Hank's last name was Taylor, of course, not Prescott, so that was not an option. After several minutes of haggling, the clerk reluctantly agreed to our admittance and placed a call to another employee who would open the unit.

"You know we have that Idyllic thing they advertise on tv all the time," the clerk commented, gesturing to the corner over his left shoulder, "but they don't stand by their protection if we allow just anybody willy nilly access, y'know. Especially right now. They got some kinda transmission problem over in that wing, so they just sent over one of their guys to work on the system. He's in there now. Said he'd be finished in another fifteen, twenty minutes at the most, so shouldn't be any problem."

Idyllic was everywhere of course, just like they advertised. Damn. T-Bone suddenly gave out a loud belch. If there'd been any question regarding my escort's and my location, T-Bone had certainly just clarified that enigma. The clerk handed me a small map.

"Ok, so you're going to make a hard left just before you get to the ramp heading down to the loading dock and follow that hallway until you get to the purple and orange Idyllic sign -- then turn right. Keep goin' for a fair stretch 'til you see another purple and orange sign and turn left again. Now you're right in front of Building G. Sounds like a longer walk than it is. Ain't too bad. That unit's G814 so continue to you get to the 800s once you're in the building -- first hallway's the 100s, don't worry -- and I think 800-825 should be over towards your right, but you should be able to figure it out at that point. It's one of the larger rentals back there, so not hard to find."

"Thanks," I nodded.

The warehouse complex appeared to have been expanded many times and boasted some of the highest ceilings I'd ever seen. Each individual unit was an immense, oblong silo. There was an odd antiseptic smell in the hallway, becoming even more pungent as we got closer to G814. It was also freezing in this part of the warehouse. The metal door to G814 had been left wide open, but the employee must have left since he was nowhere to be seen.

"Oh man, what in hell? T-Bone groaned, making a quick visual reconnaissance of the unit's interior as we stepped in. "Look at all this shit! Mountains on top of mountains of crap! I thought your husband just had a few pieces of furniture stored here. This is just floor to ceiling garbage! I can't believe this!"

I had to agree with him. It looked more like something my dad would have rented and crammed with his retro dumpster prizes as he classified them. I could see my late mother-in-law's living room furniture over to one side peeking through a monument of carpet and drapery samples, on which was then stacked variously sized Styrofoam packing squares and old aluminum tv dinner trays. Outside of my in-law's furniture, everything else smacked of my dad's calling cards. Nothing of either my late husband's or mine was visible. No question there. The rest of the unit was jammed floor-to-ceiling with my dad's massive sculptures.

"Maybe Hank was paying for my dad to well, just … store his stuff here for a while … or something…" I offered, glancing over at T-Bone. "Or maybe since the invoice was for Prescott it's actually all my dad's stuff. Maybe my husband was trying to help out with all the storage problems at my folks."

Hank had usually gotten along with my parents, although, he agreed with me that they were more like mewling newborn puppies in a discarded shoebox than adults. His willingness to pay to store my dad's oversized artwork seemed highly unlikely although I kept that opinion to myself.

"What the hell did your dad build any of that junk for in the first place?" T-Bone scowled, gesturing to a monstrous hot pink geranium sprouting at least fifty blooms, planted in a mammoth fifteen-foot high, upright avocado strangely entitled "*Beloved*".

"Props for different stage performances or trade shows. Parades. I didn't know they were being returned, though. I'd always assumed those shows had bought the, uh … creations. Then some of it was just stuff he built on speculation because he thought he could sell it," I replied, almost apologetically. "And sometimes he did … sell … some of it…."

"Jesus, Mary an' Joseph, not enough of it! Them damn books could be split up an' buried everywhere in this goddamn garbage pit! There's probably pages stuffed into those leaves up there!" he groused, gesturing again towards the outsized geranium precariously arched over us. The mellowing effect of the whiskey had now worn off. T-Bone had expected to simply waltz in, grab the listed goods and then walk out, ultimately collecting his salary from Janet Lynn, I was quite sure.

Suddenly loud rustling followed by a dull leaden thud came from behind us along the back wall.

"Shut up an' stay put," T-Bone seethed under his breath, yanking out his gun. Cursing, he thrashed his way through a mountain of battered lampshades and lumber cutoffs in the direction of the noise. I began pushing through an army of enormous spring-mounted metal penguins, positioned in closely spaced half-circles, each painted with gargoyle-like red mouths, the paint dripping down onto the birds' white bibs. My dad must have built those ugly things for some kind of bizarre *Día de los Muertos* celebration. Rarely were his creations so hideously menacing.

More loud thrashing. T-Bone obviously, but who else? Gigantic *pâpier maché* black bears were stacked almost ceiling high, one upon another, just beyond the penguins, thus creating an impenetrable interior wall. I pushed my way through the metal waddle of penguins, staying close to the edge. The sickeningly sweet antiseptic smell was getting stronger. Breathing was taking more effort. Maybe ether? I worked to stifle coughing. The stench reminded me of new tires in a car dealership's showroom -- a smell that had made me gag since I'd had my tonsils out as a kid.

More loud thuds ricocheted from the back wall of the unit, followed by someone crunching through broken glass. With effort, I pushed through the last of the penguins, but a large, aluminum foil-covered object like a space capsule suddenly loomed up, completely blocking my path. More loud panting. At least two men fighting. Maybe more. Then a loud crash followed by several muffled gunshots with different levels of retort. Two guns? A man's voice yelped in agony. Another gunshot. Then dead silence.

I was still trying to work my way around the space capsule when I realized it was my dad's newest monstrous sculpture built to look like a giant Hershey's candy kiss -- The Kiss -- as he'd named the piece. He'd received an arts' grant from the Indiana Arts Council to create this massive structure – a rarity for his projects. He'd garnered lots of lucrative corporate supporters for that one year for an interactive art gallery that was outside in a major hotel courtyard in Columbus. Based on an earlier model, this Kiss sculpture was made of heavy aluminum foil stapled over thickly rolled layers of heavy chicken wire fencing and wound around tightly inside like a conch shell. It was an interesting concept except that the wires kept breaking inside and scratching the kids trying to climb through it, so it turned out to not be very interactive and was closed off after the first couple of days. There was a hidden latch or trip wire that needed to be sprung to locate the actual opening though. Dad had shown me the trick, but as usual, I hadn't been paying much attention. The Kiss. Something twitched in my memory, but I let it go. I strained to hear anything coming from the direction of those gunshots.

Other than muffled voices somewhere in the distance far down the hall it remained quiet in the storage unit. Were both men injured? Dead? Listening intently, I moved cautiously around the Kiss, quietly patting the sides, which rattled very slightly, looking for something that might indicate the opening. The ether smell was getting even stronger. It seemed to be coming through the air vent high overhead I realized. Scuffling noises again, possibly footsteps moving in my direction. I pulled my scarf over my nose to deflect the ether as I frantically continued pressing along the aluminum shell. A thin blue chalk line, almost invisible in the gloom, stretched down about two inches long on the wires. Carefully working my fingers under the line then slowly prying open a small section, I managed to peel it apart, much like a band-aid.

I had just stepped inside the shell, reclosing the entrance as much as possible so no one could easily follow, when the lights flickered out. In complete darkness, I patted my way sideways, feeling along the ribbed support structures and sharp, bristling chicken wire stubs exposed within the interior. One of the wires caught me by surprise, etching lightly along my forehead. I swallowed a painful yelp. Thor's voice reverberated loudly in the back of my brain: what in hell do you think you're doing, Prescott? I don't know, I whispered back.

I finally got to where the conch shell wall gave over to its cylindrical center. Fishing in my pocket for my key chain, I pulled out the very tiny, attached penlight and pressed it on for a moment. Opposite me in a roughly six-foot-high space, were what appeared to be small, rather droopy, square stools looking like oddly configured mushrooms, obviously built for very young children. Feeling rather like

Alice inside some bizarre aluminum rabbit hole, I walked over to the tallest stool and carefully sat down, quickly clicking off the penlight. The mushroom was tilting, not at all well secured. Within a few seconds I was dumped off onto the aluminum-covered floor. The innards of the mushroom fell to the floor. So much for a place to sit. I felt my way to another smaller mushroom in the dark but experienced the same tilting problem immediately. Guess whatever children had used these seats had destroyed their usefulness long ago. Typically, my dad built his structures to withstand an earthquake, so the flimsy construction surprised me. Other than my heart pounding in my ears I heard no other sounds. No rustlings, no thuds, no moans, no gunshots. Nothing.

"Denise?" a man whispered loudly. "Where are you? Are you still in here?"

I froze.

It sounded like Tom Miller. But the voice was muffled. Either way I had no intention of answering. The whispering continued, the voice moving towards the other side of the room and then the footsteps seemed to continue out into the hallway. I strained to listen but heard nothing close by. I couldn't tell if any lights had come back on. Whoever had called out to me probably had a flashlight since he didn't appear to be crashing into any of the mountainous piles. I cautiously flipped on the pen light for just a moment to get my bearings inside the Kiss. The second droopy mushroom that had toppled over now revealed three five-inch in diameter reel-to-reel tapes. I caught my breath. My dad hadn't built those flimsy mushrooms -- but who had then? Hank? And if so, who'd originally tipped him off that any of my old stuff was important in the first place? Once again Dorothea Dixon's name surfaced. Some fallout she'd had with Janet Lynn more than likely. Two scheming, powerful women at one another's throats? Thor always claimed you could never trust two women with a secret. One of them always screwed things up. You might be right on this one, Thor.

My brain devolved into a demented ping pong volley. Was my husband's incredibly meteoric rise to the marketing pinnacle at Idyllic based on his recklessly attempting to blackmail Janet Lynn Webster? And where, if anywhere, did Dorothea Dixon honestly fit into this nightmare other than her annual Bimbo of the Year Award?

My thoughts returned to Hank attending that Idyllic gathering in New York City, still in pain after moving his parents' furniture and many of our own belongings into this warehouse. Somewhere during that New York visit, in my hypothetical resurrection of that visit, while he indulged in the idle chit chat with Janet Lynn, he'd mentioned that his wife's name was Denise Prescott. Maybe Janet Lynn somehow then steered the conversation around to old high school items, same as she'd done with me later at the engagement party, and Hank had mentioned the box of grade school junk including the scrap books and tapes that I'd insisted keeping. I could envision Janet Lynn's perfectly arched eyebrows lifting in what would have appeared polite interest as she carefully asked a few more seemingly benign questions … about as benign as a deadly viper. Anyone delving into the true origins of Cathy Martin's transition to Janet Lynn Webster would probably unearth countless skeletons during this monstrous woman's quest. But who could possibly have alerted Hank to the fact that Cathy Martin was in reality Janet Lynn Webster? Yet again, the equally viperous DD's name pushed itself to the top of the pile.

Known names on the death tally included the real Janet Lynn Webster, Jimmy Larkins, Janet Lynn's parents, Chomp Martin, her first husband Count somebody-or-other back in England, my husband Hank and maybe even this girl Brenda whose bones I strongly suspected were the ones recently found in the ravine near Jimmy Larkins remains. What had brought this woman to such a ruthless lifetime of deceit? With her extraordinary science and math capability, why not apply those magnificent skills to curing cancer or developing the capability for humans to live on Mars or providing ways to grow crops in arid regions so that starving children throughout the world might for once fall asleep without growling bellies?

The odd smell was finally dissipating. Only a hint remained. I pocketed the tapes, two in one pocket, one in the other, on each side of my coat. Then, as best possible, I repaired the droopy mushroom, concealing the tapes' removal and straightened the smaller mushroom with the two photo albums. I would have to return for those since they were far too bulky to conceal in my coat pocket. I was still aware of voices far in the distance but could only assume that no one remained inside this storage unit. I carefully retraced my steps to exit the giant Kiss. Once outside, I resealed the entry flap. The building was now lit only by very dim yellow security lighting that cast a sinister, gargoyle-like atmosphere to my dad's most innocent creative endeavors, never mind the metal army of bloodthirsty penguins and maniacal bears towering above me.

Listening carefully, I began moving toward the door, which was still wide open. No ether. No scuffling. No voices. Complete silence other than those distant voices echoing from another wing. Stealthily, checking both directions within the hallway, I retraced my original steps to the main hallway, intending to follow it back to the front desk. At the intersection of the next hall, however, a workman, clad in a striped, yellow vest, high on a tall ladder working in the dim yellow light, was replacing a long fluorescent tube over a set of double doors. This entry might well empty out to the parking lot where I'd left my car.

"Any possibility I could use those doors right now?" I asked, flashing a smile. "I heard the security system was being worked on … so, I just thought, well, maybe I could just boogie out through this shortcut for once."

"Sure, don't see why not," the worker shrugged, moving down a couple of rungs. "Everything's jazzed up right now with part of the electric cuttin' out for some reason. Why they want this place open twenty-four hours a day every day is beyond me. Wastes a lotta money in my book. Wait a sec while I trip the switch up top."

Moments later I was in my car, racing out of the parking lot, hoping to locate a pay phone as quickly as possible. My plan was to call the police, send them to my parents' place and then attempt to rouse Thor from an undoubtedly deep sleep, warning him that I was headed his direction. I glanced at the clock in my car. It was almost midnight. Too bad. Thor was the only person I knew who had a reel-to-reel tape player that might be able to play this older style tape. Why he'd held onto it was anybody's guess.

I didn't know if T-Bone was alive or dead. Tom's handiwork? Janet Lynn's? As I pulled out onto the main highway I was immediately enveloped by a thick, freezing fog. Dammit, I cursed at my feeble headlights. Even at low beam the visibility was only a couple feet. I crawled along, squinting through my windshield while constantly glancing in my rearview mirror.

"Intelligent criminals are seldom vicious except on special occasions."

Basil Rathbone as Sherlock Holmes in

"The Adventures of Sherlock Holmes"
(1939)

Chapter 23

A scarcely illuminated Esso sign came into view mere seconds before I'd passed the station. I quickly pulled off the highway and drove to where I thought a phone would be located. A booth was nailed on the side of the building, but the phone itself had been ripped from the wall. A dark car eased along the road as I stood there, its headlights bouncing off me momentarily. I froze watching it crawl along its path. That's just some random car heading out I reassured myself, trying to calm my breathing. Stop being so paranoid. I raced back to my car and continued to Thor's house. I would have to call the cops from there. Although I didn't remember the precise address, Thor's place ordinarily was easy to find since it was an older ranch style he'd inherited from his mom. After several incorrect fog-shrouded streets I finally pulled into the stubby driveway. Thor's car was visible in the carport as well as another car further back. I assumed the other car belonged to his roommate, although I'd never met the guy. A light through the kitchen window filtered into the carport. Simply for security or were they sitting at the table nursing a late-night hot toddy?

Thor answered my frantic knocking, wrapping an

over-large, thick flannel robe around himself.

"Geez, Prescott! Don't you think it's just a little late for drop in vis --"

I pushed past him into the kitchen and slammed the door shut, panting hard.

"I need to use your phone."

"Uh, sure, what's up? You look like you've been to hell and back."

"The to hell part for sure … but sure not back yet," I replied tersely as I dialed the police.

Unlike my exasperating experience up in Swayzee, the call went through immediately.

"What's your emergency? What town? May I have your name, please?"

"Denise Prescott," I replied. "But this is for Nashville. My dad went to a meeting and should have returned hours ago and my mom's frantic that she hasn't heard from him. But also, I'm concerned that some strange man may have forced his way into her house."

"Why didn't she call us directly?" the operator replied with obvious concern.

"She's … afraid of stuff," I stammered, "but please, sir, this is real! Could you get a car over to check on them immediately?"

"Yes, of course, Ms. Prescott," the operator answered, in a reassuring, calm voice. "Give me the address and we'll get a unit over there immediately."

"Don't let them leave her there alone, whatever you do!" I blurted. "Can you guarantee that? Please, sir? Sometimes my dad takes her over to Erskins House when she's gotten hysterical over things. She … she takes medicine for paranoia, but sometimes she forgets. Actually, most times she forgets because it makes her feel queasy. They know her at Erskins House … she even volunteers there sometimes. I hope that makes sense. Can you have the officers take her there if my dad isn't home yet? And then look for him as well? I know this seems convoluted but …" I faltered.

"We'll make every effort to do so, ma'am," answered the operator. "What's your mother's name and address -- and your name and phone? Where can we reach you?"

I finished my conversation with the operator and carefully pulled the three tapes from my coat pockets, simultaneously relaying to Thor a Cliff Notes' version of my chilling encounter with T-Bone.

"Please tell me you still have that tape player for these undersized reels, Thor," I continued. "I remember you brought it to the newsroom to validate background on some defunct radio station for an article a few years back."

"Yeah," he shrugged. "Technology's my middle name. Well, actually I don't have a middle name … but, yeah, it's on a shelf in my basement. Cold as hell down there. What do tapes have to do with your mother?"

"My mother?"

"Oh. Ok. Keep your coat on and follow me down to my concrete bunker," he replied, sensing my muddled state of mind. "Flip off the kitchen light on your way down."

His basement ran under the entire footprint of the house, eerily lit by yellowing fluorescent tubes that hummed like an angry swarm of yellow jackets while warming. Floor-to-ceiling shelves had been built around the entire perimeter. A maze of long rows divided the floor into a grid. Each shelf groaned with reel-to-reel, eight-track or cassette tapes, as well as long rows of unopened sleeves of LPs, 45s and 78 records. Most shelves were clearly identified by year. We cleared a space on his center worktable, plugged in the tape recorder and carefully wound the tape's white leader onto the empty spool. Once running, we could faintly discern a man's voice in the background under a low hum.

"I've got the volume up to max," Thor stated. "It doesn't look like there's anything on this. Just what's bleeding through after having been erased, probably at a radio station years ago."

"Wait just a little longer. Let it run. Maybe this is only what was underneath and …shhh. Ok. Wow. Oh man … that's Cathy's voice."

Just then, a young Cathy Martin began speaking. There was also a rustling of pages turning, possibly inside a notebook.

"The Story of Lady Pamela" by Cathy Martin -- So now her conversion was complete. Pamela looked smugly into the long dark mirror in her mistress' dressing room. The late afternoon sunlight cascaded from the transom window, glistening over her diamond necklace and earrings, while she slowly caressed the tight bodice of the pale, yellow silk dress until her young, firm nipples stood out prominently."

"Whoa, you girls had some pretty risqué stuff going on there …" Thor began, raising his eyebrows.

I glowered at him. I certainly didn't remember any of our recordings being anywhere near this suggestive. What the heck?

"She now looked exactly like her mistress, the Lady Isobelle. For years she'd studied her mistress' mannerisms, from that coy tilt of her blonde head under its tiny blue velvet riding hat and veil, to the unhurried way she slipped her soft kid gloves over her delicate white hands, making great show of fastening the genuine pearl buttons at each wrist. When others had remarked about the stark resemblance of late, Pamela had laughed lightly,

tossing her head with that same indifference as Lady Isobelle, even feigning her ladyship's slight lift of her right shoulder in flirtatious abandon. Every evening she swathed her hands in thick, paraffined butter to rid them of their telltale red chafing, the result of several years of backbreaking laundry work.

Suddenly, having arrived more than an hour earlier than anticipated, Lady Isobelle strode into the room.

"My God! Pamela!" she exclaimed loudly, thoroughly shocked. "What are you doing in my things? This is an outrage! Is this what goes on while I'm out riding with Sir Wexford every afternoon? No wonder my dresses have a rank, foul odor so often if you've been rousting about in them with some filthy kitchen wastrel engaged in God only knows what outrageous lust!"

Pamela looked at her ladyship coolly as she carefully removed one of the earrings, placing it unhurriedly on the dressing table, never taking her eyes from her mistress' face.

"Well?' continued Lady Isobelle, moving closer. "Answer me, girl! Are you deaf as well as unbelievably stupid?"

"Hey, anything more about those prominent nipples or that rousting in lust with the kitchen wastrel? Who cares about an earring?" interjected Thor.

"Thor …" I sighed, shaking my head. I'd always assumed that Thor was queer, but maybe I was mistaken.

"Yeah, yeah ok, sorry."

"I meant no harm," smiled Pamela, still maintaining her calm demeanor, the back of her thighs now firmly braced against the

dressing table. "Twas all in fun, m'lady. I only donned the gown for a few moments and would have carefully replaced it within your closets, I assure you. And there's been no rousting about as you call it with the lowly kitchen servants. Of that you may rest quite well assured."

"Hmmm," sniffed Lady Isobelle. "Well, that certainly remains to be seen! Remove that dress at once, Pamela! As soon as you've done so you are permanently dismissed with no hope whatsoever of any recommendation from this household, I assure you ... you filthy whore!"

"Only a whore for Sir Wexford," Pamela winked slyly, raising her shoulder coyly while removing the other earring. "And scarcely a filthy one, m'lady. He adores undressing me in your frigid finery, then we spread the gown luxuriously beneath our bodies while fully enjoying ourselves in every way you might presume ... and undoubtedly in ways you couldn't possibly fancy as well ... near the grape arbors at the furthermost woods on the estate. He laughs when he sees you in that dress a day or so later and says he loves the rich aromas of our lust wafting off your pale, chaste body."

"Get that dress off now!" Isobelle shrieked, thoroughly horrified at Pamela's vile revelation.

"Whew, seems to me your friend Cathy Martin missed her calling," whistled Thor, pausing the tape momentarily. "She should've been a porn film writer. Man, that's damned great stuff for age … what … fifteen maybe?"

"Glad you're so … invested in this, Thor," I replied in disgust.

"Hell yeah, this is great! Except, what the hell's frigid finery?"

I rolled my eyes as he let up the pause button.

"Yes, m'lady," remarked Pamela quietly. "I just need to get this top hook undone. It's always a little difficult to unhook. You see, Sir Wexford usually leaves that one open so it's easier for me to just slither out of the dress again once I'm back up here in your rooms."

"Turn around and let me start it," growled Lady Isobelle through clenched teeth. "I'll have this dress burned after you're gone anyway, but I'm certainly not about to let you exit these premises with it over your vile, putrid flesh!"

Pamela complied, turning her back to her mistress, her arms straight down by her sides, hidden deeply within the folds of the silk dress.

"The top one's done," spat out Lady Isobelle, "now get the rest of the ..."

Before she could finish her sentence, Pamela whirled back towards her, wielding a small butcher knife that was aggressively raised to shoulder level. Without the slightest hesitation, she drove it deep into the woman's heart, grinding the blade past bone effortlessly, almost completely up to the hilt for a full minute, intent upon her task. Isobelle's eyes registered the shock as she shuddered under the brutal assault of her seemingly timid handmaiden. Then soundlessly, she fell to the ground, a small puddle of blood soaking into her dark blue velvet riding habit upon landing.

"Shit," whispered Thor, pausing the tape again. "This chick's one sicko. Man oh man!"

I nodded in agreement as we listened to Cathy's voice, so eagerly engaged in relating this sordid tale. I'd never heard this story. Of that I was certain. How I came to have this tape with Cathy's and my other innocent girlhood mementoes was a complete mystery. I didn't want to listen to the story's continuation but knew we needed to do so. Without needing encouragement, Thor pressed the play button once again.

Pamela's strength came from her infamous father. Her father had at one time been the highly prized village blacksmith – known by everyone simply as The Bull -- and was the strongest man for hundreds of miles around. How many times had the rich noblemen of their town bet upon his strength when pitted against that of any man within the radius of several counties and come away extremely well-paid for their foolishly idle games of chance? His neck was the size of a large oak tree trunk, his arms were huge hams, like those you might see roasting upon the open spit of a brick-lined oven, readied for a summer fête in the town square.

But then, unfortunately, one day The Bull had lost in a brutally bloody fight against a massive toothless giant who had recently been brought into a neighboring earldom's employ. The man was much younger, deftly trained in hideously barbaric military maneuvers from abroad, unlike that which anyone had ever witnessed in Pamela's town. Her father was not only soundly, but very quickly, defeated. The lucrative betting monies now going towards this younger bull, and other blacksmiths now undercutting his trade, The Bull made himself available as a nocturnal killer for hire so that he could adequately provide for his two motherless daughters. He was known to arrive on scene quietly, dispatch his prey with swift

silence and leave without so much as the merest trace of evidence. It was rumored that even a sleuth with the capability of a Sherlock Holmes would have been flummoxed, for The Bull was such a cunning master of diabolical techniques he might well have provided the template for the evil Professor Moriarty.

After taking the broadaxe to Lady Isobelle's body, The Bull and Pamela deeply buried her remains under a low ridge on the furthest outskirts of the town, near an area that had been abandoned long ago during a cholera epidemic. They had removed the skull and severed the hands at the wrists, to completely defeat identification, and disposed of them, strewn randomly throughout forests, stream beds and caves over many acres, thwarting any detection.

"Sweet Jesus," I whispered, my hand flying to my mouth as this nightmare tale unfolded. "What kind of sick mind writes something this repugnant? And … the similarity to … my God …"

Nowadays, still fearful of night vapors and wishing to avoid the unbridled stench of an adjacent swamp, no one ever rode that direction. The rest of Isobelle's remains were dumped near the eagerly, animal-sampled remnants of an upstart boy they'd killed several years prior – a bully who had overpowered and inflicted heinous wanton acts upon both Pamela and her older sister Leah on numerous occasions. They had accosted the vagrant youth when he dared walk alone while hunting pheasant deep in the woods and made ready

dispatch. He would certainly never be missed they had mused, fully aware that many in the town would have rapturously, though silently, concurred.

****

Pamela gracefully slipped into the role of Lady Isobelle with ease. She informed the rest of the household's staff of her handmaid's disgraceful actions, stating that of course the young girl's offenses were so shockingly deviant in nature, that she had been dismissed on the spot. Lady Isobelle certainly hoped that none of the other girls would entertain such vile, appalling indiscretions in the future.

Her engagement to Sir Wexford was announced less than two months later and they were married a short time thereafter – the largest, most lavish wedding the country had witnessed since the King's nuptials a decade earlier. Wide-eyed with innocence, Isobelle begged her new husband to teach her those little tricks of pleasure he might wish to secure from those nasty, coarser women who proffered such services for a paltry fee. Reluctant at first, Sir Wexford gradually agreed to his young wife's requests. He was astounded to find her such an avid, incredibly lustful pupil, thoroughly dismissing any desires he might ever have felt to wander from her innocent mesmerizing charms.

This time I paused the tape. Thor and I sat silently, just looking at one another in shock. I broke the silence.

"To me, this is laying the groundwork to justify the murders of Jimmy Larkins and Janet Lynn Webster," I said quietly as Thor nodded slightly. "No doubt about it. If Cathy wrote this when she was fourteen or fifteen or whatever, then it's when she'd just met Janet Lynn Webster and somehow worked to make all this horror play out one way or another over the next four years." Then, as an afterthought I added, "actually, Cathy would've been sixteen, I just realized. But this tape's shocking regardless of her age."

"How do you know that?"

"What, that she was sixteen? Um, Tom Miller mentioned she was a year older," I admitted. Assuming that everything spewing out of the man's mouth wasn't complete fabrication, of course.

"Ok, I'm just gonna forget that you brought up that evil dude's name, Prescott. Let's get back on task with comparing this tape with reality. Jimmy Larkins had already been … what was that phrase she used: 'readily dispatched'," Thor stated. "I'll go with you on that. Who's this sister Leah though?"

"I've never mentioned this, Thor," I replied slowly, "but Jimmy disappeared after he'd been coercing this slightly older girl named Brenda into having sex with him. Brenda and Cathy were friends apparently, although I didn't realize that until one time when Brenda came running up to us in tears trying to escape Jimmy. I never knew Brenda's last name though. I guess there's a possibility that Brenda is supposed to be this Leah in the story even though they weren't related in real life."

"When did she come into the picture … this Brenda?" asked Thor, frowning.

"I don't remember that either," I replied, shaking my head. "But here's a strange, well, I guess what you'd call a coincidence. Cathy Martin told me that her own mother was strung out on drugs and a prostitute and had left her with her father right after Cathy was born. And Brenda's mom, once they'd appeared in town, was arrested on drug and prostitution charges so many times I think the authorities just dumped her somewhere far outside town according to the rumor. Then, later when Brenda disappeared …"

"Whoa, wait, wait," interjected Thor, "you mean this Brenda just evaporated into thin air or something? When was this?"

"There was a missing person story about Brenda in the paper before I worked there. I stumbled on the article in the archives while I was researching another missing person's story. But I don't ever remember reading anything about her having been found. None of this stuff might even intersect, you know? Anyway, by that time, they weren't even living in Nashville any longer. Then, a few months later, Brenda's mother was hit by a car while she was walking in the middle of the road one night. The police investigation was a lick and promise as my mom would scoff since Brenda's mother was assumed to have been wandering about in her usual drunken stupor. I don't know if anybody was still even looking for Brenda or if she'd just finally turned up somewhere and no one ever mentioned it. Or maybe no one believed her mom's report about Brenda's missing in the first place. The kid would have had every reason to run as far from home as possible!"

"Interesting," nodded Thor, rubbing his chin thoughtfully. "And she was older than Cathy Martin, right?"

I nodded.

"Maybe there's a third corpse down there. Brenda could be down there with Jimmy and Janet Lynn," I suddenly blurted out. "Unless that was Brenda down there in the first place and Janet Lynn is buried somewhere else entirely."

"Ok, we need to keep listening to this tape," stated Thor. "Scotch? I've got the good stuff. Right on the worktable over there."

"Sure. Two cubes, no water," I replied, nodding. "Thanks. Hey, um, do you have anything to eat? I'm starving – haven't eaten much anything all day."

"What do I look like, a Lum's hot dog lackey, Prescott? You show up at my door at midnight expectin' full service? Count yourself lucky I've even got the damn whiskey!"

"Sorry."

As Thor was fixing our drinks he suddenly exhaled loudly, slammed his hand on the counter and turned slowly to face me.

"How's this work for an explanation – hear me out on this one because it kinda fits that story we just heard. Brenda and Cathy Martin were related – you know, let's say half-sisters. Right after Cathy was born the mother takes her older daughter Brenda and simply leaves town. That older kid probably wasn't Chomp's. Who knows? That's not important. Anyway, when she returns with her daughter several years later, they don't live with Chomp and Cathy Martin. Bad blood and all that shit, you know? But Brenda and Cathy hang out together sometimes, same as you and Cathy had been doing. I mean, they had the exact same backgrounds – a father or stepfather who was the resident bullying whacko and their mother who was the official village slut and druggie. Talk about getting ostracized! But it sure as hell makes sense, don't you think?"

I nodded but frowned simultaneously.

"And, what's more, they're now associated through their business," continued Thor.

"Ok, it's a stretch but I'll go with maybe they were sisters or half-sisters. Last I heard anything about her, she was the subject of the missing person's report. What on earth makes you think this Brenda's anywhere around here now much less that she and Cathy Martin ever worked together?" I frowned again. "You've completely lost me, Thor."

"You can't figure it out?"

"Nary a blimey clue to use your phrase."

"C'mon, Prescott, you're slipping. Think hard."

I waited. Not exactly taping my foot in exasperation, but pretty darn close. I really wasn't in the mood for any of Thor's cerebral hopscotching in the middle of the night.

"Dorothea Dixon," he whispered, handing me my drink as he sat down.

"Oh, come on now! That's about as blind a leap of faith as I've ever heard, Thor!" I snorted. "How on earth do you come up with that conclusion?"

"Hear me out, ok? Everything's been status quo for the last, what, eight or ten years, right? Let's assume the two women had a major falling out way back when. Neither has contacted the other in close to a decade. Brenda's been doing her thing – whatever that is – somewhere – having arbitrarily changed her name to Dorothea Dixon. She's not aware that her half-sister, Cathy Martin, has now blissfully transformed into Janet Lynn Webster. But then, irony of all ironies, she finds out that Cathy is in line to just waltz off with the biggest pile out there … the Fowler pile including hunky David Fowler himself, voted *numero uno* Catch of the Year in *Modern Bride* magazine … and that she, Dorothea Dixon, aka Brenda, is working her ass off … figuratively as well as literally with your husband … attempting to scratch her way up the ladder to a lavish lifestyle at one of the major Fowler corporate holdings, specifically Idyllic. Both women are incredibly beautiful, downright devious, and extraordinarily brilliant. And jealous? You can bet your sweet ass the ol' DD was jealous! Good possibility I'm very close to the truth, you'll have to admit, especially if they hadn't parted on good terms all those years back."

I took a hefty swig of my scotch.

"So going along with your theory, let's say Dorothea had just recently started blackmailing Cathy – well, Janet Lynn or whatever in the hell you want to call her -- because obviously, she knew exactly who Janet Lynn really was and what's more, she knows exactly what happened to many of those people missing in action so to speak," I replied, leaning back, deep in thought.

"I'm all ears," replied Thor, sipping his scotch. "Good stuff, eh? My uncle sent this. Early Christmas present or something."

"Ok, so both women need to hide extremely sordid pasts, yes?" I continued, toasting Thor's glass. Hard liquor on an empty stomach had never been my *forté,* but I confess it tasted great.

He nodded as I continued talking.

"Let's presume that Dorothea was the one who had these newer tapes, like this one, along with various notebooks that Cathy had written while in high school. All that stuff had been stored over at Dorothea's place once everybody had started high school. Cathy sure couldn't keep anything that explosive in nature at the Websters' house or at Chomp's place! Or in her locker at school either! Too risky in case of Mrs. Webster's prying eyes, the school administration's random locker searches or any police investigations into Chomp's possibly illegal activities. Since she'd already dumped me as a friend within the first week of freshman year, immediately latching onto Janet Lynn Webster, I only retained the more innocent stuff from our early childhood. Some of my original scrapbooks contain stuff that could certainly identify Janet Lynn as Cathy Martin – like an entire page of her fingerprints pressed in blood for that matter!"

"Okay," drawled Thor, sipping at his scotch. "That doesn't really answer why she was obsessed with writing it all down ... other than the fact she's a complete whack brain spawned by the town prostitute and resident ogre and salivates over her upcoming killing sprees in print. Was she planning to publish this stuff under a pseudonym you think? Maybe planned to make a lot of money off the porno trade like I said about Lady Pamela and her fingering her --"

"Yes," I interrupted, "you don't need to go into detail."

"Well, you know – Pavlov's dogs."

"Pavlov's dogs had nothing to do with murder, Thor," I sighed. "What are you talking about?

"Yeah, yeah, sorry. It just sounded good. I snored my way through psych class. Boring prof."

I shook my head and sipped my scotch.

"Anyway, Pavlov aside, let's go through what we think we know, ok Denise?"

"I'm all ears."

"Brenda, alias Dorothea, gets herself declared a missing person by Mama the Whore and disappears with these newer tapes and notebooks, along with Cathy's older scrapbooks that were duplicates of yours. So far, so good?

I nodded.

"Cathy's life of crime allows her to take on her own Lady Isobelle character as Janet Lynn, waltzing over the pond in her namesake's body to London, after murdering the entire Webster family as well as her own father. More than likely she was scarcely concerned about Brenda's showing back up in her life anywhere in the future since she'd cast herself as Lady So-and-so of the British aristocracy. I'm liking this more and more," Thor stated, now running with the lead, whirling the ice cubes into a furious vortex in his glass.

"Yeah, ok, and then," continued Thor, "the whole London affair falls flat when she doesn't qualify for ol' late rich hubby's inheritance, so she has no choice but to head back to the States -- you know, no visa -- and quickly gets herself in line to marry into the incredibly wealthy Fowler dynasty. But, upon venturing to Indianapolis with Mr. hunky-husband-to-be a few months ago, she is horrified to discover that her half-sister, whom she may have even thought was dead, who knows, is now working in upper management in that very same firm!"

"And that my husband is even having an affair with

that same sister," I exhaled. "If you can get past a lot of coincidences, all this holds water. Going a step further, Janet Lynn is now being blackmailed by Dorothea. Whatever their original deal, it's gone beyond sour. She then poisons my husband down in New Orleans and assumes that the evidence will implicate Dorothea. But Dorothea is absolved of any guilt during the autopsy so that's a nonstarter. We don't really know the full autopsy details of course. Dorothea already had these incriminating tapes and scrapbooks that were originally Janet Lynn's safely stowed away – merged with my stuff that Hank had deposited earlier in that warehouse. Dorothea is just biding her time to turn this evidence over to the police."

"Do you think that maybe Hank and Dorothea were in on this blackmail scheme together?"

"Oh man," I began. "That thought never crossed my mind. Crap. Idiotic move on my husband's part if that was the case."

Thor poured a finger of whiskey into his glass.

"So thinking along those lines, because she still can't get her hands on the evidence, Cathy Martin is now going after *me* to find those items that Dorothea Dixon must have merged with hers. And she's really desperate I might add. Who knows what other horrors lie in these tapes or books, Thor! Dorothea already knows since she's the one who packaged them up with mine – Hank would have shown her where my feeble little mementoes were stored. Hank showed Dorothea the entrance to this giant Hershey's Kiss my dad had stored at the warehouse, and she concealed all the incriminating stuff in there. Since Dorothea works for Idyllic, which runs the warehouse security, she could gain access at any time to move the evidence elsewhere should inquisitive eyes get too close. Or freely extract it, no questions asked, right? Maybe another leap of faith in this story, but highly plausible. Poor Hank. He was really just a pawn in the clutches of these two nasty, evil women."

"Yeah, well I wouldn't go so far as saying 'poor Hank,' exactly. I imagine he got in on some mighty sizzling action doing the horizontal mambo with the DD," Thor smirked. "Remember 'poor ol' Hank' drove you crazy, Denise, and so did that worthless marriage counselor."

Ignoring Thor's last remark, I slumped back in my chair, nursing my scotch, deep in thought. The booze was undoubtedly clouding my judgment, but it was also alleviating the gnawing in my stomach. Our silence was broken by the shrill ring of Thor's telephone.

"Murder, my dear Watson.
Refined, cold-blooded murder."

Basil Rathbone as Sherlock Holmes in

"The Hound of the Baskervilles" (1939)

Chapter 24

I was grateful that he didn't answer with his usual British-flair quip: 'Thorwald's Mortuary ... you kill 'em, we chill 'em. May I be of service?'

"Yeah, she's here. Uh, yeah, sure, what's the message?" he inquired, then was silent for several minutes. "Yep. Got it. No problem. Thanks!" he said, abruptly ending the call.

"The police?"

"No, Erskins. Both your folks are over there. Cops found your dad parked outside some abandoned Shriner's Lodge over in Columbus and they brought him over about a half hour ago. Your mom had already been taken to Erskins and given a hefty sedative. Guess she was pretty … uh, hyper … going on about orange sugar that you'd stolen from her."

"Yeah, that's another long story," I sighed, rubbing my forehead. "What else?"

"Cops said your dad claimed some guy told him that the manager at the Shriner's Lodge would be along in a few minutes to order one of his art creations for their lobby. Guy never showed, though. He waited for over two hours apparently … orange sugar?"

I nodded adding, "It'll be a while before my mom gets off of the orange sugar accusation, I'm sure."

"Ok. I'll bite."

"I was certain that Janet Lynn, disguised in a brown wig, had paid a visit to my parents yesterday, expressing ridiculous homage to my dad's newest art creation, and put something in my mom's sugar bowl. I confiscated the sugar bowl because I was afraid it might be this abrin powder that the police claimed they'd found in Hank's vitamin pills, even though last I'd heard, they don't believe that he died from abrin poisoning. But now maybe they do. It's so confusing! Anyway, my mom went completely off the rails thinking it was drugs. You know, like in *Wait Until Dark.*"

"Your dad took your mom to see *Wait Until Dark*? Are you serious? That movie's scary as hell!"

"I'm sure he assumed it was some chirpy little Audrey Hepburn film."

"Geez, bad call on that one. So, where's this mysterious sugar bowl now?"

"I think under a loose floorboard in our hall closet. But I confess I don't know where I left the damn thing at this point."

"Hey, understandable," he nodded, a rare expression of concern written on his face. "So obviously you're bunking down here for the rest of tonight. You can sleep in my spare room. My roommate's out on er … extended assignment right now."

"Assignment? Is he a journalist or a cop?"

"Really can't divulge that info exactly, but yeah, something like that."

"Sorry, didn't mean to intrude."

"Ok, well in reality he's in jail right now. Trial comes up in a few weeks according to his lawyer."

Although I'm certain that surprise registered on my face, I refrained from inquiring further and gestured with my chin to restart the tape.

"I'm assuming you removed whatever tracking devices someone undoubtedly clamped on your car?" asked Thor.

"Crap. Ok, I didn't look. But you're right, I'm sure they're there."

Thor bolted outside and returned within a few minutes.

"It was a button mushroom style. A little crude for an Idyllic creation I think, so probably obtained from your local Toys 'R Us in the detective goodies section. Everything in stock from handcuffs to doggie whistles to stage blood capsules. Found it dangling conspicuously under your dashboard. Probably only emitted a really weak tracking signal so we're in luck most likely. Now unceremoniously reduced to pulp and thrown into my neighbor's truck bed. He'll be leaving for his regular scrap metal hauling route sometime in the next hour."

He refilled both our glasses and then depressed the play button. After a few mechanical clicks on the tape, Cathy's voice excitedly introduced a new tale.

"The Tragic Fire at Belsted" by Cathy Martin. Pamela's transition to Lady Isobelle continued smoothly for many months and no one suspected even the merest impropriety. That is until one day, uninvited, the real Isobelle's mother, the Duchess of Belsted, came to stay for a fortnight. Prior to her marriage Lady Isobelle had been living with a first cousin's family on an estate adjacent to Sir Wexford's. On the second day of the Duchess' visit, she had brashly walked in completely unannounced upon Pamela while her handmaiden was about to pull a new lace-edged satin camisole over the young woman's head. 'Wait just a moment,' the Duchess had barked

in her irritating, gravelly voice, as the startled servant poised with the delicate sheath still quivering in mid-air just above Pamela's head. 'How is it that the star-shaped strawberry-colored birthmark on your lower back has completely disappeared, Isobelle,' she declared suspiciously. 'Has a sorcerer seen to this inexplicable evanescence?'

'You! Girl! Do you know anything about the disappearance of that birthmark?' demanded the Duchess, whirling to face the maid. 'Exotic rubbing ointments or arsenic bleaching compounds perhaps?'

Cowering as she addressed the Duchess, eyes lowered, the servant meekly replied that she'd only been attending as a personal maid to Lady Isobelle since the week prior to her ladyship's wedding. She had never seen any sign of a strawberry-colored birthmark anywhere on her ladyship's body at any time so she could comment neither upon the fact of its existence nor of its disappearance.

"Gym class," I uttered loudly, hitting the pause button as I turned to face Thor. "I remember that Cathy Martin, Janet Lynn and I were all in the same gym class as freshmen at Columbus High. At least first semester anyway. They'd make us strip off everything after class and walk single file through that damned tunnel of freezing showers. So humiliating … well, you know …"

"Ok, no additional information needed," replied Thor. "Do you specifically remember a birthmark on Janet Lynn Webster, Prescott? I know it was a long time ago, but that might be significant. If she was writing these bizarre stories during the earliest part of your freshman year of high school, that might be incriminating right there."

Begging Thor to hear me out, knowing he would scoff

at the source -- about which I certainly held my own reservations -- I told him about the information that Tom Miller had given me from his conversations with Mrs. Webster. She was certain that the young woman now claiming to be her daughter Janet Lynn was a malevolent impostor.

Specifically, I noted Tom's comments about the broken ankle and the lack of allergic reaction to the wasp stings. Admittedly, she could have outgrown the allergy as I'd mentioned to Tom that day. But the woman posing as Janet Lynn had definitely broken her ankle as a youngster according to x-ray analysis: Cathy Martin had broken her ankle. I'd been there when that accident occurred and even had pictures of the cast. However, Janet Lynn Webster had not ever broken her ankle. And, all of a sudden I remembered that Janet Lynn Webster did have a very prominent, star-shaped strawberry birthmark low on her back, probably impossible to surgically remove without at least some scarring. I also knew that Cathy Martin had never possessed any such mark. The lack of so prominent a birthmark would have been very difficult for Cathy Martin to adequately explain.

"And let's face it," I concluded. "Surely at some point after Cathy had assumed Janet Lynn's identity, Mrs. Webster would have had an occasion to observe her daughter's backside!"

Thor restarted the tape.

The Duchess glowered at Pamela. 'Sir Wexford's father never supported his son's selection of you as his bride, which at first I found quite infuriating', she spat out loudly, daggers of unsuppressed hatred visible within her narrowly slit pupils. 'He alluded to a hideous alchemy, the blackest of sorceries in fact, the spell under which his only son had

befallen. An innocent lamb, the heir to his estate had been willfully defiled by a vile, tainted apparition posing as his son's one-time demure fiancée, according to several letters. I was obviously distraught by the man's accusations at first, but I've had my own concerns about you as well since I arrived here two days back. Who are you really and what have you done with my beautiful daughter?' she bellowed.

Pamela placed her hand lightly upon her white, silken throat and laughed softly, smiling sweetly at the Duchess. 'Why my dearest mother, I think you've perhaps forgotten – or perhaps weren't aware of the fact – that my darling husband, right after our marriage, upon learning of my chronic embarrassment of my birthmark, which of course he'd never observed prior to our wedding night, engaged the services of a magnificent renowned healer from the Orient. Twas my husband's idea, mother, not my own I assure you, to engage the healer's services. Though quite painful for well over a week, I lay in agony, wanting for my complexion to be as flawless as possible for my devoted, loving Charles, and of course, for our children who will soon be a part of our lives.'

'You're ... you're with child?' demanded the Duchess, eyes widening in a horror reflected in every crevice of her ugly visage.

'Well, there's certainly that ... possibility,' Pamela replied, eyes downcast, demurely glancing away. 'You know how it can be with a new husband who is fully captivated by his wife's irresistible charms almost every evening. One would just never know until things became a bit more, well ... obvious, of course.'

"Geez, I want that dame's thesaurus," mumbled Thor. "For a high school kid, Cathy Martin was one hell of a writer, you know? I thought you told me that math and science were her areas. I mean, even if this chick's guilty as hell, I'd pay full price any day for her stuff over that crime fiction crap they peddle at Borders. And trust me, I'm about as big a cheapskate as they come."

'I do not believe you,' growled the Duchess, 'not in the least! I'm signaling my driver to make ready my rig and am heading straightaway for Belsted,' she spat out. 'I wish to confer with the Duke regarding my suspicions and determine our course of action with respect to what I perceive as your defamatory, perpetual lies. And, most importantly, find out where you've banished my sweet, innocent daughter ... you ... viperous, prevaricating slattern!'

"Good luck with that," mumbled Thor, plopping another ice cube into his drink. "She's now a pile of splintered bones stashed in the ravine sans skull and hands. Wish I could use phrases like defamatory, perpetual lies or viperous, prevaricating slattern in a news article one day. Would probably send at least ninety-five percent of our readership scrambling for the nearest dictionary scratching their pointy little heads, y'know?"

I nodded, then put my finger to my lips as Cathy continued speaking on the tape.

Moments after the Duchess' carriage left, Pamela summoned the estate's head groom and asked that he quickly ready her own small, swift barouche. She would not be in need of a

driver, she stated sweetly, for her journey was a short one, just to visit a sick friend with a gift of jams and jellies over in the next county. The prevailing roads were quite in good condition and simple to navigate she assured him when he expressed concern, even if the horses were not familiar with the intricacies of the route. She would like to request her new magnificent, matched pair, an expensive wedding gift from Sir Wexford, rather still straining at the bit and in need of strict discipline, to be put in harness, so that her journey might be as swift as possible, she beseeched of the groom.

Prior to her departure, Pamela visited her new greenhouse that she had requested her husband have built merely for an amusement, so that she could adequately supply year-round hothouse flowers to beautify their home. The intoxicating scent of roses in January was glorious beyond measure! Nestled within that innocent glass structure, however, were cuttings of several poisonous plants, the most insidious a very rare species of belladonna or deadly nightshade as it was often called, with its telltale small black berries sweetly glistening along each stem, easily grown from a fleshy rootstock. It was said that the berry's lethal juices had been the means used by Roman empress Livia Drusilla to murder her husband, the emperor Augustus. Depending on its dosage, belladonna could be used as an intense love potion, a manner to dislodge an unwanted pregnancy, a treatment for certain intestinal disorders, and to help ease the most severe of muscle spasms. In modest application, it was surprisingly even used to alleviate a teething baby's suffering. However, Pamela's unusual cutting was not used for any of those

delicate means. She'd developed the berry for that of a quick, calculated death, completely undetectable by either the victim or any subsequent investigation of the matter.

Pamela brought along more than a sufficient number of berries to accomplish her desired goal -- that of obtaining a deep, paralyzing sleep from both the Duke and Duchess of Belsted when unobtrusively mixed with the couple's usual nocturnal sleeping draught. Neither of the royal couple could maintain a restful night's slumber without their prescribed sleeping potions, consumed each evening after several glasses of a dark, red wine richly produced within their own castle's enclave.

Once the Duke and Duchess were bedded down in their lavish separate bed chambers, the house staff quickly extinguished fires throughout the immense estate, and all was quiet within less than half an hour.

"You know, Prescott, I have to say, this just gets creepier and creepier," whispered Thor, as he paused the tape. "I really doubt that even Charles Manson or Jim Jones had their heinous acts planned out so methodically, many years in advance."

"Jim Jones?" I replied, confused. "Who's Jim Jones?"

"Don't you ever listen to your car radio?"

"Rarely."

"Oh yeah, I forgot," said Thor, shaking his head, "and you've been out of the news loop for several days. Jones was this religious eccentric with a monumental following. He encouraged this mass murder-suicide of all his followers in his commune at Jonestown out in the jungle somewhere in Africa a few days ago."

"How?" I replied, thoroughly shocked.

"Cyanide poisoning. Dumped the stuff in these huge batches he'd mixed with Kool-Aid -- you know because everybody loves Kool-Aid," he sighed. "Something like three hundred kids and six hundred adults died. Insanely sick man."

"My God, that's appalling! What's with all these sick maniacs? The world is going to hell, Thor."

"More on Jim Jones another time," he nodded, grimacing. "Getting back to Cathy Martin, that's her voice on the tape, you're certain?"

"Oh yes, my dear Watson. No question about it," I replied darkly, as I pushed the play button.

Having donned her old handmaiden attire, Pamela easily slipped past the steward, who was mindlessly flirting with one of the chambermaids at the base of the servant's stairs. She then emptied the deadly nightshade's sweet juice into the decanter from which she knew the sleeping draughts would be drawn off that evening. The bedchambers were on the far side of the castle, well away from the noise, smoke, disgusting smells, illnesses, and idle confusion of the house staff. If either of the recipients of that evening's sleeping draughts called out in agony, fingers futilely clawing at their throats attempting to regain air, a strangled voice barely audible in the stillness, no one ever knew.

In fact, no one ever knew that the couple had been poisoned at all, since less than fifteen minutes after their actual death, a small plume of smoke began to curl out from beneath each mattress. One of the many tricks The Bull had taught Pamela was how to intricately weave a tiny nest of beech twigs, long pine needles and

fireplace matches, so that a slightly smoldering ring would gradually burst from within, flaming into a massive conflagration approximately twenty minutes after having been set. By which time the person responsible would be sitting many blocks away in a crowded tavern hoisting a tankard that was almost half quaffed, easily removing any suspicion of possible contribution to said crime.

Her horses were reluctant to slow a bit along the dark road, but Pamela had urged them to diminish their pace slightly at the crest of a large outcropping high above the castle grounds. Yellow flames began almost simultaneously licking at the window curtains in the royal couple's bedrooms, quickly overspreading each room with a vibrant glow. With a smile and light flick of the whip, she urged her horses to reprise their quick gait.

She was attired in one of her favorite whisper-thin, diaphanous negligees, her white voluptuous breasts spilling out of the neckline's low plunging cut, resting supinely in her husband's warm arms for well over an hour before news of the horrible fire and her parents' untimely demise had reached the Wexford estate.

Using many of The Bull's tricks of the trade had been extremely useful for Pamela for these several years, but The Bull himself was becoming more and more of a liability, she feared unfortunately. His nightly drunken sprees and whoring bouts with lewd, talkative mouths had of late caused concern for Pamela because of his boasts that he was raising his daughter, now discretely draped in duplicitous finery, to share equally in his chicanery. Sadly, Pamela knew the time had arrived that she

would need to remove him from her life.

The tape then went blank for its few remaining minutes before reaching the end leader. Thor stopped it before it began to unspool and hit rewind. We both sat silently for several minutes as the tape whirred in reverse.

"To be continued on reel number two," remarked Thor quietly. "Well, you can bet that takes us to the true story behind Chomp Martin's demise. That is, if we care to follow. Could have used more about those voluptuous breasts spilling out of her nightgown … or even those prominent nipples in the yellow dress."

I ignored Thor's remarks. "Obviously this is Cathy's long-range plan to rid herself of Janet Lynn's parents, burn their estate including her greenhouse to hide the crime and … wow," I sighed, thoroughly disgusted. "I don't think I can stomach listening to any more tonight, Thor. This whole thing is just so incredibly sick. I'm completely numb."

"Wouldn't she have gotten insurance money for the estate?" commented Thor. "Well, unless the investigators thought the parents might have burned down their own place and staged a double suicide. I don't think insurance companies will pay out to the beneficiaries in those cases. At any rate, I think we're both completely wrecked listening to any more of this tonight. I have a 6 a.m. call at the paper. In my basement I have over two hundred reel-to-reel tapes of music, interviews and God knows what other assorted crap I've lifted off the radio and tv for many years back. Newer stuff is on cassettes, obviously. Anyway, they're in plastic boxes with the info just scrawled on the box – nothing on the actual tape. Let's randomly swap these for a couple other tapes on the shelves just to play it safe. There are three full tapes of Mozart symphonies down there, so I'll give them new boxes and incorrect ID, put those at the end and these tapes in the Mozart boxes. Sound good? I might also take everything with me tomorrow. I'll let you know."

I nodded. I doubt we said more than a dozen words to one another after that other than establishing a two-ring phone signal that he would use when calling me. He nixed the idea of my trying to return to the storage facility to retrieve any other materials without his assistance. Since the roommate's bed was piled sky high with paperwork, I bedded down in a sleeping bag on Thor's living room couch and was asleep within minutes.

Thor's double phone ring startled me awake. I'd slept completely through his departure.

"Hey Prescott," he said quietly when I picked up, "things ok?"

"Yeah, thanks," I answered, stifling a yawn as I glanced at the clock. It was just after 7 a.m. He'd already been at work for over an hour I realized.

"That's good. I've got some, uh, not so great news for you," he began slowly.

"Bring it on."

"Detectives have now re-opened abrin poisoning as the probable cause leading to Hank's death. Seems the police lab techs made an error, and the state lab discovered the miscalculation of the strength or intensity or whatever of the powders in the vitamin capsules in Hank's dopp kit."

"Shit," I swore under my breath. "Leading back to me, I assume? Why doesn't anything link to the Double D for cryin' out loud? I mean, she's the one who was doing the horizontal mambo with him again on that trip as you've so eloquently described it."

"Well," Thor continued, taking a deep breath, "this brings us to parts two and three of the bad news, Prescott."

"I'm all ears," I sighed. I definitely had a major migraine coming on from last night's booze on top of an empty stomach.

"They had a warrant to search your place overnight and found …"

"Found my mom's stupid sugar bowl with the orange sugar under the floorboards, right? Let me guess, it contains abrin, correct?"

"Yep," Thor answered. "Ample supply in fact."

"Great. Originally intended to poison my parents of course, also courtesy of my hand probably. This can't possibly get any worse. And, of course I wasn't home so that looks even more suspicious."

"Well, actually it does get worse, Denise," Thor replied, exhaling loudly. "Dorothea Dixon was mowed down by a dark car, no headlights, in that storage facility parking lot late last night. No witnesses except the one guy on security said a small Buick or Chevy hatchback went roaring through there and exited the lot, probably just after the accident. Dorothea was killed instantly according to the report that came over the wire just now. And, for what it's worth at this point, are you ready for this: her full name was Brenda Dorothea Dixon."

"Good call on that one," I sighed. "Guess you win the brass ring."

"Story that came in over the wire this morning mentioned that her mother, Sallie Anne Dixon, was also killed in a hit-and-run accident that was attributed initially to the woman's intoxicated condition – that is, she'd walked right into the path of the car. That was over in Seymour, Ohio a few years back."

"I didn't remember the woman's name, but yeah, the story jives. This just keeps getting worse and worse, Thor."

"There was a rumor that the cops have an APB out for you right now for questioning, but nothing to that effect has warbled out over the police scanner so I think that's a bum lead to be honest with you. You need to move your car behind my carport, ok? It's not visible from the street that way. It's unlikely they'd be checking out my place, but we need you to be cautious."

"But eventually they'll find me ..." I replied, my voice

now shaking. "How do I get past all of this? I mean, this whole thing is nuts!"

"Looks like Thompson just assigned me a lengthy incoming that's holding on line four, so gotta trot," said Thor. "I'll call you back in a couple hours. In the meantime, move your car but then stay hidden at my place. Don't call anyone or answer the door either, ok? Oh, and your snarling in-laws have been calling nonstop and leaving messages here in the newsroom. You need to call them. You can feed me the dimes for the long distance when I get my bill. We'll listen to these other tapes when I get back home and try to figure out our next move from there. Oh, and don't worry, I promise to come armed with a pizza this time. *Tschüss*."

Predictably, my phone conversation with Hank's parents was curt, nasty, but blessedly short. His stepmom answered the phone, quickly passing the receiver over to Hank's dad, her hand covering the mouthpiece to momentarily deflect whatever choice expletive he'd undoubtedly uttered.

"What's the damned holdup, Denise?" Bill Taylor barked into the phone. "First we get a call from those idiot forensic people of yours down there in Indianapolis that Hank's body has finally been released for transport up here and then I get *another* call yesterday that now they've reopened the investigation with this nonsense about pending results from some second autopsy that's been ordered! Something about new evidence and they were trying to trace the wrong poison," he roared into the mouthpiece.

"I don't know any more than you do," I sighed. "I'm completely in the dark, Bill."

"Then, they're now saying you're a person of interest but looks to me like you're just freewheelin' it all over creation down there same's always. *What in the hell is going on*?" He punctuated each word in this last sentence as though jabbing his index finger into my chest.

"I'm not under arrest, Bill," I replied as evenly as I could muster. "And I'm in no better position to know what's going on than you are, I confess." Then after another moment, I frowned adding, "who told you that I was under suspicion again in the first place?"

"I dunno. What difference does it make? Some guy called. American, but sort of a funny accent. Said he was from the sheriff's office down there. I don't think he gave his name just said that we were supposed to call them if you turned up here in South Bend."

I remained silent. Who might have placed that call?

"What number did he leave?"

Bill yelled to his wife who must have raced over with the information. He quickly rattled it off. It was Tom Miller's pager number.

"Probably a gelatin preparation
that melts in the wound.
That's why you couldn't see anything on Carstairs.
The murderer was about ready to get rid of the body,
and he heard the knock and became frightened."

Basil Rathbone as Sherlock Holmes in

"Terror in the Night" (1946)

Chapter 25

When I jumped into my car something seemed odd, but in my haste precisely what didn't register. The deeply frozen ruts etched into the icy ground rattled my car more than I would have expected as I steered the few feet around the carport to wedge in behind the metal shed. I crawled over the console to exit on the passenger side. Any flat foot examining his neighborhood beat in detail would more than likely spot the vehicle in a heartbeat. Hopefully, the cops wouldn't be scouring the area.

I rustled through Thor's kitchen cabinets and unearthed a partial package of very stale saltines, a jar of peanut butter, a dented can of tomato soup that was rusting on one end, and a small unopened bottle of almond-stuffed green olives. I pitched the unopened soup into the garbage to thwart any possibility of salmonella for either of us. Helping myself to the saltines, I thickly slathered on the peanut butter and consumed them along with a sampling of olives. If nothing else the olives at least helped kill the musty sawdust flavor of the saltines.

Suddenly I heard a small bump near the back door. Cursing under my breath for having carelessly spread out my feast so visibly on Thor's table, I shot into the hallway on the opposite side from the door. My heart pounding in my ears, my back flat to the wall, completely motionless, I listened. I heard another series of small bumps that seemed even closer and sensed a shadow at Thor's back window. The butter knife I'd been using for the peanut butter straddled the open jar, plainly visible from the window. Firm evidence that someone was home. There were several short knocks on the door. I remained inert. More knocks followed. The doorknob rattled slightly but as usual, Thor had left it dead bolted. If someone tried to jimmy the lock it would take a while to get it open, I surmised. If they were alone, I could ease my way out the front door while they were occupied with that task I thought, my brain edging into overdrive.

"Denise," a man's voice whispered urgently, "let me in. Please. I'm here to help you. Honestly."

Tom Miller's voice. Damn it. Just like at the storage facility last night. That idiot had undoubtedly tracked my car with some other device that Thor hadn't discovered.

I made no reply, flattening myself even closer to the wall.

"Denise … about your parents being safe? You know that they're at Erskins House now, right? I know that someone on their staff talked with Thor last night. Denise, I made that happen. You have to believe me."

Well now, isn't that just peachy keen I swore under my breath. Your remarkable web of lies continues its outrageous embellishment. Which part did you make happen exactly? Calling my father and asking him to meet you over at the vacant Shriner's Lodge for the big art buy? Listening in on my mother's and my phone conversation? Obtaining the orange sugar for Janet Lynn to deliver at my parents' house? Possibly all three? Seems you'd have had the time for it, I seethed silently.

"I know you've now heard my name coupled with this whole … operation, but you have to trust that *I'm on your side*. I'm trying to help you. I don't know what I can say or do to convince you."

And why on earth would I believe you? Miraculously, I curtailed my outburst.

"Ok, look, I know you're in there. Just listen for a minute then, ok? This is important."

I remained silent.

"When you moved your car earlier did you notice that it was really difficult to steer?"

I froze. Yes, I had. Where was he going with this?

"Janet Lynn hotwired your car last night while you and Thor were listening to those tapes. You were so absorbed you didn't even notice. How did she know how to hotwire a car? Just another little legerdemain learned from Daddy Chomp, as you might imagine. And how do I know you were listening to that tape? Yes, I confess to bugging this place quite a while back. However, without Janet Lynn's knowledge. And also, since you and Thor disappeared into his basement, I don't know what you heard on those tapes. The basement wasn't wired."

Isn't that an invasion of privacy or illegally obtained evidence or something I said under my breath?

"Janet Lynn used your car to murder Dorothea Dixon last night, Denise," Tom stated bluntly. "One of the workmen spotted your car driving from the incident. He copied down enough of your license plate number and car's description to complete the report."

"What!" I exclaimed loudly, then quickly silenced myself.

"Your whereabouts were basically unknown – you hadn't even officially signed out of that warehouse which you may or may not remember -- and the authorities know you weren't home. Since there's significant left front damage to your car -- including a demolished headlight -- that knocked it completely out of alignment, that would strongly indicate your car's involvement. The sleet may obliterate any traces of the victim's blood on the front end, but I sure wouldn't count on that."

He was quiet for several moments waiting for a reaction, but I made no reply.

"Police theorize you poisoned your husband, Denise, then brutally ran down Dorothea Dixon in a fit of rage pitted against their continuing love affair – even without full documentation regarding your addled mental state from that shrink you and Hank were consulting. Now, are you going to let me in? I can help you with this, but only if you're willing to work with me."

No dice, Louie I said under my breath. What sounded like small tools began clicking at the deadbolt. I rushed through the exposed hallway to the front door. Sleet stung my face as I tore out of the house, racing blindly down the slippery street. I cut over to the front lawns hoping my footing would be slightly more secure. My lungs on fire by the time I'd run only a few blocks, I slowed down, panting with each progressively labored step. I heard no footsteps behind me. Hopefully I'd bought myself time. Time for what exactly was anybody's guess.

Still breathing hard, I moved into a thickly overgrown section of scrub pines with tangled undergrowth on one property between two houses set far apart. Suddenly, I was grabbed from behind and roughly thrown forward onto the frozen ground just as a volley of gunshots exploded overhead.

"Jesus, Prescott," snorted an angry Tom Miller in my ear as we both hit the dirt, my cheek stinging as it scraped the icy rut, "don't you *ever* listen to anyone's advice?"

Eyes wide with fear, I stared over my shoulder at him as several more shots rang out, ricocheting loudly in the frigid air.

"For Christ's sake stay down now, ok? If you stand up at this point, I refuse to be held responsible for anything that happens to you, *verstehe*?"

The sound of the gunshots had completely paralyzed me from action. My mind was numb. What in the hell was going on here?

"Do not move. Do I make myself completely clear?" he hissed in my ear, flipping me onto my back. He then grabbed my chin glaring at me sternly for confirmation. He held a small gun in his right hand, but it was not pointed at me.

I nodded in fear, shivering in the cold as I watched him. In something of a low squat, he started a slow crab walk away from me, disappearing into a thicket of tall weeds. Then dropping onto his elbows into the dirt, he crawled along military style, or at least what I perceived as military style from the rash of war movies I'd seen. I could just barely see him through the tangled overgrowth. Several more shots rang out, scudding along in the frozen dirt. Aimed in his direction or mine? I couldn't tell. I curled up slowly into a fetal position, shivering. Guiltily I fought my distrustful instincts to banish visions of that totally staged fistfight between Cary Grant's character and that of the hook-bearing villain Scobie in "*Charade*". This was real gunfire tearing up the ground in front of me, not some kind of weird pretext related to a Hitchcock thriller.

Suddenly Tom Miller stood up and started wildly zigzagging in the direction of the gunfire. I watched in horror through a veil of tall weeds as one shot went wildly to his left and then Tom began shooting as he dove over a large bush, completely obscuring him from my view as another shot rang out. I cringed in the dirt waiting for any other sounds. Nothing for several moments except that of a renewed staccato of sleet as the wind rattled the frozen grasses all around me. Cautiously, I strained for an unobstructed view, but there was nothing except frozen wasteland riddled with high weeds in all directions. Then I saw Tom stand up in the distance, slowly placing his gun inside his slightly open jacket, which he then rezipped to his neck. As he walked towards me, I rolled over to a crouch, never taking my eyes from his face. I still didn't know whether I should trust him, but right now I doubted I had any choice. Had he shot at that other person? Was that person dead? Momentarily incapacitated? He grabbed my elbow and motioned for me to stand up to which I very slowly complied, my eyes searching his face for any explanation regarding what had just happened. The man's face betrayed nothing, however. He had either just saved my life or pushed me further down the rabbit hole into an even more deadly situation.

"We're going back to Thor's house," he stated gruffly, flicking debris from my hair, "and don't try to run from me again. You end up in another jam? Trust me, next time I won't bother to lift a finger. C'mon before you freeze to death, you idiot."

The message was delivered without any of that boyish charm he'd exhibited at the hotel in Kokomo. He was genuinely upset. Not my fault, I muttered under my breath. You acted like a jerk … you jerk.

"What about your … um, opponent over there," I interjected instead, feigning far more bravura than I felt. "Are you just going to leave him over there … dead or whatever … and that just gets tallied along with my lengthening rap sheet?"

"Rap sheet? What are you, some kind of newspaper reporter or something?" he snorted, a flicker of mirth returning in a slightly raised eyebrow. "I'll call the police anonymously saying I thought I heard gunfire in this area.

"I'm sure he was just hoping to wing you, not kill you. You wouldn't do Janet Lynn too much good if you were dead – at least not yet. Your other buddy, T-Bone or Carl or whichever one rode over with you, is probably still awaiting discovery somewhere in that twenty-foot-high penguin promenade or whatever those Godawful things are that your dad constructed," he continued. "I just knocked the wind out of him. Somebody else orchestrated the, uh, final resolution as they say. You can check my hands for nitrate residue if you don't believe me. Gun I have belongs to your good friend Janet Lynn though … so not traceable back to me. Nice to be acquainted with people in high places, you know?"

I stared at him.

"Then you *are* working with Janet Lynn you … despicable monster!" I spat out, horrified.

"C'mon, Denise," he sighed. "For a reporter aren't you jumping to conclusions? Let's get back to Thor's house before somebody else breaks in over there, ok? Don't be fooled for one minute that those two delinquent twinkies were the only ones on this extended caper. God forbid. You're shivering like crazy. I really don't need to be dealing with a pneumonia case on top of everything else with you."

The fact that we'd left Thor's house wide open spurred me to action. Tom's firm grasp on my elbow guided me over uneven ice as we walked back in complete silence. Once inside, I threw on one of Thor's jackets and began cleaning up the remainder of my tasteless snack in the kitchen. Tom sampled several olives before I grabbed the jar away from him and thrust it into the refrigerator.

I sat down on one of the kitchen chairs just as Tom's beeper sounded. He glanced at the beeper number and then started dialing on Thor's phone. Long distance. Thor wouldn't like that on his bill. The entire, brief conversation sounded like German – or Pennsylvania Deutsch possibly -- so I had no idea what transpired. He then dialed the police and anonymously reported having thought he'd heard shots while driving through the area fifteen minutes prior.

"Ok," I began as calmly as possible when he'd finished, "what happens now? Don't you think you owe me at least something of an explanation?"

"Well, yeah, I guess that might be in order," he conceded.

Silence.

"No ... 'thank you for saving my life'? Not once, but twice, Ms. Prescott?"

"Ok," I replied icily. "Yes, thank you … twice. Now, explanation please. And the truth this time. Not some ridiculously smushed up version."

"Smushed? Tut, tut, Miss Torchy Blane - Reporter. I don't think that's a particularly good verb. What on earth would your editor-in-chief say?"

Arms folded, I exhaled loudly in exasperation. Torchy Blane? Nothing like being compared to a B-level 1930s wise-cracking reporter and mediocre detective movie series that hadn't seen the light of day in decades. Where on earth had he ever heard about Torchy Blane?

"All right. The abridged version. Everything I told you about my being hired by the Websters and investigating their daughter's probable disappearance at some point in the early 1970s is completely legitimate. Same as I told you up in Galena."

"Are you really Amish?"

"Yes, Denise, I'm really Amish," he replied with a wry, lopsided smile. "And just for the record, although the Amish shun military service, most sects train their young men how to shoot a gun with great accuracy and are taught how to do so at a very young age, I might add. Coyotes, wild dogs, foxes, bears, you name it, can infiltrate our chicken coops and barnyards easily, so accuracy with a firearm is essential."

I nodded curtly for him to continue. I noticed in his explanation he'd said: 'our chicken coops.' Freudian slip perhaps. The sleet had now picked up in intensity and rattled loudly off the windows.

"As I told you before, even after the mysterious Webster estate's fire, I kept on the case, eventually buying the place when it came up for sale."

"Why?" I asked, undoubtedly sounding snottier than I'd intended. "You don't strike me as the type wanting to restore the place to its prior luxury in order to impress the little wife, assorted kiddies and beer guzzling buddies with an avalanche of poshy summer parties."

"That's rather rude, Prescott."

I let it stand. Rude, yes, admittedly. Tally one point.

"Ok, so you bought the place for … whatever purposes … and are still working the case as they say. Seems to me that once Mr. and Mrs. Websters' deaths were formally closed by the state investigators as a tragic accidental incident, you wouldn't have had any authority to poke further into the entire affair. Especially since you're not even a real detective, according to my … um, sources, that is."

"Not all private investigators are registered, Denise," he replied. "Only if they're on the full-time payroll for a major corporation, or that of the local police, state or federal bureaus. That's probably why your friend Thor couldn't find me listed anywhere," he winked. "I knew he'd checked."

Ok, tally one point for the Amish cowboy, I admitted begrudgingly.

"I didn't keep on the case -- recognized as such by authorities or not," he continued, "at least not consistently, I have to admit. But it always haunted me because I was positive that the woman who had taken over the name Janet Lynn Webster was indeed an impostor. But I'd honestly hit a roadblock and had no idea where to turn next. Believe it or not, the name Cathy Martin never came into my conversations with the Websters. It wasn't until well after their deaths when I got that phone call from that buzzard Chomp Martin that any of this started to take shape. I still wasn't putting two and two together, however, until I saw your ad in the LaFarge Sentinel or whatever. And even then, I did a lot of research on you before I bothered to contact you at the newspaper that day. I wasn't sure it was worthwhile to get involved … just with contacting you, that is… not, er, anything else."

Despite myself, I felt my cheeks burning while trying to maintain my composure.

"So why exactly did the supposed impostor Janet Lynn give me your name as the man who'd broken her heart at the University of Wisconsin? That still doesn't make a lot of sense to me."

"Maybe something of a joke. The old boo hoo hoo, my best friend took off with my guy, routine. I cried my eyes out and I don't ever want to talk about that woman again. Cue the violins. But I doubt she expected you to go searching me out, so she messed up there."

Something about this explanation didn't connect within my exhausted brain but I let it slide.

"So, do you know if Dorothea Dixon is Cathy Martin's sister?"

"I'd figured that out a while back," he nodded. "She had unexpectedly reappeared in Janet Lynn's life. A treacherous force in her own right."

"The wicked witch of the east in cahoots with the wicked witch of the west," I mumbled.

"Huh?"

"Never mind. Go on." You know about Torchy Blaine, but not "*The Wizard of Oz*". Weird.

"Dorothea Dixon demanded being a part of her half-sister's path to unlimited wealth or threatened to expose the true roots of sweet little sis. And, she had the information to make that fall from grace a loud thud to be sure. My guess is that Dorothea was continually demanding more money to keep her mouth shut. Extortion can be pretty nasty, especially among family members, right? Specific details are not necessary in my opinion. Let's face it: Dorothea had the goods on dear old Cathy and would certainly have inherited the relentless predatory mindset to use that devious information without a second thought."

The phone rang two times, stopped, and then began ringing again. Thor calling me from work. Crap.

"Um, hi," I answered, swallowing.

"Prescott, what in hell's going on?" he bellowed. "I gave simple instructions, yes? I tried to call you not once, not twice, but *three* times maybe twenty minutes ago and there was no answer! And don't tell me you were taking a twenty-minute shower! Then, I tried again two minutes ago and this time I get a busy signal. I thought we'd agreed that you were going to stay put and not use the phone. Did that request fall out of your malfunctioning grey matter?"

"There've been a few … um, developments," I replied warily.

"What kind of developments? Oh, wait, let me guess. Don't tell me that charming Wisconsin badger is panting breathlessly over your writhing naked body slathered in whipped cream on my kitchen floor?"

"Ok, c'mon Thor, listen. This is really serious. My car was hotwired and then used to mow down Dorothea Dixon last night while we were in your basement listening to those tapes. There's all kind of damage to the left front end – I mean, the thing doesn't even steer in a straight line!"

"How'd you come to that conclusion? I mean, how could you possibly know that it was *your* car specifically? Maybe you just picked up a nail in my driveway and you have a flat tire. You could have picked that up from my idiot metal-collecting neighbor. There's nothing to implicate your vehicle as a means in a homicide. Nothing to that effect has come over the scanner this morning. I can vouch for that. What they have in the way of a vehicle description doesn't necessarily even fit your car."

"My car wasn't steering right when I moved it. It's definitely not just a flat."

"Ok, if that's true then just who hotwired it? Your blue-eyed badger buddy?"

Crap, I suddenly thought to myself. Why had I believed Tom Miller when he said that Janet Lynn had driven my car or that there was even a police report on it? He'd done it himself! If he could shoot a gun he sure as heck could hotwire a hatchback Buick and drive over a defenseless woman who was frantically running in an icy parking lot in the middle of the night! Malfunctioning grey matter. Yep, Thor had called it.

"Are you there, Prescott?" he shouted in my ear.

"Yeah, I'm here. Ok, ok," I replied weakly, refraining from looking at Tom, "I really don't know where anything stands at this point. I'm just … confused."

"Ok, well, just so you know, I took all three tapes and my tape player with me this morning. Listened to that other tape before I clocked in at the desk. We were right about the plans to dump Daddy Chomp and sweet big sis Brenda Dorothea Dixon. Chomp's demise is almost exactly the way Cathy envisioned it. Looks as though she intended to poison the old man to immobilize him then leave him to freeze to death in his cabin which, if I'm not mistaken, is exactly how that one played out. But it seems that Brenda Dorothea's demise didn't quite work out the way planned. Oh, and there's a male accomplice, also. Not her husband Sir What's-his-name either, but one of those lusty kitchen wastrel guys or whatever she called 'em. Long story. I'll tell you about that one when I see you. The tapes are locked down in security here. Not exactly Fort Knox, but it's sure as hell safer than my basement."

"I think there's a chance that your place is bugged, Thor," I hissed loudly, darting a quick glance at Tom. "Not the basement, but I don't know about your phone …"

Tom shook his head theatrically mouthing the word

'not anymore' as he wandered over to the refrigerator and helped himself to more olives.

"Oh, that's just great! Is this the dreamy-eyed badger's handiwork? Tell him he's got just over three hours before I get off my shift here to yank that shit out of there or I'm clamping his charming carcass with a lawsuit the size of Texas!"

With that, a master of both metaphor and unbridled alliteration, Thor slammed down the phone in my ear.

"Tell him to include the olives on my tab," Tom winked, as he returned the jar to the fridge with fewer than a dozen olives remaining. "I always make it a practice to repay my debts. Keeps the clientele happy. In the meantime, grab your coat. We're heading back over to that storage place to pick up the rest of that information before the roads get any icier."

"*We*?" I frowned.

"Yeah, you and me, Prescott. That makes we. In my truck as well. Your car can't even move two feet right now. Obviously, Dorothea Dixon had expected to retrieve the material from the warehouse last night and our con artist friend Janet Lynn figured as much. Unfortunately for Dorothea, it looks like she led Janet Lynn right to the hiding spot, but from what I saw in Hank's storage unit, crammed with all your dad's huge uh, what do you call that stuff … displays, I guess ... she's still going to need your assistance to locate it. We need to grab the evidence before she plays the ultimate royal flush against our flimsy pair of deuces and destroys your credibility."

"I didn't know the Amish played cards," I replied curtly, nervously conjuring up a slight smile. "Sounds so … corrupt for such a God-fearing sect."

He shrugged, flashing one of his better disarming smiles.

"So that *was* you in the unit," I stated. "Did you shoot T-Bone?"

"No comment regarding that. But, hey, about playing cards, there's a lot about us you don't know," he laughed, then added seriously, "now, c'mon, get your coat, Prescott. Let's blow this joint while we're still able."

The roads were almost impassable. Tom's truck tires balked, then skidded sideways numerous times, as we inched our way to the storage building. Against the unnerving pelting of sleet now mixed with snow ricocheting off the windshield, he questioned me regarding information that would bring down Janet Lynn's house of cards. Other than the pages with our fingerprints and black stained hands stretched out towards the camera with our weird, contorted facial expressions, I honestly couldn't think of any truly incriminating details that would hold up in court. This wouldn't prove that the woman was a murderer, only that she'd illegally assumed the identity of another woman who had apparently disappeared. Those dreadful stories on the tape very likely played into all of it but only if one was able to piece it all together. Tom asked for a brief synopsis, but I begged off, stating that the content was too disgusting.

The sleet changed over to thick, diagonal curtains of heavy wet snow as we arrived at the storage facility. Tom parked the truck close to the entrance, marked by a battered sign that clearly designated the area a no parking zone. Just let them try to tow me he swore under his breath, winking at me as he killed the engine. There were only a few cars, parked far from the entry and scattered throughout the large lot, all heavily coated with ice.

Struggling against the wind, we stamped snow off our boots as we entered the large foyer. The building appeared to be completely deserted. Unlike my visit with T-Bone, there were no guards stationed along the walls, no one manning the front desk. The interior was lit by very dim emergency lighting, widely spaced along the ceiling. I realized after a moment that I could easily see puffs of my breath as well. Heat must be turned off. I was now shaking, both from the cold as well as fear. Tom put his right arm around my shoulders and pulled me close to his side.

"I'm going to take a different set of hallways to get over there to Hank's unit," he whispered in my ear. "This'll take a little longer and we'll be almost completely in the dark I imagine. You okay with that?"

I refrained from looking at his face but having no reasonable alternative, nodded. Silently moving through an unmarked service door, his arm tightened around me slightly as he murmured something about how it felt natural to have me this close. We continued down another dark hallway, lit only by the occasional ice-covered, grimy skylight lurking high above. Tom gently backed me into the wall, took my face in both of his hands and kissed me deeply. Then, brushing my hair over my shoulder he kissed me again, his hand behind my head, holding me tightly against him. Add knowing how to kiss and completely disarm a skeptical woman with knowing how to use a gun and possibly hotwire a car to this man's list of diverse accomplishments. But I offered no resistance to either the kiss or when he took my hand. Safer to just play along, Prescott, I warned myself.

We wound through a maze of hallways until getting back to the wing I recognized from yesterday. My senses fully alert, no voices, shadows or footsteps were discernable. Frowning, I glanced at Tom, but he put his fingers to his lips, shaking his head slightly. The door to Hank's unit was still wide open, same as yesterday. The same dusty security light dimly illuminated my father's bizarre panorama of oversized creations and soaring piles of his dumpster acquisitions. I pulled out my small penlight as we entered the Hersey's Kiss sculpture.

When we got to the middle of the Kiss, however, all the mushrooms had been completely flattened, their contents removed. Only the flimsy flooring remained, along with no more than a half dozen ripped pages that had fallen out from one of my old scrapbooks, peeking out from under a former mushroom. Dismayed, I picked up the scattered pages I'd harbored for over half my life. Whatever had remained under the mushrooms had vanished.

"Looks as though either Dorothea or Janet Lynn beat us to the booty," sighed Tom, whispering, appearing genuinely deflated. "My guess is that when Dorothea Dixon was killed in the parking lot here last night, she'd already stuffed all this evidence into a small suitcase or something. Then Janet Lynn runs her over in the parking lot after she leaves the building. Took, well, everything."

I sat down hard on the flimsy chicken wire and wood flooring of the Kiss. Without any evidence, my chance of disproving my involvement in either my husband's or Dorothea Dixon's murders was next to nil, forget shedding evidence on Cathy Martin's sordid history. After a moment, Tom sat down next to me.

I had thought I'd been good friends with Cathy Martin all those years back. She'd turned away from our friendship almost the moment we'd hit high school, with no explanation whatsoever. What had I done to her to warrant this kind of treatment? Not one thing came to mind. I did my best to blur the lurid headlines blaring the motives of a vindictive wife – me – repeatedly scorned by her husband and his lover, retaliating by viciously poisoning one and mercilessly mowing down the other. In its place flamed up our senior class pictures in *The Argonaut.* I reflected momentarily on the only other picture in our yearbook of a sour-faced Cathy Martin, her Polaroid camera -- looking like a square white squirrel I'd thought at the time -- nestled in the crook of her arm, pictured with the three other winning science club exhibitors.

Cathy Martin with her Polaroid camera. Her Polaroid swinger camera, an instantaneous rage that hit every department store shelf in the mid-60's. Black and white pictures instantly developed in less than thirty seconds and costing only $19.95. Point and click. Nowadays it was a much pricier full-color model to be found in those cutesy ads with James Garner and Mariette Hartley. What could be easier? I could still hear that stupid Swinger jingle that ran constantly on television with Ali McGraw strolling down the beach shooting random pictures of well-oiled, hot-looking studs with bulging muscles who were all probably queer I now realized.

"Ok, so what if," I began slowly, keeping my voice very low, "Cathy took pictures of her victims. After they were dead, that is."

"Huh?" frowned Tom, also whispering. "Man, now that's a gruesome thought. How could she do that anyway? Wouldn't Kodak or those drug store snoops find that kind of stuff when they developed the negatives and call the cops? That's pretty serious."

"Do you know what a Swinger camera was? This would be starting around 1965. You know, instantly developed pictures – lot of tv ads back then."

"No electricity in Amish homes, so obviously no television," shrugged Tom. "Also, the Amish never allow their pictures to be taken – scripture states we shun graven images of God and all that. The family I moved in with were Mennonite so yeah, they had electricity and could drive cars, long as the cars were all black, but they only listened to news reports on the radio. No television. Although allowed, Mennonites rarely posed for photos as well. Anyway, what's your point?"

"Well, during the years that Cathy and I were friends, we took pictures of all kinds of dumb stuff and had it developed so we'd each have a copy. I think I may have told you about that. It was this Kodak two-for-one deal or something. We both had photo albums and scrapbooks that were almost exactly alike."

"Ok. What kind of pictures again?"

"You know, stupid failed stunts we'd attempted like pretending we were Tarzan or Zorro, burns, scabs, weird moles, mosquito bites connected like dot-to-dots, broken toes, Cathy's broken ankle, our fingerprints and blackened fingers. I dunno, just all kinds of dumb stuff."

"And how exactly do you make a leap of faith from those innocent photos to that of photographing one's victims? Or do you mean, that she posed with their corpses after she'd killed them? That's a stretch, Prescott."

"I know, I know. But hear me out. I just thought of this. What evidence could Dorothea Dixon possibly have concealed from Cathy Martin?"

"Well, maybe she was in on some of these murders. Shot the pictures or something? Or maybe just knew about their existence. Wasn't involved personally. Dorothea, I mean," offered Tom. "Cathy could have concealed her notebooks and tapes that contained her tales of horror as well as photographic evidence of having actually implemented some of these crimes over at Dorothea Dixon's house for a number of years."

"Where? How?" I shot back quietly. We were actually thinking along the same lines, but I wanted his explanation.

"Who knows? Attic space behind a forgotten panel in a bedroom closet maybe? Basic Nancy Drew stuff. Anyway, she certainly didn't expect Dorothea to paw through her stuff. But we have to assume that Dorothea did anyway and shot pictures of everything, then returned the original items to the attic. I mean, after all, these two bitches were as crafty as heck," shrugged Tom. "And then all hell breaks loose when Dorothea starts blackmailing Janet Lynn once the Fowler marriage is announced."

"Supposedly Dorothea was one of the first women who graduated from the University of Notre Dame -- with honors to boot – so she was no slouch in terms of intelligence."

"Ok," exhaled Tom, "so, are these ... hypothetical ... pictures of corpses to be found in an album or just loose?"

"Assuming we're looking for pictures, they're probably in an album," I replied slowly. "Cathy would just go into a trance staring at our old photo albums for hours on end, thoroughly mesmerized."

"What about this?" asked Tom, picking up a small orange binder he'd discovered under a section of the flattened mushroom covering that was close by. "It looks as though whatever pictures it may have contained were already torn out."

He handed me the binder. One I'd never seen before. The same plain black photo corners we'd always used to mount our photos had survived, although some were dangling by a mere thread, but whatever photos had been in the album had vanished. And, most interestingly, they'd also left a discolored outline indicating the pentagonal shape that had occupied the space. Without question, the exact size of an early Polaroid camera's output. Right idea, Prescott, I heard Thor's voice in my head, but unfortunately, too late, Kemosabe.

"Crap," I muttered.

"Let's assume Dorothea pulled those pictures from the album – assuming they existed in the first place -- and hid them somewhere," he stated. "She rushes to the parking lot, knowing that more than likely, Cathy or Janet Lynn or whatever the hell you want to call her, is going to be out there and intends to grab everything at gunpoint. Dorothea has everything concealed in a large satchel. With me so far?"

I nodded.

"But instead of just forcing Dorothea to hand over all this stuff, Janet Lynn runs her down. Then she grabs the backpack, jumps back in her car -- well, make that *your* car -- and heads off, assuming she has everything – I mean, why would she question it? Too much to check over in a dark parking lot next to a corpse, right? Limps your car back over to Thor's house, one of her thugs gives her a ride to the airport and she's headed back to New York City on the red eye before you can say Jiminy Cricket. Arrives in time for a late-night highball with the hubby.

"But she doesn't realize until later that she doesn't have the correct photos," continued Tom, grinning, eagerly adding on to this explanation. "It's just reprints of what she's already collected. See how this could fit together?"

Had Tom's reiteration of this potential scenario flowed too perfectly, too tightly choreographed to be genuine? Just how easily had he found that binder in the first place? Something smells stinky in Denmark as my mom would have said.

"So, if that's true, then the photos are probably still here somewhere, Tom," I added quietly. "Dorothea was rushing to throw everything into a satchel. Chances are they're hidden somewhere in this structure. She wouldn't have taken the time to hide them elsewhere … at least I wouldn't think so."

A low buzzing sounded. Tom's pager. He pulled it out of his jacket and the screen was visible to me for a split second. There were three letters: JaL.

"Jakob," shrugged Tom, glancing at me once he'd realized I'd seen the image. "Jakob … Lehmann. Guess he'll have to wait awhile for a call back."

No, I seethed within, determined to keep my face completely placid. Not Jakob, Tom. Those letters stand for Janet Lynn, you liar. If the Amish don't have electricity, cars, radios, or televisions, they sure as hell don't have phones. I suspected he already knew everything about those missing photos and had led me towards this conclusion like a trusting little puppy trotting after a promised treat. Realizing her error, Janet Lynn would have phoned him when she'd gotten back to New York late last night and sent him to find me and the real goods.

Had my car been used to murder Dorothea or had Tom made all of that up? Thor claimed he hadn't known anything about a BOLO for me and he never missed a beat on the newsroom's scanner. And what's more, could all my colleagues have missed it? Impossible. No, that had been Tom's statement exclusively, along with his phone call up to Hank's parents where he'd left his pager number. After all, what was one more lie? I was now in a deserted building with an armed man with whom I'd foolishly slept just two short nights ago – a man who worked for a serial-killing female maniac with no conscience whatsoever. Once those other photos were discovered – whatever they showed -- my usefulness was history. By coercing my battered self-esteem, Tom Miller had easily broken through my usual barriers. It was imperative I remain outwardly calm.

"Maybe you could look for a better flashlight," I remarked. "This penlight is worthless. Would be a lot easier if we could see. That small room down the hall looks like a janitor's closet."

"We've got to find them," stated Tom firmly. "Everything depends on that."

Indeed it does, I said to myself, forcing myself to smile. Oh yes, Tom, indeed it does.

"In his whole diabolical career,
the police have never been able to pin anything on him.
Yet, show me crime without a motive,
robbery without a clue, murder without a trace,
and I'll show you Giles Conover."

Basil Rathbone as Sherlock Holmes in

"The Pearl of Death" (1944)

Chapter 26

Right about now, Sherlock Holmes would have brilliantly deduced the exact spot where those pictures were hidden. However, my deductive impulses were typically closer to those scattershot ramblings of Dr. Watson's than Holmes' regrettably. While Tom was searching for the flashlight, I poked furiously along the lining of the Hershey's Kiss, but only succeeded in dislodging several bits of *pâpier maché* which fluttered like confetti to the ground.

I thought back to the phone call Tom made from Thor's house, where he claimed he'd been speaking with his young Amish friend, Jakob. It had been in rapid-fire German or possibly Pennsy Deutsch, which was almost the same thing to my dreadfully uninformed ear. Back in Nashville people claimed that Chomp Martin's thick foreign accent was German, helping fuel the rumors that Chomp had been a Nazi mercenary during the war. There was also speculation that he'd been one of the notorious

Werewolves butchering Germans as well as Allied soldiers at the behest of Hitler as the Allies and Soviet troops' stranglehold on Germany became evident during those last several months of the war. You wouldn't have thought that the Nazis would have needed mercenaries I'd remembered thinking all those years back. But assuming that was true -- my memories of hearing the man speak were extremely faint, I conceded -- then Cathy would most likely also speak the language fluently. I mean, why wouldn't she?

I glanced overhead, shining my weak pen light higher along the walls of the aluminum Kiss. My dad had positioned his signature inclusion of all his works as usual: the little brass mailbox stamp holder just above my head near the end of the Kiss' paper pull. Haphazardly, the internal end of the Kiss' paper strip was taped to one side of the mailbox, presumably to hold it in place.

My thoughts drifted back to yesterday's mail, with that unsigned card's envelope boasting such an odd array of mismatched stamps yet emphasizing that I remember the stamps. And then mentioning the Kiss … but why capitalized? Other than for the chocolate candy itself, the only time I'd ever seen the word capitalized was for my dad's sculpture. And finally, there was the V for Victory. Victory for … a kiss? That made absolutely no sense. V for Victory, though. A World War II slogan to be sure, but something else? Slowly an image began to form. V for Victory was the imprint on the matchbook within which microfilm had carefully been concealed in the movie "*Sherlock Holmes in Washington*". Basil Rathbone had stated affirmatively "the man who has it doesn't know he has it."

Was there a chance that Hank had sent the card to me from New Orleans just before he died? *"Sherlock Holmes in Washington*" was the only Basil Rathbone movie he'd ever liked. Or if not Hank, possibly Dorothea knowing her days were probably numbered once Hank had been murdered? I doubted I would ever know the answer to that question.

Holding the orange binder by one end, I jumped carefully, hoping to keep the entire Kiss from violently shaking, then swatted at the stamp holder like a piñata high over my head. It dislodged after three attempts, falling with a solid clunk at my feet. As was usual for my dad's handiwork, the hinged lid had been firmly taped down. Shining the pen light closer however, the tape looked slightly crooked, possibly resealed. I nudged it slightly and the top popped open easily.

A Wrigley's PlenTpak of spearmint gum was wedged inside the stamp holder. I carefully pulled out a stick and unwound it. A slender piece of microfilm with square sprocket holes down the middle was neatly folded within. Even in the gloom I could tell there were several tiny pictures on each frame. Not a matchbook, but certainly a V for Victory, nonetheless.

Trembling, I refolded the microfilm in the silver gum wrapper, easing it back into the white honeycombed wrappers. There were seventeen white wrappers. I cautiously pulled out another piece and discovered another strip of microfilm. Two other samples yielded pieces of gum. I correctly repositioned all the silver wrappers and nestled the PlenTpak down into the bottom of my purse. Then, pressing the hinged lid of the brass mailbox until it clicked shut, I placed it to one side. I doubted that Tom would have noticed the mailbox's original position inside the Kiss and besides, there was no way I could reach that high.

I could only assume that Dorothea had taken the photos from that orange binder at a much earlier date and shot the microfilm herself. Then, wisely she continued to move the original pictures from place to place so that Janet Lynn would assume those were still the only copies. The whereabouts of those original Polaroid snapshots was anybody's guess. Maybe Janet Lynn had finally destroyed them never suspecting that copies existed until she somehow realized she'd been duped after having killed Dorothea with my car.

Shuffling footfalls warned me that Tom Miller was beginning to paw his way through the Kiss entrance. The flickering beam of a long workman's torch preceded Tom's arrival, indicating that his search had met with success.

"Any luck?" he asked.

"Not a thing," I replied, feigning complete innocence as I shook my head. "I patted all along the insides and created this sort of rain of paper bits that's all over now but I'm at a complete loss where Dorothea might have hidden those pictures in a hurry."

"Well, you know," Tom began slowly, smiling at me, "she might not have hidden them in any kind of hurry, actually. We're just kind of assuming that don't you think?"

"Meaning?" Do *not* shake, Prescott, I scolded myself.

"I mean, would she really have known that Janet Lynn was hot on her heels? Maybe she'd had a lot more time to hide those photos … you know, she'd done it days or even weeks ago."

I shook my head slowly, trying to act as though I was honestly considering this possibility. Locking its weak yellow beam in place, Tom set down the flashlight to one side and then pulled me into a slow embrace, his chin resting on my head as he continued speaking. His voice resonated deeply in his chest; I could only hope it helped mask the terrified thudding of my heart.

"I think it's safe to assume that most of those photos are still right here, Denise. Right here under our very noses, don't you think? And well … we have at least a little time for ourselves once we've located them, right?" His fingers gently raised my chin, his eyebrows lifting slightly. Definitely green eyes, Thor, not blue.

I nodded, my ear rubbing against his jacket. Stay calm I shrieked within. According to folklore, the fox can always smell when the rabbit is terrified. Do not let this man discover that pack of gum whatever you do. After a few moments, he began slowly unzipping my coat. I stepped away, somehow managing a flirtatious smile that Scarlett O'Hara would have envied, as he gently removed my jacket and tossed it to the ground. He then removed his own leather jacket and theatrically threw it on top of mine. Sweater buttons were next. First mine, then his own, once again lightly thrown, next to our coats. His mouth warmly on mine, he murmured an apology about having to leave me so abruptly at the trucker's motel, then kissed me deeply again. After we found those pictures today, we'd have all kinds of luxurious time together, right? A whole future lay before us. He was hoping that I was looking forward to those days as much as he. Warm flesh melted into warm flesh, his mouth moving slowly onto my neck, then to my shoulders, his fingers seductively exploring further with deliciously slow caresses. The irrational part of me willed him to continue; the rational part of me coldly calculated the distance between my arm and the workman's torch resting slightly beyond my reach.

It's Oscar time, Prescott! Hullo? Where are you? I could hear Thor's loud stage whisper hissing in my ear.

Tom spread out our coats and sweaters further as we lay down upon them. Something clicked in my head as I remembered that gruesome Lady Pamela story where Pamela and Sir Wexford stretched out in abandon on Lady Isobelle's so-called frigid finery. We were both now dressed in flannel shirts and blue jeans. No gun holster was visible. Meaning, it was probably in the pocket of his coat. And did it have real bullets or blanks? I was theorizing at this point, given what may well have been a completely staged gunfight outside Thor's house, that both those guns were firing blanks at the time. That didn't necessarily mean the remaining bullets within Tom's gun chamber were also blanks, however. Everyone in the newsroom had heard about the controversial gory Russian Roulette scenes in the movie *The Deer Hunter* that was set to open sometime in the next couple months. At close range even blanks sometimes had a bit of a kick, depending on the gun, especially if there was paper wadded into the chamber with the hollow bullet.

Tom pulled away and stared at me. Obviously, my attentiveness had swayed much too far from the present.

"Penny for your thoughts?" he commented, playfully kissing the tip of my nose.

"Guess I just had this … well, weird sensation that we might roll over on your gun … and it would go off or something," I replied, feigning a light laugh.

Tom moved back further, leaning on his elbow, his mouth curved into a curious smile.

"Rather an odd concern during such a heated, passionate moment, don't you think?" he chuckled. "I mean, is this how you Indiana girls react in the middle of an embrace? Worrying that the guy's gun is loaded and aimed at your head?"

There was an obvious sexual as well as chilling innuendo implicit in that sentence that I fought to ignore.

He sat up, folding his legs Indian style, and pulled over his coat. As I suspected, the gun was in his pocket. He dumped three bullets from the chamber, then, after twirling the barrel to show the chamber was completely empty, handed it over to me.

"Ah, yes, silly me, of course. Nothing to worry about," I smiled, setting the gun down between us. Nothing except this wasn't the same gun he'd used in that fight. That one hadn't been a .38 caliber snub nose pistol. Of that I was certain. Hank had bought a snub nose a few months into our marriage and kept it in his glove compartment. He'd insisted that he might need it when he left some of his late-night meetings in rougher territories.

Feigning acceptance of Tom's explanation, however, I apologized and forced myself to nestle back into his arms, whispering it would be so much more intimate without that bright flashlight. The yellow beam was so distracting, I murmured. Once darkness enveloped us, I grabbed the torch from his hands and struck him sharply on the side of his head. He slumped forward but I knew I'd only slightly stunned him with a glancing blow at best. I threw Tom's coat over my shoulders, simultaneously thrashing through his coat pockets to extract his truck keys, grabbed my purse, and raced out the same side entrance as yesterday. There was a pleasant wood smell mixed in with the leather coat that I fought to ignore. Deep within his inside pocket I could feel the other gun. Hopefully, the safety was on.

After glancing nervously around the parking lot, fully expecting to see Tom, blood oozing from his head, staggering after me, I walked quickly over to Tom's truck, flipping through the jungle of keys on his key chain. Why in the heck would an Amish detective have so many damn keys? Hank would have had a fit, complaining all that weight would strip the ignition. The snow had let up almost completely. A sliver of fog-shrouded sun was attempting to poke through the clouds, most likely the harbinger of yet another incoming storm rather than signaling the completion of the current one. As I slipped the key into the lock, I felt a small sharp ping like a bee sting ricochet off my cheek. Wasps in the middle of November? No way. I tensed, glancing in the direction of the sting. As I tried to unlock the truck door, everything around me suddenly became blurred and began to tilt. An immense drain began spinning beneath my feet. I opened the door and threw in my purse but as I tried to step up into the truck it had bizarrely moved farther away. My legs felt like logs refusing to move. The sickeningly sweet taste of a substance resembling Tang thickened my tongue. I attempted to cry out, but my mouth was filled with balls of cottony orange cyclamates. Within a moment I felt myself blacking out … slowly spiraling to the ground.

"A monster, Watson. With the chest of a buffalo and the arms of a gorilla. His particular method of murder is back breaking and it's always the same – a third lumbar vertebra."

Basil Rathbone as Sherlock Holmes in

"The Pearl of Death" (1944)

Chapter 27

I awoke sprawled on my stomach over a rough, cold stone floor. My ribs ached even when attempting to take a shallow breath. Maybe I'd been thrown in here and landed on my ribs -- even cracked one or two of them. I remembered nothing about my journey to this place but felt raw and bruised everywhere. Weak light filtered in from a small, barred window, rimmed with thick dirt-encrusted frost, high above me, but little of that beam found its way down to my battered body. I lay motionless in a swirling darkness. In agony, I moved myself over to my right side, then pushing up on both arms, gradually pulled myself to a sitting position, attempting to stifle the groans from deep within my chest. I was breathing hard, almost panting, trying to dull the painful spasms shooting from my ribcage. The taste of Tang was still thick on my tongue and down my throat. Swallowing even a small glob of mucus required complete concentration. An old Army blanket lay nearby. Shivering, I wrapped it slowly around myself, inhaling sharply with each movement.

The room was round -- a wide stone turret spiraling up into the blackness, disappearing high above the filthy window. An old silo situated on some abandoned farm property no doubt. I realized that I was only a few inches from the wall and painfully dragged myself over, forcing myself to prop my back against it and look over my prison cell – for there was no question that this was a cell.

Others had been held here I realized after a few moments. The stench of old excrement and decay filled my nostrils. Possibly from animals but somehow, I doubted it. High above to my right, a large, collapsible metal stairway tethered well beyond my reach gradually became visible as my eyes adjusted to the gloom. That's probably ground level, I thought dully. This was no animal pen. It was a human one. Any small rodents tunneling in would have been able to reverse course rather than become trapped within this stone tomb.

Were my predecessors' remains scattered about within these walls? And how many were there? Had Janet Lynn herself been imprisoned down here? And if so, how long had they kept that poor girl penned here like an animal, probably drugged, and starving to death? How long had it taken Janet Lynn to die? Had they tortured her for information? Information that would have been essential to Cathy Martin's complete metamorphosis? Falsely promising Janet Lynn her freedom after she had conveyed various tiny details from her childhood that only she would have known prior to Cathy's walking into her life that fateful day our freshman year at Columbus High?

Other than those reel-to-reel tapes of Cathy's, recorded when she was a young teen and indicative of nothing truly suspicious other than a girl's unusually lurid imagination, there was absolutely no proof of any criminal activity whatsoever on Cathy's part. And Tom, that handsome, renegade Amish bastard had somehow managed to slither through the situation completely unscathed.

There was no reason for either Cathy or Tom to return here to obtain anything further from me. Yet. They now had the last remaining vestiges of any pictures, notebooks, tapes, or scrapbooks that might have pointed an incriminating finger at Cathy Martin's true origins, or her calculated, venomous ascension to power. Completely unlike their capture and probable torture of Janet Lynn, they had already acquired everything they needed from me unless for some unfathomable reason, they hadn't found the microfilm in that Wrigley's PlenTpak in my purse that I'd thrown into Tom's truck. I was just here waiting to slowly starve to death while in too much pain to fend off the inevitable feeding frenzy of an army of rats, voraciously gnawing on my flesh. Would Cathy fabricate some kind of bizarre suicide note to be found in my apartment? Confessing that due to outrage at my husband's deception I'd poisoned him and subsequently mowed down his lover Dorothea Dixon in the warehouse parking lot? And now, in remorse for having killed them both, I was intending to poison myself at some undisclosed location. Although I was still very groggy, I could completely visualize that note – written on the scented, dusty rose stationery my in-laws had given me at Hank's and my wedding.

So many difficulties from my past were laughable right now, although my ribs hurt far too much to laugh. Maybe poison was continuing to seep slowly into my brain and would shut down all my organs within the next couple of days. If this meant that the pain from my broken ribs and the sharp teeth and tearing nails of the rats were dulled, that would be a blessing. After a few weeks, all that Cathy and Tom would have to do was come back here, stuff my remains into a duffle bag, drag that to some remote location down near any of the hundreds of overgrown creek beds to be found in southern Indiana and dump it out. Cathy had even written about that in one of our stories from so many years back. Ironically, I remembered contributing my own thoughts to that ghoulish tale!

Larger animals would continue with the scavenger nibbling where the rats had left off. *Fait accompli.* Sherlock Holmes' nemesis Irene Adler would have been so proud of you, Cathy. You've succeeded completely in acquiring unprecedented wealth, intelligence, status in society both as an accomplished socialite as well as a business investment advisor to a major corporation. Along the path you've mastered those usual hackneyed accolades awarded certain females of extraordinary beauty, poise, and grace … all honed by your relentlessly Satanic, malevolent mind.

For a long time, I just stared at the filthy window high above me, my breathing shallow, attempting to lessen the pain in my ribcage. I drifted in and out of consciousness and awoke shivering each time, further tightening the Army blanket. Maybe a day had passed now. Or maybe I'd just imagined it had passed. Had I been looking up at that window and noticed that it was completely black for a few hours? Maybe. Anything was possible. I wiggled my fingers slightly. They seemed completely numb. Either from the poison or the damp, penetrating cold. I fell asleep for what may have been a longer stretch for the window was now shrouded in complete darkness except for the bright moon's rays filtering like a brownish dust down into my cell. I heard rustling somewhere above me. The rodents undoubtedly. That they hadn't made their appearance before now was a surprise. More rustling. Slightly louder this time. Still above me. I visualized their red eyes moving toward me from all sides. Playing out like some farfetched cartoon of Tweety bird on the railroad tracks being rescued at the last minute by Bugs Bunny mere seconds before the train barreled through. Except in my case Bugs Bunny would never be showing up.

Then I thought I heard a soft footstep on the metal stairway. The moon's light had now disappeared under thick clouds.

"Denise?" whispered a man's voice. Disembodied. Had I imagined it?

I froze.

"Denise."

A gentle voice. Tom Miller. Not one to be trusted. I remained silent. Of course, you know I'm here. You dumped me down here.

"I've been frantic looking for you, Denise. I'd zipped the tracking device that had been hidden under my dashboard into my coat pocket. I've been praying since you left your coat at the storage facility and taken my jacket that you were still wearing it. I just picked up the faintest signal about a half hour ago near here. Please say something, Denise … please."

My breath came in short bursts, but I said nothing. Suddenly he flipped on a flashlight, casting an eerie, dimly lit tunnel to my far right. I recognized the workman's torch that I'd used to knock him out. The weak batteries were unable to adequately penetrate the thick gloom. He was silhouetted standing high on the staircase, moving the threadlike beam slowly around the perimeter of the stone walls. Eventually the light fell on me. I was in too much pain to move anywhere. I averted my head, refusing to look at him. My theory that he and Cathy Martin would be returning to collect my remains in a few weeks and toss them into some muddied creek bed was apparently incorrect. She must be getting impatient, decided to murder me first rather than awaiting the inevitable small rodent and insect intervention.

"*Scheisse*," he muttered under his breath. "What the hell have they done to you, Denise?"

"They?" I whispered between painful gasps.

I heard metal scraping. He must be pulling down the staircase. I still refused to look up at him. Let the knife strike without my awareness, I thought dully. Another minute? Two? What difference did it make? If I'd had the energy to laugh, I might have done so, despite the stabbing pain in my ribs.

He cautiously descended the metal stairs, each footstep emitting a hollow ringing sound. Once he'd reached the stone floor, his faint flickering shadow moved towards me. My head remained averted, my eyes now closed in anticipation of that final blow. Fully welcoming that blow, in fact. In the many cheap thriller novels I'd read, this is where the heroine suddenly is imbued with some kind of incredible reserve power, rises up with a huge, sharp rock in hand and fatally bashes in the skull of her attacker. Alas, all power was completely sucked out of me.

Tom knelt slowly beside me. I could feel his breath hot on my neck.

"Denise, oh my God," he whispered, tenderly brushing my hair back from my forehead and then gently kissing my cheek. "If only you hadn't knocked me out none of this would have happened."

My eyes still closed I made no reply. I had nothing to say to this man and his endless string of lies.

"We've got her, my dear," he said gently, easing his arms around my back, as I gasped slightly in pain. "She's still looking for the photos that Dorothea took from the warehouse, but the real proof of her identity is those sheets of hand stamps and fingerprints that the two of you made. I found those sheets after you'd left me there … some kind of brass box had fallen I think, then ripped a hole in the screening. That's how I discovered them. Do you remember making those with Cathy Martin all those years ago?"

I was far too weak to acknowledge his words. A page of fingerprints? Handprints? What on earth was he going on about?

"No," I finally answered painfully. "I … don't know anything."

"There's a page with all of your fingerprints, made in blood – both yours and Cathy's – and handprints, those are smeared with some kind of black ink -- along with your signatures from back then," Tom replied. "They can trace the DNA from the blood these days, so they'll know in short order that it's Cathy's and yours but not Janet Lynn's."

"Bloody … prints? Handwriting?" I tried to laugh, then managed to eke out, "no one's writing … looks the same as when … they were … twelve years old …"

"The signature isn't all that important, Denise, but it's on that page with her picture that you'd glued on."

"Ah," I replied, barely above a whisper, still refusing to look at him despite his arm remaining firmly around my back. "The all-important … evidence that you've … now destroyed I'm … sure."

Tom either didn't hear me or chose to continue without acknowledging my words.

"I knew she planned to follow you until you'd led her to all of that stuff. Why Dorothea took a chance to bring the rest of it to your father's storage unit that night I have no idea. That was a foolish, reckless decision. And obviously, she paid for it."

"Yes, my good friend … and savior … Dorothea Dixon. Maybe it … was just a coincidence … her adding … my husband to her … long list of … sexual conquests," I uttered, punctuated with gasps of pain.

"The one really didn't have anything to do with the other, Denise," he replied, almost tenderly. "Her parents were two of the most morally corrupt people out there. Both of those girls learned their trade at the knee of incredibly depraved people."

I laughed slightly, wincing anew at the raw spasms.

"Yes … their trade … whoring … or murdering … or?"

"No one is ever safe from that sadist Cathy Martin. I know that as well as you do."

"Keep lying … to me, Tom. It's the …icing on the …cake …."

"You really don't believe me, do you?" he whispered, kissing my cheek again.

"Not … one word."

I lay limply in his arms, silent except for my ragged breath. My eyes remained closed; my head averted. Several moments passed before Tom spoke again.

"I had to pose as though I was on her side, Denise," he admitted. "How can I make you understand? There wasn't any other way to discover just how extensive the tentacles of her vile behavior had penetrated. It's called undercover cop work."

Yes, I thought. That's assuming you were a cop in the first place which I still question. If I'd had any fight left in me whatsoever, I would have snorted at his paltry attempt at literary witticism … my journalism professors would have whacked my knuckles with a ruler. How extensive had the tentacles of her vile behavior penetrated? Maybe he was translating this from German or whatever the hell language he claimed to speak.

"Jakob's out in the truck," Tom continued. "A Mennonite friend lives a few miles from here. We're taking you to his family's farm."

I thought he'd driven Jakob back to LaCrosse or someplace. Hadn't that been the gist of the conversation that I'd overheard in that trucker's joint? What day had that been? Last week? Two weeks? Exhaustion, pain and, I now realized, extreme hunger, had pushed me into this state of inertia. The real Janet Lynn had undoubtedly been in this place – had died in this place. How easy it must have been for these monsters to promise her food or balm for her wounds or even tease her with delusional tidbits promising release once she'd reached this state of mind. Powerless, I felt myself dangerously drifting, coming closer and closer to slipping towards an inevitable oblivion.

Lapsing in and out consciousness, I felt Tom cautiously lifting me, then gently cradling me. Voice lowered as he spoke to another man in a foreign language, maybe German, who remained partially veiled in thick shadow, they slowly carried me up the metal staircase and out into the open air. From there I was vaguely aware of snow falling gently on my face, then the roar of a truck's ignition and then blissfully, nothing, as I fell into a suspended twilight sleep, induced by pain and whatever paralyzing drug still coursed freely within my veins.

Through blurred vision over the next few days, I was aware that I was lying on a small cot with sheets that smelled faintly of old lavender. The tiny room was paneled in very dark knotty pine, with an old style, hand-carved window cornice. Occasionally Tom was in the room with me, but most of the time there were several darkly attired women quietly sitting in the chair opposite my bed. I was urged to sit up and swallow some sweet tasting medicine or very warm broth, but most of the time I was sleeping, a deep dreamless existence.

*****

I awoke more fully to the rich smell of coffee. A man was sitting next to me on the bed, a large mug in his hand.

"You're really awake," he smiled, gently brushing a few strands of hair off my face.

Even though the room wasn't extremely dark, my eyes failed to fully focus. I still needed to squint to work out that it was Tom.

"Do you think you're up to swallowing something a little more substantial than thin oatmeal? I could have Frau Schmidt scramble a couple eggs – might be a little of her spoonbread left too."

I nodded very slightly, frowning, my voice stuck far back in my throat. Tom left for a moment and returned, coffee cup still in hand, and then sat down on the bed again. He set the mug on the lamp table and then, propping two small pillows behind my back, carefully eased me to a sitting position. My ribs were still sore, but I could almost breath normally once again.

"Are you up to some conversation?"

"Not really," I replied slowly, surprised how weak my voice still sounded.

"Feel like listening?" asked Tom.

I nodded.

"We need to go back to Germany prior to the start of the war," Tom exhaled, softly stroking my wrist for just a moment before continuing. "Specifically, back to an incredibly strong young man named Karl Maria Neumann who was an early recruit by Reinhard Heydrich. Heydrich was one of Hitler's most ruthless high-ranking German SS officials if you remember. It was his detailed manifest that the Final Solution aimed at total annihilation of an entire ethnic group."

I nodded again.

"How many men Karl Maria Neumann murdered is anybody's guess. He was known as a 'bull's bull', renowned as one of the roughest policemen on Heydrich's force."

"Cathy wrote about the Bull. She read it on that tape that Thor and I heard," I whispered hoarsely. "I assumed the Bull was her father. But nothing about Nazis."

"No, I doubt she'd have given all that away," nodded Tom. "Even when she was a youngster her father would have warned her to remain very secretive about that information. Karl Neumann also had the uncanny ability to speak German, Russian and Polish in a variety of European accents, thus making him an extremely valuable asset to the SS in their espionage strategies as it were. When Heydrich's men were attacked in Prague in 1942, Heydrich died from his wounds several days later. But Karl Neumann somehow managed to elude capture, possibly with the help of his mistress at that time, a well-known prostitute in Berlin, and escaped with only very minor injuries to

Switzerland. Years later, he might well have gone undetected there to live out the rest of his life in secrecy except five very wealthy Jewish men, four of whom had miraculously escaped, surprisingly maintaining most of their wealth since most Jews had been completely stripped of all their savings, spotted Neumann. The four men had settled in rural Indiana once they'd obtained visas to America in 1935. The fifth man had fled to England.

"When Karl was arrested a few years later in Switzerland over some minor village skirmish, however, a small newspaper photo somehow found its way to America where it was seen by the four Jewish men, who'd remained in contact with one another. Although the SS fugitive was a master of disguises, he was immediately recognized by the four men due to a very small tear and slight curling towards the back of his right earlobe where a dog had bitten him when he was a baby according to legend. This scar was usually quite carefully hidden by his long hair, but his head had been completely shaved in prison, revealing the tear, alerting the four men."

"Amazing they would … recognize him … after so long."

Tom nodded, then continued with his story.

"Karl was then transferred to France and tried in Paris, found guilty, brutally beaten and placed on death row in a high security prison in Berlin awaiting additional pending charges by England, France and the U.S. However, he managed to escape in 1947 and somehow found his way to America – specifically Indiana. One by one he began an almost invisible rampage, killing those Jewish men who had fingered him as well as their families. Their last names were Webber, Lazarus, Bruckner, Decker and Gartenberg, but those names probably don't mean anything to you."

"No," I shivered. "Karl Maria Neumann is Chomp, though … frightening."

Tom nodded taking one final sip of his coffee then

setting the mug over on a small table.

"Janet Lynn Webster's father's name was originally Webber. You already know how the parents were murdered. Janet Lynn probably met her demise in that grain bin where I found you. Jimmy Larkins' father's name was originally Hermann Lazarus. Jimmy was murdered and dismembered by Chomp, quite likely assisted by his daughters Dorothea and Cathy. Herr und Frau Lazarus moved a year or two later and shortly after that move their house mysteriously exploded just before dawn, killing both of them instantly."

I inhaled sharply. My arms were loosely wrapped around my still-tender ribs.

"Hiram Bruckner was the first man Karl Neumann brutally killed in this country to the best of our knowledge. That was ultimately deemed an unfortunate accident when it happened out in Spencer, Indiana. But Chomp was run out of town as a result of the jury's decision. Had the jury discovered the man's true identity, Chomp would have been swinging at the end of a rope within fifteen minutes following an aborted trial."

"I remember Cathy telling me that story many … years ago," I said slowly. "She said … someone stole a motorcycle from … Chomp."

"Fortunately, Herr Bruckner was newly engaged to be married, so his fiancée was spared Chomp's wrath. She drowned in a tragic accident several years later but that couldn't be proven as Chomp's handiwork."

"So that's three," I murmured. "You said … there were five."

"The fourth one was Harald Gartenberg, He lived in London, a cipher, claiming to be a wealthy diplomat under the pseudonym Sir Henley Clarke. He was quite wealthy, to be sure, but he certainly wasn't a descendant of any English royal line. By then Cathy and Chomp were working in tandem towards their dual interests: Cathy as Janet Lynn

Webster was attempting to marry into great wealth and influence, and Chomp was well on his way towards eradicating those five men who had fingered him."

"Sir Henley Clarke?" The name sounded vaguely familiar.

"That's who Cathy married in London. We think he died very slowly by thallium poisoning. Thallium is a slow-acting, lethal poison that accumulates in a victim's organs over several months. The most obvious sign is that clumps of hair begin to fall out from the victim's head after first being poisoned. Unlike arsenic it's very difficult to detect after death and does not change the taste of any liquid or food eaten by the victim. Even if it is detected, however, there's no antidote so death is inevitable. It's believed that someone, we'll assume Cathy herself, carefully injected the poison into bottles of 7-Up which was Gartenberg's, or Clarke's, if you will, favorite beverage."

"So now you're at four. And then there's also Hank. And Dorothea. Then Chomp was found … frozen to death. Cathy's handiwork alone."

"Actually, Chomp wasn't frozen in that cabin, Denise. That was the fifth victim, Otto Decker. Chomp killed the man found in his cabin. The authorities merely assumed it was Chomp since he was the last person known to be living there. No one could actually identify the remains."

I closed my eyes. "So then, why … did he … call you?" I whispered.

"Call me?" replied Tom.

"You said Chomp … called you … that his call … prompted you to look further."

Tom shrugged. Why was he lying, I wondered? I was certain that he'd told me the first or second conversation we'd had about Chomp's phone call.

"More importantly, Denise, we're certain that Chomp Martin is still very much alive," Tom stated coldly.

"He's done with his … five victims," I replied wearily.

"What does that matter now?"

"Not exactly. Hank was in his way as was Dorothea once they'd served their purpose."

"Their purpose?"

"To pin their murders on you so that he would have free reign to destroy all the evidence leading back to Cathy or indirectly to himself."

"Then maybe they're done," I shrugged. "Mission accomplished."

His hand moved up to my face slowly, his thumb gently stroking my cheek. Then he leaned forward and kissed me, his hand moving carefully to my shoulder as our kiss deepened. After a long moment he pulled away. As before, I felt both an incredible relaxation yet, simultaneous electric tingling from his touch, something I'd never experienced with any man. We stared into one another's eyes for another moment, then I looked away.

"Cathy's heading back there tonight intending to retrieve your body," Tom said quietly. "When she discovers she's been duped, she'll be looking for both of us."

"How long have I been here? And for that matter, where am I?"

"You've been listed by the police as missing for several weeks," he replied quietly. "Hank's body was finally released to his parents. To the best of my knowledge, the funeral service was a week or so ago in Mishawaka. I know that authorities were at the funeral intending to arrest you if you happened to show up."

"You still haven't answered where I am."

"We're up in Wisconsin right now, Denise … not too far from the Webster's property. There are a lot of bluffs here overlooking the Mississippi but very few people live anywhere close by. My guess is that Chomp is hunkered down in some crude lean-to he put together, well camouflaged, far back from one of the many dirt roads that connect this place like a beehive."

"Wisconsin? How did I get up here?"

"Probably seven hours at least of rolling around on the floor of Cathy's car. You'd have frozen to death if they'd thrown you in the trunk. They dumped you in that silo and then Cathy drove out to one of the regional airports. Not sure which one. Chomp is still up here though. He's too conspicuous to go anywhere. I haven't seen him and supposedly, we were on the same side."

I frowned.

"*Supposedly*," Tom reiterated. "Don't miss the adverb."

"Did they ever decide what had killed Hank?" I asked, closing my eyes wearily.

"They now think it was more than likely thallium," Tom replied. "Conveniently, there was a small bottle found in a plastic bag stashed all the way in the back under your kitchen sink. There was abrin found in one of Hank's vitamin capsules, but the second autopsy determined that abrin wasn't what killed him. Somebody sure as hell was determined to end the man's life, however. More than likely the thallium was the second choice. And it could be the two poisons worked in tandem with one another. I don't think that will ever be proven."

"What is thallium anyway?"

"Rat poison. It's been banned in the U.S. for the last six years, but it's still available in most European countries. As I said before, that's what they assumed killed Sir Henley Clarke, that is, Harald Gartenberg, Cathy Martin's husband in England. And it's so effective against rat infestations, that a lot of stores here in the U.S. stockpiled the stuff in their backrooms so that they could still easily sell it to their customers on the black market for triple the cost."

"So, the rat poison that killed my husband is conveniently located under my sink and my car is just as conveniently used to murder his mistress. Wow. Makes me look guilty as hell."

"We need to move you from here, Denise. Jakob and I originally brought you here because this house is only a few miles from that grain silo. You were in such bad shape we didn't want to risk moving you further. And for obvious reasons, we couldn't risk taking you to a hospital either. That would have been the first place they'd have searched."

I made no comment.

"But, when Chomp and Cathy Martin realize that you're not in that silo, they'll be after us – all of us," Tom continued. "I have something of a strategy worked out with two other detectives that I've dealt with before, but it's … really risky, I have to tell you. It's also our only practical option. Alerting area police would be a complete fiasco ... those guys are just too inexperienced. What was the name of those bumbling cops in those old silent films?"

"Keystone cops," I replied, almost managing a smile.

He shrugged. "Yeah, that sounds right. Lean on me. We only have to make it to my truck. It's parked out front."

"I can try. Where are we going?"

Without answering, he slipped his arm carefully around my back and helped me swivel my legs over to the side of the bed. I had on a large grey University of Wisconsin track suit with the requisite orange "W" above the Bucky Badger cartoon. Once I was on my feet, Tom hastily wrapped a parka around me. He told me that Jakob had locked my purse in the glove compartment of his truck. I wondered if the PlenTpak was still inside. There would be no way for me to find out. That would have to wait. I hobbled alongside Tom, surprised that I now had the energy to walk further than to the tiny bathroom across the hallway, albeit supported, which even a few days ago would have been a thoroughly daunting trek.

A blast of frigid air hit me full force as we emerged from the buffering effects of the small house. Tom pulled me closer as I began shivering uncontrollably. A young man I assumed to be Jakob helped Tom ease me up into the truck. Though a small bench, all three of us fit without any problem. Tom started the engine, let up on the clutch, and we pulled away just as fat snowflakes began heralding a windy blast from high above me. Almost immediately we began our climb into the surrounding bluffs, a zigzagged path riddled with treacherous switchbacks along the narrow dirt road. As he switched to the lowest gear, I could just barely make out a small signpost that said Bluff Hollow. I didn't know if that was the name of a place or the road. Tom had said we were somewhere near the Webster's old estate but the only name that came to mind from that trip was the name of the town. Rutledge, I remembered after a moment's mental lapse.

"*Was denkst du*?" said Jakob, glancing past me to Tom as the truck bounced over the rutted roadbed.

"I don't know," Tom replied, his eyes, after a quick glance in my direction once again riveted into the suddenly blinding snow pelting the windshield. "You tell me. That madman could be anywhere. With this weather I figured Cathy would be changing her plans flying out here, give us at least another day or two, but seems I was wrong. She's on her way," then glancing over at Jakob translating, "*sie ist unterwegs*."

"*Verdammt*," Jakob muttered, grimacing as he rubbed his forehead.

"You were supposed to be meeting her?" I swallowed, glancing at Tom's rugged profile.

"Yeah," he sighed, clearing his throat. "She owns a private plane. Pilot's on call twenty-four hours a day apparently. Her two, uh … bodyguards I guess you'd call them, were supposed to pick her up at the airport in Galena, then drive her … out here."

"Cheech and Chong," I muttered under my breath, remembering Thor's scathing review of the movie a couple of months ago, and then added, "I thought you said that you didn't know where I was being kept?"

"I didn't, Denise. Now's not the time to start mistrusting me again," he replied tersely. "When she arrived, she was going to take me there. All I knew was that they'd transported you from where Chomp had nailed you with a pygmy dart in that parking lot up to some spot here. That's the whole story."

"Pygmy dart," I sighed. Right out of a Sherlock Holmes mystery. "Let me guess: Chomp learned how to rig and shoot those while he was in the SS, right?"

Tom glanced in my direction for a moment, then shrugged. "Yeah, probably. Who knows? All I know is that I was supposed to be meeting Cathy at the entrance of the Webster place later today. From that point forward, I remained completely in the dark regarding her plans if you can believe that."

I closed my eyes in a futile attempt to again block the sickening, re-emerging image of Janet Lynn's slow, agonizing death a decade ago. What kind of monsters could so eagerly plan out such atrocities and how could Tom even have feigned any allegiance to Cathy's duplicitous plans?

Suddenly a fiery explosion under the truck's left front wheel blew us completely off the road. We careened sideways down the steep embankment, the truck fishtailing manically from the intensity of the blast over the thickly frozen, brush-covered rocks, only jolting to an abrupt stop when the truck bed banged into a huge tree. Jakob's head was crushed into the dashboard, and we were both covered with shattered glass from the windshield. Intense black smoke billowed through the broken glass. Jakob was whimpering something in German as blood oozed copiously from his forehead into a pool soaking us both. I was facing Jakob and couldn't see Tom at all. He seemed to have landed on my back. My ribs screamed with this savage, renewed assault, but my companion's injuries were far worse.

"Tom," I gasped, my voice raspy in the smoke-filled truck cab, "Jakob's … bleeding! It's bad! Oh God, it's so bad! You've got to help him! Oh God, Tom … no! No! There's blood everywhere, Tom!"

No response from behind me. Not even the slightest groan. Had dynamite been slyly hidden within the road's deep ruts, occluded by the grimy packed ice? Or had I heard gunshots first? One bullet might have hit Tom in the back of his head and others had blown out the tire. Tom lay heavily against my back. I couldn't tell if he was breathing since the car was still shuddering from the impact. Was I sandwiched between a dead man and a dying one? Two men who'd risked their lives rescuing me from that abandoned grain deathtrap, whose own lives had now been snuffed out by these maniacs?

"*Steig aus dem Auto!*" a gravelly voice barked, just out of my line of vision. A moment later a massive, craggy head, with a coal black eye squinting along the barrel of an immense shotgun, appeared just outside the battered windshield.

"*Ah ha! Ausgezeichnet!* Excellent! Eh, a … mortal … detour," chuckled Chomp, lowering the rifle, his English heavily-accented, but unquestionably tinged with mirth.

Although I hadn't seen this beast for almost fifteen years, I recognized him instantly – a man more gorilla than human by any standard. His thick mane of hair had grown into a filthy grey, tangled bush. Where his hair ended and his bristling, Rasputin-like beard began was anyone's guess, framing a dark, weather-beaten face, with a roadmap of rutted crevices that were deeply etched on either side of his nose. Intense, lidded black eyes and a permanently chiseled sneer on his thin lips were barely visible beneath the thick snarls of facial hair. Cathy's perfect model for The Bull in her sordid Lady Pamela tale. Nothing about the man looked even remotely German. Not the animal-like hair, the dark face, the black eyes … where on earth had Cathy

Martin inherited her white-blonde, blue-eyed beauty?

"*Aussteigen!*" Chomp spat out, his glimmer of humor having now evaporated. He wrenched open the passenger side door and Jakob spilled out onto the ground with a lifeless thud. Chomp grabbed my arm and yanked me off the seat. I fell out of the truck onto Jakob's limp body, my head narrowly missing the bottom of the metal door. Feeling very dizzy, I managed to get up on my knees slowly, my hands crunching in the broken glass strewn on the ground. The tips of Chomp's boots touched an expanding puddle of gasoline that was pouring out of the bottom of the truck. Panting hard, I looked up just as the truck started to shudder, then began to roll down the cliff now that the weight from within had shifted. In horror, stifling a scream, I watched it crash against another boulder, bisecting the truck bed from the cab as it continued its nightmarish spiral. The cab caught fire and almost immediately another loud blast ricocheted through the air. I prayed that Tom had died in the original explosion on the road. If not, he'd certainly not survived this last.

"*Ausgezeichnet,*" snorted Chomp again, assessing his handiwork with a smirk. He violently shoved the muzzle of his rifle against Jakob's shoulder, twisting the boy's torso backwards with a loud crack. Vacant eyes stared up at the frozen sky. Still on all fours, small bits of glass crunching into my palms and nausea roiling in my stomach, I shut my eyes attempting to block the deadly panorama of images.

Sticky with Jakob's blood, my left hand stuck to a triangular, sharply pointed shard along the ground. My fingers curled around to conceal it.

"That's why so many murders
remain unsolved, Watson.
People will stick to facts,
even though they prove nothing."

Basil Rathbone as Sherlock Holmes in

"The Hound of the Baskervilles" (1939)

Chapter 28

Chomp grabbed my right elbow and yanked me to my feet. I pulled my hands partway into my coat sleeves out of the cold, as blood congealed along the bottom of the cuffs, occasionally dripping onto the frozen ground. He then pushed me towards a narrow cave that was completely camouflaged beneath a low outcropping only a few hundred yards from where Tom's truck had careened off the dirt road. Chomp had probably set a dynamite charge in a rut that was rigged by a concealed trip wire. Then he'd hidden in the brush alongside the road awaiting our inevitable arrival. I was horrified in world history classes when I'd first read about such incendiary military tactics used so liberally in World War II and Vietnam. Since this road was probably the only one leading to the old Webster place from this direction, the stakeout was child's play.

Shoving me hard against the dark walls that led into the cave, Chomp retrieved a dimly lit, battered Coleman lantern at the entrance, then relentlessly thrust me forward into the gloom. I slipped repeatedly on the greasy, mud-slimed floor and was met each time with a harsh kick on the back of my thighs by his thick boot, which reeked of gasoline from the wreck. In agony I struggled to regain my balance as he continued pushing me deeper into the cave. After a few minutes we emerged into a high-ceilinged cavern. He placed the lantern on a flat stone jutting out from the wall like a corner shelf. Huge shadows played eerily off the rocks. As he shoved me forward again, I fell onto my hands and knees on the slimy floor.

"Aufstehen!" he snarled, slapping my face so close to my ear that for several moments my hearing was distorted. All these commands starting with *auf* or *aus* were completely meaningless to me which delighted this ogre. He grabbed my armpits and forced me high on my knees. Terrified, I kept my eyes focused on the ground, aware that he'd moved a few steps away. He returned holding something, which he threw down directly in front of me. A stool. As he straddled the low stool, he grabbed me under my chin, forcing me to look up. I kept my arms rigidly by my sides, still clasping the shard of glass, despairing of my ability to stab him in the eye since that was my only feasible course of action.

"See, I teach my Dorta an' Caterina all … eh… dey fancy, eh … tricks, ja? Dey ißt jes leetle girls an' dey know all how. Suck big. Suck nice ... long time. Ja? So good long, ja? Ah! Dey learn vey *gut* here Papa. How make Papa nice, Papa big … an' happy, *verstehe*? Mama, pssssht! She go. She angry see Dorta suck Papa big. So nice. Who need Mama? *Meine* girls dey learn *gut*! *Gut* suck!" he spat as he began unbuttoning his fly. "*Und jetzt* … now, heh?"

After a raucous laugh that echoed in the cavernous space, he uttered something else in German as he slapped my face again, opened his fly wide and pulled out his massive erection. Grabbing my hair close to the scalp on both sides he held me as in a vice, and began forcing my head back and forth, laughing.

"Look! Look! Ja? See what you gettin', ja? Nice, eh?

C'mon, you do before," he laughed, increasing the pressure at my scalp as he moved himself closer to my mouth. "Many, many men, I bet. Yankee slut, eh? But I show *besser*, ja? You like. You die happy, *verstehe*?"

Suddenly I started gagging uncontrollably, then retching. The man's animal stench thrust so deep in my throat thoroughly overpowered me. Letting go of my hair, he slapped my right cheek hard as my hot vomit spewed in waves over us both. Crazed with my own rage, I grabbed him, and without thinking rammed the glass shard deep into his engorged flesh as he shrieked, instantly pulling away from me which embedded the shard even further.

"Dreckige Hure!" he roared, falling off the stool onto the floor, writhing in pain, bathed in blood and vomit. The glass shard glistened momentarily in the lamplight as he shrieked, working to remove it all the while shrieking in German.

I somehow staggered to my feet, scrubbing my mouth against my coat sleeve in a rash effort to scour my vomit and the monster's greasy fluids that had spewed onto my face when I'd attacked. He relentlessly lumbered towards me, an enraged bear howling in agony. I grabbed the lantern from the wall, backing up slowly. Then with both hands, I threw it towards him. The lantern shattered several inches short of his feet and simply flickered out, surrounding us in a terrifying, dense darkness. He continued cursing in German and I could feel his hot, sour breath getting nearer. But then, a few seconds later, his gasoline-soaked boots suddenly ignited. A fireball rocketed throughout the cavern as he shrieked again, engulfed in a high wall of flames. Sparks liberally showered me as well and seconds later, my coat began smoldering. I hastily removed it, throwing it as far as possible, all the while coughing uncontrollably in the billowing black smoke now licked by the flames. Aided by the eerie conflagration, I scrabbled my way along the stone walls, slapping out the sparks that ignited briefly on my hair and shoulders, and hoped I was retracing my steps to the cave's entrance. I didn't remember any tunnels angling off, but that didn't mean they weren't there. Once past the fire's light, I continued in complete darkness, still choking on the smoke, groping my way along the cold walls, and praying that I was not burying myself further into the depths of this catacomb.

After what seemed to be hours, I sensed a few rays of sickly green light filtering through an entrance just ahead of me. Within another minute, a rush of fresh, icy air hit me full face. As I emerged from the cave, dazed and unable to focus my eyes, I collapsed in exhaustion against the stone entry. Before I'd even taken a deep breath, however, a gunshot whistled out high and to my right, momentarily peppering the top of my head with pebbles. I dropped to the ground and rolled quickly through icy pebbles into a tall patch of frozen weeds, and then dove behind a large rock.

Another shot ricocheted off the rocks somewhere nearby. Then another, even closer, possibly from a different angle. Had the shooter moved? Doubtful. Regardless, someone else knew I was here. No way Chomp Martin could have survived his unscheduled cremation and taken some kind of shortcut arriving ahead of me. Jakob had died practically in my arms in the truck. Tom Miller had met his end either with a bullet to his head while driving or when the vehicle had exploded into flames halfway down the mountainous bluff. No, the gunmen could only be Cathy Martin and her goons. I listened. No sounds other than the wind rattling through the icy vegetation. Another volley of shots suddenly rang out, seemingly aimed high over the cave entrance. Then a prolonged shriek of a male voice, accompanied by the loud staccato of an avalanche of large, loose rocks, came crashing down the bluff. Cautiously peering out from my inadequate shelter, I could just make out the shoulder of a man clad in a red and black jacket lying prone immediately above the cave entrance, his head badly contorted at a completely unnatural angle. Although the body remained partially obscured by the frozen bushes, I was certain it was T-Bone. Something black had tumbled all the way to the ground, several yards away from him. A gun, possibly? I was too far away for a good look.

The cold snub of a revolver suddenly nestled in behind my ear.

"Guess old Grizzly Face over there lost his balance. Fat idiot. Ok, now you, Curly Locks! Stand up. Slowly. Hands high in the air," Cathy ordered curtly, her voice sounding nothing like the soft, Southern affectation she had so adroitly crafted in her studied metamorphosis into Janet Lynn Webster. "Carefully. If you have a gun, toss it over there past that pile of gravel."

I stood up cautiously, keeping my back to her.

"No … gun," I swallowed, raising my hands as directed, her pistol pressed hard into the back of my skull.

She circled to face me keeping the gun trained steadily only a few inches from my throat. I was shaking both in fear as well as the intense cold. Her free hand expertly patted me down. I'd thrown off my coat in the fireball back in the cave and now stood shivering in the thick curtain of snow that had begun falling. Surprisingly, she wasn't dressed for this weather either – only a flimsy green peacoat, no hat and no boots, just thin socks and loafers.

"You're really an idiot, you know?" she snorted, snowflakes peppering her eyelashes. "All you had to do was just keep out of everything. I mean, how hard could that be, huh? You tell me. I had this all worked out from the beginning … well, you know that because you've now either read or listened to my stories that you and that murderous sister of mine stole, right? Or did you skip a few chapters back there? Your loss, I guess, you stupid meddling bitch. Too bad you'll never learn how the whole story ends. And my God, you stink! What, did you puke when they blew up that truck? Phew!"

"You're … you're the one who's sick, Cathy," I somehow stammered. "You're … just let me try … to help …"

"Help me? *You*?" she guffawed, the gun never moving from my throat. "I'd say your chances of getting out of this alive are less than nil Curly Locks. You've just slightly delayed the inevitable, that's all. That deadbeat Amish cowboy almost had me convinced you were now the fodder of maggots back in that grain bin. I mean, what's an abandoned grain silo doing way out here in the middle of nowhere in the first place, you know? I used to hide all kinds of stuff down there that I didn't want the Websters or anybody else to find. Then when ol' Dorta the Dimwit finds out that I'm engaged to David Fowler she gets all paranoid and greedy, steals all my stuff from the silo, and threatens she'll expose me when I discover that she's a high roller with completely bogus credentials at that Idyllic Security place. Stupid whore never even made it past eighth grade for Chrissake!"

"Can I just ask … why? Why this hatred of Janet --"

She cut me off, waving the gun in my face as she shook her head. "Bitch had absolutely no business being where she was in the first place. Too bad you didn't learn that lesson yourself a lot earlier Curly Locks! Who knows, maybe by now you'd even be married to some poor schmuck who actually loves you!"

That really stung but I said nothing.

"She was just puttin' on airs with the Websters. Didn't deserve to be there. I should've been there all along. She stole my place."

"Who stole your place with the Websters," I frowned, now thoroughly confused. "Dorothea?"

"No, of course not," she snorted. "Janet Lynn!"

"Cathy," I began as calmly as I could muster, "Janet Lynn was their actual daughter. Of course, she belonged --"

I was interrupted again by another round of Cathy's raucous laughter. She shook her head violently, the gun waving maniacally close to my nose, forcing me to take a cautious small step back.

"No, no, no, you've got it *all wrong*, Curly Locks! Janet Lynn was *adopted*! She was my identical twin sister! My ole lady hauled her ass out to this agency right after we were born and put us both up for adoption. Last thing that old whore wanted was to be stuck with two brats suckin' all day on those big titties an' makin' 'em sag further. I was supposed to be going home with Mr. and Mrs. George A. Webster, but the day they showed up with their court-endorsed, final signed papers I was really sick, so the story goes. Some kind of high fever, breaking out in these nasty, brown crusty hives. God only knows what. So, the Websters in good ol' true George and Sylvia fashion, tut-tuted about the whole deal, assumed I was just going to die and left me there. They decided they couldn't be bothered with me after that."

"You're certain about all of this?" I frowned. "Janet Lynn was adopted?"

"Oh yeah, Curly Locks. Trust me, it's real. She didn't believe me when I told her about the whole thing either. Stupid bitch. But she believed me by the end, you can rest assured about that!" she smirked.

"So … they just took Janet Lynn home instead."

"Yessiree Bob. Left me high an' dry an' expected to die. And then, of course, ol' Chomp was furious to boot when he'd found out his ol' lady had ditched the two of us. He figured she'd just headed out on one of her usual benders and left us with a neighbor. But no way by then could he get Janet Lynn back. He really wanted us both, you see. And you're gonna ask why, right? Why would a behemoth like Chomp have any interest in two daughters who probably weren't even his in the first place, right? He knew there was a great market for uninhibited little girls and then, well, twins to boot … wow! Consider those great odds, yeah? He was seeing easy street on his horizon once he had us all nice and trained up in the flesh trade … awwww, am I shocking your poor little puritanical upbringing, Curly Locks?"

I made no reply. I was more than aware of her father's disgusting initiation for these girls.

"Course, considering all that other crap he put Dorothea and me through for all those years …." She shook her head violently, then spat copiously into the snow just over my shoulder.

This woman had been deranged since childhood. She'd schemed for years to become her twin sister, dispose of the adoptive parents who'd abandoned her, and obtain what she judged her rightful, cushioned place in society. I felt hollow inside. All these murders just because her simpleminded, unsuspecting twin had in turn been blissfully absorbed into unprecedented wealth, prestige, and global respectability. She'd been dumped by the wayside, once by her real mother and then again by her adopted one. Without the slightest hint of remorse, she'd murdered both of her sisters, the Websters, her first husband, my husband, young Jimmy Larkins, Tom Miller, Jakob Lehmann and most likely a host of others who had inadvertently gotten in the way of her bloodthirsty rampage. That number didn't even begin to factor in Chomp's victims.

"So now, Curly Locks, we march into that cave, wake up ol' Chomp who's probably snoring off another hefty bender again, and dump you back into that grain silo. Then we wait several months while your meddling carcass incubates during large rodent feasting before you're discovered out near Janet Lynn's remains. See, since we're twins, no one will ever discover that those bones are actually Janet Lynn's and not mine, especially after you write out your pitiful letter of remorse, begging God's forgiveness for having killed Cathy Martin back in 1968, not to mention your having poisoned your dear hubby and fatally plowing your car into his longtime girlfriend Dorothea Dixon. I realize that's not quite the way I wrote about it back in my Lady Pamela days, but there are a few other minor discrepancies in my stories as you've probably noticed. Insignificant details."

I didn't respond. After another moment she shoved me forward towards the cave. I knew there was zero chance of escaping her grasp from inside that black cavern once she discovered her father's incinerated corpse. Only one slim possibility forced its way into my mind. Recklessly, I acted upon that impulse. Taking a couple of lumbering steps, I stumbled forward, head down, onto my hands and knees on the ice. Then, using the heel of my boot, I kicked backwards as hard as possible, aiming at her right ankle -- the one she'd broken so many years ago, praying that it was still somewhat tender after all this time. Miraculously, it landed with a direct hit. Cathy shrieked, losing her balance as she pitched sideways, falling heavily to the ground. Her revolver then discharged two or three loud shots in rapid succession, echoing sharply off the rocks. The gun fell out of her hand momentarily, but she immediately grabbed it, still lying on her left side, as I scrambled on all fours and then righted myself, racing towards the boulder next to the cave. Her next shot went wild as I dove behind the boulder. Several more shots followed, pinging off the rock mere inches from the top of my head. Had there been five or six shots? A standard issue revolver would have chambered six rounds.

"You stupid, stupid bitch!" she shouted, limping quickly towards me. "I am so done with you!"

She was reaching into her coat pocket. I was now guessing six shots. If I was wrong, I was dead. It would take her all of two seconds to reload that gun while stumbling towards me. Grabbing a fist-sized rock, I sprang out from my hiding place. She ducked sideways and my throw towards her head went way wide. I heard the newly chambered ammunition click efficiently into place. For some unknown reason, I looked down. At my feet was the gun that had fallen from T-Bone, whose body still straddled the rocks above the cave entrance. I grabbed it and pointed it at Cathy. She fired almost point blank, but her gun failed to discharge. Had the chamber momentarily jammed when she'd fallen? Shaking, I slowly raised T-Bone's gun towards her face.

"Hah! You're too chicken to use that on me, even if it's loaded! Assuming that's Fat Carl's gun, it probably ain't even loaded, you fool! Guy has the IQ of a turnip," Cathy snorted, with a chin cock at the corpse straddling the cave entrance. "And besides, even if you shoot me, I still have everything in place to prove that you're the one who originally murdered Cathy Martin as well as your stupid husband and that bimbo sister of mine. And you're gonna add me to that pile? Hah! No matter what, this is the end of the yellow brick road for you, Curly Locks!"

I cocked the gun. Undaunted, Cathy moved a step closer.

"C'mon, Curly Locks, give mama the gun like a good little girl," she smirked, her gun still extended towards me, as she limped painfully forward yet another step. "You can't win at this game. You're in way over your little fuzzy head."

My hand shaking violently, I shut my eyes as I squeezed the trigger at exactly the same moment that Cathy fired at me. The force of my gun's retort threw me back into the rocks, partially deflecting the initial sting as her bullet tore into my right shoulder, leaving my arm dangling uselessly by my side. The gun slipped from my fingers landing with a dull clunk on the frozen ground. Cathy shrieked an obscenity as my bullet winged her left thigh. Blood began seeping down her leg. But that didn't stop her from continuing to limp towards me, teeth clenched, her gun now trained directly at my head from less than ten feet. The gun mere inches from my forehead, she fired again, but the gun jammed again. With the butt of the gun, she pistol-whipped me across my face, as I shoved her away with my left arm. Blood oozed freely from my nose as I saw her stumble a few steps to retrieve my gun.

"No way this'll miss this time," she grunted, glowering at me.

Closing my eyes, I turned my head awaiting the inevitable. A sensation that blackened edges of paper were quickly curling into a towering center flame came over me. I heard a gunshot but felt absolutely nothing. A few seconds later I heard a loud thud as Cathy's body hit the ground in front of me.

I turned my head towards her and slowly opened my eyes. Standing a few feet from Cathy was Tom Miller, gun still gripped with both hands in a police stance. Although completely immobilized, Cathy's mouth moved wordlessly as she stared up at him. Guns drawn, two other men then appeared, but holstered their weapons when Tom called out to them. The men walked over to Cathy and pulled the dazed, seriously wounded woman to a sitting position, slapping on handcuffs. One of them began barking into a walkie-talkie.

Tom hobbled slowly over to me, obviously badly injured as well. But with a wispy smile curling about his lips, he gently pulled me into his arms. I fought to push back tears. My right shoulder was freely oozing blood and I felt lightheaded. How could either of us still be alive?

"How …" I swallowed, staring up at him.

"I was blown out of the truck on the driver's side and landed in the ditch when Chomp's dynamite hit," he said, hoarsely, answering my unvoiced question, while carefully wiping blood from my nose with the edge of his scarf. "There was nothing I could do to save Jakob though."

"That poor boy," I panted. "What did he get himself into with this?"

"Not a boy. Another agent. Just very young looking like a lot of Amish men. He's been working with me for a couple years now."

"Such a waste," I murmured. "That woman is a monster. She's been deranged her whole life."

"Agreed," nodded Tom with a slight smile. "I thought I'd lost you too until I heard Cathy arguing with you and those gunshots. There's still Chomp to deal with, though. Where he's hiding out around here is anybody's guess."

"Chomp's dead," I replied slowly, my voice thin, my eyes barely focusing. So much of my body was burning with intense pain right now, I was beginning to wonder if Tom's appearance was merely an apparition. A delusion. "He lives in that cave."

"You shot him?" Tom frowned.

"No. He … he burned to death," I whispered.

"You're certain?"

"It was awful … a … a fireball, Tom," I replied, swallowing hard. "I can't go back in there …"

"No, no, that's not necessary, Denise. We'll bring him out. The next place you and I are headed is the emergency room at the hospital. I'll let the other deputies book Cathy Martin."

"What about finding Janet Lynn's remains?" I interjected slowly.

"That's why I left Cathy alive, my dear," Tom replied tersely. "Plea bargaining certainly won't lessen her crimes, but it will save her from the electric chair. I expect her to cough up that location eventually during interrogation. She puts up a hard front, but trust me, she's nothing but a coward underneath."

I nodded.

"I assume you found those photos hidden back in the Kiss – the ones that Cathy was determined to destroy," Tom added, looking intently at me. "That's why you knocked me out, right?"

"Well, maybe," I replied slowly, frowning. "I'm not sure exactly …"

He made no reply.

"What happened to my purse? You said Jakob had originally locked it in the truck, I think."

"Your purse? That's way too small for a set of photos, Denise," Tom replied with a wry smile.

"So where is it? My purse, that is. Mostly I'm looking for a pack of Wrigley's gum."

"Gum?" frowned Tom, obviously confused. "I dunno. There's a chance Jakob might've filched it, I suppose … I was really surprised to see him jawing away chewing like a fiend when we were driving up those bluffs. He'd always claimed it was one of the worst habits of you English."

"Did he leave the pack in the truck?" I asked, closing my eyes. The most potentially damning evidence against Cathy Martin was probably nothing but cinders embedded in the snow at the bottom of the bluffs along with the rest of Tom's truck.

"I think he offered me a stick and then I don't know what happened to it after that. Maybe his shirt pocket? Glove compartment? Why are you asking about a packet of gum?"

"Did you ever see the movie "*Sherlock Holmes in Washington*"?

Tom shook his head.

"I'm pretty certain that it was Dorothea Dixon who had those photos – whatever's on them – reduced on microfilm, Tom. Maybe she even shot the microfilm herself. We'll never know. Anyway, they're smaller than normal width film and wrapped along with the sticks of gum inside that Wrigley's PlenTpak that was in my purse.

There are seventeen places for gum, but I don't know how many she swapped with the strips of film."

"What does that have to do with the Sherlock Holmes film?" he frowned.

"Nothing specifically. It was about two important British documents that were reduced to microfilm and clandestinely slit into an American matchbook."

"Huh. Ok. I'll go check in with a couple of our other men who are still investigating the scene back on the road. Give me five minutes. By then an ambulance should be here to take you to the hospital down in Galena, ok?"

He kissed me gently on the top of my head and began to limp slowly away, holding on to his left side. I'm trusting you, Tom, I whispered to myself. Please don't let me down now.

"Otherwise, the shadow of sudden death will be forever hanging over his head, and sooner or later ... ah, here we are!"

Basil Rathbone as Sherlock Holmes in

"The Hound of the Baskervilles" (1939)

Chapter 29

Picking up all the shattered pieces of my life after I was released from the hospital took several tedious months, including both intense physical and psychological therapy. I'd been admitted to Galena General with the bullet I'd taken in my shoulder, a broken nose from Cathy's having pistol-whipped me, three fractured and two abraded ribs, a serious lung infection that very slowly responded to penicillin, and a badly bruised kidney. I learned from Thor that my position at the newspaper had been temporarily filled, but during a brief phone conversation with the city editor, Mr. Thompson, I was assured a full-time position with benefits and that the opportunity for by-lined investigative assignments would be available for me when I returned. I was eager to return to the newspaper if for no other reason than to research and write a lengthy article about Karl Maria Neumann, also known as Chomp Martin, a man who terrorized the populace on two continents for over three decades.

The PlenTpak turned up in the glove compartment of Tom's demolished truck. Because the compartment was all metal, the slightly singed microfilm survived the conflagration. There were horrific pictures of Chomp and Cathy Martin luridly posing with various mutilated corpses including that of Janet Lynn Webster (whose remains were never located), the charred bodies of George and Sylvia Webster from the Rutledge estate fire, Jimmy Larkins, a gruesome series of dismemberment photos of an unidentified woman who may have been the corpse buried alongside Jimmy Larkins, and photos of Chomp with the five Jewish men who'd fingered him back in Europe, whom Chomp had viciously tracked down and slaughtered one by one in the Midwest and London.

David Fowler filed for divorce from Cathy immediately and refused to hire a defense lawyer for her. The court-appointed attorney attempted to prove that she was insane and driven to perform these vile acts by her terrifying father, but that plea fell flat early in the trial. The all-male jury deliberated for less than an hour before returning with a guilty verdict on all charges and the judge, also male, was far too lenient in most of our minds. Janet Lynn Webster's impostor, Cathy Martin, was sentenced to multiple life sentences in prison with no chance of parole. Exactly how she avoided the death penalty was a mystery. Since she would have been the only woman occupying a seat on Indiana's death row that might well have been a factor. She attempted committing suicide three times. Her fourth try was successful.

Chomp Martin was still barely alive when the officers found him deep within his cave, but he died very shortly thereafter. Word was sent to Berlin that escaped SS terrorist Karl Maria Neumann had at last been identified and was now deceased.

I was finally able to get my folks' place cleaned out due to Thor's energetic work detail signup of the newsroom staff over Palm Sunday weekend in late March. A brigade of mops, buckets, sponges, vacuum cleaners and most importantly, a flotilla of garbage hauling vehicles, didn't exactly render their house a palace, but it sure helped. My mom was responding favorably to a new medication for her hysteria and my dad was beyond ecstatic when he found an appreciative home at Village Hall for his completed *Fleurama* triptych.

Up in Mishawaka, Hank's dad suffered another massive stroke and was not responding well to treatment. Hank's stepmother Nancy decided that my visiting him in the rehabilitation unit would be far too disruptive, so I never spoke with the man again nor did I attend his funeral when he passed away two months later. After his death Nancy called the newspaper a few times and left messages for me but somehow, I just couldn't bring myself to return her calls. I had absolutely nothing to say to that venomous woman.

Thor and I attended several weekend blockbuster showings of old Sherlock Holmes and Hitchcock movies at the cheapie movie theater just outside town. He'd recently started dating a young woman who had been hired from The South Bend Tribune … things were already getting very serious, which surprised me. Meeting up weekly with Marcy and Linda for beer and pizza at a brand-new pizza joint in Nashville, and hanging out with several old high school friends, including Mark and Jill Stephens along with Christine Lewis, proved to be therapeutic for me as well.

And Tom? He'd fractured his leg in three places when he'd been thrown from his truck in that dynamite blast. After several surgeries and a lengthy rehabilitation, he was exhausted, but finally thinking about returning to work. He visited me a few times in Bloomington after we'd both been released from various hospitals and then I drove up to Wisconsin to stay with him for several extended weekends.

Where exactly did our relationship stand? I honestly wasn't sure. But I knew wherever we ended up, I was looking forward to the journey.

About the Author

A graduate from the Jordan College of Music at Butler University in Indianapolis, IN, Mim Eichmann has found that her creative journey has taken her down many exciting, interwoven pathways. For well over two decades, she was primarily known in the Chicago area as the artistic director/choreographer for Midwest Ballet Theatre, bringing full-length professional ballet performances to thousands of dance lovers annually. A desire to become involved again in the folk music world brought about the creation of her acoustic quartet Trillium, now in its 17th year, which performs throughout the Midwest and has released four cds. Among other varied music avenues, she's recorded two award-winning original children's cds and an album of early jazz vocals.

Her debut historical fiction novel *A Sparrow Alone* was published by Living Springs Publishers in April 2020 and was a semi-finalist in the 2020 Illinois Library Association's Soon-to-be-Famous Project Competition. The highly anticipated sequel, *Muskrat Ramble*, was published by LSP in March 2021. Both books are bestsellers.

Please take a moment to visit her author website at: www.mimeichmann.com.

Made in the USA
Middletown, DE
21 August 2022